Solve for i

A. E. Dooland

Cover design and art by Yue Li
yue-li.tumblr.com

Edited by Anne Farmer and Martina Veselá

ISBN: 978-0-9941779-4-0

ABOUT SOLVE FOR *i*

This story is a spin-off sequel to *Under My Skin* and *Flesh & Blood*—it's book three in that series. You don't need to read those stories to read this one, but you'll have a fuller understanding of all the characters if you do!

ACKNOWLEDGEMENTS

A big thank you to the wonderful Anne Farmer and Martina Veselá for their encouragement, suggestions and sharp eyes—the story would not be the same without them.

Thanks also to the thousands of people who followed *Solve for i* as a web series for all their comments, feedback and discussion. I loved reading everyone's analyses and interpretations of characters and events!

FINANCIAL BACKERS

This story was first run as a crowd-funded web series. The following people were major financial backers of this story.

Firstly, thank you to the enigmatic 'Mysterious Mitchell' and Ben Keen, my two most generous backers, and a further thanks to the other high-pledging supporters:

Sarah van der Wal
Nathan P.
Sarah Jackson
XaykWolf
Mitch Balbanero
David Goodes
J. Murley
Ray Ancheta Jr
Max Callahan
E. Brooks
Nora W.
David and Stephanie Jones
Emmalee Dirk
Brooke A. Steele
Katherine R.
Sheila Gijsens
Tsutako

Kristen Madrid
Brandon Hacker
Irian and Mai
Griffin Patrick
Katie S.
R. McCormac
Max Leviton
Sam D.
Yeon Jin Choi
Manu
Liv & Tiz
Naomi Leovao-Carpel
Ashleigh Wickens
Sten Sondre Johnson
Amy 'Starbuck' Watson
Arlena Derksen

CHAPTER ONE

Statistically speaking, the average Australian woman graduates from high school, has sex with eight different people—Aussies are the second most promiscuous people on the planet, apparently—and then she settles down and marries her boyfriend at 28.3 years old. She'll have her first kid to him at 29, her second at 32, and then pack it all in and be divorced by 40. The good news is that she'll have a further 5.3 sexual partners *after* her divorce, and she has a 1:3 chance of getting married to one of them and living happily ever after by her 50s. At this point she'll own her own house—with a 17% chance of owning an investment property, too—a car worth $13,500, and rate her overall happiness as a 7.7 out of 10.

So, according to the maths, you'd have thought that by 28.9, I would have been married, pregnant and on a smooth trajectory towards living happily ever after.

Well, that wasn't me.

This was me: hungover, sharing my rented one-bedroom flat with my grumpy old marmalade cat, and rating my overall happiness at maybe a 4.

I was a statistical outlier, that dot *way* out there by itself on the edge of the chart: a redhead (3% prevalence) with a Mathematical Science degree (1% prevalence), working in the mining industry (3% prevalence), and even if I was sort of lax with my definition of what actually constituted sleeping with someone, I had *not* slept with eight people. I hadn't even been on *dates* with eight separate people. I was about as far away from 'most people' as it was statistically possible to be.

Most regular people also didn't screw up their whole day before their alarm even went off in the morning, either. As an outlier, though, I figured I was totally capable of bucking that trend.

Which is why I found myself groaning and shielding my sore eyes from the sunlight streaming through my window at 6:30am. Gosh, my head was *pounding*, I needed to stop drinking on work nights, especially if it was getting *this* light in the morning now. Though, it... did strike me as odd that the sun was out this early in October, and I—

...Oh, no... it *was* only 6:30am, wasn't it...?

I sat bolt upright with one hand on my aching head and the other feeling blindly around for where I'd put my phone last night. Even the light of my screen hurt my eyes and I had to squint *really* hard to—*it was 7:12 already*? *No!* I was going to miss meeting Sarah!

I sprung out of bed in a panic—knocking my ankle on the bedframe and *swearing* the whole block of flats down—showered in two minutes flat and then ran around in my bra and undies looking for where I'd put my dress suit yesterday. There weren't many places for it to hide in my tiny one-bedroomer, and I found it laid out on the kitchen bench and, consequently, I also discovered why my grumpy old cat wasn't sleeping on top of me when I woke up this morning.

...because he was sleeping on my navy dress suit. All over it, with all of his long orange fur.

"*Crumpet!*" I hissed at him, shooing him off my blazer and holding it up to inspect the damage. It was disastrous. The amount of fur on it defied the amount that could possibly be attached to a single cat, let alone moulted by one overnight. "*Oh, no!*"

It looked terrible, but it wasn't like I had a choice about whether or not to wear it—I didn't have time to look for anything else if I wanted to meet Sarah at the train station! I threw it on, paused to sigh at my reflection, and then ran out the door.

I suppose I could have rushed straight to the station just to be sure I didn't miss her, but I'd been looking forward to surprising her with a drink from her favourite café—the one we always used to go to.

The barista recognised me the second I pushed the door open. "Gemma!" he said, a big smile on his weathered old face as he leant on his elbows on the counter. "Long time no see! Where have you been?" He pretended to glare at me. "Have you and Sarah been cheating on me with another café? Is it that guy around the corner? *I will take him out.*"

I had to laugh at that; I forgot how much I liked him. "No," I promised, "Sare got pregnant, and her boyfriend worries about her catching the train in the cold so he mostly drives her to work now."

The barista made an 'ah' expression. "Well, congratulate her for me!" Then, thinking for a moment, he took a huge, almost McDonald's-level enormous cup off the top of the coffee machine. "We have jumbo cup now. If she's drinking for two, maybe she should have that instead?"

It was so comically large that I just *had* to get Sarah's hot chocolate in it, and then with some difficulty I ferried our drinks to the station, and with even more difficulty, I somehow managed to awkwardly juggle them as I tapped on and went through the turnstiles in time for the 7:31. There was even a bench free—good thing, because the jumbo hot chocolate practically needed a seat of its own.

I sat down beside it, chuckling to myself about the weird looks it was getting. Gosh, Sarah was going to just love this thing; I couldn't wait to see her face when I surprised her with it! I angled myself towards the gates, trying to spot Sarah's sleek dark brown hair or hear the clip-clip of her signature Jimmy Choos on the platform. There were a lot of stylish women in suits standing around me, but none of them were her.

By the time the 7:31 pulled up and everyone piled into it, I hadn't seen her. *Someone's late,* I thought smugly as I watched the train disappear down the tracks, thinking I could finally tease *her* about being late for once. I checked my phone to see if she'd messaged me—she hadn't—and finished my latte. Never mind, we'd still make it to work on time if we got the 7:46.

By the time that train arrived, though, Sarah still hadn't.

That was the last train we could catch to work and arrive on time; the 8:01 would make us about 15 minutes late. It was really unlike Sarah to be late to work. I sat there, biting my lip and staring down at the silent phone in my hands. She *always* messaged me if she was going to be late.

She wasn't here, she hadn't messaged me, and there were way less people arriving at the station now.

I couldn't ignore the knot in my stomach. She wasn't coming after all, was she?

I exhaled, sinking down into the bench and feeling suddenly really stupid for spending $8.00 on a novelty drink when Sarah only told me she *might* catch the train this morning. It was just that I used to enjoy catching it with her so much, it didn't even occur to me that 'might' didn't mean 'would'. I thought she'd be just as excited as I was to be commuting together again...

I shouldn't have rushed, I thought as I looked down at my cat hair-covered blazer and my stockingless pale legs. I hadn't even done my makeup. That wouldn't matter for most women—especially women like Sarah who looked amazing with or without it—but because I was a redhead, everything on my face was practically blond until I de-blonded it. The people on the opposite platform were probably wondering why I had no eyebrows.

I stood as the 8:01 was announced, craning my neck hopefully towards the turnstiles one last time. When I didn't see her, I dropped the jumbo cup I'd bought especially for her in the bin beside me with a *clang*, and squished onto the train all by myself.

On the train, no one would even stand near me. Intellectually I knew that was because they had dark suits and I was basically a human-shaped orange cat, but it felt symbolic, somehow. Sarah would have found it hilarious. *It's okay, she can laugh at me about it over lunch*, I promised myself—she was so busy these days that our standing 20-minute lunch dates were basically the only time I saw her—*or at least I can tell her over lunch if I didn't get fired for being so late again...*

I leant my forehead against the closed door, and gently banged it there a couple of times. Why did I keep doing this to myself? Sighing, I stared out the window as the train departed.

I'd always liked the train ride into central Sydney from the North Shore. It went across the Sydney Harbour Bridge and you could watch the gleaming skyscrapers of the CBD approaching across the harbour. It was quite a change from what I used to see on my way into the city: I'd lived Westside my entire childhood and the view from *those* trains was basically just graffiti tags and dirty factory walls. I'd probably still be living out west, except Sarah bought a house on the North Shore about five years ago, and I struck jackpot by managing to rent a flat close by so we could keep commuting together. We did, for years.

I still found it really strange catching this train into the city without her.

It was downhill from Wynyard Station to Frost International HQ, but that meant nothing because I wasn't really a runner. In fact, Mathletics was about the closest I ever got to competitive sport. Despite that, though, I made it through the front doors before 8:45, minus my makeup, my stockings and my dignity.

I didn't really want to face my co-workers without any eyebrows, but I also didn't want to lose my job by being even *more* late than I already was, so I passed by a chemist without going in and took the service lift direct to Level 22—I know, we weren't supposed to do that, but I watched security enter the code once—and made a mad dash for my desk before my supervisor noticed I was missing from—

—he was *at* my desk, sitting in my chair.

11

Oh, no... I stopped abruptly the moment I saw him, and he swivelled slowly around to face me. "Good afternoon, Gemma," he said neutrally, his heavy black eyebrows low over his eyes.

He was like the patient, Indian version of my dad, and he had the same *you've disappointed me* frown. "I know, I'm so sorry, Anil! I'll get started!"

He was still staring at me. "Finance has been bothering me about why you're not answering your phone for the past 10 minutes, I had to come out of the big meeting to see why that was."

"I'm sorry!"

That wasn't enough, apparently. "Is there something you want to tell me, Gemma?" He leant forward and said more gently, "You've been punctual for seven years and now suddenly you're late all the time, and *look at you*," he gestured to my cat hair, my lack of stockings and eyebrows, and my generally dishevelled appearance. "What's changed, Gemma? Are you having personal problems?"

Was I *ever*... Thinking about them, I could feel my face going red.

He noticed, and spent a couple of moments staring at me. I think I'd basically imagined every possible scenario of *'You're fired!'* before he made an agreeable noise and stood up. "Get counselling on Frost's cheque book if you need it, I'll give it the sign off. But don't forget you start at 8:30." I was halfway through releasing the breath I'd been holding when he added as he walked away, "And you can take the time you missed out of your lunch break."

...my lunch break? Groaning, I flopped into my chair. So much for lunch with Sarah, and so much for my happiness level being maybe a four. It was definitely at least *minus* four right now. Or less, maybe minus a thousand.

Pushing aside the feeling that Anil had let me off way too easily for being repeatedly late, I opened my queue, feeling uncomfortable.

Not that feeling uncomfortable was that unusual for me at Frost; I was the problem child of the back office, not only because I forgot everything and never read my emails, but also because I was the only person in the whole company with a job like mine and no one really knew where to put me. It wasn't because I had a really cool, really unique job, either. Not at all. While my cohorts from the graduating class of Mathematical Science were all over the world doing super glamorous things like disaster climatology, or forensic analytics, or even cryptography for government intelligence agencies, what was I doing?

I was fixing broken spreadsheets. *Forever*.

You can't even imagine the ways in which the allegedly highly intelligent people in a Fortune 500 mining company like Frost International could mess up a single formula so that all the linked spreadsheets started turning out really obscure, really weird errors, but it was crazy. Locking them didn't help, either, because then they got upset that they couldn't make *oh my god so important changes* to things like the cell colour. I always tried to consult on this stuff when I constructed the damn things, but no, apparently being able to change the font was more important to this company than a spreadsheet that worked and continued to work without my intervention.

With a heavy sigh, I got out a notepad and began to write some of the formulas longhand so I could see where the issue was. Gosh, this was so *boring*.

Honestly, this job had seemed pretty cool when I was 21 and freshly out of uni—and it was so awesome that my friends and I could join a huge graduate program and all get really well-paid jobs together—but seven years later the last of them had left except for me and Sarah, and Sarah was getting leadership roles now. Meanwhile, I was getting nagging emails asking me for an ETA on Finance's broken ledgers.

Mid-morning, I'd gotten up to get myself a coffee and was surprised to find that our really swish pod coffee machine didn't have the usual line of people waiting to use it. In fact, there was no one in the kitchen. It was like the twilight zone; I didn't have to fight all the other women on Level 22 for the skinny milk. On my way back to my desk I suddenly realised why that was: the entire department was empty.

I stopped in the middle of the floor and surveyed the vacant workstations around me. Come to think of it, no one had said hello to me when I came in this morning, had they...?

I went back to my desk, feeling uneasy. Was there something I should to be at...? I checked my calendar in Outlook to find out, but it was empty. That didn't mean much, though, because I was pretty hopeless at accepting invitations. I supposed there was always the possibility that it was just a Risk department thing; even though I sat with them, I wasn't really part of them and they sometimes had meetings without me. I hoped that was it.

By midday when they still weren't back, though, I decided I probably needed to make sure I *wasn't* supposed to be somewhere. Maybe we had training today or something? I dialled Anil's number.

He didn't answer. I squinted, trying to remember my last conversation with him. Actually, hadn't he mentioned coming out of some meeting...? I leant back in my chair and looked towards his office; the door was closed and the lights were out.

My heart lifted. If he wasn't there, maybe I could steal a few minutes with Sarah for lunch after all...? I spent a minute or two frantically cleaning my blazer with the clothes brush, grabbed my purse and snuck over to the lift, heading to Level 36.

The first thing I noticed up there was that half of Marketing was missing, too, which was weird. The other half was full of terrifying alpha male extroverts who were eating lunch and chatting, and one of them whistled to get my attention, waved, and called across the floor, "Look who it is! Hey, Gemma!"

Oh, no. I went *bright* red. I probably should have said hello back and had some level of polite conversation with them like

14

any *normal* person would, but instead, I scuttled off and hid in the women's toilets.

Sarah hadn't been at her desk anyway, so I waited in the toilets for a few minutes, and then had to leave so it wouldn't look like I was doing anything shady in there by myself.

I hung around near the lifts for a while in case she came back from wherever she was—there was a much-frequented Red Bull vending machine there, so when people passed me I just pretended to be very engrossed in making a selection—but there were a lot of men up here and no Sarah.

Every time the lift opened I took a hopeful breath, and every time, she wasn't in it. When I'd been waiting for around 20 minutes, I conceded defeat. People were beginning to trickle out of whatever meeting they'd been in, and Anil might be back by now. I didn't want my absence to look like more than a toilet break. I told myself 'just one more minute' a couple of times, and then when those one minutes were up, I got into the lift myself, feeling like a deflated balloon.

It just wasn't going to happen today for me, was it?

I must have looked pretty sad, because a girl I kind of recognised in the lift plucked up the courage to say consolingly to me, "Don't worry, I'm sure it will all work out."

That seemed like a really nice thing to say—strange and super left-field, but nice—so I thanked her as I got out at 22. It *did* mean that I needed to look less miserable, though, if even random people I hardly knew could tell I was.

On my way back to my desk, I was just trying to pull myself together and not to look like the sky was falling in when, through the partitions, I could see a pair of long legs crossed at the ankles on my desk. They were wearing a pair of familiar Jimmy Choos.

Oh! I'd recognise those legs anywhere!

I didn't need to fake a smile anymore, that was for sure! As I got closer to my desk, I spotted that long dark hair falling perfectly over the shoulders of a neat black suit, a pair of slender wrists with stylish selection of bangles on them laced behind her head, and as I said, "Sare!" with transparent enthusiasm, she looked over her shoulder and gave me this bright open smile. It was like staggering up to an oasis in the desert.

"*There* you are!" she said, lifting her ankles off my desk, standing up a little awkwardly because of her big belly, and leaning in for a hug without even caring about the residual cat fur on me. She smelt like *Sarah*, and the French perfume I'd bought her for Christmas. "I thought you were at the union meeting. I was about to send someone in undercover to get you."

Union meeting? "Oh, *that's* where everyone is..." I said as I stepped back from her. Gosh, I needed to get this stupid *smile* off my face this very second. "I probably couldn't have gone to it anyway."

She nodded once and with purpose. "Damn straight you couldn't. We have our standing lunch date, and I'm much more important than enterprise agreements or whatever they're talking about." She flashed me a smile as she grabbed her handbag. "Now where do you want to go? Just to the food court, maybe? I'm starving and Junior here says whatever we have, it needs to be *slathered* in grease." She patted her round stomach.

'Slathered in grease' sounded pretty good to me—I hadn't eaten anything yet today—but I had a feeling the union meeting had already finished. I stopped her. "Anil saw me come in late again this morning..."

She raised her perfect eyebrows, and then laughed. "Okay, Gem, I have a question, how does a mathematician extraordinaire keep coming in late like normal people? Aren't there numbers on a clock?"

I thought about those two missed trains and the hot chocolate, and pretended to laugh with her.

She hooked an arm affectionately around my shoulder. "I love you, Gem," she said, definitely not understanding the effect those words had on me, "but you're completely hopeless."

16

She was right, I totally was. Just not for the reasons she thought.

"So, anyway, I guess you're stuck at your desk?" I nodded. She paused for a moment, deep in thought, and then leant gracefully back, picked up my phone and dialled four numbers. "Hey, it's Sarah," she said authoritatively when someone answered. "I know this is outside your job description, but can you go downstairs, grab two plates of nachos and bring them to Level 22? Thanks, I owe you one!" When she hung up, she explained sheepishly, "I have interns now, and they're all desperate to get on my good side."

I didn't blame them. "Thanks. I haven't eaten yet," I confessed, sinking into my chair as she sat herself up on my desk.

"Huh," she said thoughtfully, considering that and giving me the once-over. "...*and* you're not wearing stockings despite the fact you hate how pale your legs are, *and* you're not wearing makeup." She was waiting for an explanation.

It was on the tip of my tongue why I'd rushed to the station this morning, and I ached to say it. I couldn't, though.

At my silence, she laughed gently and warmly squeezed my shoulder. "How is someone as amazing as you so completely hopeless? Maybe I should start giving you wake up calls again."

I perked up. Waking up to her?! "That might help," I said as mildly as I could.

"Then it's decided," she announced and then tilted her head at me. "Anyway, it's been a while since I've seen you without makeup. Honestly? I kind of like the au naturel look on you."

"I don't," I said flatly. "I prefer having eyebrows and eyelashes, but I left my pencil at home with my stockings."

She immediately looked smug. "You are going to love me, then, because look what's in my handbag." She reached into it and spent a second feeling around in the bottom before her hand emerged with a dual eye pencil/mascara wand.

17

Rather than hand it to me, she gestured at my face. "Close your eyes."

Was she offering to—? "You're going to do it for me?"

"You bet. I'm the pro. Come on, close those baby blues." I couldn't close them fast enough.

Her fingertips touched my cheeks, steadying her hand on them. She did my eyebrows first—so gently she gave me goose bumps. Thank goodness I was wearing long sleeves. It wasn't until I could feel her lean away from me to dip the mascara wand that I realised I'd been holding my breath, and when she leant back in, her thumb was resting on by bottom lip. Gosh, my skin was *tingling* underneath it. It felt like the sort of touch someone would give you just before they kissed you—running their thumb over your lower lip—in this moment we were sharing, I could imagine her leaning in and touching those perfect, soft, beautiful lips of hers against—

"What is this, a salon?" That was Anil's voice. I jumped, flinging my eyes open and in my panic, the wand poked me directly in the eye. Yelping, I clutched it as he continued, "What are *you* doing down here?" That must have been to Sarah.

There were tears pouring out of my poked eye, and I could feel I was probably getting mascara everywhere. Confirming that, Sarah was looking at me and biting down on a giggle. She spoke to Anil first. "I'm just doing her makeup so she doesn't have to leave her desk for even a minute," she told him like it was no big deal. I thought it was super insubordinate before I remembered that Sarah was a supervisor now too, or a 'Lead' or whatever the Marketing version of that was called. "I ordered her lunch up here, as well. I'll be done in a sec and she can get right back to work, I promise."

Then, like nothing was wrong at all, she pointed at me. "Close your eyes," she directed. Caught between two supervisors, I opted to do what she said. I could feel my poor supervisor staring at us while she cleaned my eyes up with a tissue and expertly did my mascara again. It ruined the moment for me.

"There," she said eventually, leaning back to admire her work, and then putting the pencil/wand back in her handbag as she stood up. "I should probably head on back up anyway. Can you tell Andy to bring my nachos up to me when you see him?" she asked me, and after I nodded, she made a guilty face at Anil. "Sorry, you can have your employee back now."

"Thanks," he said dryly, and made me worry that I was going to get in trouble again. I don't know if I was or if I wasn't, but he just gave me a pointed look and went back to his office and firmly closed his door. He didn't usually do that—and he wasn't usually grumpy, either—which made me worry that he was even more angry at me than I thought.

I probably should have worried a lot more about that, but the skin on my bottom lip was still singing where Sarah had touched it, and I couldn't stop admiring myself in the reflection of the computer screen. I really liked the way she'd done it. I was busy smiling dreamily at a formula on my notepad and wondering if Sarah would do my makeup every day if I told her how good she was at it, when I began to notice my co-workers shuffling glumly back in from the union meeting.

Not that Risk isn't a mind-numbingly boring job, but they looked even more reluctant than usual to get back to it. I watched several of them sit in their chairs, run their hands through their hair, and some of them grabbed their mobiles and ducked away to make private calls.

"You look pretty cheerful today," one of my co-workers commented bitterly to me while I was watching them. "Then again, I guess you're not really *in* Risk, are you?" He turned back to his computer and opened Seek.

I just gaped at the back of his head for a moment. Had I done something to upset him...? I wasn't even sure I'd spoken to him before. He wasn't inviting me to speak to him now, either—and I wouldn't have, I mean, what do you even *say* to that?—so I just swallowed, and turned back to my formula. Maybe the enterprise agreements negotiations had failed or something and we weren't getting a pay rise this year.

A couple of minutes later when I'd victoriously discovered the missing bracket and was re-working the formula in the sheet, the guy who sat behind me—Spud, everyone called him because he was completely bald—flopped into his chair and, loudly groaning, leant back and put his forearms over his head. "Fuck it," he said through his forearms. "Fuck everything." He was in his late fifties and generally a level-headed person; it was kind of weird to hear him swear.

What was wrong with everyone?

"Are you alright?" I asked him, because he was making a really strange noise.

He took his forearms off his head and twisted to look at me. "Yeah, I'm great," he said, his voice dripping with sarcasm. "Never better. I've just found out I've worked here for fifteen years for nothing. Just fantastic."

I probably looked like a deer in headlights. "Oh, okay..."

He was about to say something, when he double-took and his expression changed. "Wait a minute, you weren't in the meeting, were you?" I shook my head. Recognition passed over his face, and he sat up. "Well, sorry to be the bringer of bad news," he told me, "but the word on the street is that Frost is offshoring half of their back office as of next year—all the non-client contact jobs. The entire Risk department is going to go. Naturally that's fucking bullshit, so the unions are bringing in the big guns to fight it in court. I don't think they're going to do anything except delay the inevitable, though."

Frost is offshoring half of their—what? "So what does that mean?"

He looked exhausted by the thought of it. "It means we'd all better start working on our resumes."

CHAPTER TWO

The only good thing about being completely doomed was that I ended up getting my wish after all: Sarah knocked off work at a reasonable human hour and caught the train home with me. Under less dire circumstances that would have totally made my night, but I kept thinking about how it might be *the last time ever* that I caught this train with her and I ruined it. I couldn't cry, though, because I didn't want to ruin my beautiful eye makeup.

Sarah looped an arm around my shoulder as we got out at our station. "Cheer up, Gem," she told me, "even if it *is* true and your job *is* being offshored, you're talented and gorgeous and we'll find somewhere else for you to work in no time."

I don't want to work anywhere else, I thought miserably, laying my head on her shoulder as we walked.

She took that as a sign I was really upset and gave me a firm squeeze. "Seriously, look on the bright side: that job has no opportunity for advancement, you didn't really have your own team—"

"—that was a 'plus'," I interrupted her. "I like working by myself."

"Well, trust me, it's way better to have people to whinge with," she told me. "I think you'd enjoy working with people if you were working with the right people."

That sounded pretty upbeat for someone who never stopped complaining about her department. "I thought you hated your co-workers?"

Sarah shrugged. "At least they answer to me," she said, and then added somewhat ominously, "until this big project is finished and I'm not Lead anymore, anyway. Then I'm by myself in a department full of misogynists again."

I lifted my head off her shoulder, brightening. "Hey, maybe we could look for new jobs together?"

She made a face. "Sorry, Gem. I feel for you, but after years of hard work I'm finally starting to get somewhere. Now is the worst time I could leave."

I exhaled. It was worth a try.

We stopped by the bottle-o on the way home so I could grab some sparkling white, and since Sarah didn't want me to drink by myself again, she invited me around to her place and added, "Rob's out of town so you can stay over if you want."

That definitely would have made my day if I hadn't been on the cusp of hardly ever seeing her again: when Rob was out of town, Sarah let me sleep beside her in her bed. I was busy buzzing quietly inside and wondering how long I'd have to wait before I declared that I was really tired, when I noticed a familiar eyesore missing from the driveway as we walked up her front stairs: Rob's banged up ute. Wait a minute... "Hang on, if Rob isn't around, how did you get to work this morning?"

She let us in and ducked into the first door off the hall to get changed, saying over her shoulder, "Min drove me."

Min Lee was Sarah's handsome and androgynous ex-co-worker who'd somehow managed to achieve something in two short months of friendship with Sarah that I'd failed to in ten long years of it: being invited to live in Sarah's spare room. It was kind of awful for me to be even a little bit jealous of that, though, because I didn't get outed at Frost as non-binary transgender, get treated horrifically and get fired like she did. Apparently, it went as high as the two CEOs, so not even her HR manager ex-boyfriend had been able to protect her and she'd ended up nearly homeless. She was getting her revenge by secretly sub-contracting the graphics she'd been originally hired for under some ridiculous and insulting pseudonym, though.

When I wandered into Sarah's living room, Min was actually in the middle of doing exactly that, hunched over her graphics tablet and squinting at her laptop screen. She didn't look up when I came in. "Just FYI, I'm not going to finish this tonight."

I blinked at her. Was she—talking to me? Or skyping someone, maybe? Reflexively, I glanced over my shoulder to see if Sarah was there. She wasn't.

"—because I've tried a thousand variations and there is no way this *essay* is going to fit on any billboard." She was apparently still trying to fit it there, anyway. "Are you sure you really need to have that part about 'surprising her'? Because the main surprise will be if anyone can actually read the text at the size I'll need to make it to fit."

When I just stood there uncomfortably, she glanced up and double-took when she saw it was me. "*Oh.*" She laughed nervously and then scratched the back of her cropped hair, looking sheepish. "Um, sorry, Gemma. Hi."

I exhaled with relief. "Thought I was Sarah?"

She flashed me a grin. "I bet you get that a lot."

For a second I thought she was totally serious, and I'd opened my mouth to tell her that one of our old friends used to mix our names up all the time at uni. I was midway through saying the first word when I realised she was *joking* because of how different we were, but I'd already made this really weird, half-a-word sound and the sentence was unsalvageable. I panicked and clamped my mouth shut, that weird sound I'd made haunting me forever.

Min just stared at me.

Sarah made it even worse. She chose that exact moment to stride into the living room and was in the middle of asking, "Hey, are we minus one small blond schoolgirl? Where's your girlfriend, Min?" when she noticed something was off and stopped in her tracks.

"She's off studying for the Psych exam she has next Monday," Min said casually, like we hadn't just been having a *really awkward moment*.

Sarah had a sixth sense for things to tease me about, though, and could basically smell it. She narrowed her eyes at us. "Spill, guys. What did I miss?"

Min briefly shook her head. "Nothing unusual, just Gemma spectacularly ruining another one of my jokes."

Ugh... That weird sound I'd made was still echoing in my brain... why couldn't I hold a conversation like normal people?! *Why*?

Sarah had been laughing, but stopped when she saw my expression. "Whoa, whoa, wait a second..." She put a hand on my shoulder and walked around me to get a better view of my face. I tried to hide my burning cheeks from her, but I couldn't. "Is that... Yes! Yes, it is! That's 46 for me!" She put her hands in the air like she'd scored a goal.

Min looked insulted. "No way, she only blushed after *I* accused her of wrecking my joke, that one's mine. Which means—drumroll, please—" she held her hands up as if to say something really momentous, "my grand total comes to 62."

Sarah wasn't backing down. "She would have blushed just from what *I* said if you hadn't stolen it from me."

I couldn't believe these two. They couldn't be in the same room together. "Okay, let me settle this: you're *both* terrible," I told them, putting my bottle of sparkling white on the table with a pronounced clonk.

They finished cackling together and Min looked properly chastised. "Sorry, Gemma," she said, and then nodded at the bottle. "So what are we drinking to?"

"My misery," I told her flatly. "I'm probably going to lose my job."

That immediately sobered her; she'd been through hell with hers. Her smile fell. "Shit, what happened? Are you okay?"

Sarah answered for me. "Her whole department's going to be offshored."

"Oh..." Min paused for a second, considering me. I was wondering if maybe I'd brought back some of the awful memories or something, when she stood up and said with exaggerated cheer, "Well, that's *fantastic.* Congratulations! This is your chance to be free from that soul-sucking purgatory forever." She took a few steps over to give me tight hug. "That's definitely something to drink to!"

I let her hug me for a second and then shoved her off, groaning. "Min, I'm actually sad about this, I like working there!"

She let me go, giving me a weird look. "Don't you *want* your soul back?"

Sarah grabbed a couple of wine glasses off the cabinet. "Her manager is one of the good ones," she told Min, putting a wine glass by the chair in front of me and another beside Min's laptop. "And so is your new one, don't you think, Min? Really good, actually. Amazing. Probably the best manager ever." She preened herself.

Min rolled her eyes again, chuckling. "'Contractor' and 'employee' are not the same thing."

"Whatever, the important thing is I'm the boss of you," she said with a big grin and an eyebrow waggle, and then popped the cork on my sparkling white. "Okay, let's get Gem drunk so she can hold a conversation without being really awkward." She winked at me as she poured us a glass each.

My stomach fluttered. I didn't even mind the 'awkward' jibe.

Min reached for her glass. "You're not going to hate us forever for drinking in front of you?"

Sarah shrugged as we all sat down at the dining table. "Well, I'd love to be joining you two, but Junior here isn't 18 yet and I don't want to break the law." She patted her belly. "Anyway, Gem, while you're letting the booze sink in, would you mind if I got Min to show me the billboards she's been working on for a sec? I have a progress report to write tomorrow. I promise that I'll give you my full and undivided attention afterwards."

I liked the promise of her full and undivided attention, so while the two of them had their heads together agonising over such critically important things as font size, I drained my glass and watched them. I had no idea what they were talking about—my eyes kind of glazed over whenever they went into marketing mode—but what I could tell was that there was a lot of brainpower right there being wasted on whether or not a diamond advertisement needed to contain the word 'surprise' or not. The more wine I drank, the more ridiculous it seemed that a pair of really great minds were being used to sell diamonds to rich people instead of, like, curing cancer or fixing the economy or something.

Then again, I was fixing spreadsheets for a living, so who was I to talk? I sighed and poured myself another glass of wine.

When they were done, Min went to top up her drink only to have one solitary little drop of wine fall into her glass. She raised her eyebrows.

I grimaced. *Whoops, I guess I got a little carried away.* "Uh, sorry..."

She snickered. "That's okay, I just made it to 63," she said with a cheeky grin, and then didn't dwell on it. "Besides, you probably need it more than I do, anyway. When's your last day at Frost? Is it soon, or did they give you lots of notice?"

"They haven't given me any notice," I told her. "There was some big union meeting today and the unions apparently told everyone what they'd sniffed out."

"Oh," she said, immediately looking a bit sceptical. "Well are you 100% sure you're even losing your job? Because the unions have been warning us we were all going to be offshored for years. Don't get me wrong, they do great work, but they're all a bunch of doomsayers."

I shrugged. "Well, I wasn't there, but everyone in Risk looked pretty sure. They were all miserable, even my boss. The whole department's going, apparently."

Sarah had been watching us, deep in thought. "Maybe Min's right," she said eventually. We both looked at her. "Like, you got told that Risk is being offshored, yeah?" I nodded. "Well, are you even part of Risk?"

I pulled a face. "Officially, I think? I'm not sure, though."

She leant forward in her chair, pointing at me. "Exactly. So even if they *are* being offshored, maybe you're still safe?" She looked at Min. "And wouldn't Henry have hinted to us anyway if something like this was happening?"

Min shook her head firmly. "No way, Henry *always* told me when we were still dating that he'd never use his position as HR manager to give me any sort of advantage over other people, so he'd be the same about you guys. He has really strong ethics about this stuff."

Sarah didn't look very impressed by his ethics. "But what if Gem asked him directly now that the word's out? Everyone knows, so just confirming her position is going isn't unfair, is it?"

Min gave us a very deep shrug. "She could ask him..."

Sarah still wasn't satisfied. "I don't get how you could not know anything though? Like, you didn't hear a phone conversation, or catch a glance at something on his desk when you're over at his house, or—"

"—*Sarah*," Min said pointedly, interrupting her. "The only thing I've noticed is that he has a lot of union meetings recently. That's about it. He literally tells me nothing, and I don't ask."

She sighed at length, and leant back in her chair. "Well, I guess I can go see him tomorrow and ask. Maybe I could read his face."

"He's not going to give you information about another employee. If anyone should go, it should be Gemma."

I'd been swimming in a pleasant alcoholic haze, but my ears pricked to attention at my name. "*Me?*"

Sarah looked a bit entertained by my reaction. "Oh no!" she said, mimicking how I said it, and then added, "You'll have to talk to a man whIle sober!"

I mock-glared at her. "I've talked to Henry before."

"—*While sober.*"

I ignored that. "But since Min says he won't tell me anything, what's the point?"

Min made a face. "He might. I don't know."

Sarah was grinning at me. "Looks like you're going to have a one-on-one with Mr HR Manager tomorrow."

I suddenly *really* wasn't looking forward to tomorrow. "But won't he be really busy?" I attempted. "Can't you ask him for me?"

Min was feeling around in her pockets for her phone. "I can ask him to put an appointment in your calendar for when he's free."

"Okay, that's settled, then," Sarah said, totally without consulting me at all. "Let us know if you find out anything, Gem. Anyway, you guys want something to eat? I'm pretty sure there are some leftovers in the fridge."

Sarah nuked a few things in the microwave for us and we chatted and ate—but Min had been compulsively checking her phone every two minutes and eventually it buzzed and she announced she needed to go and collect her girlfriend from the station.

"Can I borrow your car again?" she asked Sarah as she stood.

"Keys are on the hall table," was Sarah's automatic answer, before something occurred to her and she twisted towards Min in her chair, "Wait, how much did you have to drink?"

Min gave me a pointed look. "Not much."

I *cringed*.

"That's 64," Min said with a smirk, and then called over her shoulder as she went up the hall, "I'll be fine, Sarah."

After Min had gone, I figured I'd waited long enough for it to be realistic that I was tired, so I declared I was *oh my god exhausted* and wanted to go to bed. It wasn't even 10.

"We're getting old," Sarah said, stretching as she stood up. "I can't believe I'm actually looking forward to going to bed!"

I wished she hadn't put it quite like that, because the idea that she was in any way looking forward to sleeping beside me made me practically float down the hallway on cloud nine. Well, on cloud alcohol, anyway.

"I have some comfy old t-shirts in that drawer if you want to grab one," Sarah told me as she ran a brush through her hair, pointing me towards her tallboy.

I rifled through it for a few moments, and then came across a t-shirt I recognised: it was from this one time we were in Germany and there was a death metal band near our backpackers'. Neither of us had any idea about death metal but, just for the hell of it, we went. The whole venue stank like weed and we met this couple there who were painted up like evil KISS but who ended up having their doctorates in sociology. It was wild. Sarah bought a t-shirt to commemorate the occasion; it was really faded now, though.

I held the t-shirt up, turning around to say, "I can't believe you kept this!" but I only made it halfway through the sentence.

Sarah was topless, and facing me.

Panicking, I spun back around, my cheeks burning. My brain was screaming, '*What do I do??*' but I didn't have an answer for it, because the memory of all that tan skin and those perfect breasts was completely paralysing. I desperately wanted to turn back around, but there was no way in hell I was going to be able to do that.

Sarah noticed. "That's 47," she said smugly as she finished dressing, and continued, "It's hard not to stare at it, isn't it? It's like someone shoved a beach ball in there."

Oh thank goodness, she thought I'd been looking at her stomach!

While I was taking deep breaths and trying to get my act together, she grabbed my wrist and forced me to turn towards her, and before I could protest or say anything or recover she'd wrenched her pyjamas up and put my hand on her stomach. "There's a *human* in there. Here, feel, she's going nuts now." I was busy trying to deal with the fact I was touching Sarah's bare skin, when I felt something inside her stomach push against my hand.

29

I must have looked pretty alarmed, because Sarah laughed. "I know, right? It's creepy as hell. All I can think of is that scene from Alien."

She let me retract my hand, and then climbed under her side of the doona. It was only at that point that I realised I was staring again.

She smirked. "I mean, you can sleep in your work clothes if you like, but I think adding 'slept in' to 'covered in cat fur' is probably going to get you sent home to change."

Oh, right.

...Oh, no.

I looked down at the t-shirt. Sarah was *watching* me, and had actually started to chat about something—I think about her belly again?—but I was only aware of *every hair on my body* standing on end as I shrugged off my blazer and unbuttoned my shirt. It was only by accident that I was wearing a really nice bra—my comfy bra was dirty and I kept forgetting to wash it— but Sarah remarked on it as I unhooked it and let it fall over my shoulders. I don't know what she said; all the blood that should have been operating my ears had either rushed into my cheeks or gone down south. Gosh, I was facing her like this. She could see *everything.* Every inch of my skin and every freckle on my body was on fire for every millisecond until I'd pulled that long t-shirt over my head and climbed under the doona beside her.

It took me a moment to be able to breathe again. It didn't last long. *I could roll over,* I realised, thinking of her lying there facing me in that thin pyjama top. If I did, I'd almost be on top of her.

Suddenly, that fantasy seemed really weird and out of place; did I really just think that? *Roll over and what, Gemma?* What exactly did I plan to do to *my pregnant best friend* when I got there?

I mean, it wasn't as if I didn't kind of know what was going on with me, but it was one thing to think 'she's really amazing and I have this silly girlcrush on her' and another to be like 'okay, let's have sex'. I must have been drunker than I thought.

While I was feeling around for the lamp switch, wondering if my desire to do illicit things to her would fade when the alcohol did, I heard the familiar rattle of an old engine pull into the driveway.

My heart sank. I guess I wasn't going to find out tonight.

Conversely, Sarah sat up in bed and I had to watch her face *light up* before she *sprang* out of bed to get the front door. "Rob's back early!"

Someone whistled cheerfully all the way to the front door, and when Sarah opened it, I could hear her *jumping* into his arms and kissing him soundly on the front porch. I wrinkled my nose.

"I thought you weren't back until Thursday!" she said when they broke.

Of course he's back before Thursday, Sarah, I thought, *of course*. Because the universe wouldn't let my happiness level get above four, it was forbidden. I put a pillow over my head and groaned into it.

Rob's broad Australian accent always sounded super broad when he was happy. "Nah, they let us go early because we got everything done!" I heard them kiss again. "So I asked myself: do I want to sleep across from this bloke who snores as bad as I do, or do I want to drive for four hours and sleep beside the most beautiful girl in the world?" he said, and could hear him stepping off his Blundstones in the doorway. Before Sarah could stop him, he'd pushed the bedroom door open and then I was staring at him in his high-visibility vest with his buzzed head and five o'clock shadow. He stopped in the doorway when he saw me on his side of the bed.

I felt guilty, like I'd been caught doing something I shouldn't be. "Hi, Rob..."

Sarah peered around his big tree-trunk arms. "That's what I was trying to say: Gem's here."

He looked guilty, too. "Geez, sorry Gemma!" he said, turning around like he'd seen something he shouldn't have. "I'll get a blanket and sleep on the couch, it's cool. It was a bit *assumptuous* of me to just show up, I guess, hah! You ladies just go back to bed."

As much as I wanted to let him—as much as I really wanted to let him—he'd driven four hours to see her. They'd probably want to have sex too, because he'd been away for a couple of days and Sarah had the libido of 100 rabbits in heat. *Ugh.* "No, it's okay..." I said reluctantly, sitting up. "I've got to go home at some point, anyway. It might as well be now."

They both made a big fuss of inviting me to stay and I had to actually physically restrain Sarah from getting out the blanket and wrestling me down onto her couch, but in the end I won and they let me get dressed again and leave.

"I'm so sorry, Gem," Sarah said, giving me a big hug in her thin, practically transparent pyjamas before I left. "I hope you feel better now, anyway. I bet Henry will be able to tell you what's going on with your job tomorrow, and maybe he'll have a solution, too, and everything will be okay."

With the way the universe clearly had it in for me, I sincerely doubted there was any good news waiting in Henry's office. I forced a smile anyway, hugged her back, and then trudged out onto the street. I could hear them continuing their passionate greeting to each other in private as I left.

To make matters worse, the station was literally a two-minute drive away and Min wasn't back yet, which meant she and her girlfriend had found something else to do to with their time instead of driving back. I half-expected to walk past Sarah's car parked on the side of the road and find them necking in it.

Meanwhile, my flat was silent as I unlocked the door.

I did nearly trip over Mr Crumpet curling around my feet as I walked in, though, and he gave me this beautiful mournful mew like he'd missed me. I crouched down and gave him and cuddle. "At least *you're* happy to see me," I told him, rubbing his lovely fluffy side on my cheek.

...he struggled violently and wrenched out of my arms, retreating to his food bowl. He then sat down beside it and gave me a really demanding glare.

Of course he did. Even my *cat* didn't want my company. I filled up his kibble bowl anyway—which was already half-full, mind you—and he sniffed it distastefully and then went off somewhere to sulk that I hadn't given him wet food.

I ignored his tantrum and wandered into my empty bedroom, shrugging off my blazer again and draping it over the end of my unmade bed.

Everyone else in the known world was probably having great sex with their significant other right now, and meanwhile, I hadn't had a significant other *or* great sex since dinosaurs roamed the earth. Thinking about that, it suddenly made perfect sense why, at 28, my silly girlcrush on Sarah had begun to morph into a full-blown thing every time I was around her: I was probably so lonely I'd fall for a greeting card if it said hello to me every day. That totally explained everything.

But how was I supposed to rectify that when conversation with cute strangers was in my no-go zone? I mean, I was nervous about talking to *Henry* by myself, and not only had I met him dozens of times, but I actually had a legitimate reason to speak to him beyond, 'So, do you come here often…?'

The obvious solution was also the impossible one: I couldn't just be drunk 24/7 in case I bumped into someone I fancied and needed the confidence to say something beyond *HELP*.

I was going to need to figure this problem out, though, or everyone else was going to be well on their way to a three-bedroom house with two children and a picket fence, while I was still stuck crushing on my female best friend and sleeping alone with my ungrateful cat.

CHAPTER THREE

Henry's office was at the south end of Level 35, and the waiting area had floor-to-ceiling windows with a spectacular view of Sydney Harbour. I wasn't sure I needed *that* much sun in my face this early in the morning after all the wine last night, but at least I didn't have to sit in the main HR waiting room which was full to the brim with seething, grumbling employees who were clearly out for blood. More kept arriving in the lifts, too—and I was *super* glad Sarah had made good on her promise to give me a 6:30am wakeup call, because it meant I got in early enough to avoid wading through all those worried people to get here.

I should have been worried about my job, too. And I was—well, sort of. I'd downloaded a whole lot of statistical analyses about offshoring in Australia with the full intention of reading them to see if I agreed with the conclusions, but I'd had the first PDF open on my phone for twenty minutes and hadn't read a word of it. I had other more pressing matters to attend to.

I kept thinking about last night and the fact that I'd actually wanted to have sex with my very pregnant, very heterosexual best friend. In the cold light of day, it was an uncomfortable thing to remember, even if I'd been really drunk.

Maybe I'm gay, I thought, and then laughed at myself. Of course I wasn't gay: I'd had several boyfriends in the very distant past and, okay, those relationships hadn't gone so well, but I'd definitely been attracted to the men I'd been with. I'd also danced with and pashed loads of guys in clubs in all my years of drinking, and there'd even been a guy on the train this morning I'd noticed was kind of hot. In fact, the closest I'd gotten to a girl-on-girl experience was that one time I kissed Min—and I wasn't sure exactly where she fit on the spectrum, but it seemed to be closer to 'guy' than 'girl', so I was pretty sure it didn't count.

Yup, Gemma, you're just lonely, I reassured myself, trying once again to read that offshoring doc.

But... then again...

...maybe it wouldn't hurt to take a little peek at the stats on sexuality?

I opened my browser and googled '*what's the prevalence of female homosexuality in Australia?*' and was tabbing through the results, trying to decide if Wiki was more reliable than a government health webpage for data that I could—

"Gemma?"

I jumped and reflexively flipped my phone over. Henry was leaning out of his office right behind me, looking over my shoulder. I panicked, turning bright flaming red: he definitely would have seen my screen from that angle, and I had no idea how to explain what I was doing.

Unlike his evil ex, though, Henry wasn't running a blush tally and none of his preferred pastimes included 'affectionately' teasing me. In fact, he didn't make any sort of reference to my cheeks or indicate that he'd seen my screen. "Sorry for startling you," he said with a warm smile instead, "I promise I don't normally creep up on people. Please, come in."

Somehow managing to set aside my horror that Henry might have seen what I was doing, I stood up with shaky knees to follow him in. *Time to make an idiot of myself*, I thought, sighing internally. I was already off to a good start.

As I walked past him, though, raised voices up from the waiting room caught his attention and the warm smile fell from his face. He took a few steps out of his office to peer up the hallway, straight at the mob of anxious, frustrated people waiting for HR to attend to them. He then turned back to me with a very neutral expression. "Hmm," he said mildly, and then gave my shoulder an apologetic squeeze. "Would you mind waiting here for a moment?"

He was going to—"You're really going to go in there?" I asked him outright, surprising myself by actually speaking. Risk had been *so* angry yesterday, I had a mental image of those people tearing him limb from limb like hungry lions.

He looked unmoved. "Well, I'm not going to ask my staff to do it," he said like the answer was totally obvious. Then he straightened his tie and walked calmly down the corridor towards the lynch mob. I could hardly watch. Any second, I expected the crowd to swallow him up and start *shouting* at him, or swearing, or, like, beating him up or something...

...and then after he'd spent maybe 20 seconds addressing them all, they all hung their heads and started dispersing towards the lifts, muttering to each other.

I *gaped* at him as he returned. How on *earth* had he done that?

My question must have showed on my face. "Magic," he told me, eyes twinkling as he showed me into his office. For a second, he *really* reminded me of Min.

His dry sense of humour wasn't the only thing he shared with her—they were both six-foot-something and Korean, and, as I read on the name plate on his desk: *Henry Lee, Director Human Resources,* they both had the same surname. They also shared a lot of history; apparently Henry had been *really* in love with Min and they'd dated for ages, but then she came out, transitioned and left him for a schoolgirl literally half his size and age. Okay, so it hadn't gone *quite* that badly. Putting it that way made Min sound really selfish and cruel, but it wasn't like that at all. It was tough for both of them, but they'd come out the other side of it as best friends anyway.

Henry was still single, though, despite the fact Min had moved on. It was kind of awful of me, but I found myself being reassured by that. At least I wasn't the only person who wasn't getting anywhere in their love life.

On thinking that, though, the guilt made my blush come back with a vengeance. I sighed at myself.

Henry pretended not to notice as he rounded his desk, indicating a seat opposite him. "So, how are you, Gemma?"

Lonely and desperate, I thought as we sat down. "Good, thanks. You?"

He made a so-so gesture. "I'll be fine once I find somewhere that will rent me a suit of armour," he said with a grin. "Now, Min was very cryptic about why you needed an appointment with me."

That seemed to be a question. "She didn't say?"

"No, *he* didn't," Henry subtly corrected me, reminding me that to him and most other people, Min was now a 'he'. Min didn't mind which pronouns her friends used, and I kept forgetting that *Henry* minded, probably because of their history. I winced. Yup, there it was: me making a dick of myself. He moved right on, though. "And it would make sense if you'd wanted an appointment after this morning, but he asked last night?"

I couldn't figure out what he meant about the timing. "This morning...?" Why would that make sense?

His eyebrows went up. "You didn't see the paper?" I shook my head, and he sighed deeply. "Well, I don't normally buy it myself, but I nearly inhaled my coffee when I saw it just before..." He leant down beside his desk and snapped open his briefcase, fishing out the Sydney Morning Herald and tossing it on the table in front of me.

I picked it up. I didn't have to look very hard to see what he was referring to: plastered across the front page was the headline in big block letters, '*FROSTY CHRISTMAS SHOCK FOR 480 WORKERS'*, with various sub-headers talking about how the jobs would be gone by Christmas, and profiling employees holding their kids and worrying about losing their family homes.

"By *Christmas*?" I read aloud.

Henry's lips were in a tight line. "It's speculation," he said. He didn't sound happy. "But because of it, two thousand people are going to be lying awake in bed every night wondering if they're in the 480—and that number is fictional, by the way."

I brightened, looking up at him. "So it's *not* true!"

He made a face. "Officially, there's no comment yet."

"But *un*officially?"

"Unofficially, no one would run a story like this unless there was the possibility of changing the outcome," he pointed out. "Everyone knows Frost has been looking at offshoring for the best part of a decade. But it's still very irresponsible to make two thousand people worry before there's been any firm decisions made. Very irresponsible."

Huh. "But everyone in Risk yesterday seemed really certain they were going to lose their jobs..."

Henry paused for a moment, his brow lowering. I was suddenly aware of him watching me very closely, and I thought I'd said something wrong. "Yesterday?" I nodded. When I didn't elaborate, he prompted, "What happened yesterday?"

He was staring at me. I felt like *I* was the one confessing something; it made my voice waver. "I didn't go, but apparently in the union meeting they told a whole bunch of people that Frost is offshoring their jobs?"

His expression was completely unreadable for a few moments, and he sat back and took a couple of really obvious deep breaths. "That meeting was supposed to be about enterprise agreements, which is why management wasn't allowed to go."

I didn't know what to say. I hadn't been there, I didn't know exactly what had happened...

He was shaking his head. "I should have guessed," he said eventually, his voice hardening. "God, I should have guessed. I was barricaded with the rest of upper management in a ridiculous meeting into the small hours of last night because the MEU insisted they needed to speak with us... and of course, after the shock I got reading the paper this morning, I haven't read my emails yet or checked my messages yet..." He ran a hand through his hair. "Those sneaky bastards. I really *will* need that suit of armour."

I almost couldn't bring myself to say it in case it was super inappropriate, but I did anyway: "And I thought *my* job sucked..."

He looked up at me, surprised for a moment—in that moment, I was absolutely certain I'd made a huge mistake and insulted him—and then he broke into a smile. It was like releasing the pressure valve in a boiler. "Yes, want to swap?" he asked dryly. "I'd love to be fixing spreadsheets right now instead of this mess. Anyway, thank you for telling me, Gemma. I'm glad I heard it from you first. It gives me an opportunity to prepare for how much trouble I'm going to be in for not being able to control our relationship with the unions."

I didn't know why it would be Henry's fault that the unions were trying to protect our jobs—wasn't that exactly what they did?—but I also felt like it wasn't really my place to ask him why he'd be in trouble for it, so I didn't. "I guess you probably can't tell me if I'm losing my job or not, then..."

He gave me a gentle smile and shook his head. "But since you're here, there's other things I can do to help you plan your future, regardless of what happens with your current position."

The word 'future' reminded me of my current lack of husband, children and white picket fence. *Awesome, can you help me figure out how to stop crushing on my best friend*? I thought wryly, but let him keep talking.

"For example, I took a minute or two to have a look at your employee profile, and I noticed you haven't had a career plan in place for nearly four years." He looked a bit concerned. "Did Anil not offer to go through them with you?"

I grimaced. Anil was not the problem. "Yes, he kept asking to do them for years, but I never handed them in on time so he gave up."

He chuckled. "They're optional, Gemma. No one's going to get in trouble." He tapped the space bar on his keyboard to wake up his monitor. "Well, perhaps we could go through that process now so you have a training plan in place? Let's focus on your goals, first. Where do you see yourself in five years? Ten years?"

Married, I thought immediately, and then for some reason imagined myself side-by-side with Sarah in her bed, like I had been last night.

"Gemma?"

Crap. "Sorry!" I said, turning bright *red* and feeling like a kid who wasn't paying attention in class. "I don't know."

"You don't know?" he inquired, and I shook my head. "Well," he continued, "let me give you some ideas. Do you see yourself in management? Consulting, maybe? Do you even see yourself in a corporate job, or are you interested in branching out into teaching or research? A bachelor of mathematics *does* lend itself well to a variety of different careers."

Dad had always wanted me to get into teaching or academia. I wasn't interested. "I hope I still have *this* job?"

He smiled slightly. "You said your job sucked a minute ago."

Um. "Well, I like working for Frost, anyway."

He mouthed 'ah', and relaxed back in his chair. "Alright, perhaps we can upskill you, then. There are a number of departments that could benefit from your experience with formulas and statistics. Do you have any interest in finance? Or even something completely different like engineering or resource management? Frost Energy has lots of on-site resource engineers and a good grasp of maths is essential for those jobs."

'On-site' didn't appeal to me for obvious reasons. "Can I just get another job in this location?"

He nodded slowly. "Any departments take your fancy?"

Hah, I laughed to myself when it occurred to me. "I don't suppose you have any positions going in Marketing...?"

I expected him to immediately laugh with me and be like, 'oh, don't be silly, Gemma, someone like *you* who is the opposite of everyone in Marketing could never work there, hah hah!' but instead, he was completely serious. "It's actually funny you say that," he told me. "We used to have a young statistician working in Marketing—he left us to head to the Australian Bureau of Statistics in April and we haven't replaced him yet."

The smile fell right off my face. "Wait, really?"

He nodded. "So if you have a genuine interest in moving to that sort of job, I could speak with Anil and Omar—he's the acting Marketing manager at the moment—about seconding you there for a week or two to see if you do like it."

I knew who Omar was. I'd heard Sarah and Min talk about him. Or rather, I'd heard them talk about how happy they were that he wasn't the old marketing manager Jason, who was the one who'd bullied Min out of her job. "Wow, okay! Thanks!"

He smiled. "If you could just hold off mentioning it to Sarah and Min or anyone else until I have approval, though, I'd appreciate it. It shouldn't take too long."

He didn't have to worry, because as if I'd tell Sarah that I specifically asked. How would I put that? 'Hey, Sare, it's not enough to work in the same company and have lunch with you every day, so I put in a request to work in your department, too!' Yeah, I definitely wasn't going to say that, and I hoped Henry wouldn't. "You won't tell them I asked, will you?" I blurted out, and then immediately regretted it and returned to my regular shade of pink.

I thought he would get all suspicious and want to know why, but he didn't. He just had his usual pleasant and neutral expression. "Of course not. I'll be discreet."

I exhaled. "Thanks!" I told him, my stomach fluttering at the thought of maybe being able to *work* with Sarah full-time. Oh my gosh, we were going to have so much fun!

I was so absorbed in my excitement that it took me ages to notice he was watching me with a private smile. He chuckled when he saw me looking. "I'm going to have a really challenging day today," he confessed. "But this was a very timely reminder of why I moved into HR in the first place: having people look at me like you just did." He nodded at me and my big smile. "Thank you. I forgot how much I enjoy the basics."

I thanked him profusely as well, and since he obviously had stacks of work to do given what was going on with the unions, I floated out of his office and spent a few seconds beaming out of those huge windows at Sydney CBD.

I wouldn't have to worry about hardly seeing Sarah anymore! I felt like I could literally just leap out the window and fly through the air.

Ironically, the very person I was desperate to share my great news with was one of the people I'd been specifically instructed *not* to tell. I considered telling her anyway, but then felt really guilty because Henry was one of those people who you'd rather kick a puppy than lie to. I should probably at least tell her that I didn't have any real news about whether or not my current job was going to be offshored, though.

I took my phone out to text her on my way back to the lift, but stopped in my tracks when I saw what was still on the screen: the results of *'what's the prevalence of female homosexuality in Australia?'*.

The top result read *'Most studies find between 1-3%'*—which was coincidentally the same stat for just about all of my other variable attributes.

Gosh, I hope I'm not, I thought, continuing down the corridor at a more subdued pace. *That would make this whole thing of seeing Sarah naked and wanting to work in the same department kind of creepy.* I felt uncomfortable about that all the way back down to Level 22.

I was busy heading back to my desk and rehashing all my failed relationships to look for clues about my sexuality, when I noticed the ambient noise-level in Risk was higher than usual. That was made even weirder by the fact there were half the usual number of people sitting at their desks.

"Is there another meeting?" I asked Spud as I sat down, looking around us.

He was on Seek.com.au, scrolling through vacant positions in the commercial risk category. "Nope, about five people called in sick and another bunch of them went to have a drink at PJs."

"At 8:30 in the morning?"

He shrugged. "I think when you find out you're going to be made redundant, any time of the day is a good time to drink."

I thought about what Henry said about nothing being set in stone, but knew implicitly not to say anything. The unions might end up being right anyway, even if they were being 'sneaky bastards' or whatever Henry had called them. Instead, I logged in and opened my queue.

I'd only scrolled for about three seconds when I realised there was absolutely nothing in it. Not even Finance were complaining about their ledgers, which *someone*—and I knew exactly who—

always broke. "Spud..." I asked over my shoulder, and he made a 'hmm?' noise. "Do you know if Finance is another one of the departments who are going to lose their jobs?"

"Yup. Admin, too."

Oh. Well, that explained the lack of work I had this morning. Normally when this happened, I'd just do Risk's leftover number-crunching, except that no one was working and it would be weird if I asked to, which meant that I suddenly had free time to do whatever I wanted.

I looked furtively around me to see if anyone was sitting too close, and when I was satisfied they weren't, I got right back to the top secret research on my phone.

The numbers on sexuality were pretty comforting, actually. The percentage of girls who identified as gay was something like 1.2%, but a whopping 20% of women reported having same-sex attraction or experience. That was a pleasant 94% of same-sex-attracted women who *weren't* gay. Those were good odds for me.

I ended up downloading the full research paper and reading it through—*less* comfortingly, most of the women who reported having same-sex experiences were of the 'I had a lot of fun in my youth' variety, not actual adult women like me who were suddenly having feelings. I almost wished I'd stopped at the numbers.

I was also beginning to wish that, like this 94% of non-gay women, I'd been *way* more promiscuous at uni. Sarah had barely spent a single night with her knickers on—although, to be fair, she was a serial monogamist and was generally in relationships—but I found it much harder to find someone I was prepared to go home with. Everyone used to tease me about how picky I was. Right now I wish I'd been *less* picky, too, because then maybe I'd be one of these women who talked in hushed voices about how much fun they'd had in their youth instead of what I was now: someone who wanted to do crazy drunk college things like getting it on with her girlfriends when she was nearly 30 and everyone else was *way* past that.

Basically, all signs still pointed to ending my lonely, desperate dry spell and getting laid being the way to sort myself out. Probably anyone who hadn't had sex in as long as I hadn't would hump just about anything, including their friends. And, given that I'd expected to royally screw up my meeting with Henry and I hadn't, I felt there was hope for me managing to hold an actual conversation with strangers yet. I could just go out this weekend, try really hard not to be picky and bring some guy home.

I shared my decision with Sarah at lunch while we were sitting in a nearby foot court—minus the part about it curing my desire to hump her, of course—and she laughed openly. "About time!" she declared, hunting for olives in her Greek salad. "When was the last time you hooked up? 1801? Anyway, tell me more about what Henry said. Like, *exactly*. Word for word. People often subconsciously communicate the truth without realising it. I bet he did."

We picked apart what he'd told me about the offshoring stuff, and then Sarah tapped her plastic fork against her chin and considered it. "I'm with the unions on this one," she told me. "I mean, it sucks for Henry that he's going to get in trouble and I guess he's right about two thousand people worrying about their jobs, but if less people lose their jobs as a result, isn't it a happy ending?"

"Henry was *not* happy, though, and he knows more than he said."

Sarah shrugged. "I'm still pretty sure the unions are only trying to help you guys," she decided, and then popped another olive in her mouth, mumbling through it, "Did he say anything about your job specifically?"

Oh! I'd nearly forgotten! I took a deep breath as soon as I remembered the good news again, and I was bursting to tell her that she wasn't going to be alone in a 'department full of misogynists' anymore. I'd promised Henry I wouldn't, though. Ugh...

I managed to smother my excitement. "Um, not much. We went through a career plan, and then he said he'd speak to some other managers about looking for work in another department for me."

Sarah smacked her hand on the table. "That's it!" she said, pointing at me. "That's basically a confirmation your job is one of the ones going. Otherwise why would he bother being so helpful?"

"Because he's Henry?"

She ignored that comment. "Anyway, this offshoring stuff is a godsend. You're way better than some pseudo-IT spreadsheet fixer. Now you're going to end up with a better job, better pay and probably a better team, too."

I bit down on my smile. I was definitely getting a better team. *She's going to be such a great teammate and supervisor,* I thought, watching her mining through her salad for the good bits. Working with her was going to be like that time we'd shared a shift at an ice bar when we were travelling around in New Zealand during the winter holidays. It'd been an absolute *blast*. We'd had to wear these big shapeless parkas and fat gloves. Somehow, Sarah had still managed to look amazing in them. I'd been so jealous. She always managed to look amazing.

Today was no exception, either: she was wearing a thin pinstripe shirt with three of the buttons open and a necklace that sat directly on the 'v' of her cleavage. I'd never have the courage to wear something like that, but she was *rocking* it. With all that gorgeous skin and self-confidence, how could she not?

My eyes tracked down into her shirt. *I saw those last night,* I realised. She just had her top right off in front of—

—at that second, Sarah looked up from her salad and caught me staring at her chest.

My heart stopped. I frantically looked away, my treacherous fucking cheeks *burning* as I froze in panic. *Oh no, oh no,* I thought, *reeling*; any second that smile would fall and her expression would harden and—

"What? Did I spill food all over myself again or something?" she asked, craning her neck to look down her shirt and brushing off the swell of her stomach like there was crumbs on it. She must have actually found something there, because she laughed. "Seriously, Gem," she said, picking whatever it was off her shirt and flicking it away. "You are such a prude—just *tell* me if I'm spilling food into my rack, you don't need to stammer and blush and die of embarrassment over saying the word 'boob'!"

I should have been relieved that she thought that's why I was freaking out. I wasn't relieved, though. I seriously wasn't. My heart was pounding in my chest and all I could think of was *gosh* that was close! Too close, far too close! I didn't even want to know how weird it would get if she knew some of the things I'd thought about her. Everything had always been so easy between us, ever since the beginning. It was one of the things I'd always loved about being her friend, because I was normally so stiff around people. Not around Sare.

It haunted me for the rest of the day: how close I'd just come to wrecking 'us'. Sarah was bright, it wouldn't take her much more to figure it out.

That afternoon most people left work early, but I felt bad for Anil so I at least waited until the clock struck five to head off.

It was dusk when I got home. The last of today's sunlight was filtering through the gum trees outside and my big bay window into my cluttered and messy little living room, and my asshole of a cat was lying upside-down in a patch of it in the middle of my old couch. My place wasn't much to write home about, but I loved living here. It was close to everything, and in summer, I could stick cushions on the ledge of my big bay window and sit with it open so I had a breeze on my face. The carpet was tatty and the wallpaper was super dated, but I'd fixed that by covering my floor in assorted Ikea rugs (and, to be honest,

46

clothes and books that didn't fit on the coffee table or kitchen bench) and almost plastering my entire wall in hundreds of photos.

Most of them were me and Sarah. Some of our other friends were in them, too—people we used to see a lot more of when they were still working for Frost. Most of them I hadn't seen in months, now. There was the odd ex-boyfriend or two in group shots, some family members—my dad snuck into a couple of the birthday ones—but most of them were just Sarah and me, the two of us. In Brazil. In Italy. That one time we decided to drive around Australia in her mum's old Commodore with hardly enough money for petrol. There were even some more mundane shots: drinking on her patio at sunset, a joint selfie of us both looking wrecked during swatvac, and a picture of Sarah on a beach somewhere writing in a travel diary.

Gosh, I'd loved those. I'd tried to keep one myself when I took a solo trip to Thailand recently, but it wasn't fun filling it in alone. We'd always written in them together, with stories and anecdotes and diagrams of what we'd seen and done during the day. Late at night, when we were tired, or drunk, or premenstrual, we'd write other things in them, real things. Things we were scared about. Our hopes and dreams for the future. Everything that mattered to us.

I still had them under my bed, in a stupidly expensive fire retardant box I'd bought especially so that nothing would ever happen to them.

Remembering them was like hearing a siren's call, and I ended up on my knees beside the bed, wriggling the stupid box out from underneath it.

They were still safe inside, arranged by year. I sat and poured through them for ages, flipping the pages and laughing at memories I'd nearly forgotten. There was so much history here, in these diaries. They were the museum of our friendship, full of treasures and relics and... *fuck*, I couldn't ruin it! I couldn't ruin it like I nearly had today, because what on earth would I do without her?

I wanted a whole life with her, making new memories like the ones we already had—and I was on the cusp of another chapter in our lives, where we'd work together, as well. It would be so much fun, I could just imagine it: all the new routines we'd create and what our business trips would be like together.

I couldn't let myself ruin it. I just couldn't destroy everything we were to each other over some silly, desperate girlcrush.

I cradled the last travel diary I'd just read to my chest, hugging it there with both arms. I just needed to do whatever I needed to do to stop thinking about her like I had been recently, and I needed to do it quickly.

CHAPTER FOUR

The following morning at work, I used all of my free time to do some very important research for the weekend.

My extensive lit review revealed that 79% of men preferred a woman with her hair down, 68% preferred a woman wearing a dress, and a staggering 85% of men reacted more favourably to women with symmetrical clothes and hairstyles. Clothes that showed off a woman's hip-to-waist ratio fared better than those that disguised it (a hip-to-waist ratio of 0.67 to 1.18 was considered optimally attractive with a 95% confidence interval), and *everyone* reacted more favourably to a woman in red.

So, clearly I needed to buy myself a symmetrical tight red dress and somehow make myself look curvier than I really was.

I was scrolling through online stores with promised next-day delivery when a notification for an urgent email popped up at the bottom of my screen. It was from HR—well, from Henry—and it was addressed to 'all staff'. *It must be the official announcement of the redundancies,* I assumed as I immediately put my little red dress shopping on hold to read it.

It wasn't. It was kind of the opposite. One of the guys from Risk started reading it aloud in a really rude voice before I'd finished, too. "'HR would like to remind staff that rumours about job insecurity are not an acceptable reason to miss work or underperform, and misconduct will result in immediate disciplinary action'," he dictated, and then scoffed and added his own commentary. "What a prick, I bet *his* $300k a year salary isn't on the line."

I grimaced. This email *was* a dick move, especially since Frost hadn't officially denied the offshoring claims yet and everyone was still really stressed out. As Henry was the opposite of a dick, reconciling this long 'we will punish you' email with our conversation yesterday just wasn't happening. It didn't even sound like Henry.

"I don't think he wrote this," I said aloud without thinking, and then immediately regretted it because everyone started staring at me.

"What do you mean 'I don't think he wrote this'?" The guy asked me indignantly. "It's from his email address and it says 'Henry Lee' down the bottom."

I wasn't sure how to explain it in a way that didn't have me detailing the conversation I'd had with Henry yesterday, so I just shrugged and managed to force out of my mouth, "He's just always been really nice to me, that's all."

Someone else snorted. "I bet he has."

Even Spud joined in. "I'll give you two reasons he's nice to you, Gemma, and I bet he was staring at them the whole time," he said, more as a gentle word of fatherly advice than an attack on me. "You know he sleeps with employees, right? Be careful there. His last girlfriend was forced to leave Frost the day after they split, and she had a huge breakdown."

'He', I thought, imagining Henry correcting Min's pronouns. Everyone was still staring at me so there was no way I was going to contradict all of them, though, even if it was on the tip of my tongue: *that is* not *what happened*.

Instead, I got back to my online shopping and exited the conversation. *I can't wait to be out of this department,* I thought, and then daydreamed about working with Sarah again while I picked out dresses.

At lunch, I enlisted Sarah to help me tab through my shortlist; she had much better taste in clothes than me. While she was thumbing through them on my phone with one hand and eating an apple with another, my mind wandered back to that Henry conversation. "Why do people think Henry's a womaniser?"

She glanced up, frowning. "Where did *that* question come from?" she asked after she'd swallowed her mouthful. "Are people still gossiping about him?"

I shrugged. "I said Henry was nice, and basically got told by my co-workers he's only nice to me because he wants to sleep with me."

Sarah snorted. "Unless Henry wants to sleep with everyone, that's pretty unlikely," she said, and kept scrolling through my shortlist while she spoke. "It's just over that stuff with Min. Jason—our old boss, remember?—told everyone that Min only left after she and Henry broke up because he didn't want his ass handed to him over bullying her. People like a sex scandal more than they like other types of scandals, I guess." She stopped scrolling and nodded at my phone. "This one's good," she said, passing it back to me so I could see which dress she'd picked.

My eyes nearly popped out: gosh, it was short! Oh well, Sarah was the hook up queen, wasn't she? If she thought it would look good on me and get me laid, she was probably right. I clicked through to the check out. "Should I tell my co-workers the truth about Min and Henry?"

Sarah made a face and shook her head. "Rumours die by themselves eventually if you don't feed them."

That was an interesting idea, given all the rumours about offshoring. I thought about it for a minute or two, wondering if it kind of explained why there was no official statement about what the unions had said. "Maybe that's why Frost won't confirm or deny the offshoring stuff?"

Sarah didn't look so sure. "Maybe," she said, as we packed up our lunch to go back to work, "but I reckon there's heaps more to that story we don't know." She seemed a bit distracted, and when I asked her about it she sighed heavily. "Your co-workers aren't the only ones causing drama. Mine have apparently arranged a 'surprise' for me after lunch and I am deeply, deeply concerned."

After lunch, it was only 20 minutes before I got a cryptic text from Sarah. *"FML. Are you working late tonight?"*

I am if it means that I can go home with you, I thought, immediately cheering up. *"Probably, how come?"*

"Come up to the Women's on 36."

I glanced over at Anil's office—he had a couple of the Risk guys who'd been drunk all day yesterday in there—and then snuck over to the lift and went to go find her.

She was in the Women's on Level 36, and with her in there was an *enormous* box with an even bigger novelty ribbon stuck to it. I thought it was an inflatable paddling pool at first, until I walked around to the side of it and saw a blurry picture of naked shoulders and a baby and the words, 'Premium Birthing Tub'.

"*What?*" was the first word out of my mouth as I slid the ribbon aside so I could read it better.

"Exactly," Sarah said. I could see in the mirror that her arms were crossed. "Omar asked me yesterday in a meeting if I'd changed my mind about not taking maternity leave, and I told him no—she's due in the Christmas holidays, right? I'll get a couple of weeks off anyway—and so my co-workers thought they would use corporate funds to buy me this as a joke: a birthing tub. So I can 'pop in here and have the kid and then get straight back to work'." She looked wholly unimpressed.

I smothered a grin. It was actually an accurate assessment of Sarah's attitude towards work, but I knew she was a bit sensitive about people judging her for her decision to let Rob do all the parenting, so I didn't say anything like that. "So what are you going to do with it?"

She groaned. "I have *no* idea. They somehow managed to buy it on the expense account, so do you know how much paperwork I'd have to do to return it? And it's not like I want to draw *more* attention to that account being used for non-work-related expenses by hauling it in front of finance with a cancelled purchase order. I don't even know if I can sell it. Is it corporate property? Is it personal property? Who knows!" She threw her hands in the air. "I guess I'll take it home tonight and worry about it there."

Sarah had a meeting that finished at seven, which meant I was stuck trying to look busy until Anil left at about six. He watched me thoughtfully for a couple of seconds before he left—maybe Henry had already spoken to him about that Marketing secondment?—and then bid me goodbye.

Once he was gone I had the whole floor to myself, so I had three pod coffees (we were only supposed to have two a day), and then got bored and went downstairs to wait in the atrium café.

I was watching all the men in suits on their way home trying to decide who I'd sleep with if I *had* to, when I noticed there was a tall, slender guy in a hoodie hanging around the atrium entrance. He looked like he was trying not to be seen—he had his hood up—and I was busy jointly worrying that he was some sort of criminal and also kind of admiring how good he looked from behind when he turned around.

It was *Min*.

Whoops... I decided to pretend I hadn't been checking 'him' out as 'he' recognised me and walked over. "Fuck this place," she—he?—said with false cheer. "Is Sarah out yet? I brought the car in."

It wasn't long before she was, and the two of us awkwardly carried the birthing tub into the lift and down to Min.

Min smirked when she saw the box, but tried to conceal it. "Should you be carrying that in your condition?"

"I'm pregnant, not *dying*," Sarah told her, and then nodded sharply at a free corner. "Just help."

Min joined us in loading it into Sarah's tiny old hatchback, and then I proceeded to try and fit beside it on the back seat. Despite the number of people Sarah boasted could fit on this back seat—both sitting up *and* horizontally—there was hardly enough room for just me and the box, and I ended squished against the door.

Then, we sat in traffic for *eternity* while I slowly became two-dimensional and Min kept glancing in the rear-view mirror at the box and chuckling to herself.

Back at Camp Presti, the three of us were carrying the huge box up Sarah's back stairs and into the living room, and Bree, Min's little blond 18-year-old girlfriend, looked up from her sea of study materials spread across the dining room table as we dumped it in the living room.

It took her a second to realise what it was, and then her eyes *lit up*. "Oh my god!" she said, immediately forgetting her studies, springing up from the table, and rushing over to us with her curls bouncing around her shoulders. "You're going to have the baby *here*? That's so exciting! It's supposed to be really beautiful to give birth in the home the baby's going to grow up in, surrounded by the people who care about you!"

Sarah looked unmoved, unceremoniously tossing her handbag on the table and taking off her blazer. "Sorry to disappoint you, but I'm going to have my baby in hospital and pumped full of so many drugs that I won't know where I am or who's with me."

Bree's delighted smile fell. She glanced at the box, confused. "Then why...?"

Sarah sighed. "It's a gag present from my co-workers."

"Oh." Bree probably knew all about what those guys were like from when Min was working in Marketing at Frost. She was silent for a moment, her eyes intent on the box. "Well, are you going to open it?"

Sarah squinted at Bree. "No."

Bree was still looking at the box. "I think you should open it."

Min sighed audibly at her. "And I think *you* should get back to your prac exam so you finish it before Henry gets here to mark it." She bustled her protesting girlfriend back to the dining table and pushed her to sit down in front of her study materials again while Sarah snickered at them.

It was pretty entertaining watching Min wrangle Bree, but I was more interested in something Min had said. "Wait, Henry's coming over? When?"

Sarah stepped out of her heels, teasing me over her shoulder. "Oh no! You'd better quickly get drunk!"

Min ignored her. "Yeah, he's got a dinner meeting first but he'll be here after. Why?"

"Because she needs to know how quickly she has to leave so she doesn't need to have another conversation with him."

I gave Sarah some serious side-eyes before I answered Min. "We got an email from him at work today that I wanted to ask him about. Here," I passed my phone to Min so she could read it, and watched her eyebrows progressively travel down her forehead.

When she was done, she handed it back to me with a distasteful expression, and said exactly what I'd been thinking, "I see what you mean. Henry did *not* write that."

Sarah, who was now taking out her earrings, was less surprised. "I write stuff all the time for Omar to send out, one of his staff probably put it together."

Min didn't look convinced that was what happened, but she didn't say anything.

Sarah noticed, and stopped mid-earring removal, fixing her with a suspicious expression. "You know something."

Min was unfazed. "No, I just know Henry."

Sarah abandoned her earrings and advanced on Min. "No. That's not it. You *know* something about this union-job thing, don't you?" She turned to me, explaining, "Min was over at Henry's last night."

"Remember how I said he doesn't tell me stuff about work?"

Sarah scoffed. "Oh, come on. After all that crap went down in the newspaper and with the unions, you go over there and he *doesn't* debrief to you about it? Not buying it."

Min was unmoved. "We played PlayStation for three hours, and we went to bed," she said flatly, and then glanced at Bree who was clearly listening to us. "Also, can we maybe postpone this inquisition? I'm pretty sure there won't be questions about Henry's day on Bree's Psych exam."

Sarah reluctantly agreed to that and left Min alone until Bree was done with the prac exam. She didn't get a chance to question Min afterwards either, because Bree spent a good 20 minutes nagging her about unpacking the birthing tub until Sarah relented and helped her unpack it, and then the doorbell rang.

We all looked up. It actually was a surprise; none of Sarah's friends bothered with the *front* door anymore—we just all wandered in and out of the back one at leisure—and I hadn't heard the doorbell in *months*.

There was only one person who'd bother to ring it.

Sarah looked across at Min and then, like the mature adult she was, she shot up and ran towards to the door before Min could answer it.

Surprising no one, Henry was behind the door when Sarah pulled it open, smiling pleasantly and about to greet her.

She interrupted him. "Look, I know you're tired so I'll make this quick," she told him very seriously, "you need to tell us what's going on with the union stuff. We won't tell anyone."

Henry blinked at her for a moment, and then put his hand on the door handle and went to pull it closed. "Sorry, I think I have the wrong house."

She laughed a couple of times and then grabbed him by the wrist and pulled him inside. "Okay, not everything, but what's going on with Gemma's job at least?"

"I'd love to," Henry said amicably as he let himself be towed down the hallway by a forearm, "but I don't talk work outside work." He gave me an apologetic smile as she pulled him into the living room and sat him in a chair.

Oh. I guess I *wasn't* going to ask him about who'd written that email, then. Well, on the bright side, at least I didn't have to spend half the evening working up enough courage to start the conversation with him...

Sarah had decided to pretend he hadn't refused to discuss work. "What do you drink?" she persisted. "Gem will go to the bottle shop and buy six of it and then you can just tell yourself it's not your fault, you got drunk and accidentally told us what's going on."

He laughed, and put a warm hand on top of Sarah's on his shoulder, shutting her down. "I understand your concern, I do," he told her. "And in your place I'd probably be asking me the same thing, Sarah. You know that. But I can't say anything, Sarah. You know that."

She threw her hands up in the air. "Fine, I tried!" she announced, and then flopped down in a chair across from him. "You are a vault."

He smiled, looking genuinely complimented. "Thank you, it's one of the reasons I managed to end up as HR Manager. Now," he said, slapping his thighs and looking around the room for something. His eyes fell on Bree's study materials and the empty chair. He frowned. "Where's Bree? I thought she was doing an exam for me."

"I'm here!" Bree announced, emerging from Min's bedroom in *a bikini*. "Can we go through my prac exam while I'm trying out the birthing tub?"

We all stared at her.

Sarah snorted and started to giggle, and gosh, Min's face... It looked something like The Scream before she put it in her hands.

Henry, on the other hand, had a supremely professional expression like there was nothing at all unusual about what was going on. "Sure," he said easily.

"Awesome!" Bree declared, and then proceeded to bounce out onto the back decking where she'd dragged the tub.

Min tried to call after her, "Bree, it's cold, put on a—" The door was already shut. "—t-shirt..." she finished to herself, and then put her head in her hands again for a moment. When she emerged, she turned helplessly to Henry and said, "I'm so sorry."

He didn't look like he wanted an apology. "Come on, I want to see how she's doing with those p-value questions," he said, patting Min's back and chuckling.

After they'd gone, Sarah stood and leant right in close to my ear, whispering, "Yeah, I bet he's really curious about whether or not she knows what do to with the 'P'."

Yuck. I shoved her. "Not everyone is as disgusting as you," I told her as she laughed and slung an arm around my shoulder.

We followed them out to the decking where Bree was bent over double, trying to work out how to make the inflation pump work. To his credit, Henry definitely wasn't watching her. He ducked inside to grab a pen and the prac exam off the dining room table, and then sat down in a deck chair and began to flick through it like there *wasn't* an 18 year old in a bikini about two metres from him.

Some womaniser, I thought, leaning against the railing. If he was, he'd be checking her out right now.

It wasn't as if Bree's bikini was super-skimpy or anything— it wasn't—but Bree had one of those full-figured, cup-runneth-over kind of bodies which made almost everything she wore look slightly pornographic. I wouldn't have said she was chubby, exactly, and she definitely fell within that optimum 0.67-1.18 hip-to-waist ratio interval, but she looked soft and inviting and anyone who wasn't Henry would definitely have been checking her out.

See, I can't be gay, I thought, watching Bree. *If I was, I'd totally be ogling her while she's bending forward like that.*

Then, I double-took at what I'd just thought and made a face. *Why* did I keep thinking that when I obviously wasn't? It was almost like one of those 'don't think about pink elephant' experiments where as soon as someone said it, you couldn't think of anything else even though it was literally the most ridiculous idea ever. It really *was* ridiculous, because in my entire life it had never occurred to me to get with girls before, and I'd had plenty of opportunity to pash them at the many, many clubs I'd gone to since I'd turned 18. I was never interested.

And I'm not interested now, really, which clearly means I'm mostly straight and maybe a tiny little bit bi like almost every girl is, I decided, and then worried about the very clear memory I had of Sarah topless from the other night.

I needed to deal with this. "I'm going out on Friday night," I found myself saying. "Who's coming?"

Min had surrendered to Bree and was busy trying to unkink the garden hose for her so she could fill up the tub. "Out where?"

I shrugged. "A club, a pub, somewhere we can—"

Sarah cut in with a smirk. "Somewhere *she* can score." I gave her a dirty look.

Bree stood up from messing with the pump and looked hopefully at Min. Min shook her head. "You have an exam on Monday."

She made a face. "Next weekend, then?"

Sarah answered before Min did. "Next weekend works better for me, too, actually," she agreed, "I have reports up to my eyeballs at work and I don't want to be too exhausted to do them. Plus, Rob will be back then and he can come, too." She looked across at me. "Is it okay if we postpone your thing until next weekend, Gem? I promise I'll be more fun if I'm not totally stressed out."

I thought about how helpless I was the second I saw any of her skin. I couldn't wait that long, but what could I do, really? I didn't want to force Sarah to come with me and I didn't want to go to a bar alone. "I guess..." I said, the air slowly seeping out of my lungs.

"Okay, it's settled then, we'll all be your wingmen next weekend." She clapped me on the back. "Well, I'd better eat something and then get started on those damn reports. You want me to zap something for you, too?"

I probably could have hung around—technically these were all my friends, too—but with Sarah shut away doing reports and the others all mostly occupied, I kind of felt like a third wheel. "No, it's okay. I'll probably just head off home…" I wanted her to stop me. If I was honest with myself, I wanted her to invite me to stay the night again.

"Okay, see you tomorrow then!" she said instead, giving me a brief hug and then heading inside.

I exhaled. Well, it had been nice to spend this little bit of extra time with her, I supposed; it certainly beat just going straight home to Mr Crumpet at 5pm and watching Netflix and dicking around the internet for 6 hours. I said goodbye to the others, and then grabbed my handbag from the living room and went to leave.

Min followed me to the front door and politely offered to accompany me home in the dark. I joked, "How far do your services extend? Can I borrow you for the weekend, too?" expecting her to laugh with me.

She didn't laugh. In fact, she just watched me, looking concerned. I stopped abruptly; gosh, that sounded like I was hitting on her, didn't it? Especially after Sarah had told everyone I wanted to hook up on the weekend! *Crap!* I threw my hands up in a 'wait' position. "No, I'm sorry, I didn't mean I want you to come home *with* me or anything." *With?* "I mean, not *walk* me home like you offered to, but come back with me to, *you know*—"

"—I know," she cut me off, at least not letting me flop around uselessly like a fish out of water. Then, glancing over her shoulder to check Sarah was still in the living room, she stepped forward and closed the front door so we were alone together on the porch. "You still want to go out this weekend, don't you?"

I made a face; I'd forgotten how perceptive she could be. "Yeah," I admitted.

"It really can't wait one more weekend?"

I shook my head.

I expected her to go all third degree on me, Sarah-style, and I wasn't really sure what I was going to say if she started asking questions. I was pretty sure everything I said except the truth would sound like a terrible lie, and I usually blushed like wildfire when I knew I sounded like I was lying. I couldn't lie about this stuff, and she'd guess straight away the moment I said 'Sarah'.

She didn't do anything of the sort, though. Just like Henry hadn't yesterday, she didn't probe at all. Instead, she just nodded once, slung her hands in her pockets and took a few steps towards Sarah's front stairs towards the road. Then, she looked back at me, waiting for me to follow her.

I'd done this walk a thousand times in the dark and nothing bad had ever happened to me. "It's okay, Min, you really don't need to walk me home..."

She shrugged. "Maybe not, but if I don't, I'll worry about you," she said simply. "And I'm coming with you wherever you decide to go this Friday, too."

CHAPTER FIVE

'Guaranteed next day delivery' turned out to be a horrible lie, which meant that the first opportunity I had to try on my symmetrical tight red dress was after work on Friday.

I took off my comfy bra and put on a really uncomfy g-string so I could wriggle into the damn thing, and then spent a full minute fruitlessly trying to pull the stretchy fabric further down my thighs. It kept springing back up, so I gave up and went to check myself out in a mirror.

It was a shock to see myself in it, it looked like lingerie. Not only that, but my nipples stood out through the fabric, and it was so tight I could see my bellybutton. It was probably too tight for knickers, too, but there was no chance in hell I'd go commando in something this short. I didn't need to prove to the entire bar that the drapes matched the carpet.

I chewed on my lip, examining my reflection. I mean, I guess it was okay? It *was* a dress, after all, just not the kind of dress *I* ever wore. Then again, that probably explained why I'd been single for a thousand years.

Anyway, my 'prude' judgment couldn't be trusted on this one. I snapped a mirror shot and texted it to Sarah for her opinion.

She gave it *straight* away. *"Smoking hot!!! You're going to have your pick of the guys next weekend!"*

Yeah, 'next weekend', I thought, sighing. *"You don't think it's too much?"*

"No such thing as 'too much' with men, they love too much! Trust me, anyone would sleep with you in that!"

Anyone...? I wondered as I thought about her, and resisted the urge to invite her out again tonight. As much as she was stacks of fun and I *loved* going out with her, men always looked straight through me like I was invisible when she was around. I didn't blame them, she was magnetic. *Maybe it's a blessing she's not coming*, I tried to tell myself, taking off the dress for now.

I was shaving my legs in the bath and feeling really guilty about excluding her when she made it even worse. *"You want to come over and keep me company tonight? Rob's out of town til Monday :("*

I stopped mid razor-stroke, staring at my phone.

Yes, I thought, *and wouldn't it be better to not hide things from her, anyway?* For a full ten seconds I actually considered cancelling going out in my microscopic dress and just having a night in at Sarah's.

Then, I came to my senses. Of course it would be better not to hide things from her, but I needed to remind myself how it felt to have a man touch me so I didn't want to touch *her*. And I couldn't say anything to her about tonight, either. She'd be upset at me leaving her out, or worse: she'd start asking about why sex was so important right now. I couldn't answer that question, not without lying. She always knew when I was lying; at least, when I had to do it to her face.

Glad this wasn't one of those times, I texted back, *"Sorry :(I really would love to except I have some work I need to get stuck into at home tonight..."* while I died inside and wished I could just go over without the imminent threat of doing something to wreck our friendship. *After you get laid, Gemma,* I promised myself as I climbed out of the bath and got dressed.

I was just finishing my eyebrows when my intercom buzzed.

Min. I stood up from the bathroom mirror, took another look at my dress and suddenly felt *really* naked at the thought of her seeing me like this. It was too late to chicken out now, though, so I ducked out to the kitchen and pressed the gate switch, and then agonised about this stupid dress for the full 30 seconds it took her to get up the to my flat and knock on my door.

When I plucked up courage to open it, she was checking the time on her phone which meant I got a fraction of a second to observe her sensible dark denim jeans and casual blazer before she glanced up at me and her jaw *dropped*. "W-Whoa."

My cheeks went the same colour as my dress. That confirmed it: what the hell was I doing?! "Should I take it off?" I asked frantically, glancing down my body; my nipples were still hard. I crossed my arms in front of them. "I should just take it off, shouldn't I?!"

She quickly recovered. "No, I'm sorry, I—*god*! Okay, no. Don't take it off because of me." She laughed nervously, running a hand through her hair and trying not to look at me.

She wasn't making me feel better. "It's way too sheer, isn't it?" I asked her. "I mean..." I gestured to my nipples.

Her eyes dipped to them for just a second before she paid very special attention to looking me in the eyes. "Well, if you're uncomfortable in that, just wear something you're more comfortable in? You've got lots of beautiful dresses."

"I can't."

She gave me a dubious look. "You can't?"

I shook my head. "I spent hours reading studies about what men like, and this is it: symmetrical, tight and red."

She squinted at me. "I'm pretty sure the contents of the dress is what matters to men, and come on," she said, "wouldn't you rather be comfortable?"

Yes, I thought. *But I'd rather be a lot of things that I'm not, and one of them is 'in danger of ruining a friendship'.* "Yes, but I need to get laid," I blurted out, and then watched her eyebrows jump again while I kicked myself. Why was I so incapable of holding a normal conversation?

I didn't know what she was thinking, but she swallowed and said, "Well, if that's what you're after, that dress definitely gets your point across."

"Good," I said, hoping it *was* good, and then went to put on some matching heels and grab my handbag.

We'd only made it as far as the stairwell before I felt the wind between my thighs and stopped in my tracks. Ugh, what was I doing? I couldn't just walk around in public like this, could I? "Hang on a sec," I told Min, and went back inside to get a coat. When I came back out with it on—feeling much better, mind you, despite the fact it was way too warm outside for a coat—Min was smothering a snicker. I panicked. "What now?"

She tried not to smile too much, and nodded at the window at the end of the corridor. The light was on inside which meant it was basically a mirror.

The coat came down mid-thighs, and—happily—there was no sign of the red dress. Actually, there was no sign of *any* dress. I looked like I had on a coat and heels and nothing else.

"Great," I said sarcastically. "Apparently, I have two choices: I can either look like a hussy or a flasher."

"*Or* you could change into a different dress."

I stared at my reflection. I could, but those other dresses had never gotten me laid and this was an emergency. "I'll go with 'flasher'," I decided, and then we went downstairs to catch an Uber.

I'd decided to forgo my usual haunts for tonight—if I went to somewhere in The Rocks, half of Frost would be there and that was the last thing I needed—so we drove just past the city to Newtown. I'd only been there a few times, but I remembered there being a number of really chill places and it seemed like a really good option.

Even this late at night, the streets were bustling. At pavement-level most of the shops were open, and on the first floor of all those shops there were beer gardens, restaurants, and the odd house with washing hanging out the window. I probably would have really enjoyed the atmosphere if every single person who passed us hadn't stared judgmentally at my bare legs and stiletto heels.

The first place we checked out was a bistro-type bar full of young professionals still in their suits. It made me feel like I'd wandered off the set of *Pretty Woman*, so we left and tried the next building.

That place was even worse, because it was full of super fashionable hipsters with stylishly mismatched clothes and 100% certified vegan beers. They all looked like genuinely nice people, but I was pretty sure my fire-engine red dress wasn't going to be too popular with many of the coif-bearded men in there.

The third venue we stuck our heads in was a rooftop beer garden with live music and a more mixed crowd. It looked far more promising.

Because it was still reasonably early for a Friday night, we managed to get a table. Min grabbed us a few mixed shots and a beer for herself, downing her shots in quick succession and then holding up her Heineken. "If Bree asks, this is all I had," she told me, and drank deeply from it as she looked around us. "So, who's your type?" she asked innocently, eyes twinkling. "You know, apart from me."

I sighed at her. That was *one time*. "I was really drunk," I told her dryly, and then I realised what she'd said before that. "Wait a second, *Bree* knows you're out with me?" She nodded, and I panicked. "She won't tell Sarah?" Min shook her head. "Not even accidentally?"

Min took another swig and shrugged. "Probably not, but she's at Henry's anyway, so..."

But she's at... "So *Henry* knows, too?" I asked her, my voice shooting up an octave. I was never going to be able to look him in the face again! "But he was there when Sare said why I wanted to come out tonight!"

"He's also an adult?" She didn't look at all concerned. "Don't worry, he won't say anything."

"Yes, but he'll *know*," I said, aghast, and then *sighed*. "Great. The whole world thinks I'm a nympho. Why did you have to tell them?"

She gave me a look. "Lie to my girlfriend about sneaking out at night with a girl she knows I've kissed? Sounds like a great idea."

Okay, that was a fair point. And, I supposed with the potential Marketing secondment Henry was already successfully keeping a secret for me anyway. It didn't make the fact they knew how desperate I was any less humiliating, though.

"Anyway," Min said, turning a little in her seat to look out at the other patrons. "As I was saying, who's your type?"

I looked around us. Most people were here in groups— helpful, because it made it easier to see who was paired off with who and who looked single. Unfortunately, it also meant that to approach someone, I was going to have to interrupt a group conversation and the probability of me actually doing that approached zero. Besides, I wasn't like Sarah. I didn't pick a guy out in a crowd and then proceed to seduce him. I'd *never* flirted with anyone who wasn't already clearly interested. "Um, I think my type is people who hit on me first."

Min gave me a silent 'ah', and then chuckled. "In that case, you probably need to do something about *that*." She nodded at my coat.

I froze. Just the thought of taking my coat off and showing this entire room my nipples nearly had me breaking out in a cold sweat. Still, I was here to rescue my friendship; I needed to remember that. I drank my third shot. "Okay, but I need *way* more alcohol."

She looked at her mostly full beer and then back at me with a sceptical expression. "Okay..." she said at length. "How many this time?"

To get me out of this coat and into some guy's lap? "As many as you can carry," I told her darkly.

She spent a few seconds watching me with concern. "You don't want to maybe try somewhere else instead?" she asked. "I was reading about a place I think you might like down the road. It has great reviews."

"Unless the reviews say, 'Gemma Rowe will need less alcohol to pick up a guy here', I think I'm still going to need more alcohol."

She looked like she wanted to say something else, but gave up. "Okay, then. Alcohol it is," she said as she gave me a little salute as she headed back to the bar.

While she was gone, I had another good hard look around me. There were a few reasonable guys—I mean, not amazing ones, but I suppose if I *had* to sleep with someone...? I sincerely hoped alcohol would make my plans easier to execute, though.

It did. A few minutes after Min returned and I sculled my shots, I felt really warm. That discomfort began to outweigh my terror at all these living, breathing humans seeing my nipples, so I ended up unbuttoning my coat and standing momentarily to drape it on the back of my chair. A few eyes glanced in my direction while I did that.

I should have been overjoyed at that—this thing was supposed to catch people's attention, right?—except instead of feeling victorious, I had to fight to urge to immediately bundle myself back up in my coat. I felt naked and so, so uncomfortable.

Even more horrifying: a group of men who'd been sitting at the bar were whispering to each other, and then all looked at me. One of them stood up.

Shit.

No, no, no, sit back down! I thought, suddenly acutely aware how very much I could *not* do this. On exactly how many levels I categorically, definitely could not do this. Glancing over my shoulder towards the women's, I wondered if I could run into it without looking like I was blowing the guy off.

Too late. "Hey," the guy said, swaggering up to the table. He was probably about five years younger than me, and he carried himself with the cocky confidence of someone who knew they were hot.

I tried to speak, but this horrible croak sound came out of my mouth and I just went bright red. *Kill me now,* I thought helplessly as Min sat up.

"Hey," Min said in her gender-neutral voice, and casually held out her hand so the two of them could share a really blokey handshake. "Min," she said, and then gestured at me. "This is Gemma."

The guy *beamed* at me. "Hi, Gemma, I'm Todd. How're you doing?"

ABORT! ABORT!, my brain screamed, but I still managed a really forced smile while I sweated out every ounce of fluid in my body.

"Your girlfriend is *hot*, bro," the guy told Min, both as a deliberate compliment to me and a clear fish for information about whether we were together. "Can you teach me to get one like that?"

Smooth as silk, Min fired back, "Unfortunately, she's not my girlfriend. And I think you're off to a good start."

And I think I'm actually going to die right here, RIP, I decided, feeling actually physically sick. I could *not* do this. Who the hell was I kidding? I wasn't Sarah. Picking up total strangers was a Sarah-thing, not a Gemma-thing. If that guy touched me, I was going to need at least three years of therapy.

I stood awkwardly. "Be right back," I rasped, and then fled into the women's, rushed straight past all the girls freshening their makeup and holed up against the wall on the far side of the toilets.

I took a few breaths and put my hands to my cheeks, trying to ignore the fact the other girls were all giving me judgmental glances in the mirror. Then, because I didn't want them to think I was even more nuts than they already thought I was for wearing this dress, I turned to the mirror and pretended to be smoothing down my hair.

I'm in hell, I thought, staring at my uncharacteristically slutty reflection and imagining Min trying to entertain that guy while they waited for me to emerge. I wondered how long I'd have to wait before he'd give up and go back to his mates and then I could go straight to the airport and flee the country. I felt really guilty about leaving Min with him, really guilty. But I couldn't sleep with a stranger. Gosh, I couldn't even *talk* to a stranger, what on earth had I been thinking? And how did I really think doing that was going to help?

"Hey, wrong bathroom, buddy!" I heard a harsh voice say suddenly, followed by another girl shouting, "Dude, what the fuck—? Get out!"

I turned towards the commotion and spotted Min standing in the doorway of the women's, holding my coat and handbag and looking towards the cubicles. When she saw they were all empty, she frowned and looked across at the line-up by the mirror and spotted me. She seemed genuinely surprised to see me there. "Oh," she said, looking embarrassed. "I'm sorry, I—I thought you were really upset."

One of the women scoffed at her. "So you thought barging in here was going to make her feel better?"

I grimaced. "Come on..." I told Min, grabbing her arm and pulling her out with me. In the beer garden, the men who'd checked me out were busy laughing together at the bar, so we rushed quickly behind them and fled out to the street. The disapproving looks of strangers reminded me I was basically wearing lingerie, so I took the coat off Min and wrapped myself up again, ignoring how sweltering I was in it.

I didn't relax until we'd half-run, half-staggered several blocks away and ended up panting and completely lost. I sat at a deserted bus stop to catch my breath, my head swimming from both the alcohol and the adrenaline.

Carefully, Min sat down beside me.

"I'm sorry," I told her, feeling guilty. "You must think I'm completely nuts."

She shook her head. "I was just worried."

Hah. "I don't blame you, I'd be worried about me, too, I mean look at me..." I gestured down at my Flasher Chic. "I get dressed up in something I hate to pick up a guy I don't know, and then when I pick up a guy I don't know, I run away. I'm always having some sort of crisis when you're around."

"Is this a crisis?" She seemed genuinely interested in my answer.

I sighed. "My whole life is a crisis. To get laid I'm pretty sure I need to actually talk to people, and every time I need to talk to people: giant crisis." I groaned and put my head in my hands for a second. "Ugh! I *hate* that I can't open my mouth without degenerating into a blithering idiot... Everyone probably thinks I'm so stupid!"

She didn't look convinced. "I don't think people think that at all. I've always found your shyness kind of charming." She gave me a wry half-smile.

I looked up at her. "Great, will *you* come home with me, then?" I drunkenly joked, to horribly regret later when I was sober.

"Hmm, tempting," she shot back, fortunately playing along, "but I'm pretty sure you said you signed up for a certified guy, rather than whatever I eventually figure out I am."

"I'm so desperate I'm willing to be flexible on the minor details," I told her. "You'll do. Come on, let's go home and you can do your best to fix me."

69

I only realised my mistake when her brow dipped. "Fix you?"

Crap. "No, no, fix me up!" I tried to explain. "You know, like, 'sort me out'-'fix me up'! That's what I meant!"

She gave me a really searching look for a few seconds, and then finished with a slow nod. "Right..." She didn't say anything else, though, which made me panic that I'd taken the flirty joking *way* too far or that with the 'fix me' line I'd somehow accidentally insulted her nondescript gender.

We sat in silence for a minute or two, during which she was probably secretly judging me.

Then, I took a long, deep breath and exhaled. I should have just gone over to Sarah's, after all. "Okay, well, let's go home, I guess..." I said, standing up and looking around us to try and figure out the best place to meet an Uber driver. "It seems like a lot of wasted effort to go home before midnight, though..."

While I was feeling around in my handbag for my phone, she put her hand on my shoulder. "You sure you want to go home now?"

My cheeks flushed, there was something about her tone of voice as she asked me that... "Um—?"

"Because there's that place I was thinking we could quickly check out. It's not too far away, if you don't want to call it early..."

Oh. Well... I didn't really feel like going into *another* place, but Min had just done me the enormous favour of coming with me tonight, of not cracking it when I left her alone with that guy, and it looked like she wasn't even going to tease me about any of it either. I didn't feel like 'no' would ever be an appropriate answer, given the circumstances. "Sure."

She looked relieved. "Okay," she said, and lead me up a few blocks and then down an alley to a side-door entrance. There was a female bouncer seated at the door, complete with shaved head and surly expression, and she looked *very* critically at Min as she carded her for some reason. She didn't say anything and let us in, though.

Inside, there was a narrow hallway that led up a flight of stairs, and the dull thump of dance music drifting through the walls. It all seemed very seedy, and not the kind of place people would leave good reviews for.

"How come you want to go *here*?" I asked Min dubiously while I tried to navigate the steep stairwell as un-drunkenly as possible.

Before she got a chance to answer me, I got to the top.

Above Min's head, a rainbow flag with two linked women's symbols was hanging over the doorway.

CHAPTER SIX

All the blood drained out of my face. A *lesbian* bar?

How did she—? *Did* she—? "Why did you bring me here?" I managed. "We can't go in there!"

Min gave me a look. She very theatrically took a big step inside the doorway, pretended to look down and be delighted at seeing herself still in one piece, and then did a *tada* flourish with her hands.

I sighed at her. "Neither of us are lesbians!"

She looked entirely unconvinced. "I pass as one," she told me, "and, *honestly*, Gemma? You're telling me you've *never* been attracted to another woman?"

I faltered—because of course I had—and her face settled in a look that said 'bingo'.

My cheeks flushed and I felt an unexpected surge of panic. "Every girl is, sometimes! It doesn't mean I'm gay!"

"Uh huh, sure. Come on in." She stepped aside so I could enter.

I didn't. I just stood there, struggling with a feeling that I wanted to run back down the stairs. I might actually have done it if I hadn't been drunk and in heels. "You don't believe me? I'm not! Really, I'm not! I know you haven't seen me with a boyfriend, but I've had them, *three* of them, I just—"

71

"I had one, too, Gemma. For years."

But you're different, Min, I very nearly said and only managed to stop myself at the last second. "If you think I'm gay just because I couldn't sleep with that *one guy*, then that's *ridiculous*!"

"Gemma, you're overthinking this." She invited me inside again. "Trust me: life is way better when you try not to overthink things. Come on, let's just go on and see what it's like."

I wasn't overthinking, and I wasn't going in there! I ignored her invitation, feeling really *panicky* and really *uncomfortable* and *really* restless like I wanted to turn around and run away as quickly as possible. "Then what is it, Min? Why are you so super sure that I'm a lesbian? Because whatever it is, you need to tell me!" *So that I can make sure I never, ever, ever do anything like that in front of anyone—especially Sarah!—again*!

I didn't realise how defensive I sounded until Min looked surprised by it. She dropped her arms. "Wow... okay, if you're *that* uncomfortable with it, I'm sorry, I just thought—"

Why wasn't she answering me? "—Please, you've got to tell me why you thought I was one! Because if I'm doing it around other people, I need to *stop*!"

Her eyebrows were basically up in her hairline. She opened her mouth, considering me. "You really want to know what I think? Really?" I nodded, and she exhaled. "Okay. This whole dress thing is nuts, Gemma. You're so uncomfortable in that thing. You say you urgently need to hook up with *a man* and it can't wait a week, but why can't it wait for—"

"—Because I want to get laid as soon as—"

"—Yeah, but it's clearly not about wanting actual sex, is it? You're desperate to have sex with a man, but not because you're horny. So what's it about? What do you need to have sex with a man to prove?"

I don't need to prove anything, it's about making sure I don't try to have sex with my straight best friend, I shouted internally. *Because I will. I'll do it. And then I'll wreck the most amazing friendship I've ever had.* "You don't understand, Min, it's not about that!"

72

"Then help me understand, Gemma! What *is* it about?"

Gosh, no one could know! "I can't tell you!"

"Okay, but it's something related to this place, isn't it?"

Yes, I thought immediately, and then felt terrified by that answer, and then sick. My brain was screaming *she's wrong she's wrong she's wrong don't listen!* at full volume while I tried to smother my panic by reassuring myself, *It's okay, just like the stats I read, being attracted to Sarah doesn't necessarily make me gay...*

Not necessarily, another voice answered, *but there's a 6% chance it does, and your MO is 'statistical outlier', isn't it?*

My head swam from all the alcohol, but I couldn't ignore the crushing weight inside my chest. I didn't want to ask myself the question, I *really* didn't want to ask myself the question, but it was bubbling to the surface of my consciousness and it was too late not to:

...what if it *did* mean I was gay? What if all of this Sarah stuff *was* because I was gay?

Properly asking myself that knocked the breath out of me. Suddenly, everything I thought I understood about myself—

—no, that *couldn't* be it! I'd been attracted to men, hadn't I? I couldn't remember how it felt, so I couldn't be *sure-*sure...

But 'gay' fit. It fit, didn't it? I was so *picky* about men, but every time Sarah touched me... Was I a lesbian? Was that why I wasn't married and pregnant at 28.9?

Gosh, it was like suddenly being thrown into a vortex and churned until nothing made sense, and being so drunk made the inertia a million times worse.

Min had to reach out and grab me to stop me from falling back down the stairs. "Fuck, that was close. We are so drunk..." She looked frustrated with herself. "God, what the hell was I thinking? It was a huge mistake to bring you here, wasn't it?"

Nod your head, my rational brain was telling me, *tell her it was a mistake so she'll leave you alone, this doesn't have to go anywhere; she'll never bring it up again*. But the problem was that if I nodded my head, I'd have to go home and deal with the question by myself, because this wasn't something I could ever tell Sarah about. In fact, the only person I'd ever trust with it was right here with me.

Despite that, I couldn't say it. I stood there, *shaking*.

She had a look of real pain on her face. "Fuck it," she said, going to walk back past me towards the stairs. "Fuck it. Let's just go home. I'm so sorry, I—"

I grabbed her arm so she couldn't continue down the stairs. She looked back at me.

We stood there at the top of the dim stairwell for a few seconds listening to the muffled pound of bass through the walls. I struggled to find words; nothing would come out of my mouth.

"I'm not going to force you to tell me anything, Gemma," she said quietly when I didn't speak. "I think I've fucked up enough for tonight."

I shook my head. "You don't have to force me," I rasped. "I just—I mean, I don't know what—" I took a breath.

Silent this time, she waited for me to find a way to express what I wanted to say.

I pushed the words out of my mouth. "Let's... just have one drink here, maybe? I don't know..."

She took a step back towards me, her eyes searching my face.

I could hardly breathe. "Just—*gosh*, Min. Please, you can't tell anyone. Especially not Sarah, I don't want to have to say why."

It must have been clear what I meant, because she breathed out in a forceful sigh of relief and threw her arms around me in a tight bear-hug.

I stared into the lapel of her blazer, my eyes wide open.

Min held me for ages; and in that time, several groups of women squished by us to get out.

"I'm sorry," she murmured against my hair when we were alone again. "God, I'm so sorry, Gemma. Fuck. Part of me wondered if this whole getting laid thing was all a performance to make *us* not suspect..." She laughed nervously a couple of times. "I wanted to show you that I knew and that it's fine, I didn't mean to freak you out.'" She took a breath. "*Fuck.* Do you want to just go home?"

I didn't know what I wanted anymore. *Maybe this is all one crazy drunk hallucination and I'm passed out in bed already*, I thought ironically.

"Gemma...?"

Shit. "I'm sorry, I—" I swallowed, my head spinning. "This is all just—ugh. How did you know about me? Like, am I horribly obvious, or...?" I had a terrifying thought that maybe Sarah had already guessed and was pretending not to notice—

I felt her shake her head.

—or maybe just everyone else had noticed me staring at her cleavage or those long legs of hers? "Did you... see me do something?"

"No, it's just something I've been wondering about for a few months."

Phew; I hadn't been thinking of Sarah that way for that long. I felt reasonably comforted by the fact Min didn't seem to have connected this to Sarah, but it *did* kind of make me wonder why Min thought I was gay. Did the fact I pinged her gaydar in general mean that I definitely *was* a lesbian, after all?

I didn't even know if I felt like one. How did being a lesbian feel? A voice inside me insisted on reminding me that I most likely *wasn't* a lesbian, but was probably just a tiny bit more bi than most girls... That was still a possibility, wasn't it?

Gosh. My head. "I don't know what I am," I blurted out, because I was drunk and hopeless. "I thought I was straight..."

She laughed darkly at that. "Yeah, well, join the club," she told me, letting me go and then looking me up and down like

75

you'd check a soldier for wounds. "Just do what feels right. You can worry about what to call it later."

I can't do what feels right, though, I thought, remembering how I'd lain beside Sarah and thought about sliding across the sheets and pulling up against her, kissing those beautiful lips and that lovely smooth skin *and holy hell, that's pretty damn gay*, I realised, suddenly getting a new perspective on it, and then felt so fucking stupid for being like, 'No! I'm totally heterosexual!!!' for nearly 29 years.

But... I'd only been feeling like that about her recently, hadn't I?

...then again it had been years since I'd had a boyfriend...

I sighed heavily. My head was a big tangled mess and I almost wanted to laugh; *what a night*. "I need more alcohol," I told Min in conclusion. "Lots more."

"I know that feeling," she told me, chuckling. "You sure you want to stay here? Because I'll go home with you if you want me to. Bree will understand if I tell her you need support."

The very last thing I needed was to be at home and surrounded by pictures of Sarah while I was wide awake, and I didn't want Bree asking questions, either. She was just as nosy as Sarah was. "No..." I took a deep, steadying breath, looking at the doorway. "No. Let's... try this place. We're here now. How bad can it be?"

She gave me a faint smile and another quick hug, kissing the crown of my head. "Okay. And I'm sorry," she told me as she escorted me under the rainbow flag and inside the lesbian bar.

I didn't know what I expected in there. I knew what I hoped I'd feel: different than everyone. I hoped I'd step in there, look around and be like, 'yup, not a lesbian', but that wasn't what I felt at all.

If I thought the other bar was a mixed crowd, I didn't know the meaning of mixed crowd. Sure, they were all women—well, unless there were other people like Min—but they looked like they had been plucked from literally every category of woman on earth. There were socialites, goths, tomboys, really butch

76

diesel dykes—was that an insult? I didn't mean it as an insult—hipsters, 18 year olds, 50 year olds... they all looked like assorted characters dressed up for different novelty TV-shows congregated in one place. Min and I were swallowed up by the crowd and blended into it.

Min put her hands on my shoulders. "What do you think?" she said beside my ear.

I think it's hot in here, I mentally answered and looked down at my coat. As I was considering if I should unbutton it around all these strangers, a muscular lady in a chainmail bikini-top and hot pants walked casually past me on the way out to the balcony.

I stared at her for a second: that settled it. I took my coat off and gave it to Min, bracing myself to feel people looking towards me—

They didn't. No-one battled an eyelid; the most attention I got as we made our way towards the bar was a woman who could have been my mother turning and giving me an appreciative once-over. "Great dress, hon! If you've got the body, show it off, right?" she told me, and then kept talking to her friends. It took me a long and painful second to realise she meant the compliment *literally*. She wasn't hitting on me.

It was *bizarre*. It was like I'd wandered into an alternate dimension. I didn't feel ogled or judged at all. I suppose that shouldn't have surprised me: there were women walking around in actual lingerie in here, why would it matter if my dress just sort of looked like it?

Min was getting attention she didn't expect, too. Not that straight girls didn't occasionally fawn over her in ordinary bars—but in here they were like *moths to a flame*. No one was reading her as a man and there was a sizeable chunk of women batting their eyelashes at her. She gave me a wide-eyed look. "I'm not used to this," she privately confessed.

I was right there with her: I wasn't used to *any* of this.

We got our drinks and found somewhere to lean against the wall on the edge of the dance floor. The music wasn't overpowering like it usually was in straight clubs, but there were still loads of people dancing. Well, when I say 'dancing', some of them were clearly interpreting 'dancing' very loosely and were basically just using the dance floor as an excuse to grind up against each other. I guessed some things *were* the same in both types of bars...

It was a bit shocking to me, though, seeing it right there in front of me. There were even a few couples who had their hands up each other's tops or—it's pathetic, but I *gasped* when I saw—down each other's pants. I probably would have been way more freaked out if I hadn't been super drunk. *Those girls have sex with each other*, I realised. That was bizarre, too. I couldn't shake the weird lingering feeling that two girls having sex with each other was like eating two entrées instead of going the full three course meal—but I couldn't really explain why that was?

Maybe I'm not gay after all, I thought hopefully, before I imagined Sarah was one of those entrées.

I felt like I had no idea, though. All these girls looked really happy and comfortable in their chainmail bikinis or their bohemian one-pieces or their preppy polos and meanwhile I felt like I wasn't in Kansas anymore. If I did turn out to be like all these women, I just had no idea how to be gay. I hadn't even picked up a guy in three years and guys were basically always around with their belts half-undone, how the hell was I supposed to figure out if a girl was both gay *and* interested? How the hell was I supposed to figure out if *I* was interested in *her*? And what the hell was I going to tell Sarah, my friends and my dad if I got a girlfriend...?

Maybe I'll just move interstate, I thought, and then was horrified that it had even occurred to me to move anywhere without Sarah. But... maybe if *she* was the girlfriend...

Min's sixth drink had apparently been the tipping point between worrying about lesbians hitting on her and not worrying about it. "I like this place," she told me, sculling the last of her beer. "Maybe I'm a bit of an imposter, but I like it here."

I scoffed. That wasn't a surprise. "Of course you do, there's at least three different girls who've been looking at us and trying to figure out if we're together so they know if they should hit on you or not."

Min gave me a loose grin, her eyes twinkling. "Maybe we should kiss. You know, to throw them off."

Even this drunk, I could tell she was joking and shoved her. "You're *terrible*." She just laughed.

We didn't end up staying much longer. Without the adrenaline, anxiety and anticipation of thinking I might pick up some strange guy, and without Sarah doing her usual trick of pulling me onto the dance floor to make a drunken fool of myself with her, the alcohol began to make me sleepy. That, in combination with the rhythmic dance music, was like a lullaby.

"I'm getting old," I said miserably to Min when she noticed my eyelids were drooping.

She chuckled. "Uber or taxi?" was her response and, because it was Newtown and it was full of people, we had to wait for like twenty minutes for either. In the end, Uber won out and Min helped me climb into the back of a huge Landrover and we headed north across the bridge.

I didn't recall much of the journey beyond a hazy memory of Min telling the driver that she might need to go to Kellyville Ridge where Henry lived after we got to my place, but she wasn't sure—and for the rest of it I dozed against her while she idly stroked my hair with one hand and messaged someone on her phone with the other.

"Don't tell them," I mumbled at one point. "You promised." She just patted me in answer.

When we got to my flat, she had to help me out of the Uber, too; and up the stairs, and through my door. I was so drunk that I didn't realise I hadn't been wearing my coat the whole time until Min tossed it on the edge of my bed.

"Are you okay?" She asked as I clumsily sat on my coat, still half-asleep in my drunken haze.

"Yeah, I've been *way* drunker than this and been fine," I told her, yawning.

She gave me a look. "I mean about what happened tonight. Do you want me to stay over?"

Oh. I shook my head. "Nah, I'm going to pass out as soon as you go. Maybe before."

"Okay. Well..." She stood there for a moment, watching me for ages before she spoke. "I'm sorry for before, Gemma. Honestly. I hope you don't regret anything."

"I regret this stupid dress," I told her, gesturing at it. "That's about it."

It got a smile out of her. "Okay," she said, sounding satisfied with my answer. She gave me an affectionate kiss on the forehead, and then let herself out.

I had been planning to lie back and just go to sleep in the stupid dress when it suddenly occurred to me I hadn't seen my handbag since we left the club, and I didn't *think* I'd bought anything or checked my phone—Min had ordered the Uber, hadn't she?—I had this sudden panic that I'd left it there.

I sat up with my head swimming, freaking out, and then saw it hanging on a bed post. I exhaled with relief. Thank goodness Min had been paying attention; I was so lucky she'd agreed to go with me. I took my phone out to text her thanks, and realised I already had a text.

I opened it, wondering if Min had felt the need to apologise again for—

It was from Sarah. *"Okay so my place is empty, and since you're busy working and I could use a break, I thought I'd surprise you with some takeout from that new veggie place on the main road. Anyway I got here with all this delicious-smelling food and I'm peering through your window and I'm pretty sure there's no one here? On Friday night after dark?! I can't believe you actually went out anyway!! xD You total hussy, oh my god you have to tell me EVERYTHING in the morning!!!"*

80

CHAPTER SEVEN

Thanks to Mr Crumpet who walked all over me at 8am until I got up and fed him, I missed a golden opportunity to sleep away half the weekend and avoid thinking about the fact I'd gone to a lesbian bar. Furthermore, because I was up so early, I ended up needing to address what I'd done last night whilst also being *super* hungover.

I'd also apparently passed out without changing into my PJs last night, and so when I faced myself in the bathroom mirror with panda eyes, crazy hair and the now-crinkled red dress, I pretty much looked how I felt: like a giant mess, inside and out.

Perfect, I thought sarcastically, *if I'm having an identity crisis I might as well* look *the part.*

I had hoped a shower would fix my foggy head so I could think more clearly about the whole am-I-gay question, but I was so distracted with it that by the time I got out, I discovered I hadn't washed the conditioner out of my hair. Also, while I was worrying about whether being distracted was a sign I subconsciously knew I was gay, I nearly poured orange juice into my cereal, and then I fed Mr Crumpet again forgetting that I'd fed him only an hour ago.

When my phone dinged with a message from Sarah saying, *"Morning, Sunshine! Let me know when you're up and I'll bring you some café brekky :)"*, I basically freaked the hell out.

I didn't trust myself to reply at all, but if I didn't reply, she'd probably come around anyway. If she came around anyway, there was no way in hell I'd be able to lie convincingly to her about where I was last night—I was a bad enough liar normally without being super distracted and hungover—and I had this horrible, horrible mental image of me saying something, or even doing something to give away the feelings I'd had about her.

There was only one solution: I threw on some clothes and fled my house.

I went and loaded up on caffeine at a café—not any of the ones Sarah liked, though, because I didn't want to bump into her—and then spent a couple of hours at the local Westfield before I remembered how much I hated shopping. I'd never been the kind of person to go out and *see* things like museums or landmarks or whatever, so I ended up at the only place where I could be seedy and not judged for it: Dad's.

When I wandered into his garage, he looked like he couldn't believe his eyes. "Gemma!" he said, rushing over to give me a big hug and in the process getting engine grease from his latest mechanical invention all over me. "What brings you all the way out here?"

You're a great excuse to not be home, I thought, and then felt really guilty. "I'm a bad daughter and I don't visit you enough?"

He laughed. "Don't feel obligated to visit me, I'm not in a nursing home yet," he told me, and then added darkly, "But if your mother keeps fighting me for the house, it might be the only place I can afford pretty soon. Anyway! That's enough of that. Let me put the kettle on."

It clearly *wasn't* enough of that, though, because while he was making me tea, I got to hear all about how Mum was dating someone who *was oh my god thirteen years younger than her can you believe it* and who was apparently straight from Spain. "And do you know what she said loudly in front of me at Sandy's 60th?" he asked as he ferociously heaped sugar into his tea, "she said, 'It's nice to date someone with a *tan* for once.'"

Ouch; Dad was as fair and redheaded as I was.

"Anyway!" he said, trying to change the subject *again*, "Are *you* dating anyone at the moment?"

After his ongoing saga with Mum, that was a bit of a loaded question. I shook my head. "Nope. Still single."

"*Good*," he said with feeling, waving the spoon at me. "Stay that way. Relationships are for suckers who want to hand over half of everything they've worked their whole lives for to thieving adulterers. You're too smart for that."

Yeah... it's definitely that I'm 'too smart' for it, I thought dryly, *not that I'm hopeless with strangers or that I don't even know whether I should be dating men or women anymore...*

I briefly wondered what he'd do if I *did* bring home a girlfriend to him; it wasn't that much of a mystery, though, because Mum would definitely disapprove and that was the only thing in the world that made Dad truly happy. I could probably count on his support. Plus, he'd always really liked Sarah.

I paused mid-sip, horrified with myself for making that connection.

Dad let me hang around all afternoon in his garage while he tinkered with his latest design, and we chatted about things that weren't the fact I went to a lesbian bar last night, that I was attracted to my best friend and that I didn't know what to do about either of those things. I even earnt major brownie points for ignoring my phone while it went nuts in my bag. It was only when I was sure it was too late for Sarah to drop by that I caught the train home.

Back at my place, even my go-to movies on Netflix didn't tune me out like they usually did, because I kept noticing all the straight couples in them and wondering if I was like them or not. It got to the point where I had to turn Netflix off, get out my tablet and spend the rest of the weekend trawling through online libraries to see if there were any sure-fire tests psychologists had constructed that would give me the definitive answer on my sexuality.

By Monday, I'd not only expertly avoided Sarah all weekend, but I'd also read so many papers online that despite the fact it was Bree who had her Psych exam today, I might have actually been ready to sit it myself. I was unfortunately no closer to figuring myself out though, or figuring out how not to act on the feelings I already had.

I'd resolved to spend my train ride to work getting my story straight about Friday night so I knew what to tell Sarah when I saw her at lunchtime. You could imagine my panic when I'd tapped my Opal card and I heard a familiar voice call, "Hey, Stranger!" from the other side of the turnstiles.

Sarah was waiting there for me on the platform, giving me a big, warm, welcoming smile. I couldn't have imagined it better myself.

I stopped in place, halting the queue of people behind me.

I was so conflicted. This was exactly what I'd missed the last few months: our old routine of catching the train together. I couldn't enjoy it now, though, because I immediately worried about what I was going to tell her about Friday, and that my first thought upon seeing her was *wow, she's so beautiful*.

She had to step forward and tow me out of the way before someone yelled at me.

"Oh my god, Gem, I forgot how much of a space cadet you are in the morning!" she said, pulling me aside and giving me a one-armed hug so her bangles jingled musically next to my ear. "Don't worry, though, I've got something that'll definitely wake you up!" She'd been holding something carefully in her other hand, and she dropped her arm from my shoulders so she could try and give it to me.

It was a jumbo coffee cup, just like the one I'd missed out on giving her last week. I gaped at it.

"I know, right! Isn't is *ridiculous*? I thought I'd drop past our old café to grab you a coffee for old times' sake, and the second I saw this bathtub of a cup, I thought, 'oh my god, I have to buy this for Gem!'" She pushed it into my hands, helpfully adding, "Don't drink it all at once, though. George put four shots in it, and I think there's a fine line between 'lethal dose of caffeine' and 'enough energy to tell Sarah everything I did last Friday'..." With that, she pointedly gave me her full attention.

There it was, oh my gosh. *What do I say?! What do I say?!* my brain screamed while I forced out, "There's really nothing to tell...?"

She gave me a tired look. "Gem. That is the worst lie you've ever told."

"I'm not lying," I lied and, of course, went bright red in the process.

"Right..." she said at length, eyeing my pink cheeks. "That's 48. And I don't believe you for a second that *nothing* happened. Come on," she said, slinging an arm around my shoulders again. "'Fess up, Ginge! Tell Sarah all the dirty, dirty things you did last Friday night as penance for sneaking off without her."

There was no way in hell I was going to tell her where I'd been last night—it was only a small step from 'likes women' to 'likes me', and I'd rather anything else in the world than to damage our friendship—but I knew Sarah, and I knew she wasn't going to let go of the issue until she'd gotten a confession and a really good story out of me.

I tried the safest one I could think of, glancing around us to make sure no one could hear. "You *really* want to know?" I asked her, feigning defeat. "Fine: I got drunk off my face and when a younger guy hit on me, I hid in the toilets and then ran away."

I don't think that was the story she was expecting. She just stared at me for a couple of seconds, and then burst out laughing. "Okay, that *does* sound like you," she said, totally buying it. I could actually feel her relax against me; I didn't even realise how tense she'd been until that point. "You really honestly didn't do anything?" I shook my head. "Not even a cheeky handjob on the dance floor?" She laughed at the expression I gave her, and then spent some time looking thoughtful. "Well, what was the point of going out then? I don't get it."

Shit. I pressed my lips together, staring down at my jumbo coffee. What could I possibly tell her? "I guess I just changed my mind...?" I attempted, my voice wavering.

How closely she was watching me was making me sweat. Even I wouldn't have believed that was the full story, and I bordered on being the most gullible person on the planet. So when Sarah went, "Hmm, okay," and then shrugged and let it go, I didn't know what to make of it.

It made me uncomfortable. I felt like the conversation wasn't really over, so I tried to end it. "Anyway, yeah: I didn't pick up. Sorry to disappoint you. You went to all this trouble to give me caffeine poisoning and I don't even have a good story for you."

She didn't look very disappointed; the opposite, actually. She spent a few moments thinking about that, and then looked across at me. "Can I be honest with you?"

That question made me really nervous. "Of course?"

"I'm actually kind of relieved," she said, as if she was just realising it.

...huh? "You are?"

She thought more about it before she answered, and when she did, she sounded deceptively casual. "Yeah. When I went over to your place on Friday night to surprise you with dinner and found out you'd lied to me... it really hurt, Gem."

Oh...

"And then when I went home to my empty house and thought about that, I couldn't sleep. And when you didn't answer any of my texts all weekend, I thought you were obviously having an amazing full weekend with whoever you'd picked up." She exhaled. "Anyway, I'm not saying this to make you feel guilty or anything, it would just eat me up if I didn't let it out."

I nodded, my chest tight. That wasn't even the half of the stuff I was hiding from her... I felt a bit ill. "I'm sorry," I told her. "That's the last thing in the world I wanted."

She nodded, linking arms with me. "I know," she said. "I know."

We'd gotten on the train before she spoke again. As we were going over the bridge and gazing out at the harbour together like we always used to, she looked across at me. She had a faint smile on her face. "It's really nice to be catching this train with you again, Gem."

If I had any doubt left I had feelings for her, it was gone now. She was giving me this beautiful open expression—completely

86

vulnerable—and I'd never wanted to kiss anyone so much in my life. All I'd need to do was lean up to her, tilt her chin with my fingertips and kiss her right here, in the middle of this crowded train. I had to look away from her so she couldn't read it on my face.

I could see a ghost of my reflection in the train window, and I stared at it, lips parted. *I think Min's right*, I realised, oddly aware of the fact I was surrounded by a hundred strangers and that I might be different from every single one of them. *I think I might actually be gay.*

I hadn't recovered from that feeling by the time I got to work, even though the rational part of my brain was reminding me I had 28.9 years of experience *not* being attracted to someone who was the same gender as me and it was extremely unlikely that one single experience made me gay.

Then again, 'extremely unlikely' was basically what I traded in, and 'gay' would nicely compliment all my other outlier statistics, wouldn't it? *I could have the full set of 'different'*, I thought dryly to myself as I sat down at my cubicle and looked up to see if Anil had noticed me come in on time.

He hadn't because his door was shut.

Huh. "Is he still upset about the offshoring thing?" I wondered aloud.

Spud looked over at me and shook his head. "HR's in there with him," he told me. "Probably grilling him about what happened last week when half of his department was off getting drunk on the Frost payroll."

"Either that," someone else said from behind a partition, "or we're all about to find out we don't have jobs any more. It's *Henry Lee* in there, and why else would the *Director of HR* bother to visit Anil unless there was some serious issue?"

That made my ears perk up. Henry was in there talking to Anil? Maybe they were discussing my Marketing secondment!

"Why are *you* so happy?" Spud wanted to know, and I had to wipe the big smile off my face and pretend to be very busy.

I wasn't, though, and I kept one eye on Anil's door so that when it opened I could try and gauge if they had been talking about me after all. When they came out, though, no one so much as cast a glance in my direction. Henry was busy speaking in hushed tones to his assistant manager as he left and didn't look over me at all. Spud did, though. It was unnerving.

I was both excited and nervous to see Sarah again at lunchtime—I couldn't get the idea of kissing her in the middle of a train as it rattled across Sydney Harbour Bridge out of my mind—but she only had about three seconds to spend with me, anyway.

"I have a meeting with *Diane Frost* to discuss my reports at one o'clock," she complained dryly, trying to wolf down a half-stale sandwich in under a minute. "That woman doesn't eat and so *we* aren't allowed to, either, apparently—*oh!*" she said suddenly and sat up straight. "Speaking of eating, I nearly forgot!" She patted herself down for an envelope and handed it to me. "I was a big emotional mess this morning and nearly didn't give you this. Bree would have killed me if you didn't show up."

She kept talking while I opened it. "Henry's shouting us all to dinner at Rockpool tonight to celebrate Bree's last ever exam being over and to thank us for helping her."

It seemed a bit odd that Henry would be doing the shouting given that Bree was his ex's new girlfriend and that Min had cheated on him *with* that new girlfriend, but Henry had never been like Dad and Mum and held a massive grudge against Min over it, so I supposed it wasn't *that* weird.

Dad would still probably love him, I thought ironically as I read the invitation. They could exchange tragic stories about whose ex had fucked who over more, and I could listen and feel better about the fact that I wasn't not the only person with a non-existent love life.

"Huh," was all I said.

Sarah had been watching for my reaction. "I know, right?" she said, in a tone that suggested she'd had the same reaction to Henry's invitation as I had. "But he and Min are still really good friends, I guess. Anyway, meet you downstairs at 6:45. We can walk there together."

That was enough to make me look forward to it, even if I'd have to sit at a table with Henry and be self-conscious for an hour or two as a result.

Min and Bree were waiting out the front of Rockpool for us when we arrived—Bree shrieked and waved when she saw us— and they were both very dressed up. Min, I'd seen in a suit many times, but Bree had neatened her curls, put on a blue party dress and was wearing something other than thongs on her feet for once. She looked adorable, but that could also have been because of how excited she was.

"Thanks to you guys, I'm not a high school student anymore!" she declared and went to throw her arms around both our middles, forgetting that Sarah's middle wasn't as accessible anymore and bumping into it. "Sorry," she told Sarah, rubbing her stomach and looking sheepish.

Sarah clearly didn't mind. "How'd you go today?"

Bree shrugged. "Alright, I guess? I don't really know. I just can't believe it's all over and I did it! I made it to the end of the year!" Behind her, Min was beaming.

The only person missing was Henry. Sarah checked her watch, and looked around us. "Still waiting for Moneybags?"

Both Min and Bree chuckled at that nickname and then looked horrified at themselves. Min composed herself first. "He's in Rockpool's boardroom—*more meetings*," she said, and rolled her eyes.

Sarah glanced up sharply at Min. "Wait a minute, meetings off-site?" she asked, and was immediately suspicious. "If he was meeting with anyone from Frost he'd just have done it in the building, so why isn't he back there?" She'd clearly made up her mind as to why. "You know what? I bet it's the unions."

Min shrugged dismissively. "Well, whoever it is, he should be nearly done by now, he said he'd meet us at the table." We followed Min and Bree inside.

The restaurant looked as exclusive as its menu, and between the two-story marble pillars, the dark interior design and the haughty hostess that showed us to our table, I was scared to even touch the cutlery. I was just looking upwards at a rack of hundreds of crystal wine glasses beside us when I felt a hand on my arm.

Sarah leant over to me. "Looks like they knew you were coming," she said with a smirk, eyeing the hundreds of wine glasses. I gave her a tired look and she snickered at me. "Anyway, I'm just going to duck off to the ladies and do something about my lipstick. Be back in a sec," she told us, and disappeared.

Bree was busy drinking in our surroundings and looking absolutely delighted. "Can you imagine running a place like this?" she asked, obviously doing exactly that. "It has *three hats*!"

I had no idea what that meant, but from Bree's reverent tone, it was apparently very impressive.

Min watched her thoughtfully for a few seconds while she was gazing with starry eyes at the open kitchen, and then smiled privately to herself and went back to reading the menu. Under the table, I could see they were holding hands with their fingers interlaced. They looked so settled in their relationship; it was so weird to think just six months ago, Min and Henry had been together. I wondered how Min had figured out she liked women. I would have asked her if Bree hadn't been with us.

Min caught me looking at her and gave me a wink. I blushed and hurriedly buried my nose in the menu.

While I was looking through the menu and trying to manage my guilt over the *exorbitant* prices, Sarah appeared next to me again and sat uncomfortably in her seat. She looked like she was about to explode with something.

When she was sure we were all looking at her, she put her hands up in a 'yield' position. "Okay, I've done something I'm not proud of, and before you all judge me, I want you to know that I did it for Gemma."

My eyebrows shot up. What on—? I gave her the weirdest look. Min and Bree glanced at each other, and Min's expression mirrored mine.

"Okay," Sarah said, "Okay. So Henry's obviously meeting with the unions, right? So I thought I might just kind of... sneak over there and have a listen so I could see if I could hear anything about Gem's job..."

Min's expression hardened. "*Sarah*."

"I know, I know!" she said, sounding genuinely remorseful. "The way I figured it, there were two possible outcomes: either I'd hear something useful and then I could give Gem the heads up, or I wouldn't hear anything and I wouldn't need to tell anyone what I'd done."

There was something about the way she was listing those variables... "But you were wrong?"

She looked at me, stricken. "I was, like, *so* wrong. So wrong. Okay, so I went over there and just stood at the doorway to get a gist of what they were talking about to see if it was the offshoring stuff. But I could only hear two voices, so I thought I'd just take a little peek through the open door..."

"...And?" Bree prompted her.

"And: sorry to say it, guys, but there's no way that's an official union meeting. Henry's in there having a private dinner with the hottest woman on the planet. No wonder he's feeling so generous."

We all stared at her.

I—actually wasn't quite sure I definitely believed it? Sarah had a habit of jumping to conclusions about who was sleeping with who, especially if it smelt like scandal. "Are you sure? Maybe the union lady just happens to be attractive?"

Sarah gave me look. "Believe me. I'm sure."

Bree was looking across at Min with some concern, but Min's expression was completely unreadable. Bree turned back to us, determined. "Okay, I need to see this," she announced, and stood up.

Min reached for her arm. "Bree..."

Bree expertly evaded it. "Be honest, *you* want to know, too," she told Min, and then spun and jetted off towards the boardroom.

Min swore under her breath and stood up to follow her, and Sarah took off after Min. And since I wasn't going to be left sitting here at the table, I grabbed my handbag and followed the lot of them over to the corner where the doorway was. Besides... I kind of wanted to see what Sarah's definition of 'hottest woman in the world' looked like.

The door was open a crack, but it wasn't open enough for four faces to peer through. We all jostled for a position, and even Min eventually gave a long-suffering sigh of resignation and bent down to have a quick peek.

From what I could make out, Henry was sitting across a board table from a woman who had her back to us. All I could see of her was long black hair and a dress that was every bit as red as the one I'd worn on Friday night, but where mine was kind of tasteless and revealing, hers was haute couture, perfectly tailored, and complimented with black patent stilettos. Despite the board table and the formality of the room, I began to think Sarah might be right—no one wore something that bold to work. That was date wear, and it was being worn by someone with a *killer* body.

Wow. So while I'd been feeling comforted by the fact Henry was at least as tragic as I was and joking about his generosity, he was actually secretly dating a solid 10/10.

Meanwhile, I was probably a 7 at the most and apparently doomed to become an old lesbian cat lady while everyone else in the known world was on a smooth trajectory towards happiness and fulfilment. I was busy trying to cope with that when Bree bumped me and I fell against the door, making it creak slightly. To my horror, Henry's eyes lifted off his plate and looked *directly at us*.

"Shit!" Sarah hissed as we all stood away from the door, staring with wide-eyed panic at each other. "Go! Go!" she whispered, gesturing back to our table.

We'd begun to scuttle off when the door opened wide and Henry stepped out of it. He had a very tired expression. "It's too late for that," he told us flatly when he saw us trying to escape.

We stood in place and turned back to him, probably looking as guilty as a bunch of schoolkids caught somewhere they shouldn't be. I'd never seen him act like a manager before, but I felt like I was about to be reprimanded like an employee. He had a quiet anger that was actually kind of terrifying; I hoped it wouldn't somehow affect my potential secondment...

"This is all my fault," Sarah said frankly.

Henry looked like he wasn't interested in confessions. He gave us all a very pointed look, and then swept his arm out towards the private room with a heavy sigh. "Well, you're here now," he said, "this wasn't exactly how I'd planned to introduce you all, but you might as well come in."

We were all too embarrassed to do anything except follow his instructions, so we filed into the room like naughty children. The woman in the red dress had stood from her chair to face us, and was leaning with one hip against the table and her arms crossed over her ample chest.

I immediately saw what Sarah meant: this woman was *gorgeous*. Like, predatory gorgeous. She was very tall—maybe nearly as tall as Min and Henry?—and had a sharp face with savage features. She knew she was attractive, too: she oozed self-confidence. It was terrifying. I hoped she wouldn't try to talk to me; I had no doubt my cheeks were as red as her dress.

She and Henry shared a glance, as he indicated us one by one. "This is Min, Bree, Sarah and Gemma," he told her, and then held his arm out towards her. "And this is Natalie Heiser, partner at Heiser & Anderson, and head legal counsel of the Mining and Energy Union."

CHAPTER EIGHT

So this Natalie woman was a *lawyer*? I didn't doubt that for a second. I'd never seen anyone who fit 'lawyer' more in my life: she looked like she would eat the raw, beating heart of anyone who opposed her, and charge them dearly for the pleasure. There was a serious dominatrix vibe about her.

"Nice to finally meet you all," Natalie told us without smiling, and then looked directly at Min. "So *you're* Min."

Min's eyes widened. I felt for her.

Natalie considered her for a moment. "You don't recognise the name, do you? 'Heiser & Anderson?'" Since Min clearly didn't, she pushed off from where she'd been leaning against the table to stride forward and handed Min a small business card from her purse.

Min accepted it cautiously, her eyes dipping to read it. There was no recognition in them.

It didn't look like that was the reaction Natalie was used to. "No? We posted you an invitation to meet with us right after your unfair dismissal from Frost in April."

Now Min seemed to remember something. "Oh." She paused. "But it's not unfair dismissal because I didn't get dismissed. I resigned."

"You were forced to resign, which is the same thing as unfair dismissal in industrial law," Natalie told her, and then leant in towards her a little. "I could *cut Frost up* over what they did to you, Min. Discrimination is my speciality, and I've heard through the grapevine that you have an unresolved dispute with them. It would be *my pleasure* to take Frost to open court over it; the media would love this case, too—transgender rights are a big deal right now—and I have some old friends at the Herald who would give us favourable coverage."

Natalie may have thought she was offering Min reasons why she would want to pursue Frost, but I'd never seen more of an immediate reaction in Min than when Natalie said 'media'. Her expression was the firmest 'no' possible.

Henry noticed. "Careful who you drag into the legal system, Natalie," he cautioned her. "Not everyone shares your bloodlust."

Min looked like she was one of those other people. "Thanks for the offer," she said in a tone that held a note of the opposite.

Unfortunately, Natalie was apparently not the kind of person to take 'no' for an answer. "I'll even sweeten the deal by running it as No Win, No Fee..."

Min had her eyes on the card in her hands, uncomfortable. Beside me, Sarah looked conflicted and I could see she wanted to jump to Min's defence. However, after being caught eavesdropping, I don't think anyone of us were game to interrupt them.

"So, what do you think?" Natalie pressed, ignoring Min's reluctance.

Cornered, Min had clearly had enough. "What do I think? I think you should fire your graphic designer and let me redesign this card for you. *I'll* make sure people won't forget your firm." She waved the business card in air. "Leave this with me for a week. Excuse me, and sorry about before." Nodding politely at Natalie, she turned and made a quick exit back into the main restaurant.

Bree looked torn about staying or going—she'd been listening intently to the conversation between Min and Natalie and I thought she might've liked to have asked for more information—but in the end, she chose to follow Min. "Nice to meet you, Natalie," she said as she left, "And sorry we were spying on you and Henry before. It's only because Henry never tells us anything."

"Good to know," Natalie said dryly after she'd gone, looking sideways at Henry. "Oh, well, maybe while he's redesigning my card he'll have a change of heart..."

Henry had his arms crossed, and he raised his eyebrows at her momentarily as if to say 'I told you so'. "What did I say about pressuring him?"

Natalie shrugged. "If I always took the first 'no' as a final answer, I wouldn't be head legal counsel of the MEU," she said in a very lawyer-like voice, and then *looked directly at Sarah and I.*

Shit. I felt like a deer in headlights; we were next on the menu apparently.

"And you two... Sarah?" She said, pointing at Sarah, "and Emma, was it?" She pointed at me.

Since I was useless in this type of situation and wouldn't have corrected her, Sarah answered for me. "Gemma."

Natalie did a silent 'ah'. "Gemma, that's it," she said, while I tried to cope with all these women saying my name with their red, red lips. "Do you two work for Frost as well?"

Thank heavens for Sarah. "Yes, I'm Marketing Lead and Gemma kind of doesn't really have a department, she does her own thing. They've moved her around a few times."

Natalie didn't even acknowledge what Sarah had said about herself. "Doesn't have a department?" she asked, eyebrows up. Gosh, she was looking straight at me; I was going to die right here on this spot. "What type of work do you do?"

"She's this really incredible statistician, but they just have her fixing spreadsheets."

Natalie narrowed her eyes at me for a moment, and then I could see something light up in them. "You're Gemma Rowe," she told me while my brain screamed *WHY DOES SHE KNOW YOUR NAME?!*

"That's her," Sarah answered for me, and then, because she was Sarah and had balls of rock-solid steel, she asked directly, "Do you know if she's one of the people who are going to lose their jobs?"

Henry groaned. "*Sarah...*"

Everyone ignored him, especially Natalie. "No one's going to lose their jobs if I have anything to do with it," she said confidently, and then fixed me with a pointed look. "I trust I'll see you at the union meeting this week?"

I was gulping like a fish—I wasn't a member of the union and I didn't really want to say that—but Sarah rescued me again. "She'll definitely be there."

Natalie looked pleased with that answer. "Good," she said. "The more, the merrier. Anyway," she turned back towards Henry. "I think our meeting has apparently ended? Always good to catch up with you, Henry, and nice to meet your friends." She gave Sarah and me a professional smile and then said to me, "See you at the union meeting." It sounded more like a firm instruction than an invitation.

Henry's hand was hovering by her lower back without touching it. "I'll walk you back to your car," he told her as he escorted her out, glancing sidelong at Sarah and me as he walked past. "I'll meet the rest of you back at the reserved table shortly."

Then—*thank heavens*—they left and I was finally released from my vice and able to breathe freely again. Sarah, on the other hand, had been practically holding her own breath and on the point of explosion until they were out of earshot. "*Oh my god*!" she erupted, turning around and grabbing both my arms like she'd struck gossip jackpot. "Can you *believe* any of that?"

I still hadn't recovered. "No?"

"No is right! Wow! Henry's dating someone, she's a lawyer of the MEU, and now we know that your job is going—okay, so I know I should feel terrible about springing Henry like that, but I'm totally glad I did!"

I wasn't so glad. I'd just made an idiot of myself yet again. Natalie was exactly the type of person I would literally plan an entire day to avoid ever being in the same room with. And to top that off, making Henry angry... I was ready to go home, actually. I didn't care how nice the food here was.

It looked like I wasn't going to get that option, though, because Sarah linked arms with me and started to lead me back to the table, bubbling with excitement. "I seriously had no idea he was seeing someone. Did you? *Nuts.* At least I feel better about your job now, though."

I gave her a look. "Because there's nothing more reassuring than a union lawyer tacitly confirming your employer is trying to screw you out of a job?"

She was full of conviction. "Can you seriously think of a better person to handle the case, though? She's a shark, Gem! Imagine facing her in the courtroom: on top of the fact she's crazy intense, she's a bombshell and no one could pick up their jaws off the floor to mount a defence." Something occurred to her, and she snickered and leant in to my ear to whisper, "They're probably all too busy thinking about mounting *her*!"

For some reason hearing Sarah say that about another woman really bothered me.

Back at the table, Min had lost her rosy aura of pride in Bree and was staring absently at the menu.

"At least you know who to go to if Frost doesn't pay your entitlements," Sarah pointed out as we sat down.

Min glanced up and then shrugged. "That stuff is in the past, and I'm really not interested in crossing swords with Frost again. Frost fights dirty, and I don't think someone like Natalie would care much about anything except winning the case."

Sarah shrugged. "Maybe there would be a lot of money in it?"

"It would have to be a *lot* of money," Min said firmly. "Or there would have to be some other reason. Otherwise, no thank you."

"I'm with Min," I said. "Natalie wants to make her do media interviews."

Sarah laughed. "Oh no!" she said, mimicking me as she opened her menu again. "Not *interviews*! The horror!" She dropped the act. "Huh. I wonder if she'll want you guys to do interviews for the offshoring stuff?"

I hadn't thought of that. Oh, gosh. If there had been any sort of chance I'd go the union meeting before, it was completely gone now.

Sarah observed my expression, and pointedly said, "I guess you can tell us after you've been to the union meeting."

"I guess," I said, with absolutely zero intention of going. With any luck, I'd just end up in Marketing, anyway and none of this offshoring stuff would matter to me.

Unfortunately, Sarah read me like a book. "I knew it, you're not planning on going, are you?"

Crap. "Well, I don't know what difference it would make?" I said, instead of, 'I don't want to ever give Natalie the chance to talk to me again, especially when you aren't around'.

"But don't you want to find out more info about what's going on with your job? I know if *I* just got confirmation my employer was trying to offshore my job I'd want to know everything about it that I could!"

Min made a sceptical noise. "Not everyone enjoys working for Frost, Sarah," she reminded her.

Sarah scoffed. "Yeah, but everyone needs money, and generally keeping your job is a key part of that."

"Maybe I'll get a new job...?" I suggested, wondering what it was going to be like working in Marketing.

Sarah stopped, turning her whole head towards me and directing me a deep frown. "Wow, you've really changed your tune," she noted. "Last week you were desperate not to lose it... did something happen?"

Oh, no, was I being too obvious? Henry would kill me if she somehow guessed, and I had a feeling I was skating on thin ice with him after tonight. Crap, what could I say...?! "N-No, I was just thinking about what you said?" I tried her own line on her. "Maybe I *am* being wasted where I am now..."

She gave me a very long, very calculated look, and then looked back at her menu. "I still think you should go to the union meeting," she decided. "At least then you'll have some idea of how long you've got."

"Yeah, and you can give us more intel on Natalie!" Bree chimed in. "I want to know what she's like since Henry won't say anything. Maybe she's really lovely!"

"I think it's pretty clear what she's like," Min said dryly.

"Yeah, I don't think there's a secret compassionate side of her that Gem's going to discover at the union meeting," Sarah added, obviously assuming that she'd convinced me to go. "She's a lawyer. She fights for a living."

Bree made a face. "But she's a lawyer for the unions, right? And she does discrimination law, so obviously she's fighting for the right reasons. Maybe that's why Henry likes her."

Sarah didn't look convinced. "I think that, looking at her, we saw what Henry likes in her."

Min gave her a sharp glance. "Henry's not like that, Sarah."

Sarah shrugged. "Apparently he is? I mean, come on: what else would they really have in common apart from both being rich and hot? He's Mr Caring of the Year and she clearly has no caring side at all. I mean, did you notice?" She gestured at her round belly. "I'm huge. Women *always* comment on how pregnant I am, always. She didn't say anything like, 'how far along are you'? Or, 'congratulations'. It's weird."

"Maybe she doesn't care about children?" I suggested.

Min's mouth was in a thin line. "*Henry* cares about children," she said shortly.

Sarah reached across the table and gave Min a comforting pat. "Well, I wouldn't worry about it. They're probably just sleeping together because it's convenient." Min didn't look very comforted by that.

We politely waited for 'Moneybags' to get back so we could order, but he took a lot longer than expected. He also seemed to be concealing a smile. "I'm unhappy you all did that," he told us in a 'let bygones be bygones' voice as he took his seat at the table. "That was quite embarrassing for me."

We all apologised, and then Sarah added smugly, "You're such a dark horse, Henry. None of us had any idea at all!"

He looked up slowly from his menu for a moment, an expression of concern on his face. "Sarah, the reason Natalie and I chose to meet so far away from Frost HQ was specifically so people *wouldn't* jump to that conclusion about us having dinner together," he said. "There are enough rumours about me as it is, I don't need anyone to make it worse by inadvertently starting more of them."

Oh… okay, I admit it, I felt a little bad about the discussion we'd been having before.

While I was feeling really guilty about that, Sarah was obviously having much more trouble believing him. "Wait, you're saying you're *not* dating her?"

He didn't look up from the menu. "I'm not dating her, Sarah."

I didn't know what to make of that, but Sarah gave me a sideways look that said *oh, he's definitely dating her*, and on reflection, I tended to agree. Everything about that 'dinner meeting' was a date, and he just spent 25 minutes walking her back to her car and came back with a smile on his face. He was definitely dating her.

I suppose he couldn't say it, though, for work-related reasons. We couldn't talk about it, either, because he sat with us all dinner and clearly wasn't interested in debating the matter further. Afterwards, when we parted ways with him so Min could drive us home, it was all we could talk about. Well, it was all Sarah could talk about.

"But he could tell *us*, couldn't he?" Sarah was asking Min, leaning forward and resting her chin on the driver's seat. "We're his friends!"

Min's lips were still in a tight line. She'd been on edge ever since that 'negotiation' with Natalie. "If it has something to do with work?" she asked, and then shook her head. "He takes his ethics pretty seriously."

"Apparently not *that* seriously," Sarah pointed out. "Since he dated you while you were his employee and now he's sleeping with the opposition's legal counsel."

Min prickled a bit at that, and gave her a hard look in the rear vision mirror. "Why are *you* so interested in his love life, anyway, Sarah? Haven't you got a boyfriend of your own to spy on?"

"Yes, but I already know who Rob's sleeping with," Sarah said with a grin. "And, look, *she's* totally hot, too, but there's no mystery there."

Everyone rolled their eyes and then Min turned the radio to a very obnoxious pop music station and turned the volume way up so we couldn't continue to gossip about Henry. That was fine by me, because the more we talked about Henry scoring, the more I felt like a total loser for being the only one of us who wasn't practically married off to someone. Not only that, but I was getting a serious impression that I might have been barking up the wrong tree my entire life.

That was a scary thought, though: because according to that paper I'd read last week, if only 1.8% of women in Sydney were lesbians, then that seriously cut down on the number of women who were likely to be available to me. It was probably hardly any.

I had intended to leave that thought there, but then I kept wondering exactly how many there were likely to be, and in the end I couldn't resist: I had to figure it out.

I got out my phone and searched for the demographic spread of Sydney (8.8% were females in my approximate age bracket) and if I factored in things like probability of already being in a marriage-like relationship (63%), likelihood of working a STEM-related field so we'd have something in common (9%), and then ran that all against 1.8%, I ended up with a figure in the low hundreds. And what was the likelihood of running into those women in a situation where I *wasn't* going to go bright red and not be able to speak?

Crap, I thought, letting my phone flop into my lap. That was not a great number. *Maybe I should just give up and date boys?* I hadn't been *unhappy* with them, after all…

My phone buzzed in my hands, startling me. Frowning, I checked the message. I couldn't really think of who'd be messaging me this late except the people I was already with.

It was *Sarah*. "*Big frown you've got there... stressing about finding a new job after all?*"

I looked across at her on the other side of the back seat, and she gave me a silent smile. There was something so touching about that: the idea of her quietly sitting back while I was plugging away at my calculator app and worrying about me. I wondered how long she'd been watching for, and what she'd been thinking about while she'd been—

Shit, I was staring. I tore my eyes away from her and took a breath, trying to get my thoughts together. What had she—? Oh, she'd asked what I was doing. Well, I couldn't tell her exactly what I was doing of course, but I supposed the gist of it was okay?

I typed, "*283*," and she sent me a series of question marks and gave me a weird look. I chuckled at it. "*I realise how this sounds, but that's the number of people I think would probably be compatible with me in Sydney if I consider all the obvious variables.*"

She *burst out laughing* when she read it, and ended up awkwardly leaning across the seat and giving me a big hug until I was rosy-cheeked. "I thought you were trying to calculate your redundancy payout or how much money you had left or something!" she told me loudly over the terrible music, squeezing me around the shoulders. "Why is the number so low, though? I'm sure it's more than that."

Well, um... "I'm, erm, looking for the people with the same interests as me?" Well, that wasn't *exactly* a lie...

She scoffed. "That's a fallacy," she told me, her arms still around my shoulders. Her breath was warm on the nape of my neck. "That whole 'you must have everything in common with your partner or you're *doomed*' thing. I mean, look at me and Rob: we couldn't be more different and I used to

103

assume we'd eventually break up because of that." She patted her big, round belly. "I was wrong."

Bree must have been eavesdropping, because she twisted in her seat to peer over the shoulder of it. "Min and I do all different things, too," she told me. "And look at Henry and Natalie: can you imagine two people who are more different? I think the 'opposites attract' saying is true. Your partner doesn't need to share all your interests."

Yeah, but they have to be interested in someone who's your gender, I thought, feeling a bit tortured about the fact that I couldn't explain exactly why the number was so low. Besides, I didn't want someone who liked all different things; for example, Sarah and I had always loved travelling together, loved the same music and movies and books, even the same food—except I was still working on converting her to being a vegetarian—and we'd always been so, so close. *That* was the kind of relationship I wanted, not anything else.

"We need to get you a boyfriend," Sarah declared for about the thousandth time in my life, echoing what had been on my mind. Well, kind of.

Maybe I should *just get a boyfriend,* I wondered, ignoring the fact Min was looking right at me in the rear vision mirror. *Perhaps it would be okay?* It would certainly be easier to find one who had anything at all in common with me...

...Except the problem was that once I'd found them, I had to actually talk to them, didn't I? That was generally what happened before the relationship and the sex. It seemed pretty unavoidable.

"But I'm no good at picking up," I said, haunted by memories of last Friday. "The second anyone walks up to me I'm already bright-bloody-red and wishing I was somewhere else."

"Min and I met on the internet," Bree reminded me. "Maybe you should just go online on forums about things you're interested in and see if you can meet someone nice that way?"

That was certainly a possibility, and I'd browsed the hobby maths subreddits before in my free time, but I'd never seen any posts that weren't actually attempts to solve the formulas or critiques of other people's attempted answers. Any social chatter got down-voted into oblivion. And, I mean, it definitely wouldn't be torture to hang around on them a bit more, but how did I find out where people were from so I didn't end up falling for someone from, like, *Alaska* or something?

While I was considering that, Sarah's hand appeared in front of me. "Pfft," she said flatly. "You guys are all *amateurs*. What century are we in? Give me your phone."

I looked across at her; she had what I could only describe as an evil, evil smile. Despite that and against my better judgment, I handed my phone over.

It was only once I'd given it to her that I remembered that I'd been researching about lesbians before, and had *a horrible internal panic that she'd see it and know and our friendship would be over and I wanted to grab the phone back quickly and throw it out the window*. Trying to snatch back my phone was useless, though, because if I tipped her off there might be something to find on it she wouldn't stop until she'd found it.

So, I sat there gritting my teeth while she installed an app on my phone and then—thank goodness!—handed it back to me without uncovering any of my dark secrets. "There."

I looked down at it; it was my own Facebook profile pic on a white background. I didn't know what it was, so I frowned across at Sarah.

She was giving me a *very* broad grin. "Welcome to Tinder."

CHAPTER NINE

My blood ran cold: Tinder? The dating app? The 'you're next door, hook up with me right now'-Tinder? I panicked. I didn't want to hook up with people *right now*!

I resisted the urge to just throw my phone out the window of the car. "Why did you put me on Tinder?!"

Sarah's expression suggested I might be overreacting a little. "It's... a dating app and you're looking for someone to date?"

"Yes, but not right now at this second!" I told her, trying frantically to uninstall it. What if people could see I was on there?! "Could you maybe *ask* me before putting Tinder on my phone?"

Sarah wrestled it back from me before I could get delete the app. "You would have said no."

I made a snatch for it. "Shouldn't that be a key indication to, *I don't know*, *not* do something?!"

She put a hand on my thigh. It was enough to shut me up for a second. "Gem, I love you, but your default position on everything is no. You'd never step outside of your comfort zone if I didn't ignore you most of the time, and you'll need to step outside your comfort zone and talk to strangers to actually date them."

That wasn't fair! "I can step outside my comfort zone!"

She scoffed. "Yeah? When was the last time you did something you felt even slightly not okay about?"

Last Friday when I went to a gay bar, I thought, locking eyes with Min in the rear vision mirror. We both kept our mouths shut, though.

My silence gave Sarah the answer she expected. "Yeah, exactly. Come on, using Tinder's really easy," she told me and, figuring she'd made her point, gave my phone back to me so she could lean over to me and point at a button on the screen. "You tap that and make yourself discoverable, and swipe left if you don't like someone, and right if you do." She made the motions in the air for me. "If they swipe right on your picture, too, you can message each other."

If they swipe right on you, too, then— I looked up at her, stricken. "Wait, does this mean *they'll see my picture too*?"

She narrowed her eyes at me. "Yes, Gem. People generally like to *see* the person they're considering dating," she told me flatly.

"What's wrong with them seeing your picture?" Bree wanted to know. "It's not like you're hideously ugly or anything. What would you be hiding from them?"

My entire self, I thought. "Can you at least give me a fake name so they don't figure out who I am?"

Sarah shook her head. "It's linked to your Facebook profile, you'd need to make a whole fake—"

OH MY— was she kidding *me*? "*It's linked to my Facebook profile*?? So, like, *everyone* will know I'm hopelessly desperate?" I gave my phone back to her. "Get rid of it. Unlink it or whatever, because what if *Dad* finds out? I'm *so* not okay with—"

She pushed it back at me. "It doesn't tell people you're on there, Gem! It just takes info from there! Do you want to be single for your entire life, or do you—"

"No! But I also don't want to be in the supermarket and have people go 'is that the girl from Tinder who you swiped left on in two seconds flat before—"

There was a loud *HOOOOONK* and we both shut up for a second, blinking at each other before we finally realised the sound was Min leaning on the horn. She waited until we were quiet to stop. "Okay, kids, time out," she said to us and let a silence hang in the air for a moment before she kept speaking. "Gemma, Sarah's right, Tinder is probably a great way for you to meet people without actually having to meet them straight away. But—" she interrupted Sarah as Sarah went to agree with her, "rather than just diving straight into it, perhaps Gemma can do some research on Tinder before she activates her profile so at least she has some idea what she's doing...?"

I exhaled at length, really glad Min wasn't going to announce Sarah she was right and I needed to stop being afraid of strangers—because I already knew that, and just saying 'talk to this stranger right now!' wasn't going to change anything—and her idea sounded way better. It *would* be nice to at least have some idea at all what I was doing and what to expect on it. There were probably even some metrics I could look up. And maybe there was some way to be, like, invisible or something and just quietly look around...? "Okay, I can do that, I guess."

Sarah looked like she was going to protest, but with everyone ganging up on her, she just sat back. "Okay..." she said somewhat uncertainly. "Sorry, I was just trying to help..." She sounded a little hurt.

Ouch. "I know," I told her, reaching out and putting a hand on hers. I knew what I was like. She looked relieved at that, and turned her hand over to squeeze mine. After a moment, she gave me this *beautiful* smile.

And gosh... *I don't need Tinder*, I thought.

Her smile faded a little. "I suppose we should probably choose some good photos for your profile first, anyway..." she conceded, and stuck out her other hand for my phone. I gave it to her, and we both sat quietly in the back while Sarah went through my Facebook albums.

Bree had been watching us, and then turned a pair of positively starry eyes on Min. "You're going to be such a good dad," she told her, and Min shot her a lopsided grin.

After a few minutes of flipping through photos, Sarah grunted. "Just a question," she asked. "Do you have any recent photos of anything other than Mr Crumpet and me in your albums?" I didn't like how I looked in photos—which she knew—so I grimaced at her. She chuckled. "Thought not, but I tell you what: I know where there are stacks of photos to choose from." She then leant forward and patted the shoulder of the driver's seat, glancing at me with a smile as she said to Min, "Hey Dad, can you drop me off at Gem's instead?"

I immediately brightened.

"Sure, honey," Min responded in her best gruff dad voice, and a few minutes later, we were both climbing across the tiny back seat of Sarah's hatchback and trudging up the stairs to my apartment.

"I don't see why photos are *that* important," I was telling her as she opened my door with her key. "As long as they can clearly see I'm okay-looking, isn't that what matters?"

She stopped in the middle of what she was doing to turn to me like I'd said something positively blasphemous. "Whoa, okay," she said, hands up in a 'yield' motion, "I forgot I was dealing with Little Miss Numbers. Here's the 101 of Marketing: do not underestimate the power of a well-chosen image in selling a product. It's the difference between a successful sale and an unsuccessful one, and since Tinder has basically *no* profile section, your photos are the only thing to differentiate you from all the other stacks of cute girls. People need to look at your photo and be like 'I want to get to know her'."

I just blinked at her. I supposed I'd better start listening to all this stuff if I was going to be in her department. "Oh, okay..."

"So, let's go pick a panel of photos that'll have anyone you want eating out of the palm of your hand." She let us inside my flat, pausing for a moment to wink over her shoulder. "Or, like, eating out of wherever." She winked.

Ugh. I shoved her. "*Sare!*"

"Well, that's the point, isn't it?" She laughed, dropping her handbag on my kitchen bench and surveying my living room; her earlier comment about 'stacks of photos' might have been a slight understatement because my walls were plastered in them. "Yeah, I think we're pretty safe to find something, don't you think?" she asked me with a smirk, and then flopped onto the couch, grabbing my laptop off the coffee table and opening it on her lap. "Is your password still the same as—?" she began to ask, but then abruptly stopped, looking delighted. "Nevermind. I'm in."

I need to change my passwords, I thought, momentarily panicking that I'd left gay stuff open on there. I was pretty sure I hadn't, though, and she didn't say anything.

While she was doing that, I changed into trackies and went to sit next to her on the couch so I could read up on the torture device she'd had installed on my phone before I was forced to subject myself to it.

I was in luck: there was tonnes of reading material about Tinder, and it was all mostly statistics. I supposed with 50 million users they'd be stupid to *not* want to measure all sorts of things, wouldn't they? It was a demographics and behaviours app as much as it was actually what it advertised itself for. So, instead of reading up on how to use it, I got stuck reading usage stats (2:1 men to women) comparisons between women's and men's behaviour on the app, all the statistics about how often people matched (12% of the time), and a bunch of other stuff. I wondered what it would be like to work at Tinder and have access to all the raw data? I spent about five seconds fantasising about how cool that would be and what I'd learn about people before I realised I'd probably just end up with a longer list of other benchmarks I hadn't reached in my own life as a result.

"Wow…" Sarah was saying wistfully. I looked up from my phone; she was tabbing through photos of us hiking in the Tatra Mountains. "Do you remember this place? We were like 21 or something."

I shuffled towards her so I could see the screen better. We both looked so young; that was way back when Sarah had short hair, too. "Isn't seven years ago a bit too old for a profile photo?" I asked as she scrolled through them.

She looked a bit sheepish. "I got side-tracked," she admitted, and then switched back to the more recent folders. "Remind me never to complain about how many photos you take again, by the way."

For a couple of hours at least, we sat together on my couch and looked through most of my more recent photos, and it was such a nice way to spend an evening that I forgave Tinder for existing. Sarah's face was so animated as she scrolled through each album, and watching her eyes light up when she remembered something special that had happened, or somewhere amazing we'd been, or someone cool we'd met… it was *way* more interesting than the photos. She was really enjoying herself.

Eventually she chose three pics she thought best represented me: one was a photo of me in China during an ice festival, wearing a sunhat, sunglasses and eating an ice-cream ("It shows you have a sense of humour!"), another was one of me passed out on the couch with Mr Crumpet sleeping on top of me ("The 'aww' factor is very important."), and the third was a picture of me looking completely absorbed in a big, fat maths text book and chewing on a pencil ("It shows you're really smart.").

"And now," Sarah announced, closing my laptop after she'd uploaded those photos. "We should probably take one that's a little bit sexy to seal the deal."

'Take'? "What, like right now?"

She stood awkwardly because of her belly. "Yeah, of course! Maybe in that red dress you bought? Then you can wear it when you go on your first date with them."

Oh, gosh... "I'm not sure that's a good idea."

"Of course it's a good idea? You looked amazing in it, I have proof!" She tapped her breast pocket where I knew her phone was. "I suppose we *could* just use that selfie you took, but I think it's better if you try and look just a tiny bit seductive? Like, 'I'm cute, I'm shy, but I bet you want to nail this'?"

I may have looked a little wide-eyed as I followed her into the bedroom. "Except whatever 'sexy' is, I'm the opposite. I think I'll leave the whole red dress thing to Natalie, she can actually pull it off."

"Or Henry can pull it off, anyway," Sarah said with a smirk. "And with any luck, we'll find someone to pull yours off, too!" She opened my wardrobe door. "Okay, where is it?"

"Err, not in there," I told her, and pointed at my drawers. "It's with my undies."

She gave me a weird look. "*Why*?"

"Just wait until you see it."

She narrowed her eyes and then walked over to the drawer. "Okay, well, I'm going to open it," she said like she was issuing

111

me a warning, her hand hovering over the handle, "so if I'm going to find anything in there other than undies, you'd better tell me now..."

What *else* would be in there? "Like, dirty lingerie or something?"

She rolled her eyes and opened it. "*No*," she said. "Like a vibrator, or sex toys or, I don't know, like chains?" She laughed at my expression. "Don't laugh! I used to wonder if you didn't hook up that often because you've got, like, really kinky tastes or something..."

Hah. "I would have told you."

She was already rifling through my drawer. "Would you?" It sounded like a throw-away question, but the way she said it...

Gosh, did she know? Did she know the kind of things I was feeling for her and that I might be gay?

While all the blood was draining out of my face and I was panicking about that, it also occurred to me it might just be a comment about the other night when I went out without her and lied about it. Actually, on reflection, that's probably what it was.

...but we were talking about sexual preferences, weren't we?

"Here it is!" she announced, interrupting my personal crisis and holding the red dress up. "Wow, that *is* really thin." She paused. "*Good*. Okay, throw it on!" She tossed it at me.

I caught it. *So we meet again*, I thought apprehensively, and then wriggled into it while Sarah was rifling around on my tallboy for jewellery to match. After she'd passed me some earrings that I hadn't worn in about five years and I'd found some patent stilettos like Natalie's to match, she got right down to business.

She was like a professional photographer. Not because she took good photos—although I supposed they were as good as photos of me tended to go—but because she was super professional while she was giving me directions about how to stand, how to pose, what expression to have, etc. It was surreal being dressed in this tiny little revealing dress with almost every part of me on display while Sarah, still dressed in her full suit, manually posed me and ordered me around. In a weird way it was kind of sexy, and I bet all the photos she was taking of me were rosy-cheeked and heavy-lidded.

"There," she announced after she'd decided she'd taken the Ultimate Tinder Shot and I'd completely ruined my undies. "I guarantee you will score now. You have Sarah Presti, Marketing Extraordinaire's Seal of Approval on your photo selection. You'll have anyone you want!"

Anyone? I thought to myself, watching her as she chose filters for the photo. I sighed.

"I'll have a good think overnight about what your profile should say; you only have small amount of space and it really needs to pack a lot of punch," she told me, grabbing her handbag and giving me a loose hug while I was still in my tiny dress. Her suit fabric felt coarse against my bare skin. "Did you want to come over tomorrow night and launch it?"

Did I want to spend more time with her!? "Of course!"

She smiled at me, and I think she was about to say goodbye when her smile faltered a little.

So did mine. I also panicked and assumed it was because she'd *suddenly realised what my pink cheeks meant.* "What's wrong?!"

She took a breath, and for a moment all I could hear was the sound of my own pulse in my ears and my brain screaming that she was onto me. "Hey, Gem... can I ask you something?"

No! "Y-Yeah?"

It took her a moment, and during that moment, I'd imagined every possible scenario of her asking me if I was a lesbian and if I was into her. "Am I too pushy?"

I blinked. There were so many levels on which I didn't expect that question that I found it really jarring. Jarring, and a *huge* relief. "*Oh*," I said, laughing really inappropriately and then hating myself for being so insensitive. "No...?"

She didn't look reassured. "You can tell me, Gem," she said. "Is that the reason you didn't invite me out the other night? Because I'm too pushy about this stuff?" She looked like she expected me to deliver a killing blow on her. She was dead serious.

It was weird, because she was almost never like this; her self-confidence was something I'd coveted for an entire decade and one of the things I admired most about her.

I swallowed. "No," I told her, putting my hands on her shoulders. "No, of course not. I just—" *can't tell you the truth*, I realised.

"You can say it," her voice was really quiet.

"Say what?" I asked her. "It's not even about that."

"Then what's it about?" She locked eyes with me.

We stood facing each other. Her lip was quivering a little, and gosh, I wanted to wrap my arms around her, kiss her passionately and say, '*that's* what it's about!'. I couldn't, though, no matter how much I burned to do it. That would be the end.

Instead, I desperately tried to grapple for some at least slightly believable excuse. "I guess I'm just really stressed out over this offshoring stuff," I told her, flushing bright red. "And, you know, finding out I'm the only single one out of all of us now..."

Sarah was looking right at my cheeks. For a second I expected her to tell me exactly what I could see she was thinking—that it was bullshit—but she just swallowed and forced a laugh. "God, would you listen to me?" she said with false cheer. "Of course you are. I'm sorry for being so emo! I can blame this on pregnancy hormones, right?"

I felt sick. "Yeah, sure."

"Good," she said, and then gave me the warmest, tightest, strongest hug, that she nearly suffocated me with her big stomach. "Bye, Gem," she told me brightly with no trace of the doubt she'd expressed a moment ago. "See you tomorrow!" She showed herself out, leaving me standing uncertainly in the centre of the living room in my little red dress.

I felt terrible.

I shed all my stupid dress-up clothes and roughly scrubbed all my makeup off, sitting back down on the tiny sliver of warm couch Mr Crumpet hadn't opportunistically spread himself across. I was messing up big time, I needed to make a real commitment to this Tinder thing that everyone raved about so I could just stop messing up and get a damn partner—that was unless I really wanted to lose Sarah forever.

With that in mind, I mustered a whole tonne of personal strength and *didn't* just drown my sorrows in interesting Tinder statistics. Instead, I diligently studied how to use the damn app and what I should and shouldn't look out for.

I was busy browsing through all the options in the 'discovery settings' tab and trying to decide what my parameters should be to maximise my likelihood of ever being matched with anyone at all, when I got down to one particular option and stopped: whether I was looking for men or women.

Oh, no. I stared at it for a second. Deep, deep down inside me, I had a very strong reaction to that question: I immediately knew what I wanted to select, and, *gosh,* it was terrifying.

But what if I check it and someone sees me and sees I'm looking for women? I imagined the horrified looks of my neighbours finding out I was a *lesbian*, before I remembered that the only people I'd be matched with were other girls looking for girls, too.

But *someone might find out anyway*, I thought, worrying about it. Sarah might find out somehow if she looked at my matches... but, then again, I knew I could delete them and delete conversations, couldn't I? I'd already read about that. I could just switch it back to men and pretend to launch it tomorrow night, she'd never know.

It would be okay, I repeated to myself, no one needed to find out, and I could just stop if I really hated it, couldn't I?

Oh, gosh, I think I'm going to do it, I realised, both horrified and exhilarated. My heart was pounding as my finger hovered over the button, and in my head I could hear Sarah accusing me of never stepping outside of my comfort zone without her help. This was one thing I had to do without her, though, wasn't it? For us. I had to do it for us.

Okay. Okay then.

Oh, my goodness…

My finger shaking, I checked *'women'*, unchecked *'men'*, and tapped *'make me discoverable'*.

CHAPTER TEN

Suddenly, I felt really exposed: I was online. I was discoverable. Women were probably looking at me right now, and in the middle of that panic, all I could think about was that 'sexy' photo of me in the red dress featured in my profile and how much I didn't want anyone else—especially other women!—to see me in it.

When my first potential match popped up on the screen and she was wearing a modest dress shirt, that was the clincher. I tapped back for what felt like *eternity* until I got to the settings page and hurriedly turned off discovery.

Wow. I sat back, taking a few deep breaths as I stared at the photo of me trying to be sexy.

That photo has to go, I decided and deleted it from my profile. I hoped that nobody had seen it before I took it down. I hoped that the first potential match hadn't; I had this horrible mental image of walking down the aisle at the supermarket and coming face-to-face with her knowing she'd seen that awful photo. Or, really, coming face-to-face with *anyone* who'd seen my photo.

…Oh, gosh, that could actually happen, couldn't it? Because I was searching for people within 15km of here…?

On top of that, I had this horrible momentary panic that someone I knew would *see* me, recognise me and out me to the entire world when they found out I was looking for other women.

They would be looking for other women as well, Gemma, I reminded myself, *you're being ridiculous again.*

Well, I needed to stop being ridiculous and pull myself together. Logically, the chances of me bumping into someone I saw on Tinder approached zero. The chances of them saying something or outing me were even smaller—because then *they'd* be outed too, wouldn't they?—and, really, I had nothing to worry about.

Taking a deep breath, I ignored my panic and did the logical, rational thing: I turned discovery back on.

That woman in the modest shirt popped back up onto my screen.

I considered her; she looked nice, I suppose? I probably wouldn't have picked her as gay—or 'bi-curious', anyway, which is what her profile said she was. Suddenly, I realised my own profile was empty.

I tabbed back to settings *again* and stared at the empty text box for what felt like five minutes while a thousand million women probably looked at my profile and thought, 'What a loser, she doesn't even have a description' while they swiped left at the speed of light.

My mind was *completely* blank and in the end, I just typed, *'I'm brand new here and I have no idea what I'm doing'.*

Then, I sat and stared at that for the longest time. Was that pathetic...?

Ugh, I give up, I thought, mentally throwing up my hands. Maybe it *was* pathetic, but I was also both ridiculous and pathetic and those women had a right to know who they were considering getting involved with.

I went back to searching and back to that woman's portrait to decide what to do with her. She wasn't really my type—not that I really had any idea what my 'type' would be, but she wasn't it—so I should probably swipe left. That felt rude, though, and I didn't want to hurt her feelings. In the end, I swiped right because it seemed like the polite thing to do.

I had to swipe through a bunch of profiles of women looking for threesomes, and I'd started to worry that the 19% of women who'd had same-sex attraction and/or experience were all mostly married to men before I finally started to get some lesbians and single bi women, too.

There were actually tonnes of women on Tinder, because no matter how much I was swiping, there were still stacks more on my screen. It was kind of reassuring how normal everyone seemed. I mean, not that I really believed all lesbians were a particular way, but it was nice to have clear evidence it wasn't true. I just wasn't really sure if I was *attracted* to any of them, though. How did I tell?

For research purposes, I spent some time staring at a few super risqué lingerie shots pretty girls had up on their profile (and I'd been worried about people seeing me in a *dress*?) but couldn't figure out if I felt anything for them. In fact, I felt pretty neutral until I swiped through to someone who helped me answer the 'are you attracted to girls other than Sarah' question.

There was nothing particularly special about her at first, she had short, kind of boyish hair and a cheerful but ordinary face, and I'd been scrolling through pictures of her in a soccer game, the usual party shot with friends, etc, when I got to a photo of her in a tailored suit and ray bans, giving the camera a bit of a suave grin, and it was *hot*.

I stopped scrolling, my eyebrows up. Why was that so hot?

Maybe it's because she looks a little bit like a man there? I wondered hopefully, except she didn't, she was just wearing men's clothes but otherwise was clearly a woman. *That grin, though...*

I wanted to swipe right. It wasn't just a kind of 'I guess' moment, either, I actually *wanted* to swipe right and see where it went. But what if I swiped right and never heard anything because I wasn't her type? She was probably after other athletic girls with tonnes of energy like her and I was definitely not athletic. Yeah, I probably wasn't her type.

...but what if I was?

It made me sweat just thinking about it: I'd have to actually talk to her, and I had no idea what to talk to lesbians about. Ordinarily when I wanted to let someone know I was interested, I just got really drunk and slept with them, but it wasn't like I could just jump her while drunk because then she'd expect that to lead to sex and I was acutely aware of the fact I didn't really know what I was doing in that regard, or even if I could actually bring myself to do it at all. Imagining the finer details of sex with women was actually pretty confronting. I didn't want to think about it.

I got into a sweaty, panicked gridlock in my brain about what to do with her and eventually solved it by just swiping right before I could talk myself out of it. There: it was too late to worry about it now.

Then, while I was recovering, I went into the kitchen and had a few mouthfuls of wine to lubricate this whole decision-making process. When I got back to my phone, though, my screen was different to the way I'd left it. I unlocked it with interest, wondering what was going on, and 'It's a match!' popped up on the screen.

It's a—All the blood drained from my face. Did that mean soccer girl had swiped on me too? I was frozen with a mixture of excitement and shock and then I realised the other tiny photo wasn't of soccer girl, it was of the bi-curious girl in the modest shirt who I wasn't very interested in.

Oh. I was suddenly super aware of the fact I wasn't interested in her and now she thought that I was, and I was either going to have to tell her that I wasn't interested in her—and there was no way in the world I was going to do that—or I was going to need to find a way to get out of it.

While I was trying to figure out how the hell *that* would happen, a chat notification came through.

Shit. I opened it, but the second I had, I wished I hadn't. *'Hey gorgeous... love the freckles ;) redheads are my fave'*.

If I wasn't sweating before, I certainly was now. How could I tell someone I wasn't interested in them after they'd said *that*?

Another one came through before I'd figured out what to do. *'I'm free tonight if you'd like to catch up for a late-night rendez-vous* :) :) *happy to come to yours'*.

I wasn't—oh my gosh, was this a *booty call*? There were so many shades of 'no' that I spent a few minutes googling what to do, and eventually decided I should just pretend I hadn't seen the message and unmatch her. Maybe she'd think I'd uninstalled Tinder or something.

The second after I'd done it, though, I imagined what it would be like to be her and never get an answer for that message, and I felt like the biggest asshole in the world.

Okay, I think that's enough Tinder for tonight, I decided, hoping I hadn't really hurt her feelings. Before I got ready for bed, I did my best to delete all evidence of girls from my phone, hid my profile and reset it to 'men' in preparation of pretending to launch it with Sarah tomorrow.

Then, I lay awake for ages feeling totally stupid for not being brave enough to tell that girl that she was gorgeous but I wasn't interested.

Reassuringly, the following day on the train, my fears about being discovered and outed to the world proved unfounded: I didn't see any of the faces I'd seen last night on Tinder. No one seemed to recognise me, either, and the only person who paid me any sort of attention was a guy I accidentally bumped into who gave me a hard look that suggested my parents should be very disappointed with how I turned out.

Before I went into the office, I double- and triple-checked my phone to make sure there was no sign of gay anywhere—I had no idea how to use Tinder but I was pretty sure I'd been thorough—and then went to endure another day at work.

It was more tedious than usual because Finance and Admin were only doing the bare minimum they could get away with to hang out until their redundancies—assuming they *were* offshored—so I had absolutely nothing to fix and spent the morning imagining I was working at Tinder and had all that raw data to play with.

I wondered what percentage of people unmatched with matches? It was probably a really high number; I couldn't be the only asshole who'd ever done it. I tried googling some stats for that but I couldn't find any, and somehow I ended up side-tracked and wondering if that soccer girl would swipe right on me. According to the stats I found, women actually matched with each other far more often than men and women did (18% vs 12%), so that boded well, didn't it?

I was busy trying to figure out if there were any age-dependent variables in that—seriously, why did pop-culture articles never cite any of their raw data sources or their methodology?—when someone leant over my partition and said, "Will we see you there this time, Gemma?"

I looked up, startled. "Where?" I hurriedly hid my phone screen.

It was Anil. He was squinting at my phone, and I immediately felt really guilty for being caught playing with it during work time. "At the union meeting on Friday."

Oh, right, that; the one with scary Natalie. "*Nope,*" I said, slipping my phone into a drawer.

His eyebrows went up. "That's a pretty strong answer."

I-It was? Whoops. I grimaced, and I could feel my cheeks going red because everyone sitting around me was watching me.

He gave me a measured look—maybe Henry hadn't spoken to him yet?—but in the end, he just said, "Well, make sure you come on time to it if you change your mind," in a tone that held a note of 'and don't let me catch you wasting time on your phone during work time again'. Then, he continued en route back to his office from wherever he'd been while I wasn't paying attention.

I could still feel everyone around me staring at me after he'd gone, and just as they all went back to work, Spud said from behind me, "Are you really not coming to the meeting?"

I just shrugged as I swivelled around to him, because I was worried if I actually said something it would come out wrong again.

It turned out to be the worst thing I could have done, though, because I seemed to have struck a nerve. "What, like it doesn't matter?"

What like—no, that wasn't what I meant at all! Because he looked really angry, though, the words caught in my throat.

"I don't know, Gemma, aren't you worried about your job?" he asked me, his bushy brow low over his eyes. "All of us here are scared shitless that we're not going to be able to pay our mortgages and you're just sitting there messaging someone on your phone all morning, and now you're not even coming to the union meeting... Do you have another job lined up or something?"

Shit. I could feel my face burning. How did people read me like this?! "N-No!"

"I think you've got another job lined up," he said. "And even if I had one, too, I'd still come to the meeting to support my co-workers who don't." With that, he gave me a somewhat disgusted look, and turned back to his desk.

I felt ill. He was never like this; was I being that insensitive? I *had* been on my phone all morning, so I probably was, wasn't I? I couldn't do anything for a few minutes because I was so shaken. I felt like it was karmic punishment for unmatching that poor woman. I didn't want to look at my phone again—I bet everyone was watching me now to see if I was as bad as he said—so I tried to find things to do to my spreadsheets for the rest of the morning.

One thing was for sure, though: it looked like I was going to that damn union meeting on Friday. At least Sarah would be pleased.

I couldn't tell her straight away at lunch, though, because I was worried she'd be upset that I was planning on not going to it after I'd let her believe that I was. She gently persisted with me about why I was so off-colour until I spilt the beans, and to my surprise she *didn't* seem as upset as she had when she found out I'd lied to her about going out on Friday night.

122

In fact, she gave me a long, comforting hug—I loved that she always smelt like that perfume I'd bought her—and then said, "Spud shouldn't have spoken to you like that, but I think the universe is clearly telling you something about going to that meeting."

"I can't go to it," I lamented, still too shaken to eat my lunch. "I'm moving to a cave in the mountains where I don't have to deal with people. I'll install Wi-Fi and never leave."

"Nah, don't let one asshole colour your opinion of humanity," Sarah told me, patting me reassuringly and pushing my sandwich towards me to encourage me to actually eat some of it. "Ignore him. You might not be working with him much longer anyway, assuming the rumours are true."

"He's not a asshole, though, he's normally really nice," I corrected her, not very tempted by my sandwich. "And I *was* on my phone all morning which was kind of insensitive."

She gave me a look. "All morning? What on earth were you doing?"

Shit. "L-Looking up Tinder statistics?" I didn't have to say which statistics...

She seemed to accept my answer anyway. "Well, yeah, you probably shouldn't have done that, but that doesn't make how he spoke to you okay, either. Seriously, don't take him going off at you too personally. He's just really worried about his job and taking it out on you. Anyway! Speaking of Tinder," she said, segueing to a no less stressful topic, "I've been thinking about it, and I think I've figured out *exactly* the right profile description for you."

She made me wait until we got back to her house that evening, though—taking the train together again!—so she could check Min's professional opinion on the photos she'd chosen.

The house was chockers when we arrived; Rob was back from whatever worksite he'd been at over the weekend which meant I had the oh-so pleasant experience of watching them reunite and pash like teenagers on the front porch, and

Henry and Min were camped out on the living room couch playing some tense shooter game on Min's PlayStation.

Sarah waited until Min and Henry were finished whatever they were playing and then grabbed my phone and gave it to Min so she could check out the photos. Min threw me a silent and anxious glance before she flicked through them.

While she was in the middle of doing that, Sarah, who had been watching over Min's shoulder, made a gruff noise and leant in towards the screen to check on something. "Wait, where's the dress one?"

Oh. Oh, gosh. I completely forgot I'd deleted that one! I glanced at Henry; he had looked away to check his phone, but I had a feeling he was listening intently. It made me super self-conscious. "Well, I was thinking the other pics are enough...?"

She looked at me like I was nuts and opened her mouth to probably tell me exactly that, but something stopped her. She closed her mouth and swallowed.

Min came to my rescue. "This is a great set of photos," she said giving the phone back to Sarah. "You chose these?"

Sarah was still watching me. "Yeah," she said. "I did."

"Dare I ask what they're for?" Henry inquired politely, indicating he had been listening.

Sarah looked away from me. "Gemma's going to go on Tinder tonight to look for a date," she said with her usual cheer, but her eyes were veiled.

"Tinder, as in the dating app?" Henry clarified, and we all nodded. He immediately looked concerned. "Are you sure that's a good idea? You have absolutely no way of knowing what kind of person you're talking to."

Sarah shrugged. "You never know who you're talking to anyway, do you? You could be having a drink with an axe-murderer at the pub as well. Tinder is just the 21st century version of that. Here," she said, handing my phone to Henry. "Check out the photos we chose."

Henry didn't look any less concerned, but accepted the phone from Sarah anyway. At least with the dress photo gone I

124

didn't really mind Henry looking at them—he gave them all a seriously professional one-over with nothing more than appropriate interest—and after he'd done that, he stood up and stretched. "I think that's my cue to leave you three," he said, feeling around in his pockets for his phone and then finding it on the table. "I'll say goodbye to Bree myself on the way out." Min went to show him out anyway, and he gave my phone back to me on the way past.

That left Sarah and me by ourselves in the living room.

She waited until Henry and Min had gone before she took a breath. "You definitely want to do this, right?"

It was so weird her being this hesitant. "Yeah, of course."

We sat down together on the couch to get going.

I don't know what I was expecting. To have to act interested for her benefit, I guess? I did a bit in the beginning, but it was just so nice to have our heads together as we sorted through men that I didn't have to act for long. It was actually kind of fun.

Sarah had some seriously strong opinions about guys I honestly felt very neutral about, and there were several points we differed on: moustaches (she kind of liked them, but I *hated* them), muscles (they got an automatic yes from her, but I was indifferent) and other tiny details that I thought were important and she didn't. "Trust me," Sarah promised me. "That 'my future partner must have *these* qualities' list just goes right out the window when you meet someone. Rob ticks *no* boxes for me and he's the nicest man I've ever met."

By the end of the night she almost had me thinking I could date a guy and be fine with it—there were actually some men on there that I'd be happy to give it a shot with—but mostly, it was just *so nice* to be sharing something with her. She was forgetting to be hesitant and un-Sarah-like and had gone back to her old bossy self.

I liked it. I *liked* this Sarah, even if I'd privately swipe differently than she was telling me to.

At the end of the night, she gave me a big hug as we both yawned. "Do you want to stay?" she asked. "We can make up Rob's couch in the man cave."

Not unless he's the one sleeping on it, I thought and shook my head. It wasn't a good idea anyway; if I did that, I'd be late for work *again* and I had enough problems with Anil already. I snuck out of Sarah's before Min could insist on walking me home, and got back to my place before midnight.

It was late and I probably should have gone straight to bed, but I turned on the heater for a couple of minutes to warm my flat and then somehow ended up on the couch with Mr Crumpet on my lap, and it was therefore impossible for me to move and disturb him. He looked so happy.

Luckily, I had my phone. I didn't have any matches from tonight's foray into heterosexual Tinder, though, so it wasn't like I had heaps of people to talk to. I started to look through my likes again anyway, thinking there were some okay men there who might be really nice to get to know. I wasn't holding my breath on them swiping right on me, though, and I didn't really know what I'd say to them if we matched.

I sat back against the spine of the couch and stared at my wall, idly stroking Mr C's long fur while he purred. I wasn't *not* attracted to the guys I'd picked, I didn't think? They were okay.

It was just...

...I don't know, I'd come this far, I guess? I kind of wanted to see where this woman thing went.

Quite a large part of me hoped it was just a big mistake and I wasn't really gay after all, or at least that I was a bit bi but would be fine to live out my life dating guys. However, another part of me wanted to turn Tinder back to 'women' and see if that soccer girl would match with me.

Since I was stuck on the couch, and since there was no one looking over my shoulder, I decided to just do it. After all, what did I have to lose, right?

CHAPTER ELEVEN

Now that I knew what to expect, the whole looking-for-women-on-Tinder thing made me feel slightly less like I was about to break out in hives from the stress. Although, if I was perfectly honest with myself, it was less 'looking for women on Tinder' and more 'please god please god let soccer girl match with me on Tinder'. I wasn't sure exactly how the matching process worked, but I was pretty sure my profile wouldn't be presented to her unless I was classed as looking for women. So maybe she hadn't swiped right on me because she hadn't had the chance to yet?

I finally psyched myself up to very carefully move Mr Grumpet off my lap (and he lived up to his nickname by sooking loudly about it and making me feel like a *monster*), poured myself a big glass of festive Sav Blanc and then sat down again to start swiping on profiles while I waited.

I had to plough through a lot of women looking for threesomes with their husbands/boyfriends again first—not that the idea of a threesome was completely out of the question, it was just than meeting *one* new person was stressful enough—before I started to get to single women.

I swiped right on a biochemist, a gym junkie and an event planner, and I was just thinking that the biochemist from before would match really well with a medical researcher I'd just landed on, when I had a sudden thought that maybe that gym junkie had hooked up with my soccer girl. It would be perfect: they could do all sorts of sporty, healthy things together like go running in the morning. I'd always wanted to be the type of person who went running in the morning, but instead I was the type of person who slept in and never ate breakfast. Maybe that's why my happiness index was so low.

While I was waiting for a potential match, I eventually ran out of profiles to sort through and Tinder asked me if I wanted to widen my search parameters to find more. I didn't really, but I supposed I could be more flexible if I had to be?

After all, Min was happy with someone who was eight years younger than her, and Henry was seven years older than Min. Furthermore, one of the guys I'd dated had been 41 and married as well (although *that* wasn't a mistake I wanted to repeat) but I supposed I could go down as far as 22? Soccer girl was 24, after all.

I was just messing with the sliders and trying to decide how old was too old when my settings screen faded and *It's a match!* popped up, complete with fireworks. I stopped breathing.

I'd swiped a lot of people, so I didn't want to get my hopes up. Statistically, it was unlikely to be her. I forced myself to start breathing again anyway, repeating to myself, *it could be anyone, it could be—*

But it *wasn't* anyone. It took me two full seconds for it to sink in who 'Michaela' was and who was in that second portrait: *soccer girl.*

What?! "Oh my gosh!" I said aloud, stunned. She'd swiped right on *me*? But why? I was the antithesis of 'sporty'! I was immediately torn between being *terrified* I'd find out we didn't get along because of how different we were, buzzing around my living room in panic, and jumping up and down on my couch like Tom Cruise. She matched with me!

Okay, I was super glad I'd decided to switch my search back over to women now. I sat down on the couch with my phone in my hands and my heart in my throat. Should I message her?

I knew I probably should, but what the hell did you say to someone on Tinder? I didn't want to mess up big time and say something stupid so she'd just unmatch with me after everything.

I read through her profile a few times, trying to figure out what I could say. None of the profiles on here said anything important, though. It was all like *'late night | live life | love well'* and palm tree emoticons. Well, the ones that didn't say *'my boyfriend and I are looking for a number three for fun times!'*. Michaela's profile had *'GO MATILDAS!! You've got it this season, girls!'* (I was guessing that was a soccer team?) and that she was looking for someone special.

I'm special, right? I thought, and then sighed at myself. I was *special*, all right. In a tragic, hopeless sort of way. It also said she was 5'5", which was the same height as me. For a second, I found that really weird. I'd never been with someone the same height as me. I was used to having to kiss up at people. Looking at her body, too, she was probably even a bit smaller than me. That felt wrong, kind of. I mean, not that it stopped me from being interested in her, but it was just something to get used to about the whole girl thing, I guess. Then again, I don't know why this girl's height was an issue for me, because Sarah was the same height as me, too...

I felt uncomfortable at the thought of comparing Sarah to soccer girl. I was too excited to worry about that, though.

Any moment now, I thought, staring intently at the screen. She'd message me any second so I didn't have to. *The button's right there*, I mentally willed this 'Michaela' girl, looking at the 'why not send them a message?' button that was on my screen.

After nearly twenty minutes of nothing except me staring at my phone, she hadn't messaged me. Then, I had a sudden, horrible misgiving that maybe she'd just swiped right on me to be polite like I had with that bicurious girl I'd unmatched yesterday? It would totally serve me right if she had. I didn't want to message her in case I'd say something stupid and she'd go 'nope' and unmatch me in the same way. That would be totally depressing.

Maybe she's busy, I decided, despite the fact my brain was going overtime imagining all the horrible ways this could end that involved me feeling like I was eternally unattractive and unlovable. Trying to be mature about it instead of a nervous wreck, I decided I would go to bed and perhaps there would be a message waiting for me tomorrow.

I got into my PJs and slid under my doona, but (surprise, surprise) I couldn't sleep. Not at all. I was wide awake, and I kept checking my phone every ten seconds for the little Tinder flame in my notification panel.

I should message her, I thought. *I should just do it*. If I didn't do it, I was going to be awake half the night, rock up late to work and be in even more trouble than I already was with everyone.

I rolled over onto my stomach, phone in hand.

Oh, gosh. Okay, no, I could do this. Practically shaking, I messaged her, "*Hi… :)*"

The second I'd send it, I felt like an idiot. What the hell was that, 'Hi…'? *Wow, Gem*, I thought, *way* to be super witty and engaging. She's going to be like, 'who is this loser?' and unma—

"*Hi… :)*"

I stared at my phone for a second, stunned. Then I put my face level with Mr Crumpet's beside me on the bed and shrieked, "She's talking to me!" He didn't care. I cared, though; she'd messaged me right back, like right away. That meant something, didn't it?! Oh my gosh!

Trying to calm myself down because I was getting second-hand embarrassment from imagining what I'd look like to someone else, I brainstormed what else I could say to her. I didn't want to come across as really boring, even if I kind of was.

Before I could think of anything that wasn't really dull, though, another message came through. "*Sorry. I suck at this stuff. I promise I'm more interesting in person :("*

I was so relieved that I laughed aloud. It was nice to think she'd been worrying about the same thing! She looked really charismatic in her photos, though. I wasn't sure what I had to offer. "*I'm actually not sure I am? But people laugh AT me all the time, so I'm probably entertaining anyway.*"

"*Lol I thought that icecream pic in your profile was pretty funny :):)*"

It kind of was, I supposed. I couldn't really take the credit for it. "*I'd love to say I'm just that funny, but my best friend Sarah posed me in it. She's the funny one.*"

"*Yeah, but your expression totally made the shot :)*" she said. "*Well, that and the fact it's you in the photo… :)*"

I nearly threw my phone across the room and made another series of really embarrassing noises. She was *flirting with me*? I

130

was going to hyperventilate and die, I swear to god. I had no idea how to flirt!

We managed to start up a bit of a conversation, and during that time I learnt that despite the fact her name was Michaela, people only ever called her 'Mikey', that her dream was to one day play for the Matildas (which *was* an Australian soccer team, after all), and that she was a waitress in a really upmarket restaurant in the CBD. She'd also only just come out. *"I know it's sounds kind of stupid, but I didn't really figure it out until last year,"* she told me. *"Half my team are lesbians, you'd think I'd know, yeah?"*

I didn't think it was stupid at all. I didn't even really know what I was. *"I'm not out,"* I confessed. *"I don't really know what to come out as..."*

Even though I didn't really care about sports and she couldn't stop gushing about them, I chatted with her until midnight and then we agreed we should probably sleep.

"I have training at 7am," she told me. *"I'm going to be wrecked..."*

I winced. *"Sorry... :("*

"Don't apologise, it's definitely worth it... :)"

I made a really high-pitched screeching sound I'm glad no one could hear. I was just staring at that photo of her in a suit and waiting to see if she'd send me another message when I suddenly realised I couldn't leave her messages on my phone if Sarah was going to get a hold of it, and she would. At lunch time, she'd want to check my Tinder matches to see which boys we'd picked had matched with me.

I sighed. *"Hey, I can't leave these messages on my phone (long story), do you think we could message on Facebook or something?"*

"Lol the perils of not being out... Sure, add me, my surname is Fitzgerald."

We'd just added each other and I'd settled down in my bed to stare at my ceiling with a huge grin on my face instead of sleeping, when the flashing notification light on my phone got my attention again. I rolled over to check it. It was a Facebook messenger light. Wow. If I grinned any more, my face would *crack*.

"Listen... I have a day shift tomorrow at Chez Phillipe... you want to stop by for my end of it? I'll get the chef to cook us something amazing, he's a good friend of mine. But it's cool if you'd rather message."

She wanted to meet me?! Oh my gosh! I was no good at meeting people!

I was going to suffocate from not breathing, I swear to god. I couldn't do any of this, there were so many levels on which I seriously couldn't do this.

Despite all of them, I found myself typing. *"No, that sounds okay! Message me the details* :)" and then degenerating into a big jumble of fear and excitement in my bed.

Not surprisingly, I didn't sleep very well after that. I kept worrying that I wouldn't live up to Mikey's expectations of me or that it would be super awkward because anything that didn't follow a prescribed formula was something I was completely hopeless at. I think I probably passed out at maybe 2am, and that made me miss my alarm and my usual train, and I had to duck into the ladies' downstairs at work to put concealer on the deep bags under my eyes before I *ran* in to avoid being late. Wow, was I ever going to look attractive tonight...

Despite looking like a microwaved corpse, I floated into the office, totally high on the fact I had a date tonight with an actual real person who was interested in me, and then as soon as I got there, I remembered everyone was miserable and had to do something about my elated smile.

Because everyone had witnessed Spud going off at me yesterday for being on my phone, I put it in my drawer and tried very, very hard to ignore it all morning while I pretended to be busy. It was torture, I couldn't think about anything else except her messaging me. I was just wondering if I could maybe furtively check it when I noticed Spud wasn't in his chair, and a gentle tap on my shoulder made me jump.

It was Spud. "Hey," he said gravely. "Can I talk to you for a second?"

That sounded ominous. *What have I done now?* I thought, immediately feeling sick. Had I been looking too happy again? "S-Sure?"

He took me aside into one of the meeting rooms, spending a second checking the video conference software wasn't on. Then, he turned towards me, arms crossed.

I actually felt physically sick. I was seriously going to be sick. What could he possibly want? I'd been doing my job and I'd only checked my phone once!

"Look, I'm sorry I cracked it at you yesterday," he said, sounding very subdued.

T-That was... unexpected.

"You shouldn't have been dicking around on your phone, but that's no cause for me to embarrass you like I did. It's just I'm worried I'm going to end up on the dole and have to sell my house—the place it took me 20 years to buy in the first place. If you've got a job lined up, good on you, and it's no cause for me to go off at you because I haven't."

He let that hang for a second, and I realised it was a tacit question. I couldn't say anything about Marketing yet, though, could I? Henry made me promise.

"I don't," I lied, and went bright red.

He wasn't Sarah; he didn't guess. "I'm really sorry again, then," he said. "Especially since you're in the same boat as us."

"I'm coming to the union meeting on Friday, too," I told him, hoping it would help.

It did. He apologised again and then offered to buy me a coffee, and he didn't just buy me a coffee, either: he bought he a huge coffee and a big sugary cinnamon apple scroll to go with it. I wasn't going to be hungry for lunch!

After that big apology, I didn't want to push my luck and make Spud angry at me again for being happy or being on my phone, so I left it in my drawer.

Okay, admittedly I *did* sneak off into the bathroom a couple of times to furtively check to see if she'd messaged me—of course she hadn't, she had training and then work after—so, the second time, I spent the couple of minutes I was in there looking at her profile pictures again on Tinder. Then, I did what I knew I needed to: I finally screencapped them and deleted her as a match on Tinder.

Then, I was faced with a dilemma.

The screenshots showed up at the top of my gallery. Mikey looked quite boyish in the photo of her in the suit, and you could totally tell she was a lesbian. If Sarah found that photo on my phone, she'd immediately twig onto why I had it, because why else would you have screencapped a kind of flirty picture of a girl in a suit? I could save it somewhere where she couldn't find it, except then *I* couldn't quickly look at it while no one was looking at me at work. I didn't want to hide it or delete it, but I could 100% guarantee Sarah would want to take control of my phone to check my (now cleared) Tinder matches, and there was a chance she'd end up in my gallery. I had to delete them, I needed to be safe.

The problem was that I didn't want to. It had been ages since I'd felt like this about someone who I could actually have, and I wanted to enjoy it! Well, at least until after the date, because if it didn't work out, none of the photos or anything would matter and I could delete them and live out the rest of my days in safety as an old spinster cat woman.

I leant my head against the wall of the toilet cubicle I was in and groaned. Okay, I'd keep them at least until after the date, but that meant no lunch with Sarah. Oh well, I'd just have to deal with it. It was only one day.

"*Hey*," I messaged Sarah, at least happy I didn't need to lie to her face. "*I'm not having lunch today* :(*Raincheck tomorrow?*"

"*Wow, your team must be pretty unhappy with you! Don't worry, I'll sneak down some supplies for you in a minute* :) *I won't let my best friend go hungry!* :)"

I grimaced. "*Probably not a good idea* :(*Thanks though!*"

This time, it was longer before she replied. *"Oh... okay..."*

I could hear it in her voice, and it struck me to my heart.

One more day, I promised myself, taking a deep breath and trying to ignore the really yucky, uncomfortable feeling that had settled in my stomach before I went back out to work.

The end of the day couldn't come fast enough, and I raced home to completely turn over my entire wardrobe to try and figure out what to wear to Chez Phillipe for 8pm. Mikey had said it was an upmarket restaurant, but what did that mean? Did that mean I was supposed to dress formally? Or was work-ish wear okay? Or jeans and heels, or a giraffe onesie? What should I wear?!

After I'd piled every item of clothing I owned onto my bed to have a meltdown over *still* having nothing to wear, I wondered if I should google what lesbians wore. Then I realised that was ridiculous for two reasons: because it had backfired horribly last time I'd googled what people liked girls to wear, and also because at that gay bar there had been lesbians of every possible category wearing every possible outfit.

In the end, I decided to wear a nice blue party dress and some sparkly ballet flats. I might be a bit cold, but at least I looked really nice and the blue complimented my red hair.

It was only in the Uber on the way to Chez Phillipe that I started to, like, genuinely panic: I was about to meet soccer girl. She was a girl, and so was I, and we were going to be out in public on a date in the city and *what if someone saw us*? Or worse, what if she didn't like me? What if she *did* like me? What if she liked me and I made a huge fool of myself and she *stopped* liking me?! What if Sarah somehow found out and it ruined our friendship forever?!

When the Uber dropped me off I was in this kind of ascended state of numbness, where I was so stressed out I'd actually ceased to have human emotions. That was until I saw the cursive lettering *'Chez Phillipe'*, and then I suddenly had all the emotions at once.

Well, it's too late to back out now, isn't it? I told myself, staring up at the sign while my brain screamed that *it's never too late to back out and I could still turn around and run away RUN AWAY!*

I ignored that part, somehow managed to gather together my fried nerves, and walked in.

CHAPTER TWELVE

It took a lot of courage to just walk in through the front door in the first place, but then it turned out that Chez Phillipe wasn't right inside. I actually had to take a lift up to the 25th floor and go through the whole stress of walking into the restaurant *again*. As ridiculous as it was, I felt like as soon as I walked in everyone would swing around and look at me, like, 'that girl is a lesbian! She's here on a *lesbian date!*', but when I made it inside, absolutely no one so much as glanced in my direction.

Heart pounding, I surveyed the hordes of people, looking for Mikey's face and terrified she'd see me before I saw her. The only wait-staff I could see were an older blonde lady, a kind of dusky-looking guy with a coifed moustache and tattoos all up his ripped arms, and an Indian lady with hair down to her waist. No soccer girl.

Fantastic, there's still time to escape! my brain informed me, and I was debating the benefits of ducking outside and messaging her to say I was here, when it got worse: tattoo-and-moustache guy spotted me standing by the door and changed course to approach me. I froze.

"Hey, you must be Gemma!" he told me, extending his hand to shake. Instead of turning around and running away (which I seriously considered), I mutely shook it as he continued, "I'm Patrick, Mikey's housemate. She's expecting you! Wait here for a sec, I'll go grab her."

No, don't 'go grab' her! I thought as loudly as I could as he disappeared. I wasn't ready for this. I wasn't ready for this. I was literally going to pass out when she came out of the—

When Patrick emerged from the kitchen, there was a girl with him. I recognised the short hair with the swept fringe and that energy that had bubbled out of her pictures: *Mikey.* When she spotted me, she gave me this nervous, elated smile and I was torn between going down for the count with my brain stuck in an endless loop of *OH NO SHE'S HOT,* and doing nothing except standing there and *gaping* at her.

In the end I compromised and gave her a stupid little wave.

She gave me a little wave back, and I went the brightest, deepest red I think I've ever gone in my life; I felt like my face was about to explode. Patrick just looked amused. "I'll leave you ladies to it," he told me with a coif-moustached grin, and then zipped off to take orders.

Mikey approached me a little slowly—shyly, even?—dressed in her French waiter uniform: white shirt, waistcoat and skirt-apron. She even had a little bow-tie. It was way too cute. I kept thinking anything I said now would be stupid because the only thing I could think of was, 'you're even more gorgeous in person!', so I didn't speak.

Neither did she for a few seconds so we just stood there *super* awkwardly, blushing like crazy, before she finally said, "Hi…" Pink cheeks made her green eyes look even greener.

"Hi…" I managed, still looking mostly at the floor.

"I-I like your dress," she stammered, "that's a really pretty colour on you."

If the ground could have opened up and swallowed me whole, I think it would have been a pleasant relief. I had no idea how to take compliments. I had no idea how to return compliments, either. So, I just said the first thing that came into my head. "Yeah, blue goes really well with my bright red face."

She laughed—it was an unexpectedly pleasant sound. "Probably with mine, too," she said, and put her hands to her cheeks. "Sorry, I'm not normally like this."

"I am," I said flatly.

She laughed again and gave me a look that was—*wow*, so adoring? It had been a long time since someone had looked that way at me.

She brushed down her front. "Sorry about the daggy uniform, I'll go change," she said, still trying to smother a nervous smile, "but I reserved us a really awesome table by the window, so you can wait there, if you want. The view is really incredible at night. Here..."

She led me on my very shaky knees over to an ornate little two-person table by the window. It had really pretty provincial settings, with a lovely lacy white tablecloth and a—*gosh*, a red rose across my table setting.

My hand flew up to my mouth; there weren't roses on any of the other tables, so someone had put that there especially for me. I couldn't stop smiling as she pulled my chair out for me, draped the serviette across my lap and then stood back. "Back in a sec," she said, and then high-tailed back through kitchen.

It gave me a few seconds to catch my breath; and when I turned my head to look at this so-called beautiful view, what I actually saw was my beaming reflection in the window. Embarrassed, I tried to look less obvious.

Beyond my reflection, the view *was* great—I could see both the Opera House and part of the Sydney Harbour bridge. There must have been some festival or something going on because the Opera House was lit with different shapes and colours. I might have taken a photo of that to ask someone about later—probably Sarah, she always knew about this stuff—but my palms were so sweaty I was worried my phone would slip straight out of them.

Besides, I could hardly think of anything except the fact Mikey would be back here in a second, and I was both terrified and terrifically excited about that.

When she *did* come back, she was wearing kind of boyish jeans—she had narrow hips so they really suited her—and a very pale green shirt tucked into them on one side. She'd also slung a skinny tie around her neck and knotted it loosely at about collarbone-height, and the whole boyish, messy chic thing was just—*ugh*, she was so attractive.

"I feel a bit under-dressed," she admitted, looking down her front. "I would have worn something a bit swisher if I'd known how nice you'd look."

Apparently I was going to spend our entire date with a bright red face. "You look nice!" I protested, looking everywhere except at her and how nice she looked.

"Not as nice as you…" She said bashfully; I could hear the smile in her voice. I wished I had the courage to look up at her so I could see it.

We sat across from each other for a moment, looking in our laps with huge grins on our faces.

"So," she began, "the chef is a really awesome guy, he's actually French, and his brother owns the place. I've got him to cook my absolute favourite stuff for us, and I can't wait for you to taste it."

I was so nervous that I had no idea how I was going to eat anything, and every time I caught a little peek of that big smile of hers my chest simply inflated with air and I could hardly breathe. "I can't wait," I managed anyway.

Pretty soon Patrick came over with two bottles of wine, "Our best red and best white," he told me ceremoniously, holding up each bottle. "What's your poison, hon?" When I didn't answer—I wasn't sure which made me seem classier than I really was—he laughed. "Maybe I'll pour you a big glass of both?"

"Maybe you should leave both bottles here, instead," I managed, patting my side of the table.

They laughed like I was actually funny, and then I caught Patrick giving Mikey a private look that said *I like her*. I could have leapt out of the window and soared through the air.

While Patrick was pouring my wine and I was floating on cloud nine, it suddenly hit me like a tonne of bricks that I was sitting across the table from a *girl*. It was a *girl* I was feeling this way about, and not in a she's-just-around-and-I'm-lonely way, either. I was having, like, legitimate gay feelings for a *girl*. I managed to peek up from my lap at Mikey for a moment. She was stealing a glance up at me, too, and we locked eyes and then frantically looked away.

The butterflies in my stomach went nuts. *So I* am *gay*, I realised. I felt like I should have been maybe a bit more shocked by that discovery; I wasn't, though. I was a big ball of terrified, beaming excitement.

The chef himself brought our entrees out—cream of mushroom soup, and it was delicious—and by the time I'd managed to successfully get it down into my stomach with the butterflies, I'd relaxed a little. Mikey was nice. She was lovely, in fact. She had this adorable little laugh which she apparently did a lot when she was nervous, and a habit of resting her chin on her wrist and peeking up at me from underneath her lashes. She rolled up her shirt sleeves after she'd finished her glass of red, and that's when I got my first eyeful of her forearms. They were really defined. Like, I could see some of the muscles in them, there was a hint of muscle through the top of her sleeves, too. She wasn't *big*—she was really slender, in fact—but those muscles...

I may have stared a little. She noticed, and pushed her sleeves up a little further, giving me a shy smile. "I play a lot of sport."

I could see that; she was in great shape. Me, on the other hand? I looked down at my own squishy arms. "I don't."

That didn't seem to bother her at all. "You can hold my towel," she told me, I think poking fun at herself before she explained, "I'm around athletes all the time, I see a lot of arms like mine. I don't see a lot of arms like yours."

Oh, that made sense. "I wondered why someone like you would be interested in someone like me..."

140

She looked up at me from under her swept fringe again. "I was thinking the same thing."

With some wine in us, we got talking a little more about each other. She showed me a couple of tattoos, one for when her team made the finals, and another because she'd just really liked the design. I was interested, of course, but perhaps a little more interested in the fact she had to pull her shirt up to her hip to show me. Since when was seeing someone's bellybutton so exciting?

I'd forgotten there was more food coming until the chef bussed it out, and when it arrived, Mikey described what it was with the same sort of loving detail as Bree always did: all the French names for things, where it was from and why I'd like it. "They're all vegetarian," she told me, looking very proud of herself. "I noticed you'd liked a whole lot of animal rights pages on Facebook, so..."

Could she get any more wonderful? I was probably giving her heart eyes.

The meal was *delicious*, but we spent too much time talking instead of eating, so most of the other guests had cleared out of the restaurant by the time we were done. Mikey asked me if I wanted dessert (I explained 'want' wasn't the same as 'have any room left at all for', to which she replied, 'I guess you'll have to come back, then, because French desserts are amazing!') and so we both had coffee, instead. Even after our empty cups were taken, we still sat there, pushing the conversation.

It was difficult to ignore the other waiters hovering around us and packing up other tables, though: we were going to have to leave soon. I didn't want to, going home was the very last thing in the world I wanted right now. I could have sat here with her all night.

Mikey was watching her colleagues. "I kind of don't want to go home yet," she confessed, mirroring my thoughts. "But I hate it when patrons make us stay open late."

My heart sank. "Oh, okay..."

She took a little breath. "Do you... maybe want to walk around the harbour a bit first, though? I think there's something on tonight."

Did I? I could hardly say yes fast enough, and watching her face light up when mine did made me feel like a million dollars.

We took a lift downstairs and she showed me a secret route to Circular Quay through the back of the building. There were still loads of tourists wandering around despite how late it was, and buskers everywhere were doing an assortment of really bizarre performances.

We wandered through them pretending to be interested even though secretly we definitely weren't, we just didn't want to go home. The fact that this gorgeous woman with me wanted to do everything to try and stay in my company as long as possible just *blew my mind*.

I was already beaming ear to ear, but when I felt shy fingertips subtly reach for mine...

"Is this okay?" she said quietly besides me, and—*wow*. The butterflies were back.

I nodded. I wish I could double-nod, or triple-nod, because it was more than just 'okay'.

In answer, she slipped her hand into mine and squeezed it, and then the two of us walked through Circular Quay in full view of the entire world holding hands.

Everyone knows I'm a lesbian, I thought, walking past crowds of tourists and business people on their way home. I felt oddly exposed as if they were all staring at me, and part of me was terrified someone from Frost might see me and tell everyone— or tell Sarah!—but a much greater percentage of me was over the moon and my brain was too full of Mikey to worry much about consequences. It didn't matter who saw us anyway: I wouldn't have let go of her hand for anything in the world.

When we got to the Opera House, she led me out of the crowd and down to the waterfront, saying, "There's a little place I used to work at down here, I know everyone!" but when we got there, the lights were out, the gate was shut and the restaurant was closed.

"Rats," she said, banging the metal gate with the palm of her hand. "I was going to see if they'd let us sit out front if there weren't many people, because the view along the water is amazing."

"The view from here is still pretty nice," I pointed out, looking across at North Shore. Sarah's house and my flat were somewhere over there—too far away from the water to see, though.

It took her a moment to say it. "The view all night's been pretty nice, really..." She didn't mean out the window, either. It made my breath catch in my throat.

We were quiet for a moment; in the distance I could hear the hum of traffic from the freeway and the crowds on the other side of the quay. I was acutely aware we were all alone.

Her fingertips brushed a few strands of hair away from my face, and she stepped a little closer to me, licking her lips a little.

Oh, goodness: I knew what came next. I'd never been more ready for anything in my life.

When I looked up at her, she leant in fractionally—just to make sure I knew what was happening—and then murmured, "Is this okay?"

I nodded, unable to stop *smiling*, and slowly, so slowly, she leant across and touched her lips against mine as we stood in the shadow of the Sydney Opera House.

It was a little hard to strike a rhythm because of how much we were both beaming (and occasionally we had to stop for a moment to giggle nervously) but we managed. Wow, did we manage.

I loved how her lips felt—smaller than I was used to, and softer. I loved how shy her arms were and how they didn't just reach to grab greedy handfuls of me, but just snaked around my back and held our bodies together. I loved that I could taste her dessert coffee on her lips, and that I could

143

feel the swell of her chest against mine, and that she had this little furrow in her brow as she kissed me as if she was concentrating really hard.

I'm kissing a girl, I thought, stunned by how surreal it was, but that didn't make me want to stop. The opposite, in fact: I wanted to keep going. I wanted to keep going with her despite the fact we were both girls.

Despite being a girl too, her body was so different than mine, and even with my squishy arms around her neck I could feel how solid the rest of her was. I'd never seen a woman with a body like hers before, and I... I kind of wanted to know what she looked like. I wanted to know what she *felt* like, and I wanted to show her what *I* felt like. I couldn't stop thinking about unbuttoning that shirt and pushing it over her shoulders, and letting her unzip my dress...

I still wasn't too sure about the whole lesbian sex thing, but at that second, kissing her, I felt like I might have dropped my dress right then and there if someone could have guaranteed me that no one would see us.

No one could, though, and we couldn't kiss here forever. I was just getting up the courage to ask her if she wanted to come over, when she took a steadying breath herself and asked, "How close do you live?"

I flushed with pleasure; *she* had been thinking that, too? "Not that close, North Shore, maybe a 20- or 30-minute drive? You?"

She made the same face. "Just across the bridge, but I live in a tiny flat with two of the nosiest gayboys in all of Sydney."

"Well, I live by myself. You want to hit mine?"

Her nervous smile came back. "Is that okay? I mean, it's already pretty late..."

Was she *kidding*? It could be 4am and I'd still invite her over at this point!! "Yeah, of course. You cool with getting an Uber?"

She was, so we kissed a couple more times—back to nervous giggles again, apparently—and then I hunted around for where I'd dropped my handbag in the heat of the moment so I could get my phone out. "They're usually really quick," I was telling Mikey as I stood up. "I get them all the—"

—three messages and a missed call. All from Sarah.

The smile fell straight off my face.

"Can you give me a second?" I asked Mikey, taking a few steps away to check them.

That was really unlike Sarah. The last time she'd tried to contact me that much was after she broke up with Andrew, and for just a second, just for a tiny little second, I thought hopefully, *maybe she's broken up with Rob*! Then I felt like a terrible person. She was having his baby, she wasn't about to break up with him.

I quickly opened them. The first one was harmless enough, *"Hey Gem, Bree's cooked some three-cheese risotto and it's absolute gold! We have a bowl here for you if you want to pop around for dinner :)"* If it had been any other night, I would have. Bree's cooking certainly beat my own, and it meant more time with Sarah. *Another night*, I promised myself, and then scrolled down.

"Risotto's getting cold..." the next one read. *"We're all here waiting for you! I was also reading up on how to do really well on Tinder and I have some ideas that might help you land someone amazing!"*

Of course, I hadn't replied. After that, there was a missed call, and then an hour after the missed call, the last message said, ":("

I stared at that sad face. Sarah so rarely showed any sort of emotion that I could only imagine how bad she'd need to feel to let on that she was feeling bad at all, and whose fault was it that she felt bad in the first place?

Ugh, and I was out here in the city, having the time of my life and ignoring her, wasn't I?

"Is everything okay?" Mikey took a few tentative steps over.

I had no idea how to explain it, so I didn't try. "Yeah, it's just my best friend Sarah. She kind of doesn't know I'm out tonight." I paused. "Or that I'm into girls..."

Mikey considered that. "Are you going to tell her?" *Hell no.* I shook my head firmly, and she grimaced on my behalf. "Rough."

I nodded, and then took a long, deep breath, trying to ignore the yucky feeling that had settled over me. "Okay: the Uber."

We actually lucked out, because the Uber driver turned out to be from England and was an enormous 'football' fan. So he and Mikey chattered away excitedly about leagues I had no idea about, and it would have been a great opportunity for me to learn more about soccer (it was certainly a great opportunity for me to watch Mikey being really passionate about something), but I couldn't stop thinking about that sad face text.

I hoped Sarah wasn't crying. As soon as I thought that I realised that she probably was, and then I felt like a monster. I felt like a lying monster. She was probably shut in her bedroom, hugging her pillow and wondering why her best friend was suddenly avoiding her.

Maybe I should just tell Sarah about me, I thought, looking across at Mikey. *If it works out with Mikey, it should be easy, right? She'll never guess I was attracted to her first.*

As soon as I'd thought that, though, I dismissed it. If I introduced Mikey, then Sarah would know that I'd been questioning my sexuality for some time, and that was huge. That was a huge thing to not tell her. And because I couldn't tell her why, she'd assume it was because I didn't trust her with knowing. Nothing was more guaranteed to make her feel absolutely heartbroken.

Maybe I could at least tell her I'm questioning and attracted to some other girl? I wondered, but the Uber driver arrived at my house before I'd figured out an answer.

Mikey looked up at my building, impressed. "Wow, you live in a really nice suburb!"

I laughed once. "Yeah, and I pay for it," I told her. "Thank goodness I work for Frost!"

We had to walk up several flights of stairs before we got to my flat, and Mikey stepped up behind me to put her hands on my waist and kiss my neck while I was unlocking the door.

For a split second, I really enjoyed it—and then I felt guilty for enjoying it.

She noticed and immediately stepped away. "Hey, are you sure you're okay with this?"

I tried to laugh it off. "Sure!" I said dismissively, and before I opened the door, I warned her, "It's really messy."

She shrugged. "I'm no clean freak," she told me, still watching me a bit closely, but then laughed really hard when she saw *how* messy my place was. "It's like a girl bomb went off in here and sprayed clothes and makeup everywhere," she told me, wandering into my kitchen and looking with interest at all of my stuff. I watched her, hoping she'd ask me about a Sudoku thingy I had up on my fridge (I'd figured out the equation that guaranteed the correct figure in every square as long as 18% of the squares were already filled, and people were usually pretty impressed when I demonstrated it), but she looked past that because she'd already seen something in my living room that had caught her—

Oh, no, I'd forgotten: there were photos of me and Sarah *everywhere*.

Honestly, I'd never really thought about them before. It was normal to have photos of your best friend everywhere, because they were arguably one of the most important people in your life. But there were just so many of them. Bringing Mikey in here, I suddenly saw these photos in a different light: there were *too* many. It was weird. I suddenly felt like Mikey could see through me.

When she turned back to me, I could see she had. "Your 'best friend Sarah'?" Her smile was gone.

I swallowed, and nodded.

So did she. It took her a moment to ask, "Were you... in love with her? Is that why you can't tell her?"

Was I in—for some reason, surrounded by these photos, haunted by that sad face text message, that question *slammed* me. I felt sick. I felt sick, and uncomfortable, and I didn't want to think about it. I loved Sarah, she was my friend, of course I—*no*, I told myself. *This is totally the wrong time for me to be overthinking crap like that.* "Not *in* love with her," I told Mikey as my cheeks went pink and I felt for a moment like I might be sick. "I love her, because she's my friend. That's all."

She didn't believe me.

I didn't want to see that knowing expression on her face anymore, so I immediately pulled her into my arms and kissed her. She was stiff as a board for a moment and I thought she might tear away from me and stop everything, but she didn't, and slowly, slowly she relaxed.

It wasn't the same at first, though, it felt forced. I felt like maybe I should have explained that Sarah and I were *best* friends and we'd always done everything together—she wasn't just any old friend, hence all the photos—but no matter how I thought I'd explain it, it didn't sound right.

In the end I didn't say anything else about it because I didn't want her to worry, I just wanted to hear those shy, sweet little giggles she was giving me by the Opera House, and I wanted to make her so happy that she couldn't stop smiling again, just like I had before.

It was only when we nearly toppled over because we'd both been concentrating on other things than staying upright that she finally laughed into my lips and wrapped her arms tightly around me, just like she had before. That's what I wanted, *that* Mikey. The one who smiled against my lips like she was now, and kissed me like she had before, except here in my flat where there was no one to see us.

It was that last part that got my mind wandering back to the 'wanting more' feeling I'd had before: no one could see us here.

I toyed a bit with the lowest button on her shirt before she finally said, "You can undo them if you want..." And leant away from me so I could.

She watched my face closely as I undid them, it made me blush like wildfire, and as the fabric fell open to reveal a very faint six-pack, she was waiting for me to tell her what I thought about it. I wanted to tell her I liked it because I did, but all I could do was mutely blush and run my fingertips over all the shapes. She looked pleased anyway, and shrugged the shirt off her shoulders so she was standing hip-to-hip with me in a very plain, very modest black sports bra.

"I don't really own any nice bras," she confessed.

I bit my lip. Should I say it? "I do, and I'm wearing it right now..."

When I peeked up at her, her jaw was slack, and her eyes dipped to my cleavage.

Still biting my lip a little, I reached around behind me to unzip my dress a little, just enough to fall to my waist and show off my nice strapless bra. She watched, completely rapt, and then instead of reaching straight for my breasts as soon as she could see my bra (which is totally what a boy would do), she put her hands on my shoulders and tried not to stare down too much.

"Freckles..." She observed about my torso; I was covered in them. I'd long since made peace with that, though.

"Yeah, I'm basically a human leopard," I told her as she bent her neck down to place little tiny kisses along my neck and shoulders. I could feel her hands slipping down my arms as she did, the sides of them brushing the sides of my breasts, and, because I knew she was too shy to just grope them by herself, I lifted my hands to guide hers to where they wanted to go.

She inhaled sharply—there was that nervous smile again!—and cupped them over my bra as she leant back in to kiss me. I could tell where her mind was, though, because she kept glancing downward, and before long she was kissing my chin, across my jaw, down my neck... en route to kiss the crease between my breasts and then press her face indulgently between them.

I was silently laughing about how much she liked them (and how much I really liked that she did!) and looking over the top of her head as she—

Mr Crumpet was sitting directly opposite us, surrounded by my photos and *glaring* at me.

I must have stiffened, because Mikey noticed and looked up at me. "Should I stop?"

"It's not that," I said, and pointed. She twisted around. "My cat is watching us."

She laughed. "Maybe he's jealous?"

"Probably," I agreed, "and he's judging me. Look at him, judging me." I didn't need his judgment right now, so I went after him. "I'm going to shut him in the bedroom."

That turned out to be harder than anticipated, because Mr Crumpet had speed that belied his girth. In the end, after watching me half-undressed and trying to chase my cat around for a full minute and laughing, Mikey gingerly suggested, "Maybe *we* should shut ourselves in the bedroom...?"

That seemed like a better idea—and I really liked what it implied!—so we shut him out of the bedroom instead. Much to Mikey's amusement, my bedroom also looked like a 'girl bomb' had gone off in it, because my entire wardrobe was on my bed and I had to push it all onto the floor with the cat hair so we could hop on.

With no Mr Judgment and no photos in here, we were just getting into it again—and lying down with her, that added an extra element of illicitness that got my blood pumping—when that *little fucking asshole of a cat* starting howling blue murder outside the door. It was the most awful noise.

We stopped for a moment, mostly so Mikey could laugh. "Is he serious?"

"Be right back, I'm going to murder my cat," I told her, hauling myself off the bed to hunt the mongrel down.

He took off again when I opened the door, and I spent what felt like eternity trying to catch him and get him into the bathroom. Almost giving up, I straightened to catch my breath

150

and found myself facing the photos in my living room again. I stopped smiling.

All those photos of Sarah's happy face only served to remind me of that sad face text, and I felt like they were judging me, too, just as much as Mr Grump was. I didn't blame them: I was about to have sex while she was probably crying about me ignoring her.

It suddenly struck me how completely selfish it was of me to just let her feel like that, especially when all it would take is one simple text to let her know I was busy and that everything was okay. I could do at least that much for her, couldn't I?

I pulled my phone out of my bag, thinking I'd just text her, *"Busy, will call you very soon*! xx" or something like that so she knew I wasn't ignoring her, when I saw I'd already got a text message from her. My stomach dropping, I opened it.

"I wish you'd just tell me what I've done wrong... :("

Ugh... I leant against my bench, my hand over my eyes for a moment. I was a total selfish monster. I should have replied to her much earlier.

I didn't realise how long I'd been out there trying to figure out what to say to her until I noticed Mikey was watching me from the doorway.

She had a really strange expression on her face. I felt sick; she was reading me like a book.

I looked down at my phone. I desperately wanted to reply to Sarah and make her feel better, but it was also really rude of me to be ignoring Mikey, too, wasn't it? Mikey was my guest. Shit, I'd just have to text Sarah later. "Sorry," I told Mikey. "Sorry, I'm coming."

She didn't look very comforted as I put my phone down on the bench and walked back towards her. Before I was back in her arms, though, my phone buzzed on the kitchen bench.

I'd got another message.

I stopped in place. What if something really *was* wrong for Sarah and she just didn't want to say it on the phone?

Mikey was watching me, looking increasingly disappointed. "Go on," she said neutrally. "I know you want to get that."

Despite that visible disappointment, I couldn't help rushing back to my phone to read the message. When I did, though, it was like reading a punch to the stomach. *"Please tell me... I miss you so much..."* I think I recoiled like she'd actually punched me.

Mikey saw my reaction, and slumped. She spent a few seconds with her eyes closed, and then straightened. "You know, I think I'm just going to go." She walked over to grab her shirt off the back of the couch.

What?! "No! No, it's fine!" I told her, abandoning my phone. "I literally will just be a second, I was just going to send a quick text to—"

She stopped me. "I can guess who."

We stared at each other for a moment, and then she looked away and threaded her arms into her shirt, eyes veiled.

No. No—this wasn't happening, was it?! It was like the sudden pivot point where a beautiful dream transforms into a horrible nightmare, and I was stuck in place and unable to run away from the horrors. Just like in a nightmare, I stood trapped, open-jawed, and watching her stiffly button up her shirt.

No more adorable nervous laugh and rosy cheeks. No more elated smiles and shy eyes. When I thought about how on top of the world I'd been an hour ago, and then looked at what was happening now, I felt sick, so sick. I pulled my dress back up because I didn't know what else to do, and watched helplessly as someone incredible slipped through my fingers like sand.

Before she left, she gave me one last look. There was nothing but heartbreak on her face, and just like everything else, that was my fault.

I was shaking. "Stay," I begged her. I knew it was pointless.

"I wish I could," she told me, and I could hear in her voice how much she meant it.

The door fell gently shut behind her.

CHAPTER THIRTEEN

I tore down all those photos. One by one, I ripped them off my wall, hardly able to see through the tears in my eyes, with this horrible, horrible aching, uncomfortable feeling in my chest, and I hated it and myself and everything.

Why wasn't I a statistical average, married and pregnant with my first child like numbers said I should be? Why wasn't I doing all the *normal* things that *normal* people did? Why did every fucking thing I did have to be so far off the charts that there was hardly even a category for me? I couldn't even be straight, could I? On top of every statistical outlier I was, I *had* to be gay, too!

For a second, I wished I wasn't. Because if I wasn't, tonight wouldn't have happened. I wouldn't have hurt the sweetest, loveliest, most gorgeous girl I'd probably ever met. God knows where Mikey was going now; probably to tell her housemate how wrong they both were about me and how screwed up I was. The thought of that was almost unbearable.

I didn't know how to solve this.

Mikey was gone, and I'd made Sarah really upset. I kept thinking I should at least text Sarah to apologise, but I had this horrible mental image of her ignoring me back to teach me a lesson. I didn't want to just text her, anyway. I couldn't think of anything else that would make this horrible ache in my chest go away more than Sarah hugs.

The more I thought about it the more I was sure I needed to see her. It was another stupid decision—I already knew that as soon as I thought it—but whatever. My whole life was a mess anyway, what was one more stupid decision?

I zipped up my crumpled dress, changed my knickers, and put on a pair of Ugg Boots (which I'm sure looked amazing with my blue party dress) and then headed out the door.

I couldn't imagine what I looked like to anyone who saw me on my walk to Sarah's: panda-eyed, party-dressed and in a pair of hideous slippers, but I hardly cared. I dragged my feet all the way there and then hammered on her door, feeling like I was about to cry again. Then, when I realised it wasn't just Sarah's door anymore but Sarah-and-Rob's door, I *did* cry again.

When footsteps came up the hallway, I waited for Sarah to open the door so I could just throw myself into her arms and have her hug me while I apologised for being such a—

Min opened the door.

I was so stunned, I stopped crying for a moment.

She had the same expression, and it took her a moment to gather herself. "God, are you okay, Gemma?"

I'd been hanging out for a hug from Sarah so much that not being able to get one just made me burst into tears again. "No," I told her honestly. "Please, can I just speak to Sarah?"

Min ushered me inside, grimacing. "I wish you could, but she went for a drive," she said apologetically. "Can I help? I know I'm a bit of a poor substitute for her, but I'm here for you."

Everything felt hopeless. "I don't know if anyone can help."

"Do you want to talk about it?" I shook my head, and she was touching my hair affectionately and looking worried when her face suddenly hardened. "Wait," she said darkly, "did someone hurt you? Off Tinder, or something? Because if that's the case, I can get Henry to come and drive us to a late-night clinic that—"

"No. I just hurt everyone else."

Her expression softened and she relaxed a little. "*Oh*," she said sympathetically, pulling me into a long, firm hug so I got mascara and shimmer eyeshadow all over her hoodie. "Boy, do I know *that* feeling. Come on, I'll make you some warm tea while you wait for Sarah to come back."

The house was quiet when I followed her inside—really quiet. It was so full lately that it was strange to be reminded of the old days when it was just Sarah here.

From the lack of noise, there was predictably no one else in the living room when Min led me in; from the looks of things she'd been doing some graphics work because her laptop and tablet were set up on the table. I must have interrupted her in the middle of some Frost work or something. I felt kind of bad about that.

"Sit," she said, gesturing at the couch. "If you don't want to talk, do you want to eat? Sarah put a bowl of Bree's three-cheese risotto aside for you. Or maybe you'd like something else? Bree's fast asleep, so it'd just be my cooking, unfortunately." She looked genuinely ready to do me a three-course meal if I asked for it.

It was nice, but I shook my head. "Thanks, I already had dinner."

I half-expected her to ask me about that; it was totally clear I'd been out because of the dress I was wearing. She didn't, though. She just nodded and went to make me tea.

While she was gone, I craned my neck to get a peek at her laptop screen, just to confirm if I was interrupting her. There was just a big red square on it; I didn't know what that meant.

Min returned with two steaming mugs of tea and very carefully placed them on the coffee table, glancing up at me. She smiled slightly when she saw where I was looking. "Natalie's cards," she said about the red square. "You want to see?"

Despite how crap I felt, I actually kind of did. Min unplugged her laptop from the tablet and brought it over to me on the couch so I could get a better look. They were pretty standard business cards with the standard details, and the only defining feature about them was that they were fire-engine red.

"What do you think?" Her smile returned. "You helped inspire them, actually."

I raised my eyebrows. "I did?"

She nodded. "You remember that red dress you wore, and all that research you did about what men are attracted to? It got me thinking about how I could have people look at this card and immediately think of Natalie."

Huh. "That's kind of impressive," I told Min, meaning it.

She looked proud of herself for a moment, and then her smile faded. "Sorry, this probably isn't the best time to discuss graphic design with you..."

I shrugged. "It's nice to know I inspired *something* worthwhile."

She put her computer back on the table and then sat down opposite me, silently watched me nursing my tea for a moment. "It's hard to hear you talk about yourself like that."

"Yeah, well, it's hard to basically be one giant walking disaster who spends her time screwing things up and upsetting people, so..."

After some more quiet thought, something suddenly clicked for her. I could see it in her face. "Wait, 'upsetting everyone' doesn't have anything to do with Sarah, does it'?"

My stomach bottomed out. Sarah must have been feeling really bad if Min had noticed. "Yes," I admitted, feeling sick. "She wasn't really upset, was she?"

Min gave me a pained look. "I don't know about 'really', because she's not exactly forthcoming with her feelings, but she obviously wasn't doing so great when she went for her drive." She reached across and put a comforting hand on my arm. "Don't worry, though. Whatever it is, I'm sure you two will work it out. You're really close, after all."

Are we? I asked internally, thinking of this week versus the last ten years. Once upon a time there wasn't anything that I wouldn't have told her. But now...? Now, I felt like she knew nothing about me. She was successful, charismatic and about to have her baby with Rob; I was on the highway to nowhere and I still had no idea who I was. Slowly, steadily, she was slipping away from me.

The thought of drifting apart from such an amazing person and a defining part of my life was unbearable. All my best memories had her in them, and she was part of me; I had no idea who I even was without her.

Great, here come the tears again, I thought helplessly, and then put down my tea so I could wipe my eyes with my wrists. "Sorry..."

Min hurriedly grabbed me a few tissues. "No, it's fine," she told me, and then sat next to me on the couch and put a stiff arm around me. I thought she might have been a little unsure about how to comfort me, but she managed to try, anyway. Her hugs weren't exactly the Sarah hugs I came for, but there was something incredibly attentive and caring about Min, and just feeling like *anyone* cared about me made me *sob*. I didn't feel like I deserved it.

"I know you're probably thinking 'poor Gemma', but I'm the bad guy," I confessed, and then, because she looked so much like she actually genuinely cared, I started to tell her everything. It just came pouring out of my mouth, I couldn't stop it.

I told her about how I'd been switching preferences on Tinder and hiding it from Sarah, how excited I'd been about Mikey and how amazing she'd been, and how I'd totally blown it with her because of Sarah. I didn't tell her why or how it had been ruined, though, because I didn't want Min to know how I felt about Sarah.

Min noticed some details were missing. "I don't understand why you'd hide this all from Sarah," Min said quietly when I was done. "She's really open-minded, she didn't bat an eyelid when I came out to her as trans. And hasn't she kind of joked about your sexuality before anyway?"

Sure, she'd *joked* about it. She'd joked about her own on occasion, too. It wasn't real. She didn't really think I might not be straight. If she did, she was super forthright, she'd just tell me. She'd never been the kind of person to not say exactly what she thought. Yup, she definitely didn't know, which is why she was still happy to let me sleep in her bed, and to be naked in front of me and talk about *our* future. I was sure of it.

Min didn't press me for an answer. She was too busy frowning. "And, honestly, Gemma, perhaps you dodged a bullet with this Mikey person? Anyone who gets jealous and storms out over you worrying about your best friend being upset isn't the type of person you should be involved with, anyway."

I flinched. "It wasn't like that," I told her, feeling awful that I'd given anyone that impression of sweet Mikey. "She didn't storm out. She just got upset and left."

Min looked dubious. "Upset about what, though? How could you be upset about that? Disappointed the date ended early, maybe, but *upset*?"

I couldn't say it.

She just looked confused, both about my silence and about why Mikey had left. She didn't push it, though. "You don't have to tell me if you don't want to, it's okay," she reassured me, and looked totally prepared to drop it.

I probably should have let her, but part of me *did* want to tell her. I'd told her so much already, and I didn't want anyone thinking of Mikey as anything but the gorgeous, sweet person that she was. On top of that, I just really, really, *really* wanted at least one person in the whole wide world to know what I was struggling with. If I could trust anyone to be that person, it was Min.

Still, my throat was so dry it was hard to get the words out.

Tell her, I willed myself. I opened my mouth. I could barely hear myself. "Mikey realised something about me."

Min watched me very closely. "She did?"

I nodded. Gosh, I felt sick at the thought of saying it, but I was so tired and so angry at myself, I'd reached a point where I felt numb about the consequences of telling her, so I just said it. "She asked me if I'd been in love with Sarah."

I didn't think Min really believed it for a second; I think she expected me to continue with the story to the real truth. I could see the exact moment she realised that what I'd told her *was* the real truth, and her jaw dropped.

All I could hear was the ticking clock; I felt dizzy waiting for her reply. The silence was suffocatingly oppressive.

She didn't gape at me for long. "Oh, Gemma..." she said with such sympathy audible, and then threw her arms around me in a long, tight, warm hug, and didn't let me go; the opposite. Each second, it got tighter.

It took me by surprise; I didn't know what to make of it. "You probably think I'm stupid..."

"No, I think *I'm* stupid," she said firmly. "I should have guessed after how upset you were when you found out Sarah was pregnant. I should have known." She sounded really frustrated with herself.

"Well, I didn't know how I felt," I pointed out. "So how could you?"

She just kept hugging me. "This sounds like a conversation I once had with Henry," she told me, and then eventually pulled away. She kept an arm draped around my shoulders, though. "You should talk to him, Gemma. Not only is he an amazing psychologist, he's also been in love with someone who was the wrong sexuality to love him back."

I was a bit stung at the gentle reminder that Sarah was straight, and despite my parallel with Henry, I wasn't tempted to talk to him in the slightest. Just sitting across from him made me blush like wildfire. Telling him something this horribly private and knowing that he'd had similar personal experience would just be awkward. Plus, I didn't want my HR manager knowing what a total screw up I was in my personal life. "I don't really want to tell anyone else..."

She frowned at me. "But isn't that why you came over, though? To tell Sarah?"

My eyes were as wide as saucers. Hell, no! I shook my head firmly. "I just wanted to see her!"

Min made an 'oh' shape with her mouth. "Okay, then." She watched me for a moment, and then couldn't stop herself from hugging me one more time. "God, Gemma, I'm so sorry. This must be awful for you."

I laughed once, humourlessly. "Yeah. But it's worse for everyone else, trust me."

"Speaking as someone who's been in Sarah's position, it's definitely worse for you. I just felt awful I couldn't love Henry

159

the way he wished I could. He went through hell, as I imagine you are—but that's all I should probably say about it. It's his pain and not mine, after all." She rubbed my shoulder and stood up. "Well, I'm sure Sarah will be back soon and you can spend some time with her. In the meantime, can *I* do anything to make you feel better? Do you want that bowl of risotto after all? If you listen to Bree, apparently eating releases endorphins."

I didn't really feel like it at all, but Min was just so determined to feed me that I ended up giving in and letting her heat it up. Afterwards, while she was hovering over me like a mother hen while I ate, the unmistakable sound of Sarah's old hatchback came rattling up the driveway beside the narrow house.

I put my fork down; she was back. My heart started to pound.

Min straightened. "Well, I think that's my cue to go and join Bree in bed," she said, and then gave me an affectionate forehead kiss. "Good luck." She disappeared down the hallway to her bedroom, leaving me sitting there alone with my half-eaten risotto.

I listened to the car engine turn off, and the car door open; to the sound of Sarah's heavy footsteps up the back porch and then the sound of her keys fitting into the door. For some reason, I was *petrified* that she would come in, look at me and just know what I'd told Min. I felt like it was written all over my face.

She wasn't expecting me there, obviously, so when she entered, she started talking to me like I was Min as she pulled the door shut behind her. She was only dressed in trackies and a jumper, but her makeup was perfect. It looked like it had been recently re-applied. "Do you think you'll have the edits on that full-pager ready by tomorrow night?" she was asking tiredly as she turned around. "Because Omar said that he would..."

The words died on her lips as she turned to face me and saw it wasn't Min.

We stared at each other for a few seconds. I couldn't get over how terrible she looked: physically tired, emotionally exhausted, and completely dwarfed by her big, round belly. It looked like someone had stuck her with a straw and just sucked the life out.

That someone was me. Suddenly, my master plan of showing up here and throwing myself into her arms seemed so selfish.

She swallowed. "You *did* come for dinner after all." Her eyes dipped to my party dress and lingered there.

She's going to ask why I'm wearing a party dress, I realised. *She's going to ask me, and what am I going to tell her*? I braced for the question.

It came. "Gem. Not that Uggs aren't a great look with that hot dress, but why on earth are you so dressed up this late at night?" As soon as she'd said it, she scrunched up her face and threw her arms out in a 'stop!' motion. "*Fuck*!" she said, and it was jarring to hear her swear. "Fuck. Listen to me *prying*. You don't have to answer that question. In fact, please don't answer it."

I felt *really* uncomfortable. "O-Okay..."

For a few seconds, she just stood there, looking really frustrated with herself. When she spoke again, it was really hesitant. "You must be really angry with me..."

What? Over that question? "Of course not!"

She didn't look like she believed me. "I'd probably be angry with me."

"Angry with you for *what*? For you asking a simple—"

"You don't have to act like you're not upset, because I know that—"

Maybe she *didn't* mean the question? "I'm not upset with you at all! What would I possibly be upset at you for—"

She slumped. "For being like I am, Gem!" she told me, raising her voice and throwing her arms out in front of her. "For being bossy, and nosy, and controlling, and—"

I stared at her for a moment; I couldn't bear to hear her talk about herself like that, she'd been absolutely my hero for ten years. "Sarah, I'm not angry! I don't understand why you'd think that I—"

"Then why are you avoiding me, Gem?" she asked, a desperate note in her voice.

She was wide open to me; I had the awful feeling like I could break her with a single word. It made me sick to think about how easily I could accidentally do it. "I'm not avoiding you!"

She gave me a look, like, *are you kidding me*?

It made me panic. "I'm not!"

She took a step towards me. "I saw the look you gave me in the car, when I took your phone off you to put Tinder on it. And then the other night, when Min was oh-so subtly trying to suggest to me I need to back the hell off you...? When I looked at you, you looked relieved. I know what's going on."

I'd never heard her like this. It was crazy, and I wanted to tell her that, but I also didn't want to tell her what I was hiding from her. *Maybe I should just be honest*, I thought, and then immediately balked at that idea; then I'd lose two people in one day.

"Gem, I'm a big girl, you can tell me what I'm doing wrong. I'll listen, and I'll make the changes to myself that I need to so I can keep my best friend."

Every word felt like being slapped in the face. She was perfect to me the way she was; she always had been. "You don't need to change, Sare—"

"I do." She took a few more steps towards me. "Because otherwise why would you be avoiding me?"

I'm avoiding you because every time I look at you I want to kiss you, I thought, and then shut my eyes so I wasn't tempted to say it.

"So here's what I've been thinking," she put firm hands on my shoulders, "going forward, I'll be respectful of your boundaries. I'm not going to make you feel uncomfortable. I'm not going to force your hand on stuff. I'm going to treat you like the incredibly amazing, smart, capable adult you are, and I'm not going to be the clingy and domineering *bitch* that I've been in the last—"

"Sare, stop!" I flinched at that word; I couldn't bear to hear any more of this. "You're not a bitch, and I'm not 'a capable adult'! Look at me!" I gestured at my panda eyes and my Ugg Boot and party dress combo. "I'm a fucking wreck, I ruin everything, I hurt everyone, and I have no idea where the hell my life is going!"

Her eyes dipped to my dress; I had to at least tell her something about it as a consolation, I had to. "I'm wearing this dress because I went on a date tonight. That's why I didn't answer your messages, I wasn't avoiding you."

I didn't expect her to look as hurt as she did. She swallowed it quickly, and a whole series of other emotions played across her face. "I—thought you'd just be at home..."

I shook my head. "I wasn't avoiding you, Sarah. Of course I wasn't. I just didn't check my phone until later."

She didn't look comforted by that at all; the opposite. She looked angry at herself. That wasn't the reaction I was hoping for, so I tried to deliver my point. "You don't need to change, Sarah. Everything about you is—"

"Are you kidding me 'you don't need to change'?" She looked up at me. "You've just been on a real date—your first in, what, three years?—and not only did you feel like you couldn't tell me about it, but instead of celebrating with you, I'm totally obsessed with my own—"

"Sare, I screwed up the date! Like, you can't even imagine how badly I screwed it up! I just came around here because I wanted you to make me feel better." I put my hands over hers on my shoulders. "Because you always do, Sare. You always know the right thing to say to make me feel like everything is okay, and I really need that right now. I need you to just give me a big Sarah hug and tell me everything's going to be okay."

Unexpectedly, she teared up. Dropping her arms from my shoulders, she wrapped them around me and hugged me so tightly she was nearly suffocating me with her enormous belly. I could feel her smiling against my neck; it reminded me of feeling Mikey smiling against my lips and I felt so damn confused. I didn't know what the hell was going on.

"Thank you," she told me like I'd just given her a huge gift instead of making her feel completely fucking worthless. "I'm sorry I'm such a neurotic mess at the moment. I can't deal with anything. The doc was telling me to expect mood swings with the pregnancy hormones, but I didn't expect to feel like I can't function at all..."

See? She partially feels like crap because of the hormones, I tried to tell myself, but it didn't work. I didn't feel any better about being a walking catastrophe.

"Everything's going to be okay," she told me a bit ironically as she pulled away, giving me a wry little smile. She lifted her hand and brushed the backs of her fingers across my cheek, looking at me like she thought I was a goddamn rock star. "You're gorgeous, and amazing, and brilliant, and you'll find someone who'll love you as much as I do eventually, I promise you."

I let those words hit me where they shouldn't, because after the evening I'd had, and after disastrously fucking it up with Mikey, it just felt so good to hear her say them.

She had a sort of passionate conviction about her. "And I'll help you, Gem, I'll help you find someone. It's the least I can do after spamming your inbox with clingy, hormonal crap while you were on your first date since the turn of the century." She paused. "I mean, only if you want me to help, though..."

What could I possibly say to that? This was the happiest she'd looked all evening. "Sure!" I managed, sagging internally.

I was glad I said it, though, because she gave me one of her beautiful bright smiles. "Awesome! We'll find you someone just as amazing, and then we can do all of the stuff we've always wanted to do: double-dates, tandem holidays... it'll be really fun." I didn't know how realistic tandem holidays were with her pending baby, but now didn't seem like the best time to point that out. "I've been reading up so much on Tinder, and I have some ideas about how we could work it so you land some really awesome matches."

164

"Well, I want to hear them," I lied, trying not to think too much about the absolutely perfect match I'd already landed. No one could be better for me than Mikey, and I hadn't managed to hold that together for even one single night.

She'd brightened. "Okay! We can go through them! But do you want to get cleaned up, first? I feel like hell warmed over."

She got me her makeup wipes to de-panda myself while she changed, and then, when we were both comfortable and I'd dealt with the fact I'd need to face Tinder again, we sat down on the couch together. She pulled my legs across her lap.

I held my phone at her. "Here."

Looking proud of herself, she pushed it back. "It's your phone, you do it."

That was... odd. But okay, I guess. "Alright." I opened Tinder, and then went to the settings page. I'd set it back to 'men' when I'd deleted Mikey's match and all the other incriminating stuff. I hesitated to push the *'Make Me Discoverable'* button, though.

She was watching me. "Go on."

I looked down at the men-women toggles.

This is the moment, I thought. *This is the moment where I could tell her.*

For a second, I nearly did. I nearly let her watch me change it to 'women', and click the discovery button. It would have been *so easy* to do, so easy. *Too* easy, because then I looked up and saw my legs across her lap, and remembered her talking excitedly about double-dates and tandem holidays and I...

I couldn't do it. Because even if by some miracle she didn't join the dots as to how I felt about her like Mikey did in about three seconds flat, she'd know that I'd been hiding something huge from her. Plus—and honestly, this was the most important reason—it was so good to see her smiling

165

and being happy about my company again. I didn't want to ruin that; it could wait.

My heart sinking, I left it as 'men' and clicked *'make me discoverable'*. Maybe I could just go on a few casual dates with guys while I was trying to figure out what I needed to do about Sarah.

CHAPTER FOURTEEN

Sarah's promise that she'd found a way to 'maximise' my matches turned out not to just be vernacular: she'd actually found a formula that maximised the likelihood of a match based on your selection range, theirs, and whether you liked or super-liked them, and a whole bunch of similar variables. It was like I'd struck gold!

"How did you find this?" I asked her, a smile breaking out on my face as I looked up from my phone at her. "This is great!"

She was *beaming* at me; it was such a relief. "Told you I'd found something I thought you'd be interested in!"

She wasn't wrong. It made the whole looking-for-men-on-Tinder thing seem a little less of an exercise in pulling teeth, because at least if I had to pretend I wanted to date a man, I could test the formula and see how accurate it was.

I'd gone to grab a pen and paper so I could sit at the table to deconstruct it, and by the time I finished and went to go sit back on the couch, Sarah had dozed off. I sat down very slowly and carefully so I wouldn't move the couch and wake her. Then, while she wasn't looking, I stared at my Tinder profile page while I fantasized about being the sort of person who had the courage to walk into Chez Phillipe and apologise to Mikey.

I was nearly asleep myself by the time Rob came home. He always made a genuine effort to be really quiet, but that was like a bull making a genuine attempt to be quiet and delicate in a china shop. Even his tip-toeing sounded like stomping.

He came striding into the living room with a big smile across his face and opened his mouth to declare something—but he didn't get that far because he saw me making frantic, desperate gestures at sleeping Sarah. He looked charmed by the fact she'd fallen asleep.

"She's been doing that a lot lately," he told in the loudest whisper I'd ever heard. "Must be tiring making a whole other person!"

I would have replied to him, but I was a bit distracted by the fact he was holding a takeaway coffee cup; he'd made the noble declaration he'd stay off booze and caffeine and whatever Sarah had decided she wasn't going to have while she was pregnant. It looked like he was cheating, and that was unlike him.

He saw where I was looking. "Oh! Oh, yeah." He held it up. "It's not coffee, don't worry. There's this new age natural food shop place near where the work site is. It's not really my thing, but one of the other blokes' wives reckons this is the best milkshake in Sydney, and it's full of vitamins, too. I thought Sares might like to try it."

I was about to suggest he put it in the fridge for her when she miraculously stirred. "Milkshake...?" Rob and I laughed; and she must have been fast asleep because she seemed a bit confused about the fact I was there for a second. Then, her face lit up..

Seeing that, for just a moment part of me was glad I was here instead of sleeping with Mikey.

Sarah only had a few mouthfuls of her vitamin milkshake—"I'll give it an 8/10, but Rob's getting a 10 for effort."—before she put the rest in the fridge for tomorrow, and then wandered out of the kitchen, yawning and stretching. "I'm sorry to bail on you in your quest for love, Gem, but I can hardly keep my eyes open."

Honestly, I was kind of relieved I didn't need to pick out boys tonight. I didn't have much energy left to pretend I cared about anything except the formula. "Maybe another night."

"Definitely," she told me, and then gave me a big, long hug and practically had a snooze on my shoulder. Over hers, I could see Rob watching her adoringly and not batting an eyelid at all about the fact his heavily pregnant girlfriend was being cuddled by someone else. I wondered if that would change if he found out I wasn't straight.

After we'd all had a brief fight about how I'd get home, I eventually won and announced I would walk home like I always did. Sarah showed me to the door in consolation. There, she gave me another long hug; her belly was pushing into my stomach and making it hard for me to breathe.

"I'm glad you came over," she murmured peacefully. "I feel better."

"Me too," I told her, ignoring an unsettled feeling in my stomach.

She gave me a kiss on the cheek and then shuffled back inside.

As I walked down her front stairs, I could hear Rob's booming voice saying, "I made $2k this week, look! Maybe we can afford that whiz-bang bassinet for her after all?"

"She's not going to care what she sleeps in, Rob," I heard Sarah tell him, amusement audible in her otherwise tired voice. Then, there was a pronounced silence while they were probably kissing. It was such a domestic conversation to overhear, and it made me feel uncomfortable all the way home.

I almost didn't want to *go* home. I briefly had an idea that I'd drop past the main street and buy myself something first— what, I didn't know; I wasn't hungry, and it was too late for coffee. There was no reason to go anywhere else and I couldn't come up with one, so I just went straight home and let myself back into my flat.

Apart from the fact my walls were bare of photos, it looked the same. Eerily the same; as if I'd never brought a girl I was super into home. The memory of Mikey and I openly pashing against my kitchen bench was so far away it felt like I might have just imagined it. It felt surreal.

Maybe it's for the best that it didn't work out with Mikey, I thought as I kicked off my Ugg Boots, reflecting on how I couldn't tell Sarah or Rob I was gay yet. I would have needed to lie about Mikey, or keep coming up with some reason why I wasn't available when Sarah invited me for things. That wasn't fair on anyone.

I was just putting on my pyjamas and getting ready for bed when my phone buzzed.

My heart lifted; maybe it was Mikey after all?! I rushed to dig it out of my handbag.

It wasn't, though. It was Sarah. *"Hope you got home okay :) xx"*

That would normally make me smile; it was nice to know she was thinking about me. Right now, though, it didn't. I felt oddly numb. I didn't want her to worry, though, so I texted back, *"I did <3"* and then finished getting ready for bed.

Then, I lay down all by myself and tried to sleep.

That didn't go as planned, so the next morning when I arrived bleary-eyed, half-awake and with five seconds to spare at the train station, I almost didn't hear my name being called. I spun around, searching through the crowd.

Sarah was standing there in the middle of it—looking beautiful like she always did, even at 7:30am—with a hopeful smile and two jumbo takeaway cups. She waved when I saw her, click-clicking over to me in her Jimmy Choos to give me a loose hug and hand me my enormous coffee. "You look like you could use it."

That was understatement of the year. *"Thanks!"*

She smiled brightly; it wasn't until I looked closely at her that I realised how much concealer she had under her eyes. I wasn't sure if I felt comforted or terrible that she hadn't slept well, either.

At least with her pregnant belly people stood up for us so we could both get some seats. She was yawning as she sat down. "Sorry I crashed on you last night. Did you get any interesting matches yet, though? Anyone cute?"

I grimaced. About that... "I was actually working out the formula last night. I haven't swiped anyone yet."

"Oh," she said, and then looked hopeful again. "Well, you want to start now? It's a long trip in after all. We could do it together." I really didn't, and it must have showed in my face, because her smile faltered. "Only if you want to, though, it's completely up to you..."

Her hesitation was the final nail in the coffin. I took out my phone. "No, now's good. Let's do it."

She looked a bit surprised—maybe she hadn't been expecting me to just dive in like that?—but got into it with me, anyway.

We sat together for the whole ride with the formula up on Sarah's phone and Tinder on mine, swiping according to the instructions, even on the profiles that didn't have photos, and by the time we made it into Circular Quay, I'd reached the 12-hour swipe right limit. I'd also had a few matches, but it looked like the men I'd matched with weren't that chatty at 8am. Well, at least we'd have *something* in common...

As soon as I got up to my desk at work, I glanced furtively around me to make sure no one was looking, and then got my phone out to record the number of matches I already had. I figured I could chart how I went on a day-by-day basis and report back on the formula, maybe even fix it. I was scrolling through them when a message came through.

I stared at my phone. I couldn't deal with this while I was half-awake. However, because I'd always been a sucker for punishment, I found myself opening it anyway.

"*Hey there, gorgeous,*" it began, a universally cocky and not very convincing opener. What came next was *way* worse, though. "*Don't you work for Frost too? Risk, right? Wanna do lunch today? Or maybe dinner and breakfast perhaps...? ;)*"

My jaw *dropped*.

Shit! I felt like dropping to the floor myself, as if someone was firing at me. I looked frantically around me—was he on this

170

floor? I didn't recognise him from his photo!—and then with shaking hands, I opened up my profile and immediately disabled all of my pictures.

I couldn't do much more than that, though, because Spud and all my other cohorts then showed up for work and I had to hurriedly stow my phone in my drawer.

While I was pretending to work and worrying about that guy who'd matched with me lurking around, someone frisbeed a folded piece of paper to me. It landed beside my arm on my desk, so I picked it up; it was a printout of an agenda.

"The MEU doesn't want us circulating work emails with information about union business," Spud explained. "It's for tomorrow's meeting, I printed it for you. You're still coming, right?"

Well, it wasn't like I had much of a choice. I forced a smile. "Sure."

He mirrored my smile and nodded as he sat down at his own desk. "Awesome. Everyone's going to be there."

I realised 'everyone' now not only meant Natalie Heiser, the Scariest Woman on the Planet, but also this mystery guy who I'd matched with and, from his overly confident opening text, he was probably the sort of guy who'd feel free to just wander up to me and try to initiate a conversation. Fabulous. This was going to be a *great* meeting.

At lunchtime, I showed Sarah the profile of the guy who'd recognised me to see if she knew him. Her eyebrows rose immediately. "Wow, yeah, that's Nate from Marketing, actually." At my horrified expression, she put a comforting hand on my arm. "If you're not interested, just tell him. I doubt he'll take it personally."

Marketing?! Of all the departments for him to be from! I was going to be *working* with him! "But what if he does?!"

She shrugged, arranging her sandwich so she could take a bite. "You work in Risk, he works in Marketing. I wouldn't worry about it. Just tell him you don't want to date someone from work because it's against policy or something."

"Arriving really late is against policy, too, but everyone knows I do that all the time!"

She chuckled and reached across the table to put a heavy hand on my shoulder. "I promise it'll be okay, Gem. Guys who use Tinder are used to rejection. Just be nice about it."

I couldn't bring myself to message him straight away, though. First, I needed to sweat about it all day at work and worry about it all the way home, imagining the Worst Case Scenario where he somehow accosted me in front of everyone and publicly humiliated me. Those Marketing boys were *shameless*.

"*They're not shameless at all,*" Sarah promised me while I was texting her in the evening over a very big glass of sav blanc. "*They're actually completely obsessed with what people think of them. As long as you don't hurt their egos, though, they're pretty harmless. Just be really nice.*"

Sarah helped me compose a text: that he was very nice and probably a great guy, but that I couldn't possibly date someone from work because it's against policy, but thanks for his interest. I sent it.

I didn't get a reply that evening—which meant another night with precious little sleep—but there was one waiting for me in the morning when I woke up. I could barely bring myself to open it because I expected the worst. When I finally did, though, Sarah turned out to be right: he thanked me for being honest, told me I was totally gorgeous and then slipped in a joke about hoping he'd *'hear some news at the union meeting this morning that'd be good for both of us ;)'*. It took me a couple of seconds to realise that he meant he hoped he'd be made redundant so that he could date me, which was a pretty cheeky thing to say, but it was clearly all in good humour.

At the train station, I gave Sarah my phone so she could read it while I drank my jumbo coffee.

She chuckled at his joke and then flipped back to his photos, considering him. "You sure you don't want to date him? I mean, he gets around a bit but he's cute."

And a man, I thought. "Very sure."

She smiled at that. "Okay, then. You shouldn't date people you're not interested in," she told me, and then gave the phone back to me so I could unmatch him and then focus on my next enormous problem: this union meeting.

"Do you think he'll be at the meeting, though?" I wondered aloud as we walked into the atrium at Frost HQ.

She shrugged. "Marketing doesn't need to be there," she said, "but he doesn't need to be at my budget meeting this morning, so I don't know what he'll do."

With *my* luck, he'd be waiting for me at the door. Great. What a great week this had been for me.

While we were waiting for a lift, I was busy feeling sorry for myself over everything and stressing about what was going to happen at the union meeting, when the basement lift from the employee carpark opened across from us.

There were only two people in it: Henry and Natalie Heiser, and they were in the middle of a friendly discussion.

Natalie. My blood ran cold; I practically had traumatic flashbacks to when she'd singled me out in the restaurant. I was trying to manage those when Sarah just about gave me a heart attack by suddenly grabbing my arm. I didn't understand straight away why she'd be freaking out—Sarah wasn't afraid of anyone!—until I realised she wasn't freaking out like I was, she was freaking out about something she'd realised.

"It's an *employee* carpark!" she whispered frantically to me. "Natalie's a union rep, Henry's the employee!"

I was too full of adrenaline to think properly. "So?"

"So if she's in the employee carpark, it's because she came in Henry's car!" Sarah whispered frantically in my ear, straightening when the two of them took a step out of the lift towards us.

As they did, Natalie's eyes landed *right* on me.

CHAPTER FIFTEEN

Even though she wasn't wearing that bright red dress I'd first met her in, Natalie stood out. Not that she could avoid standing out anyway—she was a head taller than everyone else in the atrium, bar Henry—but today, she'd complimented her exceptionally appropriate dress suit with the brightest, reddest lipstick I'd ever seen. Just that tiny touch of colour against the monochrome of suits drew everyone's eyes to her. The way she held herself, she clearly knew it.

I couldn't look away, either. I was genuinely certain I was about to be eaten alive.

"Well, well, look who it is," she said as she sauntered up to me and Sarah. She paused for a moment in front of me, leaning on one full hip with a theatrically thoughtful expression. I didn't know what was going on and my life was practically flashing before my eyes until she pointed at me and said, "Gemma Rowe." Looking very pleased with herself for remembering, she then pointed at Sarah. "And Sarah Presti."

Not suffering from my Natalie-induced paralysis, Sarah played along, tapping her chin as she pretended to try and remember Natalie's name. After a moment, she shrugged. "Nope," she said with a grin. "It's not coming to me..."

Natalie laughed once. "Well, you're in luck, Ms Presti," she told Sarah, reaching into her handbag and retrieving a couple of red business cards that I recognised from Min's computer screen. "Look at what your ex-coworker just had his ex-boyfriend deliver to me."

She passed one to Sarah, who accepted it with interest. "Huh. I didn't know he was actually serious about making these, they look great."

"Don't they?" Natalie agreed, admiring the one in her hands for a moment. "He's an excellent graphic designer. What Frost did to him was criminal; quite literally, if I have anything to do with it." Then, she turned back to me. I gulped.

She'd been looking at me for what I thought was an uncomfortably long period of time before I realised at the last possible second that she was trying to hand me a card as well, and I'd been staring at her lipstick instead of looking down at her hand. Then, instead of laughing it off and accepting the card like a normal person, I panicked, froze and just stood there, dumbly staring up at her.

She looked amused. Taking a leisurely step forward, she tucked the card in my breast pocket, like I was a 5-year-old being given big-girl money for a bus fare.

Henry and Sarah chuckled—good-naturedly, probably—but it felt like everyone was laughing at me for being such an awkward loser, and I'm sure my entire face was the same colour as the card in my pocket. Why was I like this?! Why didn't I just take the damn card?!

It didn't end there. She kept looking at me. "So, are you coming to the union meeting this morning, Gemma?"

I couldn't speak. I kept waiting for Sarah to finally rescue me like she always did, but the lifeline never came. When I glanced over at her to see why not, she was beaming back at me with a proud smile that said, 'Look! I'm letting you speak for yourself!'.

Oh, no. This was the *worst* possible time in my entire life for her to leave me floundering! My face was hot, my throat was practically swollen shut, and I had Natalie's laser eyes boring holes into my skull. I looked like a total idiot in front of both Henry and Natalie.

In the end, Henry was the one who rescued me. "Perhaps she has something else on? Not everyone's going to be able to attend."

"Yeah," Sarah agreed. "I have a budget meeting at ten."

Natalie momentarily released me from her clutches to frown at Sarah. "Aren't you a team leader? Reschedule it. This is important."

Sarah took exception to that. I could see the corners of her mouth harden. "It's actually not that easy to get a time when everyone's available."

"So you pick a time when *no one* should be available?" she asked casually while I panicked about the fact this was turning into an argument in the middle of the foyer. Natalie just... wow. She just went straight for Sarah's jugular. "Besides, I'm sure Gemma would appreciate having someone there to support her when she hears the bad news. Right, Gemma?"

Everyone looked at me.

I was sweating. I wanted to defend Sarah—because, *gosh*, her expression right now—but I was worried about what Natalie would say if I sided with Sarah. She obviously had no qualms about tearing people apart in public; she was like a wrecking ball.

Henry moved in to defuse the situation again. "Gemma's entire team will be there, I'm sure they'll support each other," he said pleasantly, and then took a step towards me. "Now, if you all don't mind, I'd like to have a private word with Gemma for a moment."

Natalie put her hands on her hips and asked him very bluntly, "Do you actually need to speak to her, Henry, or is that your subtle way of telling me to shut up?"

He had a calm smile on his face, but he looked her dead in the eyes. "Do you really want me to answer that, Natalie?"

I was 100% certain I was about to be collateral damage in a huge fight between them. It was like a battle of the Titans right here in the foyer with them facing off, but instead of going off at him and tearing him to shreds like I was sure she would, she just smiled and backed down. She maybe even looked impressed. "*Fine*," she said, and then turned that sharp smile on both of us like she hadn't just been guilt-tripping Sarah. "Pleasure to see you both again. And see *you* at the meeting," she said pointedly to me before she left.

Henry waited for her to go before turning back to us with a slight cringe. "She has your best interests at heart, I promise," he said somewhat apologetically. "She can just be a little confrontational."

That was a spectacular understatement; she was gone and I was *still* sweating. As if reading my mind, Sarah said sceptically, "'A little'? I feel like I've just faced a firing squad. Can't you find less 'confrontational' people to hang out with, Henry? Someone *nice*?"

He laughed and avoided the question. "If your job was on the line, Sarah, 'nice' isn't what you'd want to represent you, believe me," he said. "Don't worry about moving your meeting, though. I'm not sure what information they plan to disclose at this union thing this morning, but I doubt it's going to resemble the actual facts."

Sarah didn't look very convinced. She turned to me, her fingers touching my arm. "Be honest: should I come with you this morning? I *could* ditch the budget meeting, I guess…"

Honestly? I would have liked nothing more than for her to be there—especially since after bumping into Natalie this morning, the prospect of coming face-to-face with her again while I was alone and defenseless was now exponentially more terrifying. I'd feel so much better with Sarah sitting beside me. I didn't want to get her in trouble, though, because her career was really important to her. A Lead ditching a budget update to go to a union meeting didn't look that great, did it? "No, it's okay."

She took a breath and nodded. "Okay," she said, sounding relieved. "Well, good luck, then. I'll see you at lunch—you can tell me all about the meeting and then we can go over your matches together."

I nodded. She gave me a brief hug and then stepped into a lift, leaving me with Henry.

He watched her go. "Matches?" he asked once she'd gone.

I grimaced. "On Tinder."

His eyebrows lifted. "*Oh*," he said, and then laughed. "I had a mental image of you and Sarah reviewing footage of you playing tennis or something similar. How are you finding it?"

"Tinder?" He nodded. I wasn't sure how to answer him, because despite how stressful it was, I'd been really enjoying it a couple of nights ago until I'd screwed everything up with Mikey. As if I could say that, though. "Fine, I guess."

He nodded slowly and looked like he really wanted to ask more questions—I wondered if Min had said something to him?—but he let it go. "Anyway," he said, taking a brief moment to glance around us to make sure there was no one in earshot. "I just wanted to let you know that I spoke with Anil yesterday and he's very happy for you to be released for that Marketing secondment. I haven't spoken with Omar, yet—I'll do that today—but I don't expect he'll have a different answer for me."

I brightened. I'd nearly forgotten about all that! Suddenly, I felt like smiling again.

Henry reacted to my smile with one of his own. "You know, Anil had some really nice things to say about you."

I my smile dropped. "*Seriously*?" Nice things to say about chronically late, eternally forgetful and hopeless me?

He nodded. "He said you're very talented, but that he thinks you might be a little bored in your current role. Which is why he's happy to release you, I'm sure." He patted my shoulder. "Anyway, thank you for not saying anything to anyone. Only a few more days and Anil will announce it, I promise."

He gave me a professional smile and then we both got into the lift and went to our respective floors. The first thing I did when I got to level 22 was retreat into the women's toilets so I could lean heavily against the vanity and recover from Natalie. Seriously, Henry had only just helped me escape from her and I was planning to put myself through all that again?!

Maybe I shouldn't go after all, I thought, staring at my pale face in the mirror. *If I'm going to end up in Marketing it's not like I need to hear about what's going to happen to my current job...*

"That's *if* they even decide to hire you up there, Gemma," I reminded my reflection. "It's a secondment, not a job offer." And what if I didn't actually like it up in Marketing?

I scoffed at myself as soon as I'd thought that; as if I wouldn't like it! Sarah and I *always* had fun together! I mean, I'd have to navigate all of those alpha men, including that guy Nate from Tinder, and Jason, Min's bitter ex-boss, and *Diane Frost,* Co-CEO who was always heavily involved with everything to do with Marketing... Gosh, when I put it like that... Maybe this union meeting *was* the right place for me, after all. Did I really want to work full-time in a department that had all those people in it?

All those people and Sarah, I reminded myself. Sarah would look after me, she always had.

I felt uneasy. Well, whether the union meeting was the right place for me or not; realistically, I couldn't ditch it without upsetting a bunch of people anyway. I'd just have to deal with being in the same room as Natalie again.

As it turned out, all my irrational fears about Natalie cornering me and mercilessly tearing me to shreds in front of everyone the second I entered that auditorium were exactly that: irrational. When Spud led us all down to the union meeting, she was already up the front at the lectern and preoccupied with reading something on her phone.

Everyone from Risk sat up the back, grumbling. "How much can the unions *really* do?" someone asked. "It's *Frost.* Frost owns like half of the world."

"Maybe they'll get us more time, though," Spud pointed out. "They dragged out the desalination dispute for years before they finally lost. It's my 19th wedding anniversary this weekend, and I promised for the 20th I'd take the wife on a big cruise. This year I'm too scared to take her to anything more than a fancy restaurant."

I wasn't really interested in their speculation about how long the dispute could drag out, so I mostly tuned out and wondered what Natalie was doing on her phone before she shushed us all and started speaking.

"I know you're all nervous about what you're going to hear today," she told us, wandering away from the lectern and into the centre of the stage. "But let me tell you that no matter what we've uncovered and no matter what Frost tries to do: the MEU is with you, and we're here to *fight* for you."

She was quite a good speaker, I thought; charismatic, animated and interesting—all the things I'd always sort of wished I was instead of awkward and hopeless. The men in the audience were certainly watching with rapt attention, but I wasn't naïve enough to think that was only because she was a good speaker. She looked *really* nice in that dress suit; it accentuated her figure.

I was just sort of idly half-admiring, half-being jealous of the definition in her calves and thighs when I noticed what I was doing.

I'm checking her out, I realised like I was having an epiphany. I suddenly understood why Henry seemed pretty keen on her even if she was terrifying: she was *hot*.

When everyone suddenly stuck their hands up in the air I realised I hadn't been listening at all, so I stuck mine up quickly so I didn't look out of place.

A unanimous show of hands made Natalie flash her perfect teeth in a big smile. "*Excellent*," she said like she meant it. "We'll figure out the most disruptive time to go on strike and then we'll let you all know!"

Oh. I looked around me at all the men giving each other high-fives and cheering. I think I'd just agreed to strike. So that's what the meeting had been about...

After it had finished, everyone was in a much better mood, despite the fact the MEU apparently hadn't given us much more information about who was going to lose their jobs. The boys from Risk all went to lunch to pick over the contents of the meeting at some flash new popular restaurant Spud recommended and they invited me too, but I declined. I didn't want to be late to meet up with Sarah.

When I spotted her waiting in the atrium, she looked really stressed out. She rushed over to me as soon as she saw me, her heels clicking on the tiles. "Are you okay?" she asked, grabbing my forearms and looking me up and down.

It was downright weird to see her so worried; normally if she knew I'd be trapped in a room with someone who made me uncomfortable, she'd just tease me about it. This was new. "It was fine, Sare."

She didn't look convinced. "I should have come," she said with conviction. "As much as I hate to say it, that Natalie was right, I should have. As soon as I walked into my meeting, I was like, 'Sare, why are you doing this?' and then for the whole of the damn budget meeting I was off with the fairies because all I could think of was that Kraken eating you alive, or you hearing terrible news about your job, or something like that, and all I could think of was *my* agenda, and *my*—"

"Sare, it's fine, I—"

"No, seriously. Hear me out. I've been avoiding union stuff because I was pretty closely associated with all the drama that went down with Min at the beginning of the year and I was selfishly thinking of myself and my career instead of my *best friend*, and—"

"Sarah!" I said, grabbing *her* forearms. "It was *fine*, she didn't even look at me! We voted to strike or something, but otherwise nothing happened."

For a moment, I don't think she believed me. She watched me very carefully, and then when I nodded in confirmation, she finally relaxed. "Huh," she said, considering that. "A back-office strike? That'll suck. I hope it's not at a time that impacts the massive project I'm running. When is it?"

I shrugged. "They haven't decided yet."

"Well, keep me posted," she said, and then exhaled. After a moment, she laughed at herself. "Oh my god, Gem. I've been so worried about you and what Natalie might do to you. I'm ridiculous. Of course nothing happened." She slung an arm around my shoulder and led me out of the atrium to have lunch.

We ate at Subway—Sarah had apparently been craving the double chocolate cookies for days—and then we went over my matches as promised. Without photos, I actually got hardly any. The ones I got opened up every chat with, "*pics???*" It was disappointing.

"Someone should tell the Tinder-formula people that their formula is missing a variable," I said dryly, unmatching all the men who'd rudely demanded pics. I wasn't interested in people like that. The trouble was, there wasn't much to choose from. There was *one* message from a guy who'd at least opened with '*hey there!*', but when I tapped through to his profile, I found myself eye-to-eye (so to speak) with a large, HD-quality dick pic in all its glory.

Sarah nearly spat out her cookie. "Oh my god!" she angled my phone so she could see it better.

"Charming," I said, not that impressed.

Sarah wasn't, either. "I don't know why they all think we'd like that," she told me, zooming in on it anyway like it was a lab specimen. "Dicks are so weird-looking. Rob sent me a shot of his once and I was like, 'thanks but no thanks, it's better in person'."

I made a face. I did *not* need to know that. "That is *too much information*."

She laughed at my expression. "At least I knew whose dick it was when it arrived in my inbox!" she pointed out, and then gestured at Frost HQ above us. "That mysterious dick could belong to anyone in this building, and you'd never know who."

That was a kind of disturbing thought. "They know who I am, though."

"You removed all your pictures," Sarah pointed out. "That's why no one's talking to you anymore."

"Yeah, but 'Gemma' isn't exactly a common name, even without them."

She considered that, picking out a chocolate chip and eating it. "I've always thought it's kind of weird Tinder forces you to use real names. At least mine is 'Sarah', I guess. Like half of Australia." She thought for a moment, and then shrugged. "Just disable your profile when you're close by work, maybe? That way you can keep everything the same and keep your photos up without worrying."

"Too late. I've already been propositioned by people who work for you."

Sarah laughed. "If it's worrying you *that* much—and I get it, matching with Nate is kind of close to home—you could just set up a fake Facebook and make a new Tinder account. But seriously, I think the best thing to do is just turn Tinder discovery off when you're in range of work, that way you can leave your name and photos and stuff all the same. You'll get more matches that way, trust me."

As much as Sarah was quite possibly right about leaving everything the same, after that whole Nate thing *and* the unheralded dick pic, there was definitely no chance in hell I was leaving my Tinder profile as it was.

On the train on the way home I set up a dummy Facebook account (and after some deliberation, I chose the name 'Kate' because I'd always kind of liked the idea of being a Kate), and then copied most of my description across from my other Tinder profile, but added, "*If the first thing you do is ask me for pics, we're probably not going to get along*'. Then, I deleted it. It sounded rude. Besides, it was kind of a good filter, wasn't it? Men who asked for pics right up were clearly only after one thing, and since we'd established I was hopeless around men who wanted to straight-up screw me, it was better to screen them out from the start.

As soon as I got home, I set up my tablet and swiped according to the formula (I was probably going to have to make some small adjustments to it to factor in my profile with no images, since that clearly impacted on my ability to maximise my matches), jokingly texted Sarah that her best friend's name was now 'Kate' and then went to have a shower.

While I was getting undressed, I felt something sharp poke me in the chest and remembered Natalie's business card was in my breast pocket. I fished it out and spent a second reading it and thinking about her lipstick before I stuck it to my fridge with a magnet and went to have my shower. It might come in handy one day if I ever needed a lawyer.

By the time I'd washed up and climbed into my PJs, Sarah had replied. *"The whole house voted and we prefer 'Gemma'. Plus what am I going to do about this tattoo if you change your name? ;)"* She didn't have a tattoo, she was just being silly. I laughed anyway, and had sat down to think about something witty to reply to that when I realised I was smiling.

This was fun. It was like it *used* to be between us: so easy and comfortable, and all because I was back to dating guys again.

Maybe it won't be so bad dating guys? I wondered, briefly reflecting on my previous relationships. My immediate thought was that none of them held a candle to Sarah or Mikey, and I'd known Mikey for what, three days? Still, maybe I'd find someone nice and then I could sort of see how it went. A mediocre relationship would probably be worth it if it meant that everything between me and Sarah went back to normal again. Heaven knows I'd been royally screwing everything up with her while I was trying to date girls...

I was chewing my lip and trying to think of something funny to reply to Sarah so I'd make her smile too, when I matched with a 'Stephen'.

I was tempted to ignore that and finish replying to Sarah, but despite being wholly uninterested in whoever Stephen was, I figured I should probably check it and at least record his stats so I could start repairing the formula.

Interestingly, when I opened his profile, he didn't have pics either, so I checked his age because my range was set kind of broadly. He was only in his early 30s. That wasn't *too* bad; he was older than me, but there had been an age gap of several years between me and Mikey as well, and it had been absolutely perfect anyway.

I was just scribbling all his details down on an envelope (I wasn't sure which stats would be important for the formula yet, so it was better to record them all) when he messaged me. *"Good evening :)"*

Huh. I considered that. It was kind of a bland opener, but it certainly beat sending a graphic shot of his erect penis or demanding pictures of me. I decided it deserved a reply. *"Hey! :)"*

I waited for a little while for him to respond to that while I checked his profile. *'Brand new to this!'* it read. *'Old-fashioned man looking for a nice woman for friendship or perhaps more :)'*, and that was it.

I stared at it. What did he mean by 'old-fashioned'? Like, women-belong-in-the-kitchen old-fashioned, or I-won't-try-to-screw-you-on-the-first-date old-fashioned? I hoped the latter.

Hmm. Well, maybe he'd do, at least for some time while I figured out how I was going to tell Sarah I liked girls. Because as much as every part of me didn't ever want to do that, I probably needed to get onto that soon or I was going to ruin our entire friendship while I was, ironically, trying not to ruin our entire friendship.

Yeah, I might as well talk to this guy. What did I have to lose? Chances were me and him wouldn't even hit it off anyway and I'd just end up with something to discuss with Sarah in the morning.

I took a deep breath and tapped 'reply'. *"So, what do you do, Stephen? :)"*

CHAPTER SIXTEEN

If I'd expected to stay up all night chatting to Stephen like I did with Mikey, I was sorely mistaken.

I assumed we'd go through all the usual get-to-know-you stuff: the basics of what sort of people we were, what our jobs were, what our hobbies were, all that. But that wasn't what happened at all. I had a brief conversation with him in which I basically learnt absolutely nothing of substance—such a change from talking to Mikey, because she'd been so open—and then we had this patchy conversation where he replied every ten or fifteen minutes and then later at around 10:30pm he apologised about needing to get back to work and just stopped responding.

I frowned at my phone. What kind of 'professional' job (that was all he would say) had him working this late at night?

When I went around to Sarah's on Saturday morning to brainstorm the answer, she had a million suggestions for me. "Maybe he's a hospital doctor?" she offered while she and Min were seated at the dining table with their heads together over some materials for her big project. "Or an air traffic controller? Or some sort of rostered engineer or something?"

"Maybe," I said vaguely, not convinced. None of those seemed like a good fit.

"Or a police officer? Or a lab tech? Or—"

"Okay, you've made your point," I told her from the couch, sighing and reading over his messages again. Maybe he'd hinted at it?

Min didn't look up from her screen. She'd given me a very pointed look when I'd told them about Stephen but had otherwise reserved her judgement on the fact I was intending to date guys again. She had something to say about this issue, though. "I know this is kind of harsh, but did you maybe consider he was just making an excuse to stop talking to you? If he was taking ages to reply, maybe he was talking to lots of other women."

I appreciated her concern, but I didn't think that was it. "No, he seemed really polite and pretty keen to chat... just distracted. And he was apologetic about needing to go," I said. "Plus, he obviously wants to keep his job a secret, so it's got to be something a bit embarrassing or a bit shady, don't you reckon? So what's a bit embarrassing to talk about that has you working late at night?"

I shouldn't have asked it like that. "Maybe he's a stripper," Sarah suggested with a smirk. At my aghast expression, she took it a step further. "Or a *private* stripper, if you get what I mean. Hey, at least he'll be good in bed, right?"

I recovered from mental images of gold G-strings and baby oil. "Yeah, thanks for your valuable input, Sarah."

She made pistol fingers at me and then went back to watching Min work. "You're welcome. It's probably something really benign, though. Maybe he's an accountant or something and he's worried if you find out he's really boring you won't be interested?"

"Maybe," I said doubtfully. "Do accountants work that late, though?"

"They do if they work for Frost," Min pointed out, "or for themselves." She made a frustrated noise and sat back, running her fingers through her hair, irritated. "Exhibit A," she said, gesturing to herself. "I work for Frost and myself, and I feel like I've done nothing but these fucking brochures for 24 hours straight. What is sleep? Who knows. When I close my eyes, I just see emails telling me to change things completely."

Sarah slung an arm around her shoulders and gave her a hug. "Not much longer. I just need to get these designs to Admin on Monday so we can ship the brochures out and have them ready for when the ad campaign goes live in two weeks."

"Your ad campaign would be fine *without* brochures," Min informed her. "I've been on projects where we didn't do print material and still exceeded our sales targets."

Sarah shrugged. "Yeah, but this is my first project as Lead, and everything has to be by the book. If I screw this up, I can kiss my career at Frost goodbye. I'll be stuck as an entry-level Marketing clerk for eternity."

Min ran her hands over her face for a moment. "Wow. No pressure, though, right?" she said miserably, and then got back to work.

I was scouring the Tinder messages from last night for clues about Stephen's profession when Bree, who was trying to teach Rob how to cook so he'd be a good housewife for Sarah once the baby was born, leant out of the kitchen. "I had an idea!" she announced. "Maybe this Stephen guy is a celebrity? Or someone famous? That's why doesn't want you to guess anything about him!"

Hah. That was a pretty nice idea, but, "With *my* luck? That's *way* too good to be true."

Bree shrugged. "Well, it might be something like that?" She was fanning the air with an oven mitt. I realised I could smell smoke. "Anyway, lunch is going to be a bit late because Rob burnt the kebabs. Like *really* burnt them, don't worry if you hear the smoke alarm. So we're having noodles instead."

By the time they'd finished those and ferried the bowls out to us at the table, I was still no closer to solving the Stephen mystery.

"Maybe he just hates the internet," Rob suggested, insisting on eating his own charred kebabs. "I hate talking by text message, it takes too bloody long to type all the letters. I'd much rather pick up the phone and talk if I want to know something."

Min swallowed her mouthful. "Or, perhaps there is no big secret after all, and he's just really private? Not everyone wants to tell strangers on the internet everything about their lives." She put her fork down and frowned at me. "Anyway, why does it matter so much? Is a guy you've talked to for an aggregate 15 minutes worth spending all this energy on?"

I was about to say that I was just curious, when Sarah answered instead. "Because he's a *puzzle*," she told Min, grinning. "And Gemma loves to solve puzzles, it's her MO." She looked at me. "Speaking of solving things, how's that Tinder formula you're trying to fix coming along? Finished yet?"

I laughed once. Spoken like a true non-STEM person who didn't understand how experiments worked. "I need *way* more data before I can even think of trying to find patterns or averages in it. I'll probably need to get two weeks' worth at least."

Sarah looked really amused by that. "Well, you'd better not get too attached to the enigmatic Stephen then."

She had a point, and I *did* have a number of new matches and unread messages that I was ignoring. Since there was a lull in the conversation while everyone was eating, I opened them one by one, jotting their stats down on the back of a used envelope while I did. I was just working through them when I opened up what looked like a fairly innocuous profile and got another charming surprise: a guy holding a dead rabbit in one hand and a rifle in the other. *Ugh*.

I made a disgusted noise. I needed to add 'Vegetarian' to my profile. "*Why*?" I asked him rhetorically. "Why would you think someone would want to see that?"

Sarah dropped her fork immediately. "Is it another dick pic? Is it awful? Show me!"

Suddenly, everyone was interested in my phone until they saw what it *really* was. "I'd almost have preferred it was a dick pic," I said glumly, and then accepted my phone back after they'd passed it around.

"He looks okay, though," Rob pointed out. "He's not ugly or anything. And he's smiling. Maybe he just hasn't been around people who'll let him know that shooting animals for fun isn't right? His parents might be farmers."

"My mum was a farmer back in Serbia," Bree said primly. "And she didn't shoot animals for fun."

Sarah reached across and put a heavy hand on Rob's shoulder. "Rob, babe," she said, "I love you and I love that you think literally everyone is nice, but some people are *not* nice, and I doubt Gemma wants to hook up with a guy who shoots fluffy animals as a leisure activity."

"I don't," I said, just to make that perfectly clear, and then something occurred to me. "Wait, maybe *Stephen* is one of those 'not nice' people? What if I date him and find out he's as shady as he seems?"

"Then you'll get to add 'sadist' to your list of 'People Gem Has Dated Who Are Bad for Her'," Sarah said cheerfully, clearly not worried it was actually going to be the case.

Min sounded darker. "Don't sound so happy," she told Sarah. "Because let me tell you what it feels like to know your best friend is dating a *sadist*."

Sarah spluttered her noodles. "You mean Natalie?" She laughed. "They're probably just sleeping together, I wouldn't worry. I don't even know how well they get along, because Henry even had to apologise to us yesterday because of how rude she was. Didn't he, Gem?" She looked at me.

All this talk about Natalie reminded me of sitting in the auditorium yesterday and perving at her legs. I definitely didn't have anything useful to add to the conversation after that mental image, so I mutely nodded.

Min didn't look very comforted, though. "I just don't trust her," she muttered as an afterthought.

Sarah snorted. "Well, you can't hate her *that* much, you just did $1000 worth of graphics work on her cards for free."

"It wasn't for free, she insisted on paying me," Min corrected Sarah. "And Henry *does* seem to like her..."

"But you don't trust her," Sarah finished. Min's lips were pressed in a tight line. Her answer was clear.

I didn't think I had any concerns about her trustworthiness—she seemed pretty upfront to me—but I still didn't really want anything to do with her. She was everything that made me feel uncomfortable about people: confrontational, super confident, domineering...

But she has nice legs, I reminded myself, as if there were any legs in the world that were nice enough to compensate for the other things. Besides, Mikey had nice legs, too, and she was everything I liked in a person.

I sighed at length—it was too late to dwell on that now, though, wasn't it? I'd screwed it up with Mikey, and here I was with a phone full of men, sitting across the table from my female best friend whose equally nice legs were crossed at the ankle and in calf-length Ugg Boots.

While I was reflecting on the muddle of it all, my phone vibrated in my hands; I could see the Tinder flame in the notifications panel. I thought it was probably just one of those many matches I couldn't have cared less about, so I opened it.

It was *Stephen*. I leant forward towards the screen. *"Sorry to disappear on you last night, I just had a few things I needed to take care of* :)" he began. After all this talk about shady people, I found that a bit ominous. *"How are you?"*

"Suspicious as hell," I said aloud, and then looked up and realised I had four people staring at me. I went bright red. Whoops.

Sarah and Min glanced at each other. "I think that's one each," Sarah said with a grin. "What am I up to, 69?"

Min snorted. "Nice try. Thirty-something."

"Forty-nine," I corrected her. "And Stephen messaged me."

That got their attention. Sarah's eyes grew super wide and she made a 'continue' motion with her hand. *"Well?"*

"Well, he said he just had some 'things to take care of', last night."

Completely dead serious, Bree said, "Maybe he's an assassin. Those type of jobs really exist, you know."

Min gave her a weary look. "He's not an assassin."

Sarah was ignoring them and staring at me. "What are you waiting for? Ask him what 'those things' were!"

That seemed like a fair instruction, so I did. He replied, *"Boring, menial tasks. You wouldn't find them interesting* :)"

I read it out to everyone. They all looked at each other. "Okay, he sounds like he's hiding something," Rob agreed. "You should just straight up tell him he should tell you the truth."

Yeah, confrontation wasn't something I was a big fan of. "What if he's not, though? I can't just accuse him of lying." I tried to think of a non-aggressive way to phrase it. *"Would you mind telling me what you do for a living?"*

It didn't work. *"Only if you tell me first! Sorry, just not a big fan of sharing my details with strangers, that's all. There are a lot of people who aren't that happy with me at the moment."*

Curiouser and curiouser. Well, I wasn't saying anything if he wasn't. That wasn't fair. Plus, who were all these people who disliked him? This was *so weird*.

Before I could declare that I gave up and I had absolutely no idea what was going on with him, another message came through. *"But if you'd like to meet up for dinner tonight, perhaps I can tell you in person."*

Tonight??? I practically screeched. I needed *way* more time than six hours to mentally prepare myself to spend time alone *talking to a total stranger*!

Because I wasn't speaking, Sarah leant over to read my screen. She made the noise I nearly had. "Oh my god! Well, that settles it, you've totally got to go. It's killing me, you've got to find out what his deal is." She paused, looking a bit uncertain. "That is, if *you* want to..."

I definitely didn't want to, I wanted to hide under my bed. I gulped.

She saw it in my face. "Erm. Don't worry about it," she told me, and then pretended to dismiss the suggestion. "Ignore me, you know what I'm like about this stuff..."

It was how her smile suddenly faded that settled it for me; she'd been smiling so much while we'd been talking about it before. I took a deep breath. "No, I'll do it. I'll go."

She brightened immediately. "Oh my god, really?" She pumped her fists. "*Yes*! I'll help you dress up—I have tonnes of clothes that don't fit anymore that I've been thinking would really suit you. I'll do your makeup and everything, you're going to look so amazing you'll have him eating out of the palm of your hand, and he'll tell you whatever you want to know!" I sincerely doubted anything she could do to my appearance would counteract the fact I'd be a blushing, mumbling wreck, but I really appreciated her vote of confidence.

After we'd all finished lunch, Min immediately stood with her empty bowl. "Hey Gemma, you want to give me a hand with washing these up? It's the least we can do after being cooked a delicious meal." She looked directly at me, like *you'd better not say no*.

Uh oh. I definitely knew where this was going. I reluctantly followed her into the kitchen and as we put the empty bowls in Sarah's sink, Min double-checked we were alone and crossed her arms at me. "You want to tell me what's going on?"

I grimaced. I supposed pretending I didn't know what she was talking about was pointless, wasn't it? "I thought I'd give men another shot..."

"Did you," she said flatly. She didn't look very impressed.

"It never hurts to be sure, right?"

"It doesn't," she agreed, "when there is only one person involved." She spent a minute watching me while I felt like I might be about to get the third degree. I was almost bracing for it, but when she spoke, her voice was surprisingly mild. "Look, Gemma, I've been in a relationship with a man I wasn't attracted to before because I thought I could push past the fact I wasn't attracted to him. I couldn't, and we both got hurt."

Ouch. I understood those tightly crossed arms, now. "Well, don't worry, I won't lead Stephen on like that. It's just dinner. He might not even like me anyway."

Min didn't appear to think that was very likely. "Just be careful, okay?" Then, she gave me an impromptu hug.

Sarah interrupted us, entering the kitchen with a handful of dirty tea cups. She stopped in her tracks, smirked, and said as she passed us en route to the sink, "Careful, Gem, Stephen will get jealous."

Min gave me one last heavy look, and then pushed up the sleeves of her hoodie and got stuck into the dishes before she and Sarah got back to work for the afternoon.

I probably would have had plenty of time to go home and shower and maybe get some of my own clothes and makeup—

Min and Sarah worked on those brochures all day—but I thought since I was going to head up to Marketing shortly I should probably hang around and try and passively learn from watching them. Gosh, it was boring, though. The graphics stuff took so long. On the bright side, it gave me plenty of opportunity to agonise about all the things that could go wrong on this blind date I was about to voluntarily subject myself to.

By the time Min had declared she'd had enough of the 'fucking brochures', I'd already decided exactly what I thought would be the three worst (realistic) things that could happen: him shouting at me in public, him being loud and over-the-top like one of those scary men in Marketing, or him throwing himself at me so I had to spend the whole time we were having sex trying to figure out a polite and non-confrontational way to turn down the sex we were having. His wouldn't be the first bathroom window I'd climbed out of.

When I told Sarah those scenarios as she was picking out clothes for me to try on, she laughed. "Gem, I promise you that the worst thing that can happen is that you won't click," she said, holding out a black chemise. "What do you think?"

I shook my head. "Colour looks better on me. If I wear black, I look like I have no boobs."

She considered it. The no boobs problem was an alien concept to her. "Shouldn't you wear something formal, though? If a restaurant is listed as 'top floor', or wherever he said it was, it's going to be somewhere really nice."

I sighed; maybe she was right. I held my hand out. "Okay, let me try it on..." I could feel her eyes on me as I pulled off my t-shirt and buttoned the chemise closed across my front. I then presented myself.

She made a face, staring at my front. "Okay, you're right." Her eyes were twinkling.

I picked up one of the pillows from her bed and smacked at her with it. "Thanks so much, *friend*."

She shrieked and darted away. "Kidding! Kidding! It looks fine. And you know what? Some guys are into chicks with no—*help!*" I smacked her again.

She rounded the bed with surprising speed for someone who had a belly her size, a beautiful open smile on her face as she braced for me to chase her. I didn't, because I was suddenly struck by how much fun I was having.

This was the way Sarah and I always used to get ready for dates: laughing together, chatting, and dressing each other. Well, usually it was *Sarah* getting ready for her date, but this was nostalgic nonetheless. Everything felt so easy again, just like it always had; like I hadn't nearly fucked everything up by falling for my straight best friend. Tonight made me feel like I could put it all behind me, even if I did still have feelings for her.

Maybe I wasn't really attracted to men, but everything else about dating men was so much better. I was really glad I'd decided to do this.

After Sarah and I had chosen an outfit (colour after all, a turquoise dress she loved and couldn't wear anymore) paired with the black ballet flats I'd worn over, I sat still while she pampered me: straightening my hair, doing my makeup and painting my nails to match the dress. I would have been completely happy if my Saturday night had just been that: her dressing me up like a doll. I wished she could do it forever. Unfortunately, I kept needing to remind myself that this was all in preparation for me to meet a total stranger, by myself in a place I'd never been to. That ruined it a little.

When she was done, she took a few snaps of me on her phone—"So I can admire my handiwork!"—and then a selfie of us together, which she uploaded to Facebook immediately. We both looked gorgeous because she was so good at doing my makeup, and it was probably one of my favourite ever photos of us together.

I set it as my Facebook profile pic while she was driving me into the city, and then spent a little while staring at it. We both looked so happy.

My mood sank as we drove over the bridge, though. The Sydney skyscrapers loomed in the background and reminded me that I'd shortly leave Sarah's side and be in the cold company of someone I didn't know anything about. He could be anyone.

"I hope he's not dangerous," I told Sarah after we'd left the bridge and were sitting at traffic lights. "Like what if it's a trap or something? I don't know anything about him, he could kidnap me and get away with it."

Sarah gave me a wide-eyed look. "I bet nothing like that will happen, don't stress about it," she told me. Later when she was circling for a park, though, she added, "Can you text me ten minutes in and just let me know you're okay?"

I'd expected her to dismiss my anxious nonsense out of hand like she always did, and the fact she wasn't doing that at all made me worry even more. Gosh, anything could happen to me, couldn't it?

I almost didn't want to get out of the car when she'd found a park. "Maybe you should just drive me home," I said as we both peered up at the building that the restaurant was supposedly at the top of. It was really tall.

"It'll be fine," she told me, not committing to it. "And, look, I'll wait here until you've told me it's okay."

It was a No Standing zone. "You're going to get a ticket."

She looked across at me and gave me a faint smile. "Yeah. But it'll be worth it."

It felt so good to hear her speak like that about me, that I had to hug her. "Thanks," I said, holding her tightly for a moment. "Well, here I go, I guess..."

I got out of the car, waving goodbye to her and walking one foot in front of the other into the building. It was really swanky; marble everything, stainless steel fixtures and fresh flowers. There was even a doorman who opened the door for me.

The name of the restaurant was printed beside the top button on the lift—at least I knew I wasn't being lured into a drug den or something—so I took a deep breath and pressed it.

An older couple got into the lift with me halfway up, headed to the restaurant, too. The woman complimented my dress, and then asked, "Meeting someone special?"

I went red. "I hope so," I managed anyway.

They laughed good-naturedly and then got out before me when the lift arrived at the top floor. "I hope he's nice!" the woman told me as they approached the doorman.

The 'he' stood out to me in a way it never would have before; it was jarring. I wondered what this old couple would have thought if they'd seen me with Mikey? I was glad I didn't have to find out.

"Name?"

I snapped back to reality. The doorman was looking right at me. *OH GOSH.* "Um," I don't think Stephen had said what the booking was under? "Stephen, maybe? I don't know his surname."

The doorman gave me a very judgmental look, and then ran his finger down the screen in front of him. "We don't have a booking for anyone by that name."

I frowned. "Maybe it's under his surname?"

"We take both names for bookings. Is there someone else who might have used their name for the booking, instead…?"

No, I didn't think that was likely. I was just feeling deeply uncomfortable about what might be about to happen and worried that I *was* about to be in trouble, when I happened to look past the doorman and spot a man waiting just inside the door.

He was dressed to the nines in a very sharp suit, holding a big, expensive-looking bunch of flowers and sporting a warm smile. His eyes landed on me at the exact moment I recognised him, and his smile fell in an instant. He glanced self-consciously at the flowers in his hands.

It was Henry.

CHAPTER SEVENTEEN

"'*Kate*'?" Henry asked me, his voice straddling two octaves.

I gaped at him, frozen in place. So 'Stephen' wasn't a hospital doctor, or a male stripper, or a serial killer or any of those other things we'd wondered about: he was *Henry*. HR Manager Henry, Min's ex-boyfriend Henry, and out of the millions of people in Sydney I'd somehow ended up on a blind date with him. How the hell did this happen?!

The doorman looked between us. "Is there something wrong, Ma'am?"

I shut my jaw. What should I say?! What did people say in situations like this?! "I-I don't," I began, my cheeks burning. "I mean I—I don't—"

Henry stepped forward to rescue me. "Everything's fine, thank you," he managed, still looking shell-shocked.

The doorman didn't look convinced. He didn't say it, though. "Well, if you'd like to wait by the bar, then," he pointed, "I'll have a waiter show you to your table right away."

Henry had to lead me away from the door to get me to move. He was shaking his head. "God, I should have told you what I looked like. I should have asked what *you* looked like…" He laughed nervously. "I didn't want 'Kate' to think I'm superficial!"

I didn't know why I didn't ask myself; I guess I didn't think it would make a difference. I was only here because Sarah was so into the idea of solving Stephen's mystery. Well, it was solved, and in a million years I'd *never* have arrived at this answer.

'Stephen' noticed my silence, and as soon as we were far enough away for the doorman to hear, he stopped, turned and faced me square on, putting his hands on my shoulders. "Look, Gemma," he said quietly, "don't feel obligated to stay. I'm happy to have dinner with you anyway as a friend—god knows I could use a drink after that surprise!—but maybe you'd prefer to just pretend the whole thing never happened and go home?"

I didn't want to stay in this whole awkward situation, but the chances of me looking Henry in the eye and saying 'Yeah, I'm not interested in dinner with you even as a friend' approached zero, so instead of saying anything, I just stood there mutely and hoped that maybe the building would collapse or something and I wouldn't have to answer him.

He read between the lines, standing straighter and nodding. "Alright. It's okay, I'll cancel the booking and we'll call a taxi. I'm sorry." He looked down his arm at the beautiful big bunch of red tulips he was holding and sighed heavily. "Oh well, I suppose these will look nice in my hallway…" He forced a smile. "Come on."

There was a slump in his walk as he led me back to the door, cradling the flowers. It seemed such a shame to waste them. And he was dressed up so nicely, wasn't he? It even looked like he had a fresh haircut. He'd put in so much effort to present well for 'Kate'. I felt sick.

Henry ignored the doorman's clear disapproval. "Look, something's come up at the last minute and we'll need to cancel our booking. Is that too much of a problem?"

The doorman forced a smile of his own. "I'm sorry to hear that. It's no problem at all, but you do forfeit your $100 deposit if you cancel within 24 hours of your reservation."

That was the final straw, I didn't want him to *hate* me. "It's okay, we'll stay," I blurted out, before I even realised I was going to speak.

They hadn't been expecting that I would, either, and both turned their heads to stare at me. My throat closed over.

It felt like *eternity* before the doorman looked back at Henry, like, 'well?'

Henry gave him a thin smile. "False alarm, apparently," he said, and then took my arm and ushered me back towards the bar where we'd been asked to wait.

I was still stuck on that $100 deposit issue; a place would have to be really popular and really fancy to be able to do that. I hoped Henry didn't feel like he was wasting money on me. "It's not too expensive here, is it? We can split the bill if you want..."

He shook his head. "I'm happy to pay, it's the least I can do after causing this whole mess." He stood for a moment, looking down at himself and laughing openly. "Wow," he said, grimacing. "How embarrassing. Well, I feel like you know all my secrets now. Oh! that's right..." He remembered the flowers he was carrying and presented them to me. "These are for you, I suppose." He was smiling.

They weren't for me, they were for 'Kate'. I took them anyway—because what else could I do?!—but he was watching my reaction to getting them and I felt like anything I said or did would be the wrong one. I hated getting presents in public; my cheeks were as red as the bouquet.

"They're pretty," I said hoarsely. I hoped it was enough.

It must have been, because his smile deepened, and the warmth in it made whatever was left of my soul wither and die inside me.

We got shown to our seats—a really nice 'lovers' table by the huge windows that was separated from the main restaurant—and I let myself fall into my chair. Henry fumbled with the wine menu and hurriedly selected a white for us (I think just to get rid of the waiter) and then we sat there for a moment in silence.

"Well," he said at length, looking at the romantic setting around us. "This isn't exactly how I'd imagined this evening would turn out."

I felt so guilty. I had no idea what to do, so I apologised. "Sorry..."

He shook his head shortly. "Don't be. *You* were the one who was asking me questions. I should have just answered them."

It took me a few seconds to work up the courage to ask, "Why didn't you?"

"With the whole offshoring business, there are a lot of people who would like to see me suffer," he explained. "Employees have complained to me about their colleagues pranking them on Tinder before. I figured if someone *was* pranking me, though, they probably wouldn't go as far as to meet me in person—that would definitely get them fired."

Oh. That made sense. While I was wondering whether I should tell him about why *I* had a fake profile and if he'd even be interested in the reason, I glanced up to see him waiting patiently for me to reply. It was reassuring. I took a breath. "When I went on Tinder with my real name, I *did* match with someone from Frost."

That made his eyebrows jump, and he blew a stream of air through pursed lips. "My worst nightmare," he said, and then laughed nervously. "I already have enough of a reputation as it is, I don't need anything fanning those flames! Frost is an absolute rumour-mill and it's a tough culture to crack." He looked up at me for a moment. "Which is why I'd appreciate if you could keep this mix-up to yourself, if that's alright."

That was very alright. I wasn't keen on telling anyone myself; people would laugh, and the thought of that made me feel pathetic and hopeless. I nodded.

He relaxed a little. "Thank you," he said. "And really, I'm genuinely sorry for all this, even if it is a nice opportunity for me to get to know one of Min's good friends better. Let's just treat it as a lovely night out with a new face, shall we?"

It was actually really flattering to be called 'Min's good friend'. I nodded.

He gave me a broad smile in reply as the waiter returned with the selection of wines Henry had wanted to sample. We were forced to go through this whole process of trying of them before we were allowed to select one—Henry seemed to genuinely be doing it and not just pretending like I was so he didn't look uncultured—and when the waiter went to pour our glasses for us, Henry stopped him. "We'll take the bottle," he said, receiving it from him. The waiter nodded smartly and went to ferry away the other wines and fetch us a cooler.

As soon as he was gone, Henry filled our glasses to the brim. "I figured we might both need more than one drink."

He wasn't wrong. I lifted my full glass, wondering how quickly I could get it into my bloodstream. "It would be rude if I just sculled it all in one go, wouldn't it...?"

I was joking, but his eyes twinkled. "I won't tell if you won't," he said as we clinked glasses, and then right in front of me in this expensive restaurant, he poured his expensive wine down his throat like a broke uni student during happy hour. I was laughing too much to copy him; I kept forgetting that despite the fact he always seemed so responsible and mature, he had a sense of humour like Min's.

After he was done he waited for me to do the same, and then poured what was left in the bottle level in both our glasses and we finished that, too.

When the waiter returned maybe a minute later with the wine cooler, he carefully lifted the bottle from the table to place it on the ice. The surprise showed on his face when he realised it was completely empty.

"You were right," Henry told him with a completely straight face, "the local Pinot Gris *was* an excellent choice."

That might not have got a chuckle out of the waiter but it got one out of me, and while the waiter went off to grab us another bottle at Henry's request, I watched a cheeky grin settle on his face as he reached for his menu.

I unfolded my own. Maybe tonight wouldn't be so bad, after all.

It was actually quite difficult to decide what to eat; there wasn't much vegetarian range but everything in it looked delicious. Henry hadn't eaten here, either, so he didn't have any recommendations. "The review said the steak was delicious, but that's not much use to you," he admitted. "I would have chosen somewhere different if I'd known 'Kate' was a vegetarian."

I grimaced; I hoped he wasn't angry 'Kate' hadn't told him. "No, it's fine, this place is great," I said quickly, and then looked out across the floor of the restaurant. It was filling up fast. "And judging by how popular it is, I'm guessing that whatever I pick will be good."

He looked up at the floor, a slight furrow on his brow. "Yes, there are a lot of people here," he conceded, surveying their faces with some concern as he closed his menu. "It's a very popular place, I hope we don't see anyone we know. Anyway, I think I'll go for the gnocchi. You?"

I'd been planning on having the gnocchi too, and I thought it would be too weird if I chose the same thing so I had to spend another two or three minutes *sweating* and trying to make a choice while he patiently waited. At least my wine was starting to sink in.

By the time the waiter returned to take our orders and deliver us our second bottle, I'd settled on another pasta dish and was already feeling pleasantly tipsy. Henry offered me a refill, and it seemed impolite to say no, so I let him. At least he just poured a normal-sized glass of it this time. I sipped at it so I had something to do with my hands.

"Well," he said, leaning back in his chair. "Is it rude of me to ask how you've been finding Tinder? Aside from bumping into that fellow from Frost, that is."

I was a bit lightheaded. "Next question," I said, and only realised after I'd said it that it sounded less self-depreciative than it did outright dismissive.

Henry looked a little taken aback. "I'm sorry," he said quickly, "that's none of my business. Well, then, how do you feel about—"

"No," I interrupted him, but then didn't know what to say after that. He stopped speaking, and for a moment we sat there in awkward silence while I panicked about what to do. At least this time he didn't have to rescue me. "I-I just meant that it hasn't gone that well," I managed to say with the help of the wine I'd had before. "Not that you're not allowed to ask..."

"*Ah*," he said, and then relaxed again. "Well, I'm sorry to hear that, then. Same for me, actually: 'Kate' was the only match I've had so far, and I'd begun to think I shouldn't have started using Tinder after all."

"Why did you?" I wondered aloud. "You seemed like you hated the idea of it before."

He laughed at that. "I still don't like the idea of it," he admitted. "But Natalie practically bullied me into using it and she's a woman who's very hard to say 'no' to."

I laughed at his choice of words; 'bullied into Tinder' was *exactly* what had happened to me. "Sare was exactly the same when she told me to get it!"

Recognition passed across his face. "Oh, so *Sarah* wanted you to use it?" he asked, and I nodded. "Well," he said, "that makes a lot of sense."

I... wasn't sure what to make of that comment. When I looked up at him, worried about it, he didn't seem like he was going to push that point further. I was probably being paranoid, anyway. Everyone knew how awkward I was, it was probably something to do with that. Anyway, he'd said something else I was interested in. "Natalie uses Tinder?"

He laughed. "You'll need to ask her that yourself."

Yeah, there was zero chance of that happening. I couldn't even be in the same room as her. "I bet she gets lots of matches," I said as an afterthought, "she could just post a picture of, like, her ankles or something random and every man on the planet would be drooling over her...."

Henry probably gave me the best answer I was going to get by looking really surprised and then laughing. "I am *not* getting involved in this conversation. She's a professional contact."

"Who bullied you into putting Tinder on your phone."

He sucked air through his teeth. "Touché," he said. "But could we leave that conversation here, please? The last thing I need is for some rumour to get started about Natalie on Tinder. She'd sue the pants off Frost."

I found his choice of words very amusing; mostly because I doubted she'd need to sue anyone to get their pants off. Gosh, though, I must be *drunk* to be thinking like that...

When I lifted my glass to see how much I'd had since he'd filled it, it was nearly empty. Oh, dear; I tried to remember what we were talking about before I'd got stuck on thoughts of Natalie and pants being lost. "Um. I wouldn't tell anyone she's on Tinder, you know. You just kind of told me that she is."

He shook his head. "Two people talking about something is how rumours spread, and I've seen many, many careers ruined over them at Frost. Mine's not going so well as a result of them, either."

That, I found hard to believe. "But you're one of the upper managers there, isn't that the definition of 'going well'?"

He smiled tightly. "We'll see how long it lasts."

I balked at that. "But no one could fire you over some rumours, though, right? That's ridiculous!"

He shrugged, taking a slow sip of his wine and carefully considering his words. "When an employer wants to get rid of you, everything is an offense." He sighed. "Getting fired by Frost *would* be the kiss of death for my career. I haven't worked anywhere else in a decade."

"You could leave first, maybe?"

He laughed shortly. "You sound like Min," he said, and then shook his head. "No. I'm going to stick it out. That's what my lawyer tells me to do, anyway." He exhaled. "Natalie thinks it will all blow over, and I'm inclined to agree as long as I'm careful not to do anything else to feed the rumours about Henry Lee, Womanising Director of HR."

I spent a few seconds thinking about his predicament and wondering what I'd do in that circumstance. "I don't think I could stay if people were spreading things about me," I confessed. "I mean, I get why you are: you have this amazing job and you're super successful. I just fix spreadsheets."

"Not for much longer," he reminded me.

I managed a smile. "Oh, yeah, the Marketing secondment..." For some reason, I couldn't work up as much enthusiasm as I'd had initially. Perhaps because I was starting to feel really drunk, or perhaps because in comparison to HR Manager of a Fortune 500 company, 'Marketing Clerk' sounded pretty unimpressive. Especially when I thought about where I always assumed I was headed. "Everyone said I'd probably end up in ASIO," I found myself telling him. "Or running the Australian Bureau of Statistics or something..."

Henry looked sympathetic. "Is that what you want?"

What I want... I laughed once, humourlessly. "I don't know what I want," I told him honestly. "I just thought whatever I'd be doing at 28 would be more than this."

He laughed gently. "I hear you," he said frankly.

I wouldn't have been so familiar if I weren't quite as drunk. "Says Mr. Millionaire HR Manager."

Thankfully, he didn't look bothered at all. His usually ever-present smile did fade a little, though. "Don't assume I'm living my dream, Gemma. I'm really not."

I didn't understand. Did he want to be CEO or something? "What else would you be?"

He opened his mouth to answer me, and then changed his mind at the last second. "Well, something else. It's a bit depressing."

He couldn't just stop there. "What, though? You can say it, I promise I won't tell anyone."

He drew a long breath. Honestly, I didn't expect him to answer me. I thought he'd make some excuse or say he didn't want to start more rumours about himself or something like that. When he looked up at me, though, I could see from the resignation in his eyes that he was going to tell the truth. "If I could be anything, I'd be 'Dad'." He sounded wistful. "Or 'Husband', at least. And one day, far in the future when this nightmare at Frost is way behind me, I'd be 'Grandpa'."

Oh... I felt awful for asking. Looking at him sitting there, he painted a stark picture: in his nice suit, with his brand new haircut and the beautiful flowers he'd bought. It suddenly made sense why he'd put in so much effort for 'Kate' even though he knew nothing about her. But instead of sitting across from Kate, someone who he'd maybe hoped would turn out to be the woman he married and had those children with, he was sitting across from me, an awkward, closeted lesbian, and finishing his third glass of wine as he leant heavily on his elbows.

And at 35, he was even closer to the edge of the bell-curve than I was with his personal life. There was something like a 95% confidence interval for a man being married by 35; he'd somehow slipped through to defy the odds. For a moment, I felt both comforted by his situation and horribly guilty that I was.

A silence stretched between us; I think he misinterpreted that. He had another big gulp of wine. "Listen to me! Clearly I've had too much to drink. Sorry, Gemma. I didn't mean to ruin our conversation by lumping you with all my personal tragedies."

"No..." I didn't want him to feel worse than he clearly did. "I'm a tragedy, too." Even this drunk, it took a moment for me to work up enough courage to say it. "You know how I said I had bad luck with Tinder?" He nodded. "Well, I didn't, not really. I met someone really awesome. Like, *incredible*. We totally hit it off." I could still remember every single part of what it had felt like when Mikey had reached for my hand at Sydney Harbour. "On the same night I met that amazing person, I completely screwed it all up and they walked out on me."

"It sounds like a big misunderstanding," Henry observed.

"It wasn't," I said flatly. "She was right."

As soon as those words had left my mouth and I realised I'd said 'she', I think all the rosy colour drained from my cheeks and I went white as a sheet. I looked up at him, *horrified*, but absolutely nothing about him was surprised, or shocked, or anything like it. I could have told him what the time was and he'd have nodded in the same way. "May I ask about what she was right about?"

I... why didn't he comment on it? Did he already know? I would have asked how—maybe Min told him?—but I was distracted by his question. In a million years if someone had asked me, 'would you answer Henry if he asked that?' I never would have believed them if they'd said I would. Still, I think

207

encouraged by the fact he'd said 'she' without even blinking, here I was, opening my mouth and saying, "She was right about me being in love with someone else." I paused for a moment, unsure if I should elaborate, but then I did, anyway. "Someone I can't ever have."

His face softened, and he gave a bit of a wry chuckle. "Well," he said, with great gentleness in his voice. "Have you ever found your drinking buddy in me, Gemma." He held his glass out in invitation for me to clink. "Cheers to our terrible choice in partners." There was such acceptance of me in his smile.

I felt tearful, almost. There were a million ways he could have responded to finding out (or having confirmed?) that I was gay, but this was the way he did. I clinked my nearly-empty glass with his and then drank the rest of it, hoping I *wouldn't* cry. I felt such affection for him.

His smile deepened as I did—little crinkles formed at the corners of his eyes. He had such a lovely smile, and after how well this evening had turned out, I really just wanted to hug him; I probably would have if we hadn't been in public. I was just gazing at him and imagining that, when with a sudden, terrible shock I realised what I was doing. I was gazing at him.

You're just drunk, I thought, admiring his profile as he checked his watch and turned his head towards the kitchen. *It's not real, you'd probably throw yourself at anyone right now, Gemma. Especially someone who was this nice to you.*

I decided the real test was whether or not I'd want to kiss him; when he looked back at me and smiled again, I realised I probably would. He was actually pretty cute, and he was so, so lovely.

I swallowed. That was... Wow, I didn't know what to do with this information. I'd literally just come out as gay to him, what the hell? Was I *not* gay after all? Was I just drunk? Or was I actually just so starved for attention that I'd consider sleeping with anyone who was nice to me?

His smile faded. "Are you alright?"

I closed my jaw. "Yeah. Just—" *Confused as hell*, I thought. "Just thinking I've probably drunk too much."

He chuckled. "Yes, I'm not sure how wise the second bottle was. Whoops. Well, I'm sure the food will sober us up." He paused, and then added a little shortly, "Assuming it eventually arrives, that is. Perhaps they're understaffed?"

When a waiter approached us, Henry and I both assumed it was to inform us of a delay on our meals. Henry had opened his mouth to say something forgiving about it being fine and that we could see how busy they were, but the waiter gave him an apologetic look and turned to me.

I blinked. Me?!

"Ma'am, I'm sorry to disturb you," he said. "But there's someone waiting at the door."

"There is?"

He nodded. "A woman who says she's very worried about you and only needs to speak to you for a moment to make sure that nothing terrible has—"

He didn't reach the end of his sentence before I realised *exactly* what was going on. "Oh my gosh!" I hissed, interrupting him and clumsily springing up from my chair. "I forgot to text Sare to tell her I'm okay!"

CHAPTER EIGHTEEN

I sprung up from my chair, accidentally knocking into the table and nearly sending the super expensive silverware all over the ground. *Oh my gosh* how could I have forgotten to text Sarah?! She was probably worried sick! I had to go let her know everything was okay and 'Stephen' wasn't a crazy axe-murderer!

I was a bit unsteady on my feet, so I half-ran, half-staggered back towards the doorway. Sarah was out there in the lobby wearing her big comfy jumper and her Ugg boots, fidgeting nervously and, boy, did she ever look relieved the second she saw me.

I felt terrible. "I'm sorry!" I called to her before I even got there. "I'm so sorry! I completely forgot!"

209

She threw her arms around me as I got to her, squishing me up against her big belly. "I hate you!" she said into my neck. "Oh my god, I totally hate you! I've been *stressing out*, and these damn hormones are turning me into a wreck, I swear to god, I was like, 'something's wrong, Gem's been kidnapped by a serial killer!'"

I grimaced. I still couldn't believe I'd forgotten. "I got a bit distracted..."

She immediately pulled away from me, giving me a very pointed look. "And a bit drunk, apparently, you smell like wine." She paused, her smile fading. "I hope this Stephen guy isn't trying to get you really drunk."

I laughed at the suggestion. Henry didn't seem like the type. "No, he's had as much as I have."

She didn't look convinced. "Men can have more, though..."

I hugged her again; she was normally so pragmatic. I kind of liked this new, protective Sarah. "I'm fine, seriously. No one's trying to take advantage of me. I'm just a space cadet who completely forgot to text her best friend."

Sarah looked like she had more to say, but with considerable effort, she managed to leave it and move on. "Okay, I'll trust your judgment. And, speaking of judgment, what's this Stephen guy like after all this? And what *does* he do for work?"

I opened my mouth. *I should tell her it's Henry*, I thought, but then half-remembered through my very alcoholic haze that Henry said something about not wanting me to tell everyone. I closed my mouth again. Whether there was a distinction between 'anyone' and 'everyone' I couldn't tell, but I also didn't trust my judgment at this blood-alcohol reading.

I decided to play it safe so I could check with Henry first. "He's fine, and he's a manager at his work and he just didn't want his employees to find out," I explained. Then, because I didn't want to lie anymore before I'd spoken to Henry, I added, "but I'll tell you more later. I should go back in."

She clearly wanted way more detail than that, but instead of probing like she usually would have, she took a long slow breath, and then released it. "You know what? I'm not going to grill you, even if the suspense is literally killing me. I'm going to let you enjoy your date." She gave me another hug, and then stood back. "Fancy place this Stephen guy brought you to, though, isn't it? I googled it; apparently it's the hottest place in town at the moment, everyone's coming here! Obviously he wants to impress you."

I forced a laugh. Poor Henry. "Yeah...."

She spent a couple of seconds affectionately fixing the way my hair fell over my shoulders. "Anyway, I'll leave you to it. Tell me *everything* in the morning, okay?" Giving me a little salute—she'd picked that habit up off Min—she stepped into the lift and the doors closed.

It took me a few moments to recover after she'd gone. Should I have just told her it was Henry? I felt like I probably should have; once upon a time, it wouldn't have even occurred to me *not* to tell her.

I sighed and turned to go back inside. Henry—along with *everyone* in the restaurant—was going to think I was *nuts* for just running off like that...

I was side-stepping through the tables and hoping no one would recognise me as the girl who'd been running through them earlier when someone *did* recognise me and grabbed my arm. "Gemma!"

I *yelped*, and was just going bright red and apologising for the loud yelping when I realised who had grabbed me: sitting at the table I'd been edging past was Spud, all dressed up, with a woman I recognised from the photos on his desk. Oh, no...

He was beaming. "Whoops, sorry for scaring you!" He laughed heartily and introduced me to his wife 'Elaine'—at least I think that was her name, I was too busy freaking out to remember that clearly. Whatever her name was, she smiled and nodded politely at me, her long chandelier earrings brushing the modest neckline of her evening dress. I would have admired how she was dressed if I hadn't been *horrified* they were here.

This couldn't be happening. I was drunk and hallucinating, right? There *couldn't* be people from Frost here, no matter how popular this place apparently was! I glanced up at Henry over by the window; he was sipping his wine and checking his phone, oblivious.

Spud was used to me being speechless. "Isn't this place great? Great place to take my wife for our 19th anniversary," his tone darkened, "while I still have a job and can still afford to, that is..."

His wife looked just as sober as he was on that point, addressing me. "Lovely to meet you, Gemma. Is this whole offshoring nonsense taking your job, too? It's appalling."

Oh, gosh. "I-I'm not sure."

It seemed to be the right answer. "That's just it, isn't it? HR isn't telling anyone anything. It's appalling, simply appalling." She shook her head. "Anyway, you look very nice, that's a lovely dress! Are you out with someone special tonight, too?"

All the blood drained from my face.

To my horror, Spud latched onto my silence. "I think that's a 'yes'," he said smugly, as he and his wife merrily laughed. He clapped me on the arm. "Well, it's about time, Gemma! I don't think you've dated anyone the whole time I've worked with you! Are you going to bring him over and introduce him to us?"

"W-We were about to go, actually..."

"Well, drag him past the table on the way out, okay? I'd love to meet the man who finally tamed you!"

No, you definitely wouldn't, I thought, *panicking* and trying to figure out how the hell I was going to get out of this situation.

Spud found my horror entertaining. "Hah, that looks like a 'no', doesn't it?" he asked his wife. Then, he leant forward on the table. "Why not?" he asked, acting like I had an entertaining, juicy secret. "Is he a *secret* boyfriend?

"No!"

They laughed pleasantly. I glanced up at Henry, trying to figure out how I could possibly get a message to him that we needed to leave immediately before Spud saw us together, but I looked for just a tiny little bit too long. Spud noticed.

He laughed, turning his head in what felt like agonising slow motion, and I watched as his eyes searched the area before finally settling right on Henry.

It took a moment for it to register, and then his laugh abruptly stopped and the smile fell right off his face. When he looked back at me, the blatant shock in his expression took five years off my life.

His wife didn't understand. "What's going on?" she looked across at Henry, too. "Who's that? He looks nice."

I didn't want to wait for Spud to reply. Every nerve in my body was *screaming* for me to get out of there *get out of there GEMMA GET OUT OF THERE*! "I-I have to go!" I stammered, and then took off, drunkenly stumbling over the leg of someone's chair as I fled the restaurant.

I didn't get very far because my handbag was still at the table, but I did make it out into the foyer of the top level again. I backed up against the wall beside the lift to take inventory on what had just happened.

Spud was here. He'd seen me with Henry. Of all the goddamn nights in the entire year to pick this exact restaurant, he'd picked *tonight*. I laughed bleakly; what were the chances of that?! They had to be miniscule, this had to be a one-in-a-million occurrence. Then again, who the hell was I? Everything about me was a one-in-a-million occurrence, if someone had calculated the probability of a person existing with all my characteristics, the likelihood would have been so close to zero it would be infinitesimal. 'Unlikely' was my MO; if there was a distant chance of anything, there was a direct correlation between how obscure the thing was and how likely it was to happen to me. It was practically my superpower.

I would have laughed a lot more at the irony of it all if it had only been *my* problem: but this time, Henry had been sucked up my end of the bell curve, too. His comment about his career being on the line if anything else happened with

213

him and an employee was fresh in my head, so if Spud said anything to anyone, Henry was in deep trouble.

When I realised what that meant and what I'd have to do, I felt a bit ill. I was going to have to confront Spud and whatever reaction he was going to have so I could ask him not to say anything, wasn't I?

While I was pressed up against the wall and talking myself out of assuming a secret identity and fleeing overseas instead, a familiar and concerned face appeared by the door of the restaurant. "Gemma?"

Henry; I had this sudden vision of telling him what had just happened and not only making a terribly embarrassing night even worse for him, but also of him being really disappointed with me for not immediately being able to come up with some casual lie about why we were here together. I could never think of the right thing to say, never, and the thought of letting him down felt like kicking a puppy; I had to try and sort this out so I didn't need to.

I'd already worried him. "Are you alright?" He was one of those incidental-touchy people, and so as he approached me, his hands went to my shoulders. "Did something happen with Sarah?"

"I'm fine!" I said quickly, terrified he'd guess why I was out here. "Sarah's fine!"

He gave me a look. "Well, great..." he said uncertainly. "So, would you like to—"

He was gesturing back into the restaurant, and we couldn't go back in there. Not while Spud was there! "No, I think we should go. Now! I'll pay you back for the $100 deposit and the wine. I'm sorry I ruined everything!"

His mouth opened, and he stared down at me for a moment, eyebrows up. "Um. This is rather sudden." He took a moment. "And what do you mean 'ruined everything'? Because you want to leave, you mean?"

"Yes." That certainly beat telling him what had actually just happened.

He spent a few seconds just frowning at me, and then shook his head. "Well, okay," he said slowly. "If that's what you want. Let me just go and get—" He was turning to go back inside.

"No!" I said, grabbing his arm. "Can you stay here? We can get *him* to get our stuff." I pointed at the doorman, who gave me a really strange look.

Henry gave me an equally strange look. Anyone else probably would have refused to leave without *grilling* me; Sarah certainly would have. Henry didn't, though. He just raised his eyebrows. "Alright, then..."

He arranged for one of the waiters to bring out my flowers and my handbag. Along with those, the waiter handed me two warm little boxes.

"I figured we shouldn't miss out on this food, since it has such a good reputation," Henry said gently as he ushered me out on my shaky knees to the lift, and then took everything from me because I was honestly an inch away from dropping it all.

It was a long way down to the ground floor, and while we were standing silently side-by-side and I was wondering how the hell someone hopeless like me was going to confront Spud, I could feel Henry looking at me with concern. Before the doors opened on the ground floor, he said gingerly, "Gemma, would you mind if I asked you a question?" Wide-eyed, I shook my head. I hoped it wasn't going to be what I thought it was. "Did you tell Sarah that it was me in there?"

...Oh. At least that was *one* thing I could answer truthfully. "No."

He exhaled and gave me a weak half-smile. "Thank you," he said, looking forwards again and visibly relaxing. "I shouldn't be relieved about that, but I am. Sarah is a lovely girl, but I get the feeling sometimes she doesn't know when the teasing goes a little too far."

He wasn't wrong about that but *crap*. Just: crap. There was my answer about whether or not I could tell Sarah who

215

'Stephen' was. Was there anyone I *wasn't* hiding stuff from right now?

I spent the remaining seconds of our lift ride trying to decide if I *should* tell Henry what had happened after all; but if he'd looked that relieved when he found out Sarah didn't know we were there together, I didn't know how he'd react if he found out that someone who wasn't a good friend of ours knew. Nope, I didn't want to let him down if there was a chance I could sort this out without involving him.

After he'd hailed us a taxi (he didn't trust Uber drivers), he spent most of the ride back clearly worrying about me while I felt progressively worse and worse, and then he absolutely insisted on making the taxi wait while he got out and showed me up to my flat. I practically needed to close the door on him; then I felt really bad about that and texted him to thank him for what had been a nice night before I'd ruined it.

"*Don't worry about it, Gemma! After what you disclosed to me before, the timing of your decision to leave seems pretty significant. I completely understand. Let's do this again when you're feeling better, alright? On purpose next time, though :) - H,*" was his reply.

I stared at that reply. '*...the timing of your decision to leave seems pretty significant*'? As in, right after I'd rushed out to... Sarah... he meant?! My stomach dropped into my feet. That wasn't even the reason that I wanted to leave this time, how had he—? Was I *that* bloody obvious?!

I couldn't deal with this right now. There was no way, I was too drunk. So, I made the incredibly healthy and emotionally mature decision to knock myself out with another couple of reds and then crash in bed without taking off all the beautiful makeup Sarah had lovingly applied for me.

At least the following morning when she'd texted me to ask if she could come around so I could *oh my god, tell her everything*! I wasn't lying to her when I texted something to the effect of, "*can't, hungover, kill me,*" and then turned over and put the pillow over my head.

When I did finally manage to drag myself out of bed, I had cold restaurant leftovers for lunch and dinner while sitting in my dark living room, a sea of old photos of Sarah and I that I'd pulled off the wall all around me. I gazed down at them while I was eating.

I couldn't put her off forever, so if Henry didn't want me telling her he was Stephen, I didn't know what the hell I was going to say to her. She wouldn't accept 'no comment' as an answer to *tell me about him*!!' even if she *had* made that pledge to not grill me like she used to. There wasn't a single question I could answer about him without lying to her, and not only would she know I was lying immediately by the colour of my face, I just really didn't want to lie to her anymore. I'd had enough; I was hiding enough from her already. I was sick of it.

In the end, I managed to delay the inevitable until I was less hungover by promising Sarah I'd tell her *everything* at lunch on Monday, hoping I'd have some sort of genius brainwave about how to deal with both Spud and Sarah by then.

However, for a person all the teachers universally agreed would go very far in life, I didn't get very far on that one simple point, let alone with the rest of my life. Instead, I spent most of the evening staring blankly at the screen of my phone and forgetting I'd googled *'how to have a difficult conversation with a work colleague'* and not clicking any of the links.

Therefore, despite giving myself until the following day to think of a way out of this mess, by the following day, I had achieved exactly 0% of that goal. So, to avoid bumping into Sarah at the train station in the morning and being put on the spot with no idea what to say, I managed possibly for the first time ever in my life to catch a really early train into the city. I got into work super early and sat alone at my desk, staring at my blank computer screen.

Spud would be in soon.

This was it; my palms were actually sweating. It was silly, I shouldn't be this worried: catching him early and alone gave me a *prime* opportunity to take him aside and tell him that Henry wasn't 'womanising' me—or whatever he clearly thought—but we were there as friends and nothing more.

...'friends' who just happened to be sitting at the 'lovers' table, and I just happened to have a big bunch of red tulips next to me. Shit. It didn't look good, did it?! What if he didn't believe—

"You're in early!" I jumped; that was Anil's voice. He looked a little surprised, smiling broadly over the partition at me.

"Yeah, I caught an earlier train," I said like that wasn't blindingly bloody obvious, and then felt stupid for saying something so redundant.

He didn't act like I had. "Big day?" he asked with that same smile.

I didn't know what he meant so I just laughed nervously—I mean, of course it was a big day, today was the day when I either saved Henry's career or ruined it, and saved my friendship with Sarah or dug the hole even deeper—but I couldn't really say that. I hoped awkward, high-pitched laughter would suffice.

He seemed to think we'd just been exchanging pleasant small-talk, because he chuckled back and then headed off into his office. I was trying to figure out what to make of that conversation when the lift opened and I heard Spud's unmistakable voice as he was chatting to whoever had ridden up with him.

As soon as I saw him approaching me, I was suddenly extremely aware of how I could *not* face him right now. Or ever, really, but 100% definitely not right now.

So, instead of being a functional adult and calmly asking Spud if I could discuss the little misunderstanding we'd had on Saturday, I dealt with this predicament like I dealt with all my problems: I scurried away and went and hid in the women's toilets.

It was pathetic. *I* was being pathetic. *Gemma, get your act together*, I ordered myself, staring at myself in the mirror. *Go out there, say 'Spud, may I talk to you for a second?' and then explain that there's nothing going on with you and Henry.*

"There's absolutely no way he'll believe me, though," I complained to my reflection. My ever so helpful brain supplied a crystal clear memory of him scolding me about not going to the union meeting—with every fibre of my being, I did *not* want him to do that again. That had been awful.

Maybe I should just write him an email instead? I wondered, before I realised putting in writing that I'd been out at night with the HR Manager was a colossally terrible idea if I was planning on trying to actually *save* Henry's career.

Or, maybe you should stop finding excuses not to do it and actually do it, Gemma, I told myself, and then put my face in my hands and groaned. Why was I like this?! Why couldn't I just walk out there and handle the situation like normal people?

Not only did I not manage to convince myself to speak to Spud, I didn't even manage to convince myself to leave the toilets. It got past the point where I should have started work, and by the time someone knocked on the toilet door, I'd already decided that assuming a secret identity and disappearing overseas was the only possible solution to all of this.

"Gemma," that was Anil's voice, "is everything okay?"

That is generally a pretty dangerous question to ask me, boss, I mentally answered, but seeing as he *was* my boss, I needed to pull myself together and get out of here, anyway, or I was remove the element of possibility from the whole offshoring equation and *definitely* lose my job.

When I opened the door, probably white as a corpse, Anil was standing there beaming at me.

It was pretty uncharacteristic of him—especially since the offshoring stuff started—and I didn't know what to make of it. To make it even more confusing, everyone in Risk was gathered around the meeting table in the middle of the room, all waiting for me. They all looked at me as Anil and I walked over to them.

My face and ears burning, I stared at the tips of my ballet flats and the grey carpet beneath them. Spud was sitting there somewhere...

"Well, now we're a full team," Anil said, and thankfully people turned to look at him instead, "I have a short announcement to make before my meeting with HR at ten which is probably going to be very bad news. I thought we'd start off the day with something positive! Well, positive for one of us in particular." He looked right at me. A knot began to form in my stomach. "Gemma has some fantastic news to share, which I'm sure she'll be happy for me to say on her behalf."

I realised what this was about, and turned my head to *gape* at him. Oh, no. No, no, no. *Now* was when he was going to make the announcement?! Now?!

He didn't notice. "As you may or may not know, Marketing lost their demographer in April and they hadn't managed to replace him. Our Gemma, being the industrious person that she is, has made an arrangement with HR to be seconded to his position to see if she likes it—I'm sure she will!"

They didn't look as excited as Anil was. One of the guys even piped up with, "I bet she'll like keeping her job ever more. Marketing isn't on the chopping block."

There was a murmur of polite laughter and then Anil nodded. "Yes, that's why it's *good* news. The timing couldn't be better! Will you all join me in congratulating her in her potential new role?"

Everyone started half-heartedly clapping—it was hard to clap for someone whose fortune was better than yours, I guess—and I happened to accidentally glance up.

Spud wasn't clapping. He was glaring directly at me.

All the blood drained from my face. Anil patted me on the back and said something nice—'We'll take you up there after lunch', I think?—but I couldn't focus on it. Not with the way Spud was looking at me. As the crowd dispersed, I turned to make my getaway. I didn't want Spud to say anyth—

"Oi, *Gemma*!"

Oh, no...! I tried to walk faster.

"Gemma! Can I have a word about this little 'arrangement with HR'?"

I'm ashamed to say that I panicked and started *running*. Literally, jogging across the office; everyone was looking at me and I didn't want to wait for the lift in case he caught up to me and accosted me in front of everyone, so I just slipped into the stairwell.

Behind me, I could hear someone asking, "What was that all about?!" and Spud's dry voice answering him. I shut the door before I heard exactly what he said; but I knew what it was. I knew exactly what it was. Spud was telling them what he'd seen on Saturday night.

I'd missed my opportunity to ask him not to.

CHAPTER NINETEEN

I stood for a moment in the stairwell. *I shouldn't just stand here*, I thought, standing there anyway. I knew I should actually *do* something, but I had no idea what.

Sarah would know what to do; whenever our travel plans went awry, she always stepped in, took control and took care of the situation. She'd open her perfect mouth and all the right words would come pouring out of it so easily, even when it was big things like getting us on the plane we should have boarded 15 minutes ago, or organising a couple of days' extension on our visas when we'd accidentally overstayed. It was always such a relief.

I should ask her, I decided, *and I should really tell her about Henry being 'Stephen' before she finds out from someone else.* She could tell me what the best thing to do was before it was too late to do anything at all.

Wow, yeah, I felt better: that's what I'd do.

I couldn't text her right now, though, because in my panic I'd very intelligently left my handbag in the office with Spud.

So instead of walking back in there, I dragged myself down 22 whole flights of stairs to the fire exit in the atrium; Sarah would probably grab hot chocolate number two in an hour or so from the atrium café, I could meet up with her then. After all, it wasn't like anyone would be looking for me; Anil had a meeting with HR, and Risk would probably think I'd already gone up to Marketing. So, I sat down at the café to wait for her.

By 10:30—well after hot chocolate o'clock—I'd run out of complimentary magazines and newspapers to read, and she still hadn't come down. I kept watching people flood out of the lifts, listening for the click-click of her Jimmy Choos and looking for her lovely dark brown hair, but I didn't see it.

By lunchtime, she hadn't come, either.

I fiddled anxiously with my bracelet. It was unlike her; if I wasn't at my desk and hadn't answered my phone, she'd come looking for me. *Maybe she's texted me to say she couldn't come?* I wondered. I wasn't going back up there alone to check my phone, though, and I didn't want to walk into Marketing by myself, either. But it was nearly 1:30—she wasn't coming. Why wasn't she coming?

Something occurred to me: what if someone *already told her* about Saturday night and she was really angry? I stewed on that for a couple of minutes, before I decided that it was pretty unlikely the rumour had travelled *that* fast.

...then again, something being 'unlikely' was the story of my life, wasn't it?

Groaning, I rested my forehead on my hands on the café table for a moment. Since every minute that passed diminished my chances of salvaging Henry's reputation and career, I knew I couldn't wait any longer: if Sarah couldn't help me out, I was going to have to tell the very man himself, and I was going to have to do it now.

He's going to kill me, I decided, stepping into one of the lifts and pushing the little '35'. It travelled upwards slowly—again, one of those things where the speed at which you need to get somewhere inversely correlates with how fast the lift actually takes you there—and then ten or eleven years later, the doors opened to the steel-plate sign 'Human Resources – Frost Group'.

At the end of the corridor, Henry's door was shut.

I stopped. *Well, I guess he's busy now*, I found myself thinking and wondering if I should come back later. I almost talked myself out of telling him, but then I managed to get a grip; whatever he was doing, he'd want to know what had happened on Saturday night *more*. I needed to interrupt him.

Still, my hand was practically shaking when I knocked on his door.

"Just a moment!" he called, and then I heard him finishing up a phone call. "Come in!" He sounded cheerful.

Oh, no: he was *happy*. I pushed the door open.

"Gemma," he said in greeting, a big warm smile on his face. "Anil told me he made the announcement this morning."

I nodded and forced a polite smile. "Yeah..."

He returned it with a real one. "Great! Sorry if it seemed a little sudden, I just thought you could use a little pick me up after how off-colour you were on Saturday! I pushed it through last night to cheer you up."

Oh... I grimaced. "Thanks..."

He noticed my hesitation and his big smile faltered. "Should I have left it after all? I thought it would make you feel better..."

I felt like I was *already* kicking a puppy. *Say it*, I willed myself, *tell him*, but I literally couldn't look into those big brown eyes of his and tell him I was about to destroy his career. Especially given that he'd apparently been working on building mine all Sunday. "No, it does make me feel better..." I managed.

He softened. "Just nervous about your new job, perhaps?"

"Yeah," I told him as if that was the reason—it was true, I guess, but also only about 5% of my actual problem right now. Or maybe 0.5%. I sighed at myself.

He let a long silence stretch between us to give me the opportunity to talk, but I think he didn't want to make me feel awkward when I didn't, so he spoke. "Well, you know I'm

223

here if you need someone to listen, Gemma," he promised me, and then gestured across from him. "Please, take a seat. I assume Marketing sent you up here to sign the secondment agreement? We can do it now, if you like."

I didn't have the heart to correct him about why I was there, so I sat opposite his desk as he handed the agreement across to me. I tried to pretend I was reading it (I couldn't concentrate), and then just signed it and pushed it back across the desk.

"Is there anything on there you have questions about?" he asked, standing briefly to make me some photocopies. I shook my head and accepted them from him as he sat down again. "Fair enough, it's all pretty straight-forward. I tell you what, though: Marketing will love getting you up there so quickly! It's a very important week for them because they're in the middle of a big project. An extra set of hands will be appreciated."

He gave me some other info about it, too—to be honest, I wasn't really listening. *Come on, Gem*, I was willing myself as I stared at him. *Say it. Tell him that Spud saw us.*

I only realised he'd stopped talking and was watching me again when it suddenly occurred to me that the room had been silent for several seconds. I went bright red.

His comforting smile returned. "Everyone's always nervous about a new job," he said, "but I imagine it's much harder for someone who's as introverted as you are." There was such warmth in his voice. His smile deepened, and then he sat back and slapped his palms gently on the desk. "Anyway, I hate to kick you out when you're clearly not feeling 100%, but I need to make a few phone calls and I have a meeting in ten minutes. Perhaps we can catch up a little later to have a proper talk, if you'd like one?"

Oh... "Okay," I found myself saying as I stood. "I'm sorry I interrupted you."

He shook his head. "Don't be, I'm sorry I can't spend more time with you right now! Anyway, I'm sure you'll enjoy your new role in Marketing. I hope it's what you're looking for." He smiled; I just grimaced.

As I was walking out the door, eternally disgusted with myself for failing at adulthood once again, it occurred to me that this was going to be another moment like before with Spud. A moment when as soon as I'd walked out the door, I'd massively, massively regret not finding the strength to speak to him when I needed to, which was now, not later. *Not* after I'd spoken to Sarah or hidden in the work toilets for several weeks: right now.

But he's going to be angry, I found myself thinking, and with that warm smile so fresh in my memory, it was hard to even *consider* saying anything that would wipe it off his face.

...on the other hand, nothing would wipe it off his face like *losing his job*, especially after he told me on Saturday it was the one thing in his life he was proud of.

Shit. No, I couldn't leave this. I couldn't.

"Henry?" I spun around; I could hear the desperate note in my voice.

So could he. He looked sideways at the phone receiver he'd just picked up, and then very slowly put it back in its cradle. "Yes?"

Oh, gosh. "I need to tell you something..."

His eyebrows lowered ever so slightly. "Alright." He gave me his full attention.

I hadn't thought about how to say it, and when I opened my mouth, it wasn't like when Sarah opened hers. The right words didn't just flow out. "I-I'm sorry," I stammered. "I really am. I should have told you, but I'm totally hopeless. I thought that I could handle it by myself, but I don't know why the hell I thought that because I can *never* handle anything by myself, and I should have known I wouldn't be able to..." I felt breathless.

"It's okay, Gemma," he said slowly. "Take your time."

Just say it, I mentally berated myself, and then took a deep breath and opened my mouth again. "Someone saw us on Saturday night!"

225

His eyebrows finished their journey down over his eyes. It felt like eternity before he spoke. "Someone from Frost?" he asked carefully.

I nodded. "Spud from Risk."

Recognition flashed across his face. "Oh..." He spent a second thinking about that, and then his eyebrows flew up again. "So it *wasn't* seeing Sarah that made you want to suddenly leave?" Something else occurred to him and he looked horrified. "Oh, no, and your secondment was announced this morning!"

I had to close my eyes for a moment. And he'd been looking so forward to cheering me up... "I'm sorry. I'm so sorry, I should have said something—"

"Why didn't you!?" He sat back in his chair, agape. I could feel him *looking* at me.

"I'm sorry, I thought I could take care of it myself, but—"

"*Fuck*, Gemma..." He took a breath. "If you'd told me on Saturday night, I could have delayed the announcement about your secondment instead of putting extra effort in to push it through early so it looked like—" He could hardly say it. "Like I requested sex from you in exchange for job security!"

I felt sick. "There's got to be something we can do, right? I meant, nothing actually happened between us, so—"

"That doesn't mean anything. Well, not outside court it doesn't, and that's where I'll be judged. Just—" He rubbed his brow. "Do you still have all the messages we exchanged on Tinder?"

That reminded me that my phone was still down in Risk. "Yeah, do you want me to get my phone now? Because I don't—"

"No, just don't delete the messages, okay? Because this might actually end up in court, I might need to litigate Frost to keep my job. Fuck, my boss is going to *ream* me." He ran his hand over his face. "*Fuck*!"

A tense silence stretched between us; his eyes tracked through the air as he tried to figure out what move to make. The smile was definitely gone now.

Eventually, he spoke. He sounded calmer. "I'm sorry, Gemma. I didn't mean to be short with you just then, it's just..." He exhaled at length, and then shook his head. "Look, the more I think about it, this probably would have turned into a rumour even if we'd waited to announce your secondment. Spud would have joined the dots anyway, so maybe I'm overreacting." He looked up at me. "Do you think he'll say anything to anyone?"

I winced, remembering him doing exactly that. I nodded.

He sighed audibly. "Well. Let's get Anil back up here and see what can be done about it."

...back up here? "From Risk?" He nodded at me. "Do you think..." Gosh, it sounded like a stupid request on top of everything, didn't it? "D-Do you think you could ask him to bring my handbag up?"

Henry already had the phone against his ear and he was giving me a long frown, but when he invited Anil up, he finished with, "Oh, and would you mind bringing Gemma's personal belongings with you, too?"

The way he phrased that meant that when Anil arrived at Henry's door with my handbag, he was pale. "Is everything okay?" he asked, looking between us and handing my bag to me.

Henry shut the door behind him. "Not exactly."

Anil gave me a very wide-eyed look and then sat beside me at the table.

Henry explained what had happened—coming right out and confessing that we'd both been using Tinder under pseudonyms. That made Anil's bushy eyebrows shoot up, and guaranteed I was going to spend the rest of the conversation beetroot-bloody-red. Yeah, what I really wanted was my boss, who probably already secretly thought I was a failure at life, knowing that I needed to use Tinder to meet people...

"...and so you see our predicament," Henry finished, sitting back. "I was hoping you could shine a light on the best way to manage that information in your team."

227

I wasn't really sure what I expected from Anil—he'd always been pretty nice to me?—but I *didn't* expect there to be zero sign of suspicion on his face. He didn't look like he doubted Henry's far-fetched story about what had happened at all. In fact, he smiled a little. "Sorry," he said, trying to wipe it off. "That's rude of me, isn't it? It's just that what are the chances of you meeting each other anonymously?"

I actually knew the answer to that, I'd tried to work it out. "Something crazy like one in 250,000." As soon as I'd said it and they both *looked* at me, I realised Anil's question was 100% rhetorical. I went even redder and then continued to make it worse. "S-Sorry," I mumbled, trying to explain myself. "It's just that if you take the number of users that fit my parameters and the likelihood that someone with swipe left on—" Gosh, was I *hearing* myself? "—I mean, never mind."

They both smiled very briefly. Henry rescued me. "It's just very bad luck at very long odds, I'm afraid."

Anil nodded slowly, sobering. "I'm sure there's a solution to this," he said eventually, and then turned to me. "Would you mind if I had a word to Henry alone? It feels odd discussing staff in front of other employees."

I obediently took my handbag and went and sat outside Henry's office, listening to their hushed voices inside. I tried to figure out what they were saying for a couple of minutes and didn't get anywhere. Sighing, I looked down at my handbag.

My phone was in there.

Even though I could finally check to see if Sarah had messaged about lunch, I almost didn't want to; because what if she didn't come because she'd heard that Henry was 'Stephen' and was upset I hadn't told her first?!

Well, she's definitely going to hear it from someone else first if I don't tell her soon, I reasoned, and took the damn thing out.

I had a missed call and two messages. The first was a text saying, *"Late lunch? I'm having a big meeting now – maybe like 2ish?"* I'd nearly let out a big, fat sigh of relief... right up until I opened the second one. *"Gem. Why didn't you tell me... :("*

Shit... of *course* someone had told her about Saturday night already, of course... Henry was right about this place being a rumour mill. Ugh. I replied, *"I really wanted to, but Henry told me not to :(It's actually just a big mix-up, though, can I tell you everything over lunch?"*

"... Oh? 'A mix-up'? You mean it's not true? That's weird, everyone is talking about it like it's some big, secret deal you made to keep working at Frost."

Everyone? Oh, gosh... *"No, trust me, it's not. Can you tell them it's just a rumour? I don't want it spreading out of control..."*

"Yeah, of course, I'll do that now." There was a pause. *"Wow. I know this shouldn't be a relief, but it is :) It's soooo awful feeling like you're keeping secrets from me."*

She didn't message me back straight away, and I stared at my phone, feeling uneasy. Despite clearly being a little hurt... she was taking it kind of well. Really well. She'd gotten upset over a *lot* less recently...

While I was wondering why that was, another text message came through. *"Okay, are you SURE it's not true?? Everyone here is pretty convinced..."*

"Yeah, it's just because Spud from Risk saw Henry and I at the restaurant together on Saturday night and of course jumped to the conclusion that I was sleeping with him for job security or whatever," I messaged. I was typing, *"I'll tell you more at lunch, meet me downstairs!"* but I never got to send it, because she sent one first.

"...Wait, what???????"

There was a pause between messages, and in that pause, my life flashed before my eyes.

"What the hell are you talking about?? I was talking about the Marketing secondment that just got announced!" Then, *"...Weren't you with STEPHEN on Saturday night??"*

Oh...

Oh, no. I'd done it again.

While I was *gaping* at my phone, Anil stuck his head out of the door on his way out. "Henry wants a word with you."

I looked up at him, aghast. Sarah was going to *kill* me.

I didn't want to be rude, though, so since there was no way I could figure out what to message Sarah right now to undo what I'd just said, I numbly stood and walked back into Henry's office. I think Anil said goodbye to me, but I didn't realise until it was too late for me to say it back without it being weird.

Henry looked glum, but he still managed to note my expression. "Are you okay?"

Okay? Hah. "Sure, if by 'okay' you mean 'World's Biggest Screw-Up'."

Despite his furrowed brow, he still managed a reassuring smile. "Making one mistake isn't screwing everything up. Everyone makes mistakes."

I appreciated him trying to comfort me, but Sarah... I could feel my phone vibrating in my bag; she was trying to call me. It was louder than usual, and I was just wondering about that when I realised *Henry's* mobile was on vibrate and ringing too; it was travelling ever so slightly across his desk as it buzzed. He was trying to ignore his, just like I was mine.

He noticed my eyes on his phone. "That's Sean Frost, my boss," he said, nodding at it. He swallowed. "I'm not going to answer it until I feel comfortable with what approach to take about this restaurant business. Anil thinks Spud will probably cool down and the whole thing will blow over, but I'm not so sure. I think we should do something now." His phone fell silent for a moment, and then started to vibrate again. He flinched.

I did, too. "Well, what do you think we should we do?"

He looked up at me. "I think we should go and ask Natalie that exact question."

CHAPTER TWENTY

Henry did actually have a meeting that he needed to go to, but when I asked him if I had to go back to work as well, he gave me a dramatic look like *heaven forbid*. "What kind of manager would I be if I forced you back into a workplace where you felt uncomfortable?" he asked, and then shook his head. "That's a recipe for a Workcover claim. Take the rest of the day off and then I'll meet you at this address at about 5:30pm." He opened his drawer and handed me one of Natalie's little red cards. "What's your mobile number? I'll text you if I'm going to be late." After that, I was free to go.

It was weird having the afternoon off. I'd been working full-time since I finished uni, and since I usually saved up all my annual leave for big overseas holidays with Sarah, I pretty much never had workdays free. I felt like a ghost, wandering aimlessly through shops while I waited for 5:30pm to come so Henry and I could meet at Natalie's office.

Her firm, Heiser & Anderson, was in a building on the east edge of the CBD, just north of Hyde Park. They shared it with a couple of other law firms, and when I walked into the modern foyer which had an open café like Frost HQ, everyone in there looked well-dressed, confident, and as sleek as the interior design. I immediately felt out of place and tried not to make eye-contact with any of them in case they realised I was an impostor.

It was lucky there was a little waiting area I could tuck myself away in, because Henry ran a little late. "I had to make sure I didn't bump into anyone who was trying to intersect me on the way out of work," he said cryptically, and exhaled at length. "Shall we?" He gestured towards the lifts. He was a little breathless.

I let him escort me into one as he tucked his car keys into his pocket. He *seemed* calm, but it must have been all for show because he missed his pocket and dropped them on the floor. I went to pick them up for him and we both ended up crouched on the tiles for a second.

At least it made him laugh, if nervously. "I'm sorry, Gemma," he said a little stiffly as he stood. "I'm not usually like this."

I let him help me up. "Are you okay?"

He laughed a couple more times, and then gave me a strained smile. "No, not really."

I felt awful for him. *I really should say something comforting, seeing as this whole thing is my fault,* I thought, and then, as if on cue, my mind went immediately blank. *SAY SOMETHING!* my brain was screaming, but that was all I could think: that I *should* say something, but I couldn't think of what to say, so nothing came out of my mouth. In the end, I was just staring at him in panic while he looked elsewhere and pretended I wasn't. It was an awkward silence.

I looked forward at the stainless steel doors, watching the numbers above them light up. I hated that I could never say the right thing; it was what had gotten us into this whole mess in the first place.

Upstairs, the Heiser & Anderson offices were decked out in slate grey and tennis green—kind of a bold choice, I thought— but it made the place seem really young and fresh. Everyone on that floor looked rather young and fresh, too, and the receptionist was probably the oldest of the lot. She was still friendlier than the ones at Frost. "Henry!" she said, recognising him. "Take a seat, would you? Natalie's still on that video call. Would you like some tea or coffee while you wait?"

He glanced at me in question, and I shook my head, so he looked back at her and said, "We're both fine, thanks, Kathy," and then led me to the little waiting room by reception. It overlooked Hyde Park. Outside, the street lights were starting to turn on and there were hordes of business people pouring out of every building and swarming across the roads. No one from this particular office looked like they were going anywhere, though. I guessed that was something Heiser & Anderson and Frost had in common.

232

"Henry, Gemma. So sorry to keep you waiting." Even though I was facing away from her, I recognised that sinuous, self-assured voice. It made the hairs on back of my neck stand on end.

As I turned towards her (and definitely *didn't* jump out the window to escape like I wanted to), Henry was already standing in greeting. He looked relieved. "Thanks for seeing us at such short notice, Natalie."

She briefly returned his smile. "It's always a pleasure," she told him as she invited us into her office. "Anything to get my teeth into Frost. The MEU oversees 14 corps and no one even comes *close* to the complaints and conciliations we need to run on behalf of Frost employees."

The view from Natalie's windows was pretty great as well, but I was too nervous to appreciate it; I was so busy worrying that I'd fall over, drop something, or say something stupid that I tried to pay very close attention to what I was doing so none of that happened. As a result, I missed the first half of something she said to me. "...having you here as well, actually."

Was she talking to—*Oh, no*, she was looking right at me. I froze in panic; how did I make it look like I'd been listening?!

She laughed at my expression and sat opposite us in her big leather executive chair, apparently entertained. "I said: 'Gemma, it's a nice change having you here as well'." She looked me up and down. "I do like that blouse, blue is a good colour for you, too. Where did you buy it?"

I was practically sweating. She was wearing red again, was she teasing me? Transitioning back to my own shade of red, I managed to say hoarsely, "P-Probably Target?"

She laughed like I'd made a joke. "Yes, their new designer ranges sometimes have some great pieces. Especially last season," she said like she thought I wore designer clothes, like I followed fashion seasons and like my blouse was *less* than five years old which it definitely wasn't. Then, she leant in like she was going to share a naughty secret. "Don't tell

233

any of my rich corporate clients I occasionally shop at Target, though. They all think I buy *haute couture*." Laughing, she pushed her sleek black ponytail over her shoulder which made me stare at her exposed collarbones. Even *they* were elegant. Honestly, it hardly mattered where she shopped. With a body like that, she could wear a hessian sack and look amazing...

She sat back and crossed her long legs so one stockinged knee peeked over the edge of her table. "Anyway, it's getting late and I made you wait long enough, so let's get straight to business. What can I do for you two?"

Henry gave her the abridged version of what had happened on Saturday night and the consequences at work after Anil's announcement, and just before he'd finished, she had to stop him to clarify, "Okay, so you both made dummy Tinder profiles specifically to *avoid* this exact situation and ended up matched anyway?" She was actually watching *me* very closely. I didn't understand—did she not believe us or something?—and the discomfort of being scrutinised made me go red. That, of course, made her suspicious. She squinted at both of us. "Why do I feel like there's something you two aren't telling me?"

Henry glanced perhaps a little nervously across at me, and she noticed. It took her a fraction of a second to form a conclusion about that, and a smile grew on her lips. "*Oh.* Come on, you two. Off the record: you're dating now, aren't you? Despite what happened?"

Henry stiffened again, going as red as I was. "I'm never dating another employee, Natalie. You know that."

Natalie noted his cheeks, fifty shades of smug, herself. "As usual, your lips say no..." She looked across at me, and I gulped. "Gemma will tell me, won't you, Gemma?" she asked, leaning in like we were sharing another secret. "*Are* you with Henry? Because I don't mind if you are. I'm just curious."

Eyes wide, I shook my head.

She squinted at me a second before clearly opting to believe me. "Huh, okay," she said, and relaxed back in her chair again. "I would have sworn that's what you were hiding. Oh, well; you would have made a cute couple. Anyway, would you mind telling me what's being spread around Frost now? It's hard to know what the best course of action is without knowing exactly what the slant is. Is it 'Henry is taking advantage of vulnerable female employees' or is it 'Gemma is sleeping her way to job security'?"

Henry exhaled at length, clearly very relieved we were back on topic. "Well, it hasn't gone too far yet," he said. "I mean, apparently Sean knows about it, somehow. But judging by my trip downstairs in a packed lift this afternoon, not many people do. No one looked at me, or was whispering about me or anything like that."

Her eyebrows lifted slightly. "Excellent," she said, sounding pleasantly surprised. "You probably won't even need my legal advice if we can get the jump on the rumours. That's where we need to start with this, not the courts. Courts would be overkill, overkill screams 'guilty', and you don't want people assuming you're guilty if for some bizarre reason you plan to hang around in a job where your boss is actively trying to sabotage you."

Henry ignored that last part. "It sounds like you deal with this situation a lot."

She gave him a bit of a raised eyebrow about glossing over the sabotage thing, but let him get away with it. "You could say that," she said dryly. "Of course, it's much harder to manage when the two people involved actually *are* sleeping with each other. But it's tricky anyway."

"So, what's your advice?"

She tapped a finger against her red lips, thinking. "Well, my *legal* advice is to keep and back up all records of every conversation you've both had electronically or otherwise. Don't be seen in public alone together, don't communicate using work email, and don't call each other using work mobiles. Don't confirm or deny anything, just say you're sick of talking about it if anyone asks."

"But in your *non*-legal opinion...? You must have some idea about how these things usually go."

That smile crept back. "I sure do. My *personal* opinion? You'd be better off trying to frame this rumour to make it seem ridiculous than you would be seeking legal advice. For example," she pointed at me, "Gemma, do you think people would be willing to believe this 'Spud' person just got rejected by you?"

I blinked. "No, he's married."

She scoffed. "That doesn't mean anything. In fact, it makes the rumour even juicier, and juicy rumours spread faster."

I shook my head; I didn't think it would work. "He's really not like that."

She made a face. "Alright, then. What are people's general feelings towards him? Do they dislike him enough to believe whatever negative stories they hear?" I shook my head again; he was pretty well-liked. She exhaled audibly. "Okay," she said, and kept thinking.

While she was brainstorming possibilities—they all seemed pretty full-on, I didn't really want to ruin Spud's career or anything—I tried to work up the courage to say something about it. After all, the covering up and lying about things I'd done recently had just exponentially multiplied all my original problems.

Eventually, I managed to say, "Can't we just tell everyone the truth?"

Natalie looked at me like I had three heads. "Sure," she said flatly, "if you want absolutely no one to believe you and to make it all worse. No one is interested in the truth unless it's better than the rumour—trust me on that one. I've been managing industrial disputes for fifteen years."

Well, that shutdown just about guaranteed I wouldn't say anything else for the entire meeting. "Okay, sorry," I mumbled.

I don't think she noticed. "Okay, so Min's your mutual friend..." she was thinking aloud. "Do you think Min would mind saying he's dating Gemma for a while? That's juicy, and it has the added benefit of making Henry look like a jilted lover who's trying to make peace with both of you."

Min and... oh, *gosh*. The thought of that made me blush like wildfire; Min probably wouldn't mind—I was actually fairly certain she (he?) wouldn't—but *Bree* certainly would.

Henry gave me a cautious look, considering that. To my horror, he said, "Well, Min and Gemma *do* have some history..." After some thought, though, he made a face. "God, what on earth am I thinking? Let's leave Min out of this. He's been put through the ringer at Frost enough."

Natalie nodded once, "Understandable," and then looked across at me for a moment, eyes alight with curiosity. I knew exactly what part of that she'd latched on to. "*Really*, though. You and *Min*?"

My cheeks burning, I shrugged lightly.

She spent a couple of moments closely watching me, and then relaxed back in her chair, eyes still fixed on mine. "Interesting," she said neutrally, and then mercifully looked away. I released a breath I wasn't aware I'd been holding. "Maybe we can use that..."

While I was taking a few slow breathes and recovering from that confrontation, I realised Henry was also quietly watching me. He was deep in thought.

That, Natalie noticed. "Henry?"

He frowned, glancing at her, before turning back to me. He opened his mouth, but it was a couple of seconds before he spoke. "Gemma, would you mind if I told her about you?"

I flinched; after saying it like that, I didn't think he really needed to articulate it. It was kind of obvious Natalie had been questioning my sexuality a second ago, anyway. Grimacing, I nodded.

Henry looked back at Natalie. "Gemma recently discovered she isn't interested in men."

That... wasn't exactly how I'd have said it. 'Prefers women', maybe? 'Likes women'? Or maybe he *was* right, after all.

Anyway, for Natalie's purposes I don't think the distinction was necessary, because a dark smile was already growing on her lips. "Oh, that's *perfect*," she said firmly. "Absolutely perfect."

The colour drained from my face. I didn't like the sound of that.

She looked resolute. "We can just bring forward your coming out to *right now* so it rescues Henry's reputation."

Bring forward my—Oh, no. Oh, gosh, no. My ears started to ring.

I hardly heard the rest of what she said, but it was something to the tune of, "Honestly: it's quite simple. All we need to do is somehow link your sexuality to the dinner with Henry, let the rumour spread for about a week—just enough for this sex-for-job-security rumour to die a quiet death—and then after that, just very casually confirm you're gay if people ask. Once people think it's not a secret anymore, they'll stop being interested in it and it will blow over. Don't confirm straight away, though, it's got to be a secret to spread." She looked very pleased with herself. "Look at it this way, Gemma: not only would you be saving Henry's reputation and possibly his career, but if anything at all goes wrong with your coming out, it will give me a delightful excuse to sue the pants off Frost for making a workplace that's unsafe for people of diverse sexualities, and we'll all walk away with a *lot* of money. It's win-win."

It didn't feel win-win. I was still stuck on the part where *all of Frost* was going to find out this very, very private secret about me. Everyone looking at me, whispering about me, knowing what I felt about women...? Fuck, *no*! I didn't want that! With the power of a thousand burning suns I didn't want that! I'd never be able to show my face at Frost again!

Henry was watching me. "Natalie, that's *not* going to work, and I'm *not* going to let you do that," he said brusquely. "Min was outed at work and that was the centre of all of his—"

"It wasn't Min's choice and he had a manager that bullied the entire department anyway," Natalie cut him off. "This is not the same situation."

"It clearly is," Henry told her, gestured at me. "Look at her! 'No' is written all over her face, coming out isn't something you can just tell someone to—"

"How about you let her answer for herself, Henry?"

They both looked at me; my breath caught in my throat.

Henry's brow had a deep crease in it. "No, because it's my responsibility not to allow my employees to be exploited by people who have something to gain, Natalie, and it's my responsibility to not exploit them myself!"

Natalie was sceptical. "How exactly are you exploiting her? She created this situation by not giving you critical information, this is an opportunity for her to fix it. Doesn't sound like exploitation to me." She was still calm. "So, what do you say, Gemma?"

Before I could speak, Henry interjected. "Natalie," he said in a cautionary tone, "I'm not going to let you do this."

She rolled her eyes, looking very slowly back at him. "Oh, would you get off your white horse for five seconds? She doesn't need anyone to rescue her, she's capable of making her own decisions about what *she* wants." She looked back at me. "So what do you say?"

I say you clearly are very mistaken about my ability to make decisions, I thought, my lips practically fused together.

Henry didn't waste any time in turning back to her and saying something like, "Natalie, that's really unfair," and then both of them—high powered, corporate professionals— started straight up arguing about me like newly divorced parents. Honestly, it was how Mum and Dad used to argue and it made me feel just as uncomfortable, even if these two weren't calling each other names like Mum and Dad did. I couldn't run away and hide in my room now, either.

I'd never seen this side of Henry before; I knew that later, he'd be really embarrassed about it and I was embarrassed now on his behalf. I also felt awful that I'd put him in a situation where he was stressed out enough for that total self-assurance and calmness he always had to crumble away. He was clearly blaming himself for this whole thing.

That's what it was about, wasn't it? He was blaming himself for something that was *my* fault, that *I'd* caused. Deep down in the pit of my stomach, that made me feel really gross, and the more I thought about it, the more I preferred Natalie's plan. The idea of people whispering about me for a week seemed far more tolerable than the knowledge I'd have to live for the rest of my life knowing I'd ruined Henry's reputation and career if I didn't go ahead with it.

I knew what my answer needed to be, but, *gosh*, it made me feel ill. I closed my eyes. "I'll do it."

They both fell silent, and by the time I opened my eyes again, Natalie was giving Henry a look like 'see, I told you!' and Henry's frown was even deeper. He looked deeply concerned; it was pretty clear what his assessment of my decision was.

When Natalie's hand touched mine, I jumped. I hadn't realised she'd been leaning across the table. "Don't worry, Gemma," she said firmly. Her fingernails were *really* red. "If this backfires and people make you feel at all uncomfortable, I'll get you a six-figure settlement for the trouble."

People always make me feel uncomfortable, I privately thought, and sighed. I mean, money would be nice, but I was worried about what sort of things would need to go wrong for me to be eligible for *that* sort of money. I didn't want to think about it.

Plus, leaving Frost would mean leaving Sarah.

...Sarah.

I'd almost forgotten about what happened today; I looked down at my bag where my phone was, imagining that, on top of everything else she just found out, she learnt her best friend was gay when some random person made a joke in the lift about it. It would absolutely break her heart.

Henry and Natalie were busy discussing something again—probably me—when I opened my mouth. They both went quiet to let me speak. "Can—Can I ask for something, though?"

Natalie gave me a lavish grin. "A negotiator. I like it."

I—didn't know what to make of that. It made me blink at her for a few moments. "Um. Can I just have, like, maybe a couple of days to do something first?"

She pursed her lips. "Not really, time is on our side at the moment."

Oh... "24 hours then, maybe...?" Was I asking too much? "Or 12? Or something?"

Watching me again, she leant back in her chair and crossed her legs, considering the request.

Henry spoke first. "Come on, Natalie. It's the least we can give her after we're *forcing* her to—"

She cut him off. "No one's forcing her to anything, Henry," she said dismissively, and then pressed her lips together and nodded. "Okay, 24 hours should be fine. I need to have a think about how we disseminate this information anyway." She looked amused. "I don't suppose you want to spend the next 24 hours looking for a woman to strategically be seen with, do you?"

Hah. If only she knew how disastrously bad I was at picking people up... I didn't end up needing to reply to that anyway, because after that, Natalie spent a few minutes with Henry arranging a time to call him tomorrow and then making sure she had my number, too. We agreed that on Wednesday morning, we'd go ahead with whatever Natalie had decided was the Right Thing to do. Honestly, it felt like doomsday. The clock was ticking.

Henry had brought his car over, so he offered to drive me home after the meeting had finished.

As we were going to leave, Natalie stopped us. "Oh, by the way," she said casually, as a matter of course, "I realised this is short notice, but these sort of things really have more impact if they're sudden. I'm sending out Union Call to Action tomorrow: if Frost doesn't sign on the dotted line to keeping all current positions on shore for at least two years, we're going to call a strike from Thursday."

Thursday? We both stared at her. Henry was the first to react. "You know they'll never agree to that, Natalie."

There was that dark smile again. "Then I guess all of Frost back office is on strike from Thursday."

Henry took a breath. "Look, there are a lot of big projects running at the moment, there's going to be a big impact on business. Can't we just all take a step back and discuss this?"

—there are a lot of big projects running—Something suddenly occurred to me. Oh, no... Hadn't... *Sarah* said something about this being a critical week for her Marketing project?

"But Sarah's project needs Admin support!" I blurted out. "She won't be able to get all her print material out on time without it!" As soon as I closed my mouth, I felt stupid. That was the point, wasn't it?

Natalie looked unfazed. "If she relies on Admin that much, I'm sure she'll appreciate the fact we're fighting to keep their jobs in Australia," she rebutted me easily. "Perhaps she can even support them *and* you and strike with us."

I also clearly remembered Sarah saying if her project didn't go according to plan, it was unlikely she'd ever be selected as Lead again, too. Her career was *so* important to her; as important as Henry's was to him. I felt sick. "Can't you wait for that? Like, even one week?"

Natalie shook her head. "Like your rumours, time is an important factor in this one. Anyway, just thought I'd give you the heads up," she said nonchalantly, and then briskly ushered us out the door.

We both stood outside her office for a moment, shell-shocked. Could this week get any worse?!

Henry recovered first. If possible, he looked even more stressed than he had when he'd gone in. He didn't say anything, though, neither of us did. Not until we'd gone down into the basement car park, climbed into his car and were stuck stationary in Sydney peak hour traffic.

"*Fuck.*"

I smiled a little; that was pretty much where I was at, too: *fuck*. My smile faded quickly.

He looked across at me. "For what it's worth, I'm sorry you had to be present for all of that. Natalie and I don't see eye-to-eye very much."

Hah. *I'm used to it*, I thought, remembering Mum and Dad arguing for my entire childhood, and then apologising for arguing in front of me for my entire childhood. "It's okay."

He shook his head. "It's not." He picked at the steering wheel with his thumbnails, shifting tensely in his seat. "There's just got to be another way, though," he said, shaking his head, "you *shouldn't* have to come out, we don't have to do what Natalie—"

"Henry, it's totally okay."

His eyes searched mine for a moment. Then, he sighed at length. "I just don't want this to go wrong and ruin *two* careers; Min still gets nightmares from some of the things that happened to him after he was outed."

I thought about the alternative. "Well, I'd rather have those than nightmares about how I ruined someone's life because I was too scared to do anything to fix it," I told him candidly. And, even though I wasn't sure I'd ever want to, I added, "I have to come out at some point, anyway. I might as well do it now and save your career." It was mainly to make him feel better.

He spent a few minutes digesting that as we inched forward in the terrible CBD traffic. After a little while, he turned back to me. "Is it rude of me to ask why you need the extra 24 hours?" He paused. "Is it because of Sarah?"

I pressed my lips together, looking at my hands in my lap, and nodded. She was *not* going to have a good week this week...

He looked forward again, mirroring my nod. "How much are you going to tell her?"

That, I was trying to avoid thinking about. "I don't know."

While we were sitting at traffic lights he spent a little while watching me, but we were across Sydney Harbour

243

Bridge before he spoke again. "I've tried to kiss Min twice since he broke up with me. We were drunk both times, but I still knew what I was doing." He let that hang in the air for a moment, looking thoughtful. "But it's not weird between us now because of that, not at all. We're too close, and someone who's open-minded, mature and who loves you isn't going to feel anything except compassion for you if you love them unrequitedly." He glanced across at me, smiling faintly. "If the friendship is that important to you both, Gemma, I promise you, you'll work through it. Nothing, not even one of you briefly falling for the other, will change the lifetime of treasured memories you'll make together and share."

Unexpectedly, that struck me. I hadn't expected something that was *his* story to strike so close to home for me, but it did. It got to the very core of what I was afraid of: what it would mean if we couldn't work through it. If things did get weird between us.

Our lives were so different, these days. She was about to embark on the next chapter of hers: having a baby. Probably getting married. She'd already bought a house and been promoted and done a million 'next chapter' things in her life while I was still stuck desperately at the gates, waiting for my gun to finally go off.

And all the things we used to love—our amazing holidays, our wild adventures, drinking really huge and irresponsible amounts of alcohol: that stuff was in the past. She said it was just on hold until her baby was old enough, but I doubted Sarah was going to stop at one baby. I knew she wanted three, so those days were over. Deep down, we both knew that.

And if those things were gone, and she was in a different phase of her life now, without me: what was left?

I knew the answer: I was left. I was left by myself desperately missing the old Sarah, my old best friend in the whole wide world.

I looked down at my handbag. On impulse, I reached down and retrieved my phone so I could look at that selfie Sarah has taken of us on Saturday night. It was there, smiling at me from the top of my gallery, but I couldn't open it. Staring down at that thumbnail, I wondered if it was going to be the last photo of us together.

There was no stopping this now, though. Even if Natalie came up with some other plan, it was time Sarah knew. I'd screwed up enough—I just wanted all of this mess to be over. I wanted all the messes I'd created with all my stupid terrified bullshit to be over. I was exhausted.

Swallowing back tears, I opened messaging. *"Sare, there's something else I really need to tell you. Can you come over tonight?"*

"At the OBGYN."

That was cold. I guess I deserved it; at least she was talking to me. *"Afterwards?"*

"Afterwards I'm busy."

The beginning of the end, I thought, remembering her beautiful smile from that photo. *"Sare, I have something I really need to tell you. I know I screwed up, but please let me do this properly..."*

We were nearly back home at my place by the time she finally replied, *"Maybe tomorrow night."*

I think Henry accidentally saw that last message as he pulled over beside my house. "It's okay if you don't want to come in tomorrow," he said. "I'll sort things out with Anil and Omar."

It was tempting not to. It was *really* tempting not to, but if Sarah was finding out she was going to lose all the staff she needed to complete her project on time, I couldn't *not* be there. Especially if I was going to dump a whole lot of other crap on her tomorrow night, too. I had no idea how I was going to deal with everyone else at Frost, though, but I had to be there for Sarah. "No, I'll come in."

He frowned. "Are you sure?" When it was clear I was, he sighed. "Okay, but if you feel uncomfortable at all, just take sick leave, alright? I'll sign off on it, no questions asked. I won't have you going through what Min did."

I nodded, putting my phone in my handbag and my handbag in my lap. I sat for a minute in the passenger seat with his engine running quietly in the background. "I'm sorry," I told him, eventually. "You know, for everything."

He smiled tightly. "If both of us get through this in one piece, I'm going to crack open a bottle of really expensive, really alcoholic champagne, and I hope you'll share it with me." He paused; there was a slight smile on his lips. "Even if it *is* only because you don't want an old man to drink alone."

I had to chuckle at that. "It wouldn't be because of that," I told him warmly, and we smiled tiredly at each other.

"Well, with any luck it'll all go smoothly and we'll have worried for nothing," he told me as I got out of his car and bid him goodbye. I agreed with him to make him feel better, but that reference to 'luck' made me uncomfortable.

This was me we were talking about: if there was a way for something to go wrong, it would. If there was a tiny outside chance at all something terrible would happen, it would happen, and Natalie was about to raise the stakes a thousandfold.

I just really, really hoped she knew what she was doing.

CHAPTER TWENTY-ONE

That night, I couldn't sleep. It wasn't just the fact I needed to come out to Sarah, either; I kept thinking about all the horrible things that could happen at work. I wasn't sure which part was worse: knowing everyone might be whispering behind their hands and judging me, or the fact that I knew Sarah was going to have a *terrible* day and a large chunk of it was my fault.

The whole thing stressed me out, and I kept asking myself why the hell I was thinking of going to work in the first place— after all, Henry had said it would be okay if I called in sick. I couldn't do that to Sarah, though. Bailing on her in her time of need because of my own problems wasn't the answer.

It did mean that I couldn't sleep, though.

At about 2am I got sick of staring at the ceiling, and wandered to the kitchen with the intention of downing a bottle of sav blanc so I could at least get *some* rest. However, when it came to pouring it, I ended up just staring at the bottle. Did I *really* want to be super hungover on the day I finally came out to Sarah?

Like you're going to be sober when you actually say it, anyway... I thought ironically, and poured myself a mugful, leaning against my kitchen sink in my PJs and preparing myself for how gross it tasted to drink in one gulp.

I probably would have just done it without a second thought, but when I looked down, I noticed that I'd taken out an old, stained Garfield mug to drink it from. A kid's mug. It wasn't exactly what most adults would drink their wine out of; then again, statistically, most adults were married, pregnant and happy right now, and not gay, alone and self-medicating with cheap wine out of ugly children's mugs at 2am.

Also, most adults don't need to suddenly come out to everyone at 28, I reasoned, and just poured it all down my throat. I'd made all the wrong decisions about everything anyway, and it wasn't like drinking myself to sleep tonight was going to be the one that ruined my life.

Of course, I changed my tune in the morning when I woke up with a pounding headache, but it was a bit too late to feel sorry for myself by that point: I had way bigger problems to face today.

My first one was which department to go to when I got to work. I stood in the lift, worrying about which button to press.

There was no chance in hell I was going to go to Risk, no chance in hell. Not before Natalie had exacted whatever plan she was concocting to get rid of the me-sleeping-with-Henry rumour and it had all blown over, because Spud would eat

247

me alive. The trouble was that if I wasn't going to go to Risk, where *was* I going to go?

I could probably go straight to Marketing, I thought, my finger hovering over the '36'. But did I really want to walk in there by myself? I wasn't sure if Sarah would be in yet, and in the event that the me-and-Henry rumour had already made it upstairs, I wasn't sure how I was supposed to fend for myself without her. Marketing was a bunch of men who had the collective sensitivity of a charging rhino.

Henry would know what to do. Unfortunately, Natalie's advice had been to not be seen alone together, so there went the idea of paying him a quick visit in his office.

The only solution I could think of was just presenting at the HR reception and explaining my situation. So as much as I didn't really want to wander in there like a lost little kid, I pressed '35' anyway.

As hoped, the receptionist got a proper adult to come and collect me. "Hey, you must be Gemma!" A deep male voice with a heavy American accent asked me from the doorway; Omar, the acting Marketing manager was standing there, leaning casually on the doorway and directing me a very white-teethed smile. He even *looked* like a salesman as he extended his hand towards me. "Omar. I've seen you around. How are you doing this morning?"

You don't want me to answer that honestly, I thought, while I forced a meek, "Fine, thanks," and stood so he could lead me up to level 36.

He was one of those people who *talked*—a salesman thing, I guess—and since I wasn't one of those people, I just gave him a thin smile and nodded politely while we caught a lift up. It probably would have been kind of comforting that he was completely happy to just fill the airspace by himself, except I kept worrying about what was waiting for me upstairs.

Marketing was only one floor up, so I didn't need to wonder for long. When the lift doors opened, it was to an entire department full of people. Worse: everyone was clearly expecting me, because when people looked up and saw who it was in the lift, they all started standing from their desks and walking over.

Suddenly, there were at least 20 smiling men converging on me as Omar basically pushed me out of the lift. It was like standing in a room with the walls closing in.

I couldn't be here. I couldn't do this. Beside me, the women's toilets sparkled like an oasis in the desert; it would be so easy to just duck in there and wait until everyone had dispersed. I'd done it before so many times when I was up here looking for Sarah that these guys probably all thought I had a bladder problem.

I hesitated, though: wasn't running off how I got into this whole big mess in the first place?

I hadn't answered that question by the time I was engulfed by clerks. They swarmed around me, grabbing my hand and shaking it and greeting me and telling me all their names—so many names, I was never going to remember any of them?—and asking me various questions. How long was I up here for? Had I been told which project I was on yet? Was I from Sydney originally? I didn't know who to answer first, and when I opened my mouth to try and answer any of them, someone else asked another. In the end, I couldn't say anything. I was frozen in place with my cheeks burning. There was so much noise!

"Look, Ian, you made her blush, dude!" someone called across the crowd, laughing.

Omar actually had to hold out his hands to shut them all up. "Okay, okay, pipe down, all of you! I know you're excited we have a brand new team member, but I've got about ten minutes to show her around so if you could let me get on with it..."

As they all backed away, I realised my next problem: what was going to happen after ten minutes?! If Omar was going to abandon me, I hoped Sarah didn't hate me too much to chaperone me on my first day. I looked around for her, thinking that she probably would have found the whole engulfed-bybuff-men thing hilarious if she hadn't been upset, but she was nowhere to be found.

Eventually, while Omar was teaching me how to use the flashy new coffee machine in the kitchen (a very important feature of Marketing, apparently), I worked up enough courage to ask where she was.

"Oh, yes, Sarah!" he said, frothing the milk like a pro. "She's probably downstairs in Admin—we just took a big shipment of print material that needs to be sorted and mailed to vendors before Friday, so she's probably explaining to the staff down there all what they need to do."

Oh, no—I'd almost forgotten. The staff that would be walking off their jobs tomorrow because of the strike.

Omar saw my expression and mistook it for simple discomfort. "Don't worry, though, she'll be up for the big meeting we have first thing."

'Meeting first thing'? "Oh, a union meeting?" I asked, wondering if Natalie was planning to tell everyone face-to-face.

I only remembered that Marketing wasn't affected by the offshoring when Omar frowned at me. My question must have been really left field, because a couple of the other boys who were waiting for the coffee machine looked at me like I was nuts, too. As if I wasn't red enough already...

"No," Omar said slowly, "just a project update meeting. Why?"

Crap. "No reason!" I said quickly, returning to my usual shade of red, accepting my latte from him, and then following him to the meeting room.

Just as I'd feared he wouldn't, he didn't sit down with me and protect me against his staff. Instead, he left me sitting there with a bunch of them while he went to 'just quickly do something' before the meeting started. Everyone was looking at me, and I had a feeling they might want to actually talk to me if I wasn't careful, so I took out my phone and pretended to be super engrossed in what was on my screen.

I thought it was going pretty well until, in my peripheral vision, I saw several guys stand up from the other side of the table and start walking towards me.

I stared at my screen, my eyes widening. *No*, I willed them, *no, don't talk to me, don't talk to—*

"Hey!" One of them greeted me, proving I needed to put more work into cultivating my 'unapproachable' visage. "'Gemma', isn't it?" He pulled out a chair, spun it around, and sat astride the backrest.

They all sat around me in my preciously guarded personal space, smelling like a cologne department. I put my phone away because I couldn't very well keep staring at it while they were talking to me, but when I looked up, to my *abject horror*, I recognised one of them.

It was Nate from Tinder.

They introduced themselves—I didn't hear their names because I was busy listening to the sound of my pulse hammering in my ears. Nate didn't look angry; he didn't look anything. But he certainly didn't have the same charming grin as his four colleagues.

Has he heard the rumour about me and Henry? I wondered, desperately trying to read him. I couldn't, and it made me sweat. If he'd heard it... well, I'd told Nate I didn't want to date him because he worked at Frost. Gosh, I *hoped* he hadn't heard it...

"—so you're the new John, right?" The chair-guy asked. I'd never heard of 'John' before, but I guessed he was the previous demographer, so I nodded. So did they. "Good, John was shit," he said abruptly, and they all laughed. "I heard along the grapevine that you're *really* good at what you do."

I... didn't like the way he'd put that. Maybe he was just being flirty—? Like that made it better, though: I was in shy girl hell anyway. I was blushing, I was sweating, and Nate was watching me with a really strange expression.

The guy who was talking to me was one of those people who knew they were really attractive, which made him

251

terrifying. His charming smile was as impossible to look at as the sun. "So, what *is* it you do, Gemma? Because rumour has it that you're not a marketing clerk."

My throat was dry. "I'm a statistician."

He feigned interest in my answer. "Cool," then, he leant forward. "You must be really smart, right?"

I felt mildly ill. "I guess?"

"I was always terrible at maths," he told me. "I used to bribe my classmates to do my assignments. Maybe we could come to *that* sort of arrangement, yeah?" He flashed that blinding smile at me.

Was he...? I internally dismissed that: there's no way someone would hit so openly on a co-worker. He must just be making small talk. "I don't think—well, I'm here specifically to do your maths?"

They all laughed like I'd said something really funny, and then they all shoved the guy who'd been speaking to me. "Owned!" one of them told him, and then turned to me. "What Ben here *really* wants to know is if you'll have coffee with him."

'Ben' turned that grin on me. He was about to speak, when *Nate* interrupted him. "Yeah, man, I don't think she's interested."

Ben gave Nate a look; he obviously didn't appreciate that interruption. "What, are you a chick-whisperer now?"

Nate was looking directly at me instead of at Ben. All the blood drained out of my face; I had no idea what he was going to say. "Not exactly."

Everyone was starting to listen to him. I glanced around the room; there was nowhere to escape. All these men were sitting all around me, fencing me in.

Nate kept going. "Yeah, I hear that she doesn't date people from work," he said, and there was something about his voice... The men sitting around me were all sort of frowning at him, waiting for him to explain himself. He locked eyes with me. "Unless they can save her job, that is."

Oh my gosh, he *did* know.

I gaped at him. He was going to tell them. He looked me directly in the eyes—actually he looked kind of *hurt*?—and I think he was just figuring out what to say when Ben spoke first. "Dude: just *what*?" he said, clapping Nate on the back. "What the hell 'save her job'?" He looked at me, and then something occurred to him. "Wait... Do you guys have history or something...?"

Before Nate could answer that, a familiar feminine voice suddenly interrupted us. "Okay, enough chit-chat, let's get going with this meeting so I can get back down to Admin ASAP."

Sarah!

Oh my gosh, I could have hugged her! She bustled past us up to the head of the board table and began to set up her laptop. The boys all sobered up, turning forward in their seats to face her.

I had a big smile all ready for her—gosh, I was so thankful to her for saving me from that!—and I couldn't wait for her to look at me so she could see how appreciative I was. But when she finally did, I didn't get the reaction I expected.

She didn't smile back. In fact, she looked really guarded, like she was hiding what she really felt. She nodded at me to acknowledge the 'thank you' anyway, but when I looked closer at her, I could see she had a layer of heavy eye-makeup on. She only did her makeup like that to either hide that she hadn't slept, or that she'd been crying. I didn't feel good about either of those possibilities.

Omar came barrelling into the room a few moments later and closed the door. "Sorry everyone! Sarah? Have you already properly introduced our newest team member?"

Something passed across her face. This time, she forced a big, bright smile anyway—she even managed to feign some ceremony about the whole introduction—but it felt a bit off. It was pretend. She didn't feel like smiling.

Most of the meeting wasn't that important to me; I only half-listened. Sarah was pointing at some Gantt charts and delivering her update on where her project was at—a really critical point, apparently—when, across from me, one of the men made a sudden exclamation.

"*Fuck*!" He was looking at his phone.

I was embarrassed on his behalf; were they allowed to just openly swear in front of their boss like that?!

Omar didn't appear very bothered by the swearing. "Something to share, Carlos?"

'Carlos' looked up. I had a feeling Omar's question was more of a 'shut up' than a genuine question, but he answered anyway. "Yeah," he said, "Admin's going on strike."

There was a pronounced silence.

Suddenly, everyone was paying attention, especially Sarah. I held my breath. She leant forward, frowning deeply. "What? When?"

He put his phone down, and there was defeat in his voice. "Close of business tomorrow."

I could see the colour draining out of Sarah's face. "You're joking." He shook his head. She reached for her phone in disbelief and tabbed through to her own email—like everyone else in the room was doing—her eyes tracking backwards and forwards as she read it.

While I was watching her and worrying about her, Omar spoke up. "Hey, Gemma—"

Me?! I looked over at him, saucer-eyed.

He was frowning. "This might seem like a really strange question, but did you already know about this? You mentioned a union meeting this morning…"

Shit! I glanced over at Sarah as she looked up sharply from her phone. Oh, no…

Omar noticed my expression. My answer was obvious. "Don't worry, you're not in any trouble! I was just hoping you'd be able to give us more intel about how long they're planning to go for, etc."

Locking eyes with Sarah, I swallowed. "No, I only found out they were doing it really late last night," I rasped. "I don't know any more. I promise."

The hurt on her face was *so* transparent. I could see exactly what she was thinking as she gaped at me: *you knew, and you didn't tell me. How* could *you*?

It only lasted for a second, and then she closed her jaw. "I'm going to go call the MEU and find out what the hell's going on," she said resolutely, and then high-tailed out the door. I think I was the only one who noticed how hard she shut it.

I wanted to go after her. I wanted to explain to her that I'd planned to tell her, and I'd texted her to come over, and—gosh, I really just wanted to hug her and apologise for *everything*! I wasn't sure she'd welcome that right now, though.

Omar looked like he'd aged about ten years in the space of 20 seconds. "*Fuck*," he said at length. "Sarah's project's on some *really* tight deadlines. Can we get casuals?"

Jason, Min's old boss, answered. "It takes at least two days to get the recruitment agencies on board, vet casuals and train them up," he said. "Not to mention it's an exorbitant staffing cost to expedite the whole hiring process. We wouldn't be looking at less than $100k for the contract."

"Well, Sarah decided to spend $100k on these damn print materials and I'm not going to lose that budget," Omar told him, and then ran a hand over his face. "*Fuck*. Okay, meeting's over. I need to talk to Diane."

Before he went to go do that, he hurriedly set me up at my workstation: a little cubicle in the corner with dual monitors and a space-age-looking scientific calculator. Fortunately, everyone else was too busy discussing the strike and how it impacted them to care much about me right now. For that, I was grateful.

I couldn't see Sarah straight away, though. She wasn't at her desk. I sat at my own desk feeling terrible; not even the awesome calculator helped.

I should have texted her about the strike last night, I thought. Although, what would have that achieved except to guarantee she wouldn't sleep a wink? *I should have done it anyway*, I decided, shaking my head. Now look at what had happened...

When Sarah did reappear, it was from the direction of the women's toilets where she definitely hadn't been calling the MEU, and she had another fresh layer of eye makeup on. She was walking towards me in a really deliberate way, like she was psyching herself up to speak to me.

I took a deep breath. As she arrived, I began to blurt out, "Sarah, I tried to invite you over, I wanted to tell you everything that I—"

She threw her hands up to stop me from talking. "Please," she said in a very measured voice. It wavered a little. "Please, I can't deal with that right now. Not at work. Let's just go over what I need you to do so I can go back to dealing with the strike."

"But—"

She stopped me. "Gemma, I can't. Please." She couldn't even look at me.

It was like being punched in the stomach. *But I want to help*, I thought, *I'm here to support you*. I didn't say it, though.

She made me log in and open some spreadsheets, spending a few minutes explaining what the department had needed me to do today. I listened, but I was mostly watching her while she spoke. She was being completely professional and courteous, but there was none of her usual warmth. None of her usual silliness or humour, and that cheeky smile she always gave me was nowhere to be seen. There was something empty about her.

I was looking at the face of my beautiful best friend—someone who I loved with all my heart—but to anyone else watching us, we could have been perfect strangers.

"If you have any questions, come ask me," she said, but it seemed a bit hollow. I nodded, and so did she, before returning to her own workstation. There were already people standing up to go speak to her as she sat down.

256

After that, she didn't speak to me. She didn't have lunch with me, either—no wonder, really, everyone was so busy—and I mostly sat away in my corner with my spreadsheets, alone. I didn't really have any sort of problem with this arrangement, but the men kept looking at me like they might come over. I was especially worried that Nate would try and confront me again; fortunately, he seemed pretty busy with the impending crisis.

Later, when Omar dropped around to check on me, he explained that Sarah had told everyone statistics took a lot of concentration and no one should disturb me.

That was nice of her. I watched her from across the office, wishing I could thank her. She didn't look at me, though; she was really busy. I exhaled, and turned back at my own computer. This wasn't at all how I imagined working with her would turn out.

As much as I didn't want home-time to come because of what I needed to tell Sarah tonight, when 5pm rolled around, I figured I might as well leave because I was done with everything and wasn't any use to anybody right now. I had to walk past her desk to leave.

She didn't look up as I passed her, but I could see her fingers pause on her keyboard, so I stopped.

Taking a careful breath, I asked gingerly, "See you tonight?"

"Tonight?"

I frowned. She'd forgotten? "Yeah... you said you were coming over so I could tell you something important?"

There was a long pause, and then she twisted right around to look at me. "You mean that 'I need to tell you something' thing *wasn't* about the strike?" I shook my head, and her eyebrows went up. "There's *more* you haven't told me?"

Oh... "Y-Yeah. It's not about work, though..."

She sat back, eyebrows high. Then, she shook her head in disbelief. "Jesus, Gemma."

A silence stretched between us. It took me some time to work up the courage to say, "I know. I know I'm terrible. But you'll still come, right?"

She pressed her lips in a thin line and shook her head.

"But—"

She turned sharply around to look up at me again. "Gem, I actually can't deal with any more of this right now," she said, emotion audible in her voice. "Like, how much more am I going to find out you've been hiding from me? Please, just—I've got work to do. Just let me do it." Then, she turned back to her desk, drew a long, steadying breath and kept typing.

The conversation was over. There was no point in me standing behind her chewing my lip afterwards, so I just left and caught the train home by myself.

My house was quiet as I changed out of my work clothes into trackies and sat down on my couch. I felt like I could use a hug, but Mr Crumpet was asleep in the last patch of sun on my bay windows and he'd be grumpy and not very cuddly if I bothered him now.

I shouldn't have gone in, I thought. *I should have taken Henry's advice and called in sick—then Sarah wouldn't have found out I knew about the strike. I wouldn't have made things even worse between us while I was trying to do the right thing and make them better.*

What a terrible day to need to come out to her, though; like, it had to be on the day she found out the make-or-break project for her career might fail, *after* she'd found out her best friend was still lying to and hiding things from her. It was nuts, no one would expect this to work!

The more I thought about it, the more it seemed really insane that I thought I'd be able to tell her tonight. As soon as Natalie told us she'd decided to call the strike, I should have made the connection between that and me coming out to Sarah, and I should have asked her for at least another 24 hours. After all, when I'd first asked for 24 hours, I didn't know I'd be competing with the strike for Sarah's time.

I turned my phone over in my hand, thinking. Maybe… Sarah would probably have figured out what to do about her staffing issue tomorrow, yeah…?

I could just delay coming out to her by a *little* bit. Yeah, even just putting it off by one day would probably help, right?

The chance of me calling Natalie directly about it approached zero, and it still took me a good fifteen minutes to get the courage to call Henry. He answered straight away. "Hello, Gemma. How did it go with Sarah? Are you alright?"

I grimaced; his faith in me was painful. "It didn't, she's busy because of the strike." I jammed my eyes shut. *Say it*, I willed myself. "Do you… think I could have just one more day? Like, surely one more day won't matter, right?"

There was a long, telling pause. "Are you having second thoughts about coming out to everyone, Gemma?" he asked. "Because if you are, you don't have to do it, I'm sure if we speak to Natalie, she'll—"

"It's not that. I just need one more day."

There was another long pause in which I could almost *hear* him trying to second-guess what I was saying, "Well, if that's definitely the case and there isn't any other reason you'd like to delay it, I'm sure Natalie will understand. It's a very big thing you're doing for me, after all. I'll ask her."

Oh, gosh. *Natalie.* "Okay…"

"I'll call her. Be in touch shortly," he said, and then wished me goodbye and hung up.

I put the phone in my lap and stared at it, waiting for Henry to call back. *Please let Natalie say yes*, I thought, staring at it. *Please, please, please…*

When it rang again, I dove on it and was about to swipe to answer when I noticed the words '*Private number*' in the caller ID section.

I had Henry's number saved.

It's Natalie! I realised, and nearly threw my phone across the room and scuttled under the couch. I didn't, though, but I

259

didn't do much better than that, either: I sat and mutely stared at it while it rang and rang and then rang out.

As soon as it fell silent, I felt the familiar weight of guilt and regret settle on me: that had been probably my one chance to get extra time to come out to Sarah, and what had I done? I'd freaked out and *missed out*. That's how all this crap had started in the first place!

I was busy groaning into my hands and hating myself when it buzzed again.

Don't you bloody miss that call again, Gem, I told myself and forced myself to answer. My hands were sweating so much that I was worried it would slip out of them like a wet bar of soap.

It was a second before she spoke. "Gemma." Even over the phone her charisma was horribly oppressive; she might as well have been standing over me wearing full leather. "I just got a very interesting call from Henry, and I wanted to have a quick chat with you about it."

"O-Oh?"

Oh? *Oh?!* That was the best I could do?

"Mmm-hmm. He said that you have something 'very important' that was causing you to need to defer the disclosure tomorrow. I was just a little curious about what could be *that* important."

Then, she waited for me to explain while I sat there, grimacing. There was no point in hiding the real reason from her, was there? Despite that, it took me a few false starts to get the words out of my mouth. "I need to come out to Sarah first, so she doesn't find out from other people."

There was a long pause.

I could practically *feel* her judging me. "It's just with the strike, she's really busy, so..."

"Yes, I can imagine she is," Natalie said conversationally. "But we're on a tight timeline here, so if you'd still like to fix things for Henry, I'm going to need you to sort this out tonight."

But—"But she's just got too much on her plate at the moment!"

"Is she going to have *less* on her plate tomorrow after Back Office has walked out?"

260

...good point. I couldn't say anything to that. "No, I suppose not..." I admitted, but then panicked at the thought of calling her again now. "It's just she's been really stressed out lately and—"

"Gemma." There was that tone again. "Can I ask you a question?"

I felt like I was in trouble with a school teacher. "Yes?"

"How important would you consider fixing Henry's reputation?"

That was a no-brainer. "Very important?"

"And how important is coming out to your friend before everyone else finds out?"

Again, "Very important?"

She didn't even pause. "Then why are you avoiding doing both?"

Ouch. Bullseye. "I'm not avoiding them, I'm just picking the right time to—"

"When is the right time? Because it's not going to be tomorrow. I don't know how long Back Office will elect to strike, but I can guarantee you Henry's reputation will already be in tatters by the time your friend has Admin on call again, if that's what you're waiting for."

As soon as the words had come through the receiver, I knew her logic about timing was absolutely watertight. It made me wonder what I actually *had* been waiting for, because I don't know on what planet I thought Sarah would be in a better headspace tomorrow.

"So," she said, after giving me a few moments to let her point sink in. "I'm going to need a firm answer right now if you're going to pull out of helping Henry, because I'll need to plan something else. What would you like to do? Would you still like to fix this mess?"

I exhaled. There was only one right answer. "Yes..."

She made a satisfied noise. "Okay, I'm glad to hear it. In that case, I'll give you a call tomorrow at about 9am so we can discuss how to disseminate this 'not interested in men' thing, is that alright?"

No, I thought, worrying about Sarah. But there wasn't much I could do.

"Okay, I'm not hearing a 'yes'. Are we still on for tomorrow, Gemma? Because I'd hate for you to make another decision you'd regret."

I pressed my lips together. "Yes, it's alright."

She pretended not to hear my hesitation. "Okay, good. I'm glad we sorted this out. Speak with you tomorrow." With that, she hung up.

I looked down at my phone as the screen went dark, and then put it in my lap.

Shit.

So I *wasn't* getting extra time, and Sarah *was* going to find out when everyone else did unless I told her tonight. Those were the only choices, weren't they? Tell Sarah tonight, or Sarah finds out from someone else tomorrow. The answer was clear: if I wanted to stop the carnage, I needed to tell her now, regardless of how upset and stressed out she was. It would be worse if I didn't tell her, I *needed* to tell her.

Taking a breath, I looked down at my phone.

Call her, I ordered myself while I just sat there, not calling her. I didn't want to do it. Like, I really, really didn't want to do it. Every part of me was noping the hell out of there, and after not being able to explain to Natalie about *why* I didn't want to do it, I didn't really understand what my problem was.

Henry was right, Sarah would probably be *fine* about the fact I was gay even if she guessed that I was into her—I accepted that now. I mean, she wouldn't be fine about the fact I was telling her under these circumstances, but the alternative was worse.

So if I now knew that was the case, I just... Well, I didn't understand why I had this enormous block about telling her. Why I'd always had it, and why every part of me was like *NO!!!!* when I thought about opening my mouth and saying those words. I didn't understand. I kind of wasn't sure I wanted to.

I couldn't focus on that right now, though, could I? I just need to do it. I could worry about the details later.

Feeling ill, I forced myself to unlock my phone, shakily dial her number, and put the handset against my ear. I could hear the bell toll with every ring.

Finally, she answered. "Yes?"

My heart was pounding. "Sare, I need you to come over after work tonight, because I really need to talk to you." Before she could say no, I cut her off. "I know you're super busy, and I know I've been lying to you and hiding stuff from you, and I know everything is terrible, but trust me that everything will be way worse if I don't talk to you tonight..."

There was a long, drawn out pause where I had no idea what her answer was going to be. I even wondered if she'd hung up already. In the end, though, I think in my heart I always knew what she'd say. "I seriously don't know when I'll be done here, Gem..." '*But*', I heard in her voice. *But I'll come.*

Gosh, I think I was so relieved I actually *smiled* for a second. I didn't mind waiting up. It was just a few more hours out of my entire life. "It doesn't matter," I promised her as we said our goodbyes. "I'll be awake."

CHAPTER TWENTY-TWO

Sarah wasn't kidding about how late she needed to work. The clock ticked past midnight while I sat there on my couch, chewing my lip and staring at the door. It was so long that the two glasses of wine I'd had for courage wore off, and I realised with mounting horror that I'd need to come out to Sarah *sober*. Without alcohol, I had no idea how to say it to her. Most of all, I just hoped I *could* say it. I kept imagining her yelling at me, or crying, or—just turning around and walking out on me like Mikey did last week.

While I was remembering that and worrying that's how tonight would end as well, I heard the click-click of high heels on the pavement outside.

Immediately, my heart started to pound. *Shit.* I closed my eyes and took a few deep breaths, waiting for her to let herself in.

Instead, she knocked.

In all the years I'd lived here, I don't think she'd ever done that. It didn't bode well. My knees were stiff as I stood up to open the door to her.

She was just standing there in my doorway, still and silent. I was so used to her bustling into my kitchen, chatting, laughing and full of energy, that it felt surreal to see her completely devoid of it. What struck me was how tired she looked; tired, and worn down. She was normally so vivacious and so beautiful—she was still beautiful, of course, but tonight she looked like a wilted flower.

When she finally spoke, her voice was quiet. She wasn't looking at me. "Work is hell," she said, I think to explain why she was so late.

I could imagine it was. "Thanks for coming anyway."

She walked slowly past me into my kitchen and hovered there, uncomfortable. "Well, you said it was urgent, so..."

"It is." I closed the door behind her, and leant on it.

She turned back towards me, handbag still under her arm. She didn't put it down; she clearly wasn't planning on staying long. "Can I ask something, though? Am I going to be really upset by what you're going to tell me?"

I swallowed. "Maybe."

She pressed her lips together for a moment. "Then does it really have to be today, Gem? After the day I've had, I just have *nothing* left in me. I don't know if I can hear it."

Sarah... "Yeah, it does."

She sighed and nodded slowly, looking back down at the floor, eyes glazed. A long silence stretched between us.

After today, I felt like I owed her a proper explanation for why I'd dragged her here. I took a steadying breath. *Here I go,* I

264

thought. "Sarah, I—Tomorrow I have to tell everyone at work something, and I wanted you to hear it from me first."

She looked up at me, frowning a little. "It's a *work* thing?" I shook my head. "But you have to tell everyone at work anyway?"

I nodded. "Yeah, it's something I'm doing for Henry."

She gave me the strangest look. "*Henry*—?" She stared at me for a moment, and then something dawned on her face. "Oh my god, Gem, are you *pregnant*?"

That question was *so* unexpected that I couldn't help but laugh for a second. "*What*? Sare, I think you probably need to be able to talk to guys to end up having sex with them! I haven't been so good at that lately..."

She didn't look convinced. In fact, her expression hardened. "I'm pretty sure you and Henry were having a conversation at the restaurant Spud saw you two at..." She paused, I think trying to decide if she should continue, "...that you lied to me about and told me was some random Tinder date."

Wow, that stopped me smiling pretty quickly. Shit. "Oh, no, Sare. No! That was just a coincidence! We were both using fake profiles, and then when we met up and saw it was each other—"

"—you still lied to me anyway when you came out to let me know you were okay."

I grimaced. "Well, Henry said that he didn't want me to—"

"—And that was *after* lying to me about that other time you were out at night, too. I think I can see a pattern here," she told me. She didn't really sound angry, though, just tired. Just really, really tired. "Look, Gem, if you're dating Henry, if that's the *big secret*, Min's probably going to struggle a bit with it, but in the long run I don't think any of us are—"

Huh? "But I'm actually *not*!" I told her. "I'm not! I'm telling you the truth!"

She looked directly at me. "And, after the past month, you can see why I'm having trouble believing it."

...*Ouch*, that was a fair point. I exhaled. "Yeah. I guess I can."

We stood there, watching each other silently again.

Eventually, she sighed and looked away. "Actually, you know what, Gemma? I'm too tired to get into this tonight. Just tell me this bad news you need to tell everyone so I can go home and collapse in bed."

I inhaled sharply. "Well, it's not bad news, exactly..."

"Whatever it is," she said flatly.

Oh, gosh. "It's just that you're going to be upset I didn't tell you earlier."

"Gemma, I think I'm too burnt out to feel very much at this point. Just say it."

Now that I felt like I was on the spot, I felt that familiar panic, and familiar desire to change the subject or go to the bathroom— "I'm really sorry I have to do it right now, on a day when everything is really terrible for you—"

"Gemma, will you just *say it*?"

"—but Natalie thinks that if I do it, it will kill the rumour about me sleeping with Henry to save my job—"

"Gemma, I swear to god I'm about to *strangle* you, will you just tell me whatever Natalie or Henry or whoever wants you to say to everyone so I can just go home and sleep?"

Just say it, Gemma, I willed myself. *Just open your damn mouth and say it!*

This was it, I'd come this far, it was too late to go back.

I closed my eyes, opened my mouth and *finally* pushed the truth out of it. "Sarah, I'm going to come out to everyone so they don't think I'm sleeping with Henry, and I didn't want you to hear it from someone else tomorrow. That would be awful. So, yeah, Sare, I'm not straight. I'm—" Gay? Bi? *Questioning*? "Well, I'm not straight."

My words hung in the air for a moment.

I was too scared to open my eyes—I'd said it! She knew!— but after a long silence, the suspense got the better of me and I slowly peeked through my lids.

She didn't look surprised.

266

That made *me* surprised, and I blinked at her. There wasn't any trace of shock on her face, she just looked really sad. I didn't expect that, not at all. It could only mean one thing. "Wait, you *knew*?"

She shrugged like I'd just told her about the weather. "I wondered."

What? Was I *that* obvious? I was beginning to think everyone knew! "Then why didn't you say anything?"

"What would I say? 'Hey, Gem, you were looking pretty hard at Bree's rack just then, maybe you're bi?'" She shook her head, exhaling. "Honestly, I didn't think you knew." Her expression faltered when she looked back up at me. "And I always thought you'd tell me when you *did* figure it out."

Oh... "I was actually planning on telling you, Sare. I promise."

"But you didn't until now."

"No, because I—"

"But you didn't. I was just something to take care of at the last minute so you didn't feel guilty about it. And actually, after everything, after ten years... that really hurts, Gem," she said, the hurt she spoke of audible in her voice. She spent a few seconds dwelling on that, her jaw set. "And what did you say before? That *Natalie* told you to tell everyone? How does *she* know, are you seeing her?"

What? "No!"

"Okay. Then that means you chose to tell her. You chose to tell *Natalie*, the person who orchestrated all the seven hells of crap that's going on at work for me right now before you chose to tell me, and you can probably imagine how that makes me feel. I mean, what else am I going to find out you've hidden from me, Gemma?" She was looking to me for an explanation. "What else am I going to find out my supposed best friend has decided not to tell me?"

The 'supposed' stung, but I didn't answer. I couldn't answer, because there was just one thing. *The* thing. The reason I'd been fucking everything up for the past three weeks.

When I didn't say anything, she shook her head. "I think that's what hurts the most out of everything: a month ago, I would have sworn that there wasn't a single thing I didn't know about you, because you always told me everything. I just—Gemma, I don't know why you'd tell *strangers* before me?" She took a step towards me. "What is it, did I give you the impression that I'd have a problem with it if you're bi?" I shook my head. "Then *why*?"

All of these questions had the same answer, but I couldn't give it to her. I couldn't.

She wasn't going to leave it, though. "Seriously, Gemma, say it. Tell me the reason. Even if it's going to hurt me, just say it, because I just don't understand."

I stiffened. "I can't."

She pressed her lips in a thin line and shook her head in disappointment at me. She turned away, I think to express her disgust—but she froze mid-turn.

Something had caught her eye in my living room, and she turned her body towards it, *gaping*. When I looked up, I saw why.

I'd forgotten that I'd torn down all our photos, every single one.

She took a few astonished steps towards the bare walls, staring up at them. Then her eyes dipped: surveying all the discarded piles of photos on the coffee table, on the armrest of the couch and on the floor. I hadn't actually put them down there; Mr Crumpet must have knocked some of them off the surfaces I'd piled them on, and then proceeded to walk all over them. They looked like rubbish, discarded and covered in cat hair. It must have seemed like I didn't care about them at all.

"You took them all down?" she asked, a raw note in her voice. "You took down all the photos of us together?" When she looked back at me, I could see the heartbreak plainly on her face.

I couldn't explain it to her.

At my silence, her face *crumpled*. Dropping her handbag, she bent awkwardly down on her hands and knees with her big belly, hurriedly collecting the photos off the carpet. She was facing away from me. "At least let me keep some of them if you're going to *throw them away*," she said bitterly, picking them up off the floor and carefully brushing the cat hair off them.

I felt numb. Like I was watching something happen in third person—like it was all rushing past me and happening *to* me and I was a bystander. "Sare..."

She was lifting them up to the light as she cleaned them— pictures of our adventures. South America. A photo of us in funny hats from her 21st. A picture of all the old crew in our graduation gowns, throwing our hats into the air and *cheering*. She gathered them all up in desperate handfuls, as if she was worried they would disappear if she didn't.

"I'm not throwing them away..."

She stopped collecting them up for a moment, looking down at them in her hands. "It feels like you are," she said. I couldn't see her face. "It feels like that's what's happening here."

I felt sick. "That's not what's happening at all, I just decided to take them down and—"

"Throw them all over the room, Gem? Really?" She twisted back towards me. "You just came home one day, completely unrelated to the fact that you've been pushing me away for the past month, and decided you'd like to tear down every single photo of us?"

I didn't know what to say, but I didn't want her to think that I didn't care. "I know you think I'm trying to push you away, but—"

"—can you stop pretending that isn't what's happening, Gem? I try to help you, and you push me away. I back off, and you push me away. I feel like I've tried *everything* to be the kind of friend you want me to be and still you're going out to bars without me and lying about where you are. Still you're choosing to tell total strangers intimate things about you before you tell me, your best friend of *ten years*. How is that supposed to do anything except make me feel like you don't want me around and don't care about—"

No! "—I do care, Sarah! And you're not doing anything wrong, it's just—"

"—it's just that things aren't the same anymore, are they? I know they're not." She was close to tears again, spending a couple of seconds looking down at all the photos of our adventures in her hands. "I know things are different than they used to be now," she told me in a wavering voice. "I know I'm not Sarah-who-drinks-half-a-bottle-of-vodka-and-then-goes-skinny-dipping anymore. I know I'm not 'Hey, wake up! Let's drive to Perth tomorrow!'-Sarah anymore. I know I work 24/7 and I have *this thing* inside my stomach and I go to bed at 9pm now," she said, the tears finally welling in her eyes. "But inside, I'm still Sarah who's Gemma's best friend. I'm still Sarah who would do anything for Gemma. And it just *really fucking hurts* that even though I'm right here, even though I'm doing everything possible to try and keep you, you don't seem to want me anymore."

Nothing could be further from the truth! "Sare, that's not it at all!" I told her, desperate for her to listen to me. "That's not it at all! I don't care which Sarah you are, you're perfect, you're the best friend I've ever—"

She flinched as I said 'perfect'. "If that's true then I just can't understand why you're pulling away? Why it feels like you'd rather be around anyone except me and talk to anyone except—"

"I want to talk to you! That's why you're here!"

She shook her head at me. "No, I'm here because you felt you *had* to come out to me. Not because you thought 'I know who will love and support me no matter what sexuality I am, Sarah will', but because you went, 'well, I suppose Sarah *should* find out a few hours before the entire—"

"Stop it, Sare, you don't even know why I *couldn't* tell you, or why I—"

"—then *fucking tell me*, Gemma! Fucking tell me why you've been avoiding me, and hiding things from me, and lying to me, and pushing me away for the past—"

The words just came tumbling out of my mouth before I even realised what they were. "Because I've been bloody *in love with you*, Sare! And I'm trying to get over you so I don't ruin our friendship and make it weird, and I suck at doing it, okay? I keep messing up. I keep messing it all up but I'm trying because the worst thing I can think of in the world is to lose you, because I don't even know who I am without you!!"

I—

Oh my gosh, what had I—?!

The second I'd said those words, the second I saw the transparent shock on Sarah's face, I clamped my hands over my mouth and stare at her in wide-eyed panic. I regretted saying it. I regretted inviting her over. I regretted *everything* that might happen now I'd told her, but I couldn't shove the words back into my mouth now, they were out there.

She'd heard them, and she was frozen for what felt like eternity, gaping at me.

I couldn't bear it. "There," I said quietly, dropping my hands. "I guess now you know why."

It took her a while to process it all, long enough that I wondered if she'd say anything at all. It was so quiet that the only sounds I could hear was the humming of my old fridge in the kitchen, and the ticking of my clock.

Eventually, Sarah drew a long, slow breath. "Did you always—? I mean, from the beginning?" she asked, shell-shocked. I shook my head. "How long, then?"

I shrugged. I wasn't sure; it was hard to pinpoint when I crossed the threshold between 'love' and 'in love'. It had been like slowly boiling a frog in water. "I don't know."

She looked up at me for a moment, worried. "We were friends, though, weren't we? Before you felt—?" I nodded, and she looked somewhat relieved. Sitting back on her heels, she carefully put the pile of photos she'd collected on the coffee table beside her, gazing down at them while she was deep in thought.

I had *no* idea what was about to happen.

She looked back up at me. "So *that's* why..."

I could barely speak. "That's why...?"

"Why you were avoiding me: you're trying to get over me." She looked deeply troubled by that idea, bracing herself on the couch and pushing herself awkwardly up off the ground. She spent a moment quietly watching me. "So what happens now?" she asked. "Should you maybe have a break from me?"

I felt like I'd been punched in the stomach. Gosh, no. No, I didn't know what I'd do without her! "I don't want to have a break from you!"

"But maybe you *need* to have one? It might help. I had one from Andrew after we broke up..."

And she wasn't friends with him anymore. He'd moved to another country. Suddenly, the prospect of her walking out that door and closing it behind her seemed very real. Tomorrow, I might wake up in a world by myself. I'd tried everything, everything I could think of, but it didn't matter. I was still going to end up losing her. And it was because of something I couldn't control.

Fresh tears welled in my eyes. It wasn't fair. I didn't *ask* to be this way. I didn't ask for any of this. It just wasn't fair.

"I've tried so hard to figure this all out," I found myself confessing to her. "I've tried everything I can think of to try and get over you so I'd never have to tell you and it would all just go away. But despite being *Genius Gemma*, despite having more maths awards than can fit on a mantelpiece, none of those 'advanced' problem-solving skills helped me with this at all."

She seemed surprised by that. "Why wouldn't you want to tell me, though, Gem? Why is that the worst thing you can imagine?"

"Because I didn't want to lose you over it!"

"Are you *kidding* me?" she asked, but her voice was gentle. "Why on earth would you lose me over it?"

"Because you know what I'm thinking when I look at you!" I told her, throwing my hands out. "You know what I've *been* thinking about you. You might feel really weird around me now, like you don't know what I'm thinking if we hug, or if we touch, or if I accidentally see you change. It might be awkward and you might *hate* that."

To my surprise, she scoffed. "Gem, you're always awkward as hell, and I've never hated it," she pointed out. "So I take it that means you don't want a break from me?" I shook my head. "Then what *do* you want?"

That, I knew. "I just want everything to go back to normal, like none of this horrible mess I created ever happened."

She had a private smile. "You *did* create a pretty spectacular mess," she acknowledged, almost sounding impressed by it. I gave her a look, and she sobered. "Seriously, though, Gem. You're unique. I *love* being your friend. We click so well and we have so much fun together that I just know in 50 years' time, I'll be lying on my deathbed with a great big happy smile, looking back on my wonderful life and all the amazing things we did together." Without any hesitation at all, she took my hands in hers. "I've been spending the last month feeling like that future was slowly slipping away from me. So, yeah, I won't lie, it's kind of a shock to find out why you've been avoiding me, but honestly, if there has to be a problem between us, I'm so glad it's *this* problem." She squeezed my hands. "Because at least you're not thinking, 'I don't care about her'."

I was going to cry. "It's not that," I told her. "It's *definitely* not that. I *do* care about you."

"Yeah," she said simply. "And I care about you, too. I care about you, and us, and our amazing friendship way too fucking much to let this one thing break it up. And that's how I know we're going to get through this, Gem. Because we both want to. We'll figure it out together."

She was smiling at me; that's what got me. I'd told her everything—*everything*—and she wasn't walking out that door. She wasn't leaving. She wasn't avoiding me, or shying away from my touch, or acting like our friendship was somehow tainted. She was just smiling at me, and there was a look of perfect acceptance on her face.

It was too much; my fresh tears spilt. "I'm sorry, Sare. I'm sorry this happened, I know you're straight, I knew it couldn't go anywhere, but..."

"It's okay, Gem," she told me quietly, "we'll get through this." I could already hardly see through my tears, but when she wrapped her arms around me and hugged me tightly against her and her big belly, I couldn't hold any of my relief in: I started *sobbing*.

The tears just wouldn't stop. Everything I was afraid of, everything I thought would happen and everything that I thought would be over—it was okay. Despite all the stupid mistakes I'd made, it was okay. She was still here with me, hugging me, comforting me, and telling me how much I mattered to her.

I felt like the *luckiest* person in the whole wide world.

She didn't let me go for ages. "I'll help you get over me," she promised. "I'll help you find someone who'll love you like I can't. Because there's so much about you to love, Gem, and you're going to find someone who sees all that and who *isn't* straight, and you'll absolutely set them on fire."

She didn't even know about Mikey—but that was who I immediately thought of. It was an odd turn of events to be hugging Sarah and thinking of Mikey, instead of the other way around. "I already did, kind of..."

She pulled slowly away, hands still on my shoulders. She looked interested. "Yeah?"

I nodded, wiping my eyes on the backs of my hands. "That failed date last week. It was with a girl."

"Oh?" she brightened. "Well, what's she like?"

I gave her a look. "*Failed* date, Sare. She walked out on me."

Sarah scoffed. "Gem, you think a project is ruined if it has one single typo."

"Typos *do* ruin equations."

She rolled her eyes. "Yeah, okay, Einstein," she said dismissively. "Anyway, my actual point was that you always jump to the worst conclusions. Maybe she's waiting to hear from you? I mean, what happened?"

I grimaced. "It was the night you were texting me upset, and then she saw all the photos of you on my wall and guessed…"

Recognition dawned on Sarah's face. "So that's why you took them down…" Her relief was palpable. "Anyway," she continued, "everything's sorted out with me now, so…" She made a 'go right ahead' gesture with her hand.

"Mmm," I said neutrally. The fact I'd finally told Sarah didn't change what had happened with Mikey last week, so I wasn't very optimistic.

She looked like she wanted to discuss it more, but a big paralysing yawn interrupted her. She let it. "God, I feel like I've run a marathon," she confessed afterwards, and then laughed to release some tension. "I'm so glad everything's sorted out, Gem, but I'm going to actually die if you make me go home. Some poor jogger will find my corpse tomorrow, halfway to my house, because I died of exhaustion before I got there, RIP."

It was so wonderful to hear the old Sarah talking to me again. "Then don't go home. I'll sleep on the couch."

She gave me an odd look. "Since when did you ever sleep on the couch when I stayed over?"

Oh. "Well, I just thought…" Now that she knew what I was thinking about her…

She scoffed. "Well, you thought wrong. Your bed is enormous, and if we're able to somehow push all the dirty clothes off the other side of it, there's always been room enough for me." She gave me a cheeky grin, just like she always used to. I knew it was on purpose.

And—gosh, I loved her for it. I really loved her. Everything was so perfect, that even if I'd tried to imagine the best possible way tonight could have turned out, I wouldn't in a million years have imagined it would end up like this. With her climbing into bed next to me like nothing had changed.

She did push the clothes off my bed—right onto the floor. Mr Crumpet promptly nested in them and we had to step carefully over him while we got ready for bed. Sarah didn't duck into the bathroom to change (although she did turn around, but I think to avoid torturing me), and then we climbed under the doona and turned out the light.

Then, we lay there like we had a hundred times before, chatting, laughing and gossiping until she finally fell asleep.

I stayed awake and watched her for a little while—how soft her face looked when she was sleeping; how much younger she seemed. I let myself drink in how beautiful she was one last time before I let it all slip through my fingers like ashes scattering on the wind.

It was time to get over her.

Side-by-side, we fell asleep, and I finally, *finally* lay that beautiful, impossible dream of my best friend and I to rest.

CHAPTER TWENTY-THREE

It was surreal waking up beside Sarah again. She was fast asleep being the giant bed hog that she'd always been, and it was nice being able to laugh about how some things never changed and not having to worry that they *would* change.

We were okay. She knew everything, and we were still okay. That was such an enormous relief that I didn't want to get up straight away. I wanted to lie here and be relaxed around her for once, and I thought I'd just close my eyes for a second before I—

"Gem?" Someone was gently shaking me. "Gem, I just wanted to say goodbye before I left."

Sarah? She was leaving *now*? I scrambled to push myself upright. "What do you mean 'goodbye'?! I'm coming with you!"

When my eyes cleared, I saw she was fully dressed with her handbag over one shoulder. Behind her, the sun had suddenly risen.

She looked sceptical about me coming with her. "The train leaves in 15 minutes," she told me, checking her phone. "I need to be at work much earlier than normal today, and I can't miss my eight o'clock meeting. I've got all this stupid strike crap to try and deal with."

Oh, that's right. Well, she wasn't going without me, not even if she was leaving really early! "Don't worry, I'll be dressed in five!" I promised, and then rushed around my place, showering and dressing and tripping over everything to produce a somewhat professional outfit before we rushed out the door. We had to hightail to the train station—we did make the train, thank goodness—but when I saw my reflection in the train doors closing behind us, I wished I'd told her that I'd meet her at work.

My hair was frizzy because it wasn't straightened, I wasn't wearing makeup, and for some unfathomable reason, I'd apparently decided a navy shirt and a red tartan skirt matched. Today, of all days, I had to do this to myself. "Great," I said flatly, staring at my reflection as the train left the station. "I'm going to... *do what I have to do* today looking like the giant mess I am."

Sarah glanced up. "'Do what you—'" she repeated, frowning, and then it twigged for her. "*Oh,* you mean come out to everyone," she said in a really loud voice.

I panicked, looking frantically at all the people around us. "Sare! *Shh!*"

She scoffed. "Look, no one's listening," she promised, getting right back to her phone. She was already knee-deep in urgent emails, apparently. "And you look fine."

Well, no one around us *appeared* to be interested in what we were talking about... I still didn't like discussing it in public, though. "I do *not* look fine. I should have worn my navy dress suit."

She gave me a knowing glance. "Gem, I'm pretty sure even the perfect outfit wouldn't make what you have to do today any easier."

Valid point. "Maybe not, but at least *I'd* feel better…" I sighed at my reflection. She was probably right, though; having a different skirt on and actual eyebrows probably wouldn't make the difference. "I don't even know what Natalie wants me to do," I confessed, trying to smooth down my hair anyway. "She said she'd tell me when I spoke to her at nine this morning."

"Whatever it is, I'm betting being dressed up isn't the answer." Sarah put her phone away with a groan, giving up on her emails. "She'll probably just get you to 'reply all' to a private email or something. I doubt it's going to be anything too dramatic."

I hoped it would be something like that. Something that didn't involve me needing to actually speak to people or be the centre of attention. Natalie's other ideas had been *way* too extroverted for me. "You know, she wanted me to pretend to be in a relationship with Min so that I had a good reason to be out with Henry."

Sarah smirked. "You'd probably both enjoy that a little too much for Bree's liking," she said, and then sobered. "How would that be coming out, though? I don't think the troglodytes at Frost would be able to make a distinction between 'transmasculine' and 'man', so dating Min for you would be kind of straight."

I shrugged. "Well, it was either that or just find some random girl to be seen pashing—that was her other suggestion."

Sarah's ears piqued at that. "Well, maybe you could recruit that girl you like to help you out? What was her name? 'Mikey'?" She grinned. "It would give you a reason to message her…"

I grimaced. "If I message her, it should be to apologise for paying more attention to you on the last half of our date than I did her."

That didn't make her back down. "Well, 'I want to apologise' is a good opener."

Man, I wished that would work, I really did. She'd been great. I shook my head. "I messed it up, Sare. The last thing I need to

278

do is be like 'Hey, remember how much I hurt you? Well now I need to use you for something, aren't you glad to hear from me?'"

Despite saying that—and meaning it, I couldn't do that to her—thinking about Mikey had me reaching into my handbag to grab my phone and see if she was still following me on Facebook. I just had *this feeling* if she was still following me, it would be a sign that—

She wasn't still following me. I exhaled; that was that.

"Look on the bright side," Sarah told me, peering over my shoulder. "At least she didn't block you."

"That's a bright side?"

She ignored me, squinting at the screen. She reached out to pull it a little closer to her so she could scrutinize the display pic. "Huh. She's cute, Gem."

I gave her a sideways look. "Can we *not* torture Gemma?" I asked her. "I blew it. I'm better off just leaving her alone."

Sarah shrugged. "Suit yourself," she said. "I just thought it would be really convenient if you could make up with her and, like, make out with her right in front of Frost or something." She exhaled. "Oh, well. Plenty more fish in the sea."

It was a pity the other fish were all nothing like Mikey. Or like Sarah, for that matter. "Yeah," I said half-heartedly. I probably sounded half-hearted, too.

Sarah considered me for just a little too long. "Hey, do you still have Tinder installed?" she asked, and when I rolled my eyes at her, she held her hands up in a 'yield' position. "No—don't look at me like that. Let's just take a peek at the other fish, okay? Maybe it will cheer you up, and honestly, I need something to distract me from this horrible mess *Natalie* has created for me at work, so..."

My first thought was a firm no; after all the drama of the past couple of weeks, I wasn't that keen on wading knee-deep into Tinder again. I wouldn't have, but it suddenly struck me that Sarah was casually trying to help me find *a*

279

girlfriend. Like it was totally normal, and exactly like the way she had tried to help me with guys. She might have been doing it for exactly that reason too, to show me she was 100% supportive. That in itself kind of warranted a 'yes'. And I *was* supposed to be actively moving on from Sarah, wasn't I...?

I sighed heavily. My heart wasn't really in it. "Okay," I said, opening the app and reactivating my real profile again—the one with my actual name. "Maybe I'll get lucky and someone from Frost will recognise me on Tinder and *that* can be the scandal..."

"I don't know any lesbians at Frost," Sarah mused while I changed all my settings to women. "I always thought that woman on Reception might be one. The security guard."

I knew the one she was talking about. "Maybe," I said, thinking that the woman was probably just butch because she had a physical job. Then, I took a deep breath as the first match popped up. Surprise, surprise, it was a married woman looking for a threesome.

"She might still be okay for a public pash right in front of Frost, though, right?" Sarah pointed out.

I gave Sarah a tired look and swiped left.

We kept swiping through women until we arrived at Wynyard station, and as we stepped off the train, Sarah's somewhat cheerful mood darkened. "I don't really want to go to work today," she confessed as we tapped out through the turnstiles. "But I suppose if I want to be a manager, this is exactly the kind of situation I need to figure out how to handle, isn't it?"

I didn't understand why people wanted to be managers; life was stressful enough already without volunteering for more. "I'm sure you guys will figure something out," I promised her.

She didn't look convinced. "We'll have to, or that's my career."

Sarah arrived in time for her eight o'clock meeting. On his own way in there too, Omar dropped some demographics data on my desk and asked me to crunch it. As per usual, though, a non-maths person massively overestimated the time it was going to take me to finish a simple task, and I had it all done and dusted in about 15 minutes. That meant I was sitting at my desk while everyone around me was working like a maniac.

Any other normal adult would have asked her colleagues if there was anything she could do to help them—and I really should have done that—but that meant actually speaking to one of those loud men who—

Wait. I stopped myself right there. Wait a minute, Gemma.

It was *this* sort of ridiculous crap that had gotten me into so much trouble in the first place, wasn't it? Avoiding the hell out of everything normal adults did? And it wasn't like asking these Marketing guys if I could help them with any work was *anything* like telling my best friend I'd been in love with her, or—I gulped—whatever Natalie was going to have me do to start rumours about my sexuality. Honestly: come on, Gem. It was *one question*. I could do it.

I still felt like I was walking the plank as I pushed myself up from my desk with shaky knees and selected the oldest, least threatening-looking Marketing clerk to go up to. Ian, I think he'd introduced himself to me as yesterday.

He didn't notice me standing behind his desk so I just stood there awkwardly for a few seconds wondering what the hell to do, and when he did notice me, we both jumped. He laughed. "Sneaking up on me, Gemma!"

Oh, gosh. "U-Um, I wasn't—!" What could I say to that?! I tried to force a laugh too, but it sounded panicked. And now he was looking at me and expecting me to say something else, but I couldn't figure out what to say. I was in too deep, I couldn't get away now. I had to say something! "Hi."

He laughed, a hand on his chest. "Hi! You gave me a fright, there! What can I do for you?"

Okay. That hadn't gone as badly as expected, maybe if I just... "I was wondering if you had any—I mean, everyone is really busy, so—"

"Sorry? Speak up, I can't hear you."

Shit. "I-Is there anything you—?"

"*Pardon?*"

281

I tried to belt the words out. "Is there anything you need help with?"

He laughed. "Sorry, you've got such a quiet little voice! Unlike the rest of *these* idiots," he nodded at his incredibly loud, extroverted teammates. "Can you do anything for me? Well," he tapped his chin, "I need this week to be over, pronto. So, if you can use that maths brain of yours to figure out how to fast-forward time, that would be amazing."

I-I didn't have any idea what to say to that. "That's physics." ...*Shit*.

He didn't seem to mind that I'd just corrected him. "Well, it's all numbers and weird symbols to me," he said. "But no, I don't think there's anything you can do," he paused. "Unless you want to go get me a coffee, that is." He waggled his eyebrows.

...I really didn't. I didn't feel like I could say 'no' to that, though, because I was new in the department and he was much older than me and therefore possibly quite senior, so I ended up agreeing to do it. Unfortunately, while he was writing his new-age weird coffee order down, word got out I was going on a coffee run downstairs. Before I knew it, I had like ten orders and my purse was heavy with random coins and notes.

Somewhat serendipitously, there was only one barista in the atrium café which meant that I'd be oh-so-horribly 'stuck' down there for ages waiting for her to fill the orders, and not upstairs contenting with all the extroverts. Breathing a sigh of relief, I leant against the counter and pulled my phone out to pass the time.

Tinder was still open.

Well, I *had* promised to try and get properly over Sarah, hadn't I? I didn't really have anything to lose by just taking a peek who was on.

Glancing furtively around me to make sure no one could see, I started swiping profiles while I waited for all the coffees to be done.

I was just sipping my own coffee and idly wondering whether Mikey was using Tinder again too, when I swiped through to a pair of long legs in black stockings. It was a photo where the head had been cropped out, but I could see the woman had long black hair, a *killer* figure, and was reclined on a couch in something similar to the Little Red Dress that had caused me so much distress a couple of...

...hang on, I kind of *remembered* those patent stilettos from—I glanced down at the name of the—*Natalie*, 36.

My stomach *dropped*.

No way, I thought, hurriedly flicking through the photos, looking for one of her face so I could confirm it *wasn't* her and laugh to myself later about how I'd thought this profile was *the* Natalie. There wasn't one, though. Well, I supposed Natalie was a kind of common name for someone to—

—'*professional woman who works long hours looking for discreet and discrete hook-ups. Not ruling out relationships, but not looking for them either. You tell me your kinks, I'll tell you mine ;) No more photos provided: if you want to see what I look like then you'll just have to bite the bullet and meet me in person*'.

That certainly sounded like her! I didn't know how old Henry's Natalie was—I supposed about 36?—and if she *wasn't* 36 then at least that would give me the definitive answer on whether or not *this* Natalie was Natalie Heiser. I mean, those long legs certainly looked like hers, but... Gosh, it was absolutely killing me! I wanted to text Henry to ask him how old she was, but I'd also promised Natalie that I wouldn't contact him on his work mobile, so...

So... I took a big gulp of a breath. I could ask *this* Natalie myself, couldn't I?

As soon as I'd thought of doing that, *every single neuron in my brain* started screaming blue murder and telling me to delete Tinder, to format my phone, to proceed immediately to nearest bridge and fling myself off, but...

Despite the fact I was sweating buckets, despite the fact I definitely, definitely couldn't handle the fallout, I found myself swiping right and telling myself, *don't worry, Gemma, it's probably not her, there's no way Henry's Natalie would be this*—a screen popped up with '*It's a Match!*' on it.

I grabbed my phone with both hands and *stared* at it, mouth open. You had to be fucking—

A chat notification popped up and with shaking fingers I tapped to maximise it.

I knew my answer immediately.

"*Well, fancy meeting* you *here ;)*"

CHAPTER TWENTY-FOUR

It *was* Natalie Heiser.

I gaped at my screen, so confused; wasn't she sleeping with Henry?! She *had* to be, otherwise why were they so familiar with each other? It didn't make sense at all!

I opened her profile again just to see if I'd missed anything— gosh, and got another eyeful of those amazing legs—but it didn't seem at all like she was experimenting or looking for a number three for her and Henry at all. It was very clear that she knew what she wanted, and that was another woman.

...and she'd swiped right on me.

Oh my—no, this couldn't be happening. It couldn't be. Maybe she was just being friendly? I had no idea what the etiquette was for matching with people you knew on Tinder, maybe she was going to just say hello?

Yes, it was probably just that. I took a long, deep breath, slowly exhaled and replied, "*Hello :)*"

She replied immediately. "*Hello ;)*" Why was there a winky face?! "*So, do you come here often…?*"

I-I didn't know what she—wow, that seemed very flirty, didn't it? I had to wipe my hands on my skirt. Was she teasing me, maybe? I wanted to ask her if she was, but I didn't really know how to ask the question or what to say or what to *anything* and I ended up just typing, "*You swiped right on me?*" and then the very second I'd sent it I massively regretted it. 'You swiped right on me'; Gemma, *really*??

"*Yeah. I believe you're supposed to do that when you see a very attractive woman on here ;)*"

I gaped. Okay, now I *knew* she was teasing me. My photos were 'nice', they were 'cute', but they most certainly were not 'very attractive woman'-level. She was probably just complimenting me to make me feel good about myself. That was nice of her, I supposed.

...or maybe she *was* teasing me? This whole thing was way, way, way too stressful.

While I was panicking about what to say next, another message came through. "*Isn't that why you swiped right on me, Gemma?*"

I went bright red. Oh, no. I didn't want to insult her by saying it wasn't—because she *was* very attractive, after all—but I was completely incapable of flirting so I just decided to keep it simple. "*I just thought maybe I recognised you and was going to ask if it was you after all.*"

She didn't waste a second. "*So which part of me did you recognise...?*" she asked. "*There are no pics of my face in there ;)*"

I... I decided to carefully side-step her question, even though I immediately knew the answer. Flirting wasn't a forte of mine. "*Is that because you don't want people to know you're...*" How should I ask it? "*...looking for women, too?*"

"*Wow, you are new to this.*" Wait, what about what I'd said had 'new' written all over it?! "*No, I've been out for 20 years. Everyone knows why I specialise in discrimination cases. I've just been working with industrial law long enough to know sexy pics with your face attached inevitably become blackmail fodder.*"

Oh. That made sense. Well, all of it except the part where she said 'everyone' knew about her being out. Then again, I was always the last to know everything, so I supposed it wasn't that surprising that—

"*So, my meeting doesn't start for a good five minutes... ;)*" That winky face was stressing me out. "*It seems a little unfair that you've seen compromising pics of me and I haven't seen any of you. I need you to fix that for me, Gemma.*"

Even reading her saying my name made me sweat. I sweated even more when I remembered that I actually *did* have a 'sexy' pic: the one of me in the red dress that Sarah had taken. But there was no way I could show anyone *that* picture!

"*I hope this silence is you looking through your gallery for inappropriate pics to text me ;)*" There was a pause. "*Or actually taking one for me right now.*"

I didn't... Well, I supposed—I mean, I *had* seen pictures of her in what was basically lingerie, hadn't I? Maybe I should send something to her...?

I opened my gallery to take a peek at that photo of me in the red dress again; you know, just to check if it really was something that I could never, ever send to anyone. As I opened it, I braced myself to feel the same deep discomfort as I had right after it had been taken, and I—

—didn't, though. Huh. I chewed on my lip. It was quite a nice photo of me, really? I mean, not the kind you'd share around, but it was sort of sexy, and Natalie had asked for 'inappropriate'. She'd probably like it—it was probably exactly the sort of photo she was after.

Oh, gosh. I took a nervous breath. Was I actually considering sending this photo of me in the sprayed-on, skin-tight, tiny little red dress to drop-dead gorgeous *Natalie-fucking-Heiser*?!

I knew the answer to that. I knew it immediately, and thinking about it gave me butterflies. I *was* considering it. I was considering sending this sexy, revealing photo of me to the hottest woman in Sydney because she wanted one. Imagining what she might do with it once she'd got it was kind of—well, fucking terrifying. Terrifying, but terrifying in a really *hot* way.

I wasn't sure if I was more frightened or more excited by the thought of it. Before I could talk myself out of it, I'd tapped 'share' and texted it to her.

As soon as I'd sent it, I half-panicked—what if she *was* just teasing me, and right now she was laughing at how awkward and hopeless I was, and how someone like me had thought I was anywhere in the stratosphere of her league?!

Heart pounding, I gripped my phone with both hands, biting my lip and staring intently at the screen until I got an answer. I don't think I'd ever sweat so much in my entire life.

It felt like eternity before another message came through. *"So, did I tell you I have a thing for freckles, Gemma?"*

She did?! I was disassociating so much I think I may nearly have phased into a different dimension. *"I have lots of freckles."*

"Yes, I probably can see almost all of them in this fabulous picture ;)" There was a pause. *"But you left your face in it, Gemma. That's no good at all, you've really put yourself in a very compromising position. You'd better do everything I say so this picture doesn't end up anywhere you don't want it to... ;)"*

If I gaped any wider, I think I might have dislocated my jaw. This was too much. Too, too much. I had no idea at all how to reply to any of it—I was so, so out of my depth!—but fortunately, while I was panicking and sweating, and—well, trying to decide if she was even maybe half serious about that threat, she messaged me again. *"...and now everyone's clocking in for my meeting. What terrible timing. I suppose I'd better get back to work."*

I breathed a huge, long sigh of relief.

"Do you remember that restaurant Henry and I were in couple of weeks back?"

Huh? The one where we got caught spying on them? "Yes?"

"I'm in the boardroom there. My meeting should be done by 9:30—come down here and speak to me in person. It's better if we have confidential discussions away from Frost HQ ;)"

I inhaled all the air I'd sighed out again. Oh, no—meeting her in person after what we'd just been messaging each other?! I should figure out some way to just make it a phone call so I could—

"Excuse me?"

I jumped. Wide-eyed, I looked up towards the person who'd been speaking to me.

It was the barista. "All your coffees are done. Do you need help carrying them upstairs?"

Had she seen any of that? Could she have guessed what was going on?! "S-Sure? I mean, I don't—" *Get yourself together, Gemma.* "How much does that come to?"

She looked mildly amused. "You've already paid."

As soon as she said that, I remembered trying to divide up everyone's money earlier. Practically forehead-slapping, I grimaced. "Oh, yeah..."

She looked a bit smug, but didn't say anything else as she helped me ferry all the coffees upstairs. Thank goodness she didn't try to speak; small talk would have been totally beyond me right now. I could hardly get my head around what I'd just learnt and what had just happened.

Natalie was gay. And not just gay: gay and potentially hitting on me. I felt like I was in the twilight zone. Since when was someone like that interested in someone like me? It didn't make sense at all unless she *was* teasing me, and I couldn't stop bloody thinking about it!

I needed to sort my head out before I got to Marketing, though, because if the barista was smirking at me and probably wondering how someone as scatterbrained as me managed to get a position in a Fortune 500 company, I didn't want everyone in Marketing to think that as well. I had enough trouble looking them in the eyes as it was, and it was going to be hard enough after rumours were circulating about my sexuality. I didn't need them to think I was hopeless as well.

I managed to pull myself together to start dividing up all the change (I'd written a big comprehensive master list of how much people had given me and how much change they needed) but no one seemed to care about money, and after everyone had walked off with their coffee I ended up with a purse full of everyone's loose coins. I tucked it all away in my bag, feeling awkward.

While I was torn between worrying about what would happen if they wanted their money later and worrying about the fact I had to meet Natalie *in person* in like thirty minutes after we'd both seen racy photos of each other, Sarah finally got out of her meeting.

She looked tired again. Really tired, in fact. In hindsight, I should have asked her if everything was okay with her project and been a good friend to her, but instead of doing anything supportive, I rushed over to her and frantically whispered something to the effect of, "Natalie is gay and she found me on Tinder!"

Sarah stopped in place and blinked at me. Then, glancing furtively around us, she dragged me away from prying eyes. "*What*?"

I held my phone up. "She found me on Tinder. She swiped right on me. I sent her the red dress photo but I think she might just be messing with me and now I have to go to a restaurant to meet her?"

Sarah's expression... After a second, she closed her jaw. "Gemma, I love you, but I think you've finally lost the plot."

I pushed my phone into her hands. "No, I'm serious."

She didn't look convinced. "Natalie is definitely sleeping with Henry," she said. "Are you sure it's not some other Natalie you found? Or someone who just looks like her?"

"I'm 100% sure!" I unlocked my phone and showed her Natalie's profile. "Look!"

Sarah took my phone from me so she had a better view of my screen and could tab through Natalie's photos. As she looked at them all and then read our messages, her eyebrows slowly rose all the way into her hairline. "Oh my god."

"I know!" I said. "I told you! She's *gay*!"

"Well, apparently," Sarah said, and then looked up at me for a second, spun. It took her a moment to process it as she went back to reading the messages. "Also, Gem, can I say it? You are officially the most awkward person in the world. She's literally throwing herself at you and you're like, '*I just thought maybe I recognised you...*'"

Ugh... "Really?" I asked, cringing. "Don't you think maybe she's just teasing me, though? Or being friendly because she knows me?"

Sarah gave me the longest, hardest stare.

"She might just be complimenting me to be nice?"

"No, Gemma, no. This," she said, holding my phone my face, "*this* is a woman who's telling you in every possible way she's up for it."

I still felt like it couldn't possibly be happening. "Are you sure? Because I have to go meet her about the whole Henry thing at a restaurant in like twenty minutes, I don't think she'd really be seriously hitting on me knowing that?"

Sarah clearly disagreed. "I think you're about to get nailed in a restaurant bathroom."

Oh, my—"That would never happen!"

Sarah held up my phone again. "Gemma. Are you telling me you're saying no to *this*?"

"I'm telling you she's just messing around!" I said, and then accidentally thought about 'being nailed in a restaurant bathroom'. The mental image was way too confronting even for me to imagine. "I can't believe this is happening!"

Sarah was shaking her head. "Neither can I, actually...And *Natalie,* of all people?" She thought about something and then laughed darkly a couple of times. "In that meeting, we were all bitching about Natalie and how unions are literally the devil."

I made a face. "You know she's doing it to try and save people's jobs, right?" I reminded Sarah. "It's just a pity that it's *your* project that her strike interrupts."

Sarah shrugged. She didn't look very comforted. "I'll tell myself that while I watch my career go down the gurgler," she said, and then sighed. "Look. I get it, I get all the reasons why she called the strike, but I'd be lying if I said she was my favourite person right now, even if she *is* Henry's...well, 'friend', and even if you're probably going to end up doing her in the broom closet or something. Seriously, though," she said, looking at me, "can you do me a favour? When you *do* end up nailing her, could you do it *really damn hard* as revenge for when she—"

—I nearly had an aneurysm. "*Sarah!*" I half-shrieked, interrupting her and looking frantically around us. No one was listening. "I'm not going to 'nail' her! I can't even talk to her! I have no idea what's going to happen when I need to actually look her in the face after she's seen me in that dress!"

Sarah was smirking. "Let me tell you what's going to happen. You're going to take one look at each other and then she'll throw you down on the—"

I frantically tried to shush her. "*Sarah!*"

She was laughing. "Okay, okay. I take it back. That's not going to happen. You're going to walk casually down there like you haven't been drooling over each other and have a professional and important conversation about how she's decided you're going to come out to everyone so you can save..." Her words trailed off as her expression suddenly changed. "Oh my god."

I felt uneasy. "What?"

She looked at me. "Gem, it should be her."

"What should be her?" I hoped she didn't mean what I thought she meant...

Sarah put her hands on my shoulders. "It should be her that you pash outside of Frost, or whatever. To come out to everyone."

All the blood drained out of my face. "I'm not pashing anyone outside Frost, Sare! Especially not Natalie!"

Sarah was on a roll, though. She wasn't going to be dismissed that easily. "No, hear me out, Gem!" she said, hands still on my shoulders. "Natalie said it's got to be something that out-rumours the you-and-Henry rumour before it takes hold, right? What better rumour than pashing the union's *female* head legal counsel?"

I felt sick. "Sare…"

She was getting more and more excited as she kept talking. "Oh my god, though! If people think you're with Natalie, no one will think it's Henry that got you the job, they'll just think that Natalie somehow forced Henry to do it to save your job! And everyone thinks the unions are corrupt and evil anyway, so it's not like it's going to affect her reputation! It's *perfect*!" She was practically shaking me. "It's totally perfect! She's even already into you!"

My ears were ringing.

The worst part of all of it was that the moment she'd said it, I knew she was right. It *was* a good idea. "Oh, no…"

"Oh, yes!" She was beaming as she put her hands in the air. "Yes! I'm a genius! Am I a genius?"

"No, you're a monster," I told her, and then closed my eyes and put my head in my hands for a second. She was going to be the death of me. "Sarah, I can't even talk to her!"

She scoffed. "Who needs to talk? All you need to do is kiss her!" she dropped her hands. "Seriously, though, I've heard you talk to her before." She meant that one time Natalie had practically eaten me alive in the atrium at Frost, and it wasn't a great example. "You'll be fine!"

I completely disagreed with her, but when Sarah got like this, there was *no* disagreeing with her. And after the past couple of days of watching her be really stressed out and really upset—all mostly my fault—I didn't really have the heart to put my foot down on this one. She'd been so very supportive of me after I came out to her. Besides, I knew Natalie was *not* her favourite person, and I had a feeling she was going to get some serious Schadenfreude out of the fact that Natalie would be part of the rumour mill, too. That in itself made it worth consideration.

If Natalie agreed to do it, that is, and that was a big if! An even bigger if was if *I* was going to actually be able to even broach the idea with her at all. I had a feeling I'd come face-to-face with Natalie after our torrid chat on Tinder and just turn around and bolt in the other direction.

Sarah was standing in front of me and waiting for my answer with a great big smile on her face, though. She looked so excited about her idea, and I could feel my resolve crumbling. This was going to be one of those things I couldn't get out of, wasn't it?

What was I doing?! "Okay," I said, still feeling sick. "I'll ask her."

Sarah fist-pumped, and then spent a minute or two gushing to me about how she thought it should happen and demanding that I tell her every tiny detail of what *did* happen at the restaurant before she got called away to deal with the Marketing project crisis 'Ms Evil Incarnate' had caused.

...Leaving me alone and realising that it was time to go and *meet* Ms Evil Incarnate at that restaurant.

Oh, no. I wiped my hands on my tartan skirt. This was the end for me.

Feeling like I was walking the plank (and spending every step of the way needing to convince myself to not just spin around and run in the opposite direction), I made my way to the restaurant.

Before I went inside, though, I ducked into a pub next door to spend a few minutes staring at my eyebrowless reflection and frizzy hair, and wondering how anyone on the planet could possibly find me attractive. It was a mystery. I mean— they must, mustn't they? I'd had boyfriends and stuff before, and Mikey had obviously been really into me, too. Natalie was a whole different ballgame, though. I felt like the ugly duckling beside her, and I still couldn't shake the thought that she might be just teasing me, after all.

Part of me almost hoped that she *was* teasing me; I'd much rather come out by accidentally hitting 'reply all' to an email or leaving my unlocked phone with Tinder open somewhere than by getting handsy in public with the scariest woman on the planet.

I checked my phone: 9:28am. Oh, gosh. I needed to go in there.

Wetting my hands and trying in vain to smooth my frizzy hair one last time, I left the bathroom. *Help*, I thought, and with shaky knees walked into that restaurant.

This early in the day there was no one on the door; there was just a barista at the bar. He was taking advantage of the post-coffee-rush lull in business to wipe down the benches. He smiled at me as I walked over to him.

My voice was shaking. "I-I'm here to meet someone for a meeting? In a meeting room?" I immediately wished I could sew my mouth shut. Real smooth, Gem. I was going to *nail* this thing with Natalie for sure.

He pretended not to notice. "Only the boardroom is being used at the moment," he said, politely gesturing towards where I knew it was. "Would you like anything brought in? A coffee?"

Still recovering from my complete inability to form proper sentences, I shook my head—there was no way I could put anything in my stomach at a time like this—and then walked slowly and deliberately over to where I knew she was.

The door was partially closed, just like it had been then.

Taking a deep breath, I peeked through the crack.

Natalie was seated at the end of table with a slender notebook, her chin resting on an elegant wrist as she watched her screen. She had an earbud in one ear; I could tell by the white cord trailing down her neck. There was no one with her; her meeting must have ended already. I would have been relieved by that if I hadn't suddenly realised that meant I needed to go in there right now. Right now?!

I can't do this, I thought, eyeing those legs that I'd already seen most of, and that gorgeous body I knew was under that dress suit. It was all too real, and I was lightyears away from being ready to actually speak to someone who looked like that!

It was only when I caught myself thinking things like 'she looks busy' and 'I shouldn't disturb her, I should just leave' that I reminded myself it was making the same excuses that had caused me to be a walking disaster in the first place. Putting things off, waiting until the 'right' time. Well, this *was* the right time, wasn't it? Those rumours about me and Henry were on the cusp of breaking: it couldn't wait.

Honestly, she'd invited me down here. She was alone. She was probably just watching videos or doing work while she waited for me and—wow, she was gorgeous, and *terrifying*, and she'd seen me in a tiny little dress and I'd seen her in less than that, but none of that cancelled out the reason I was doing this.

I'd come out to Sarah for this. I'd promised Henry I'd do this. I had to actually do it, even if I was *fucking terrified*. *Now* was the time.

I think I must have been white as a sheet as I lifted my hand like it weighed a million tonnes and knocked lightly on the door. I had to knock a couple more times for her to hear me.

She looked up. As soon as she saw me through the partially open door, my heart started hammering in my chest. I felt like I was standing in a spotlight. Then, something worse happened: when she silently beckoned me in, she smiled slightly and *winked*.

I gulped. I wasn't sure my legs were going to manage to get me inside; my knees were shaking so much I worried they might lock up. Somehow, I managed to push the door open and take a few hesitant steps towards her.

Her video was still running on her screen. She didn't make any move to pause it, to take her earbud out, or to say anything. She was just faintly smiling and watching me. She was also nodding for some reason. For encouragement, maybe...?

Staying silent was just about the worst thing she could have done, because then I was standing there also silent, sweating, shaking, panicking and thinking *I have to tell her Sarah's idea! I have to tell her Sarah's idea!—oh, no, I'm going to have to kiss her?*—but I couldn't speak, and when I opened my mouth all that came out was, "I-I have an idea, and—well it's—I'm not s-sure you—"

I was going to lose my nerve if I couldn't just spit it out!

She held up one finger and gestured at her laptop. "Can it wait just a minute, Gemma?"

No, I thought, *it can't, because every time I put something off it ruins everything and I never do it*! Second by second I was thinking I should just leave her to her video and leave her at this restaurant and run away as fast as I could—

—*No*! Sarah was right, pretending to be with her was a great idea and it would definitely solve the whole rumour about Henry—and Sarah would enjoy 'getting back' at Natalie—*whoa*, she was *hot*, wasn't she?—and nothing was coming out of my mouth and the only words that were ringing in my head were Sarah's, "All you need to do is kiss her!" and with all the panic and all the brain fuzz and this really attractive woman giving me bedroom-fucking-eyes in front of me before I knew it I was like *just do something, Gemma*! And I—couldn't say anything, but I had to do something! *I had to do something! I couldn't put anything off any more!* And I—

I leant forward and pressed my hopeless mouth against her perfect red lips.

W-What—

—what had I just—?

She froze. I did, too; I was just as shocked as she was. For a second we were just staring wide-eyed at each other over our noses, lips pressed together.

Then—she did it first—she closed her eyes and leant firmly into the kiss. I was panicking so much it took another couple of seconds to really believe we were doing this, and then I closed my eyes too. It was actually a huge relief not to have to look at her.

Her *lips*—was I *really* kissing them?—they were soft and full and tasted like coffee. She smelt like coffee, too; coffee, and French perfume and *wow*, I was kissing Natalie Heiser! I'd done it! I could feel her long black eyelashes fluttering against my cheek and one confident hand reaching up to cup my jaw. I didn't know where the other one was, but I felt her chest heave as she drew a deep, guttural breath like she was getting *really* into it, and I—

I pulled away because I needed to breathe and I didn't want to pant in her face like a dog.

For a moment, we just watched each other. Despite her momentary surprise before, she was now *completely* composed. Chuckling and glancing at the screen, she reached a thumb up to her mouth to correct her smudged lipstick. Her video was still playing.

"Well, that was a little unexpected, apologies," she said, using an unnervingly professional voice. It took me a moment to realise she wasn't talking to me. She was talking to her notebook.

I looked at her screen, because I didn't understand why she'd speak to—there were several faces there. And a list of names, and a little microphone icon and I—

All the blood drained from my face.

She was on a video conference call.

"Gemma," she said evenly, gesturing at her screen. I could hear a note of amusement in her voice. "I'd like to introduce you to the entire Administration management team at Frost International."

CHAPTER TWENTY-FIVE

There were so many faces on her screen; some of them I recognised, some I didn't. Most of them had the same horrified expression I had.

Natalie, herself, remained unreadable. "Will you excuse me for a moment?" she said calmly and professionally to the gaping participants. Then, she muted the microphone, closed the screen and turned in her chair towards me.

I gulped. "I'm sorry!" I stammered, my life flashing before my eyes. "I didn't mean to—I mean, I didn't know you were—"

"Gemma," she said firmly, cutting me off. She let a pause hang in the air for a moment as she locked eyes with me. Then, she smiled. "That was *perfect*."

—*what*? I didn't—"It was?!"

She nodded. "Oh, yes. There's 18 supervisors, managers and team leaders on that call, and they're all meeting later today to discuss the terms of their strike. Plenty of opportunity to gossip, and from those expressions, they definitely will," she said indulgently, and then gave me a measured look. "Why? You didn't think that went well?"

"I didn't know you were on a video call!" I blurted out. Then, something occurred to me. Did she just say—? "Wait, you were *expecting* me to do that?"

She shrugged. "Well, it did occur to me that it would be a good opportunity," she agreed, while I gaped at her. "I figured you'd only do it if you felt comfortable with it." She considered me for a moment, eyes narrow. "If it wasn't to out yourself, though, why did you kiss me so suddenly?"

My cheeks returned to their usual shade of red. "I-I didn't really know what to say?"

She raised her eyebrows at me, like, 'are you serious?' and then laughed a few times. "Well," she said eventually, looking very entertained. "I suppose it doesn't matter how or why it happened, does it? I think we can safely say that no one's going to care at all that you had dinner with Henry after *that* little performance."

I blinked at her. But... "You don't mind that they all saw? Won't it get you in trouble?"

She scoffed. "With who? I specialise in discrimination law. If any of those people have an issue with me kissing a beautiful woman off work premises, they can meet me in court." Did... did she just call me *beautiful*?! "Now," she said, slowly and regally standing to her full height. We were toe-to-toe, and she was so tall I had to tilt my chin back to look up at her. "Since I'm apparently taking a little break from my meeting, where were we...?"

She took a step towards me, and reflexively, I took a step back. And another, and another, and then the backs of my thighs hit something and I had nowhere else to retreat. She didn't break eye contact as she pressed her hips against mine and pinned me against whatever was behind me. I couldn't look away from her. It was like being hypnotised.

She's going to kiss me again, I thought, and then all I could look at were her lips. She wet them as I watched. Her chest heaved against mine—even though her breasts were nearly up in my collarbones—and I could feel the shape of her body through her dress suit. She leant down towards me, her hot breath on my lips and her fingertips sneaking underneath my blouse and then she *chuckled*, a low, deep sound in the back of her throat.

Her lips were *millimetres* from mine, millimetres. So close I could feel the warmth radiating from her skin. I wanted to close that distance and press my mouth against hers but I was paralysed, frozen solid by that oppressive charisma. I waited and waited and waited for her to stop chuckling and dancing around my lips and to just *kiss* them, to take me, and to just *nail* me right here in the restaurant just like Sarah had said and any second now, any second, she'd—

—lean back, smirking at me.

299

I stood there for a second, reeling, mouth still open as I stared at her.

She wasn't reeling, though. She was in complete control once again. She touched the corners of her lips as if to check her lipstick, smoothed down her shirt, and straightened. "Anyway," she said, like she hadn't just been casually torturing me, "I should get back to my meeting, they'll all be waiting for me." She took a few steps back to the table and sat down. "How's my lipstick?"

I swallowed. Honestly? Still a little smudged. "Um...?"

She laughed. "Perfect," she said, turning back to her computer. Before she opened the screen, she said very nonchalantly, "If you're interested in picking up where we just left off, I have a gap between a meeting that finishes at 9:30pm and after-dinner victory drinks with a large client at 10pm. Come to my work."

The idea of going anywhere right now seemed foreign to me; I could barely move from whatever furniture I was up against.

The invitation she'd just delivered didn't make it any easier, either; it was unmistakably a booty call, and the idea that *Natalie Heiser* would be interested in my 'booty' was still completely beyond my comprehension. I didn't have much time to get it into my comprehension, though, because she opened her screen and unmuted her mic.

"Again, sorry for the interruption," she said smoothly to the video feed, putting the earbud back in her ear. "I believe we were discussing contract lengths, Dixon?"

To my horror, I realised I could see myself over her shoulder in her camera, and so could everyone else. I looked like I'd been well and truly *ravished*, and I had lipstick all around my mouth from when I'd kissed her.

Oh, no! Blushing the same colour as Natalie's lips and fuelled entirely by embarrassed panic, I managed to push myself off the—serving table, it ended up being, and hurtled towards the door. I glanced back at her as I left; she looked over her shoulder at me with a faint smile while she kept talking in her super professional lawyer voice. She held that eye contact for just a *little* bit too long. Oh, gosh.

High-tailing to the bathroom, I spent a good minute or two staring at myself in the mirror and trying to come to terms with what had just happened. I had her bright red lipstick around my lips. The fact she'd put it there *by kissing me back* still hadn't sunk in yet. It was there, on my chin, like hard evidence that a very attractive woman had kissed me.

She wants you, I told myself, completely spun out by that. I was—well, look at me. I looked down my body. I was wearing mismatched clothes, I hadn't straightened my hair and other than her lipstick, I wasn't wearing makeup. I was also my usual bright red, eyebrowless self. Not exactly screw-supermodel-lawyers material, was I? And yet...

"Maybe she has a thing for redheads?" I wondered aloud; I was still convinced that was the only reason I'd ever gotten laid in uni. She *did* say she liked freckles...

I took a few handfuls of toilet paper and cleaned off the lipstick, and then walked in a complete daze back to Frost.

I was momentarily worried that I'd arrived back at work to find that in the space of 10 minutes, the entire company was talking behind their hands about me pashing Natalie on video, but when I walked back into Marketing, no one looked up. They all had their heads down working solidly on the crisis the strike had caused.

Sarah was still in her meeting. I sat at my desk for a few minutes, still totally spaced out, and then made a really bad decision to text her. I probably should have been a mature adult and waited patiently for her to be available, but apparently, I wasn't. Besides, I'd just pashed *Natalie Heiser*, and that seemed like something Sarah would want to know ASAP. "*So, uh, I just kissed Natalie while she was on a conference call to Admin management...*"

Ten seconds later—not even ten seconds—the door to one of the meeting rooms flew open and Sarah was rushing towards me, eyes wide.

I felt guilty. "Isn't that important?" I asked about the meeting, looking over her shoulder as she grabbed me by the wrist and dragged me away from everyone.

"Yeah, yeah, I'll go back there in a second," she said, waving her hand dismissively, and then held me at arms' length and looked me critically up and down. "Oh my god, you *did* just get nailed in the restaurant, didn't you? And what the *hell*? You kissed her on video? Just like that? That is so unlike you!'"

I grimaced. "Well, I didn't know she was on a conference call when I did it, I just kind of panicked and, well, it kind of just happened..."

That made her laugh. "Okay, that sounds more like you," she acknowledged, and then shook her head, expression intense. "What on earth, though—like, for real? You kissed *Natalie Heiser*? Demon Seductress Lawyer-Natalie Heiser?"

I laughed at that scarily apt description of her, and then gave Sarah the abridged version of what had happened. "So, like, what now?" she asked when I was done. "Are you going to date her? Marry her? Have hot seductress lawyer babies, or what? Jesus Christ, I can't believe it. That woman isn't a real human."

"No, I think she wants to just hook up," I said, thinking that Natalie wasn't really the sort of person I could imagine myself ending up with anyway. I'd be too afraid to come home. Sarah seemed pretty relieved by my answer, too, even though she was obviously trying to hide it. "Sare, you don't have to pretend to be happy for me just because I might finally get some, I know she's not your favourite person with the strike and all."

Sarah made a face. "Yeah, I am happy you're not, like, falling for her or something," she agreed, "Kill me: I'd rather my best friend goes out with someone who *isn't* indirectly ruining my career, and maybe even someone I actually like as a person? But, Gem," she said, taking me by the shoulders again. "Come on. She's hot, even I can admit that. You should definitely sleep with the evil hot lady. Make it bondage. Beat her up for me."

I laughed at that, and we stood against the far wall of Marketing, giggling like schoolgirls. It was like uni all over again.

"So did she invite you over later, or...?" Sarah asked when we'd stopped tittering.

Oh, yeah. That reminder sobered me pretty quickly. "Tonight at her work."

Sarah's eyebrows shot up. "Wow. Well, good luck."

I hadn't even gotten that far yet. "So you definitely think I should go?"

She gave me the most bizarre look. "Gem, are you kidding me? How often do regular mortals get to hook up with people like that?" She patted my shoulders again. "Come on, get that notch on your belt. You can tell your grandchildren how you nailed a 10-out-of-10 lawyer and it was the best sex you ever had. Anyway," she checked her watch, "I do need to get back to that meeting. Don't disappear, though. We need to discuss this a *lot* more. I want a blow-by-blow." She paused. "Or, like, the lesbian version of that."

She wasn't kidding about wanting to discuss it more, either. Her lunch break was about 4 minutes long and consisted of her shovelling salad into her mouth and mumbling through it, "So do you think she planned that whole kiss thing all along?" while I struggled to understand her. I hadn't even managed to get to an answer yet before she'd asked me *another* question, and then another, and then she had to go before I'd answered any of them.

"Honestly, I'm just so happy you're getting some, even if it's with demon lady," she told me, giving me a quick hug before she went in for a serious meeting with Diane Frost. "When Diane murders me for messing up this huge project, at least I'll die knowing my best friend finally got laid." I think she was more excited about it than I was.

Me? I... wasn't so sure. None of it felt real because I was sort of 100% convinced that I'd say or do something stupid and it wouldn't happen anyway. Another part of me kept thinking it was a trick, like a big 'Gotcha!', and someone would jump out and tell me I'd been punk'd or something.

I hoped it wasn't the case, though. There was a little flame of hope inside me that was like, 'Someone gorgeous is attracted to you!'.

Mikey was gorgeous and attracted to me, too, I reminded myself, remembering how it had felt when she'd reached for my hand and given me a coy little sideways glance. I caught myself daydreaming about that memory and had to forcefully push it aside; there was no point in dwelling on that now, was there? I'd wrecked my chances with her. Now I needed to try and not do the same with Natalie.

I didn't like my track record on not wrecking things. As a result, I couldn't focus all day and I had no idea how I managed to do any of the piles of crap Marketing was heaping on my desk. Somehow, I chewed through it—luckily, I'd always been able to do stats in my sleep—and when the clock ticked past five and Sarah was nowhere to be found, I realised it was time to leave work.

Time to go home and get ready for tonight.

As I walked out the door, the prospect of sex with Natalie got a *lot* realer. Especially when I got home and saw the red business card Min had made for her under an old Garfield magnet on my fridge, and *especially* when I got a text message and casually picked up my phone to read it, assuming it was from Sarah.

It wasn't. It was from Natalie.

I would have had a drink before reading it if I'd had any alcohol in the cupboard—what if she was cancelling? What if she *wasn't* cancelling!?—but the message just said, "*The after-hours security code for the door is 655143. See you soon, Gemma* ;)" ...which meant it was time to go through the whole shaving, plucking, moisturising routine before I got dressed.

My wardrobe was a catastrophe. Most of the clothes from it were actually beside my bed rather than hanging up in it, so I went on a journey through the laundry piles on my floor to try and find something to wear. I felt like it had been so long since I'd slept with anyone, I didn't know what was expected of me anymore. And were women different than men? Should I wear something different than I would if I was hooking up with a guy?

'I should wear something nice' was about as far as I got, and my eyes fell on the blue party dress I'd worn when I met Mikey.

I reached out and touched the fabric; I liked how it felt. It seemed a little... I don't know, too 'first date', though? Like something you'd wear if you wanted someone to like you enough for a second date.

A second date wasn't on the cards with Natalie; she didn't really seem like girlfriend material. She'd made it pretty clear what she was *really* after, and that was sex. I should probably wear something a bit sexy, right?

Immediately, I thought of the red dress.

I laughed at myself for even thinking about wearing that stupid dress again after the disaster of a night I'd had last time I wore it... and then I stopped laughing, because I was actually seriously considering wearing it again. I kept thinking back to Natalie's reaction to that photo of me in it, and back to that sudden realisation I'd had when I'd looked at the photo again: *I actually look good here.*

Maybe... I could just try it on to see...?

I had to burrow deep down to where I'd buried it in my underwear drawer. When I pulled it out again, it seemed much more innocuous than before; just a piece of fabric like all my other clothes. After a moment spent considering it, I stepped into it, wriggling it up over my hips and then standing in front of the mirror.

Just like last time, I could see my nipples through the material again; and my bellybutton, and my hipbones, and...

...and that was it. I didn't panic about that like I had last time. I didn't feel uncomfortable, or overexposed, or like I should immediately take it off and bury it back in the depths of my underwear drawer to be hidden forever. I just felt like me, but in a tight red dress that showed off my body. Maybe I *could* give it another chance, after all?

Certain I was making another terrible decision with the dress, I put on dark stockings so I wouldn't look like a flasher when I put my coat on this time. Then I straightened my hair, did my makeup, and stood in front of the mirror again, just to see if I was kidding myself.

I didn't think I was. I mean, empirically, I probably looked quite good, didn't I?

I decided I needed a sample size bigger than one for a proper conclusion, so I took a mirror selfie for Sarah to scrutinize and texted it to her. She replied immediately. *"You know, in 10 years' time I'm going to hate myself for being at work right now instead of helping you get ready for the hook-up of the century."*

I chuckled at that. *"Saving your career > helping me dress up for Natalie."*

"Yeah, well, it's not saved yet, and if my career fails anyway, I'm going to regret not just throwing it all in and being over at your place tonight," she told me. *"Oh well, at least one of us is having some good luck for once. And you look amazing, Gem. Totally amazing. She is one lucky lady :)"* That made me smile; I'd almost forgotten how great Sarah always made me feel about myself.

I looked back at the mirror and for just a moment I saw myself how she did: *amazing*. Like I was someone loveable, and like someone *would* find me attractive one day, even if she couldn't herself. It was that last text from Sarah that solidified my decision to wear the little red dress tonight, after all.

I finished getting ready, and when my Uber arrived, the driver looked me up and down as I got into her Jeep and, despite the fact I was wearing a coat over my dress by that point, she said, "Woo! Go get it, hon!" which made me go bright red and laugh nervously. I stopped laughing kind of abruptly when I realised she probably assumed it was a guy I was getting it from, and to avoid any questions about 'him', I pretended to be really interested in my phone as we drove into the CBD.

The sun had just set as we drove across the Sydney Harbour Bridge; all the buildings were starting to turn their lights on. Frost HQ loomed over them all on the skyline, its big snowflake-diamond logo lit up against the sky. The last sets of people in work suits were pouring into buses and trains on their way home, and a younger crowd was starting to gather on the footpaths near bars and pubs, drinking and laughing.

The driver dropped me off at Heiser & Anderson. At this time of night, there was no one there.

When I nearly face-planted the closed glass doors, I remembered Natalie telling me I'd need a security code to make them open. I found a keypad next to the door and punched it in, walking into the foyer.

My heels clicked on the marble floor, just like Natalie's and Sarah's always did. I liked the sound; it made me feel like a proper adult as I stepped into the lift and pressed the button for Heiser & Anderson's floor.

It was only when the doors closed that I suddenly realised *Natalie* would be up there. She'd be up there alone. We were about to be alone together, and—oh, no. I knew what was going to happen. My stomach promptly started to tighten.

I could leave, I thought, she'd only said that I *could* join her, right? If I *wanted* to...? I had to talk myself out of just turning around and going home, because I'd come this far. I'd kissed her already. I knew she was interested. And, really, casual sex was always a bit blah, wasn't it? Like, she knew I was brand new to this, so she couldn't really expect that I'd have any idea how to—

The lift doors opened.

—Oh, no, I bet she was totally expecting great sex and I was going to horribly disappoint her, wasn't I?!

I stood inside the lift for a moment, heart pounding, looking forward into Heiser & Anderson's offices. The waiting room was dark; the only lighting in the reception was from outside and the emergency '*Exit*' sign by the stairwell. There were two lights on further down the hallway, though, and as far as I could tell, it was almost empty.

Despite that, it took a *lot* of gentle coaxing (and several presses of the 'open doors' button) to get me out of that lift.

My heels sank into the plush carpet as I walked towards the unmanned reception desk. Without a receptionist, I wasn't sure what to do. Probably not sit here in the dark? I checked my watch; 9:31pm. Her meeting might already be finished.

I looked up the hallway towards where the two lights were; one of them had a closed door with a red sign that said '*meeting in progress*' on it. Inside, I could see someone pacing behind the frosted glass and hear a muffled voice; and with rising panic, I realised it was *her*. It was Natalie.

She'd walk out of that room at any moment.

I didn't know where to wait for her to do that, because the reception area was unmanned. She'd left her office door open, though, and that light was on, too.

My heart in my throat, I took a few careful steps down the hallway, wondering if she wanted me to wait in her office. I mean, she'd left the light on, that was a sign, wasn't it? It just felt a bit rude, wandering into someone's private office while they weren't there.

I looked behind me at the waiting room again; it was so dark, I didn't think I was supposed to wait there. I almost did anyway, to avoid doing something wrong.

Before I made a decision, though, I noticed there was a piece of fabric hanging on the door handle of her office; it hadn't been there last time Henry and I had been here. My curiosity got the better of my anxiety, and I took a few ginger steps forward, peering down at it. My heart nearly stopped when I realised what it was.

It was a blindfold.

CHAPTER TWENTY-SIX

You had to be kidding me; a *blindfold*?!

I'd never done anything like that—never—and I suddenly felt like I was stuck in one of those nightmares where I arrived at an exam, sat down and then realised the questions were 1000x harder than the ones I'd been studying. I was *so* out of my depth.

I could just go now, I thought, looking back over my shoulder at the lift. I didn't think Natalie had seen me yet, so I could just tip-toe out and pretend I was never here.

Then again... I looked down at the blindfold. I mean, she couldn't really do anything too kinky in her office, could she? The carpets here were so nice, and from what I'd seen of really kinky stuff on the internet (research purposes only, I swear!), it looked kind of messy. She was probably too responsible to do anything like that at work.

Maybe I'm just overreacting and it's not even a blindfold, I thought, reaching out to pick it up. I was probably jumping to conclusions and it was just a scarf or maybe a—*nope*, it was definitely a blindfold. It even had soft satin eye pads.

Well, shit. I was about to be trapped in a room with someone who purchased luxury sex toys and brought them to work.

I put it carefully back on the door handle, arranging it as if I hadn't touched it, and looked through her door into her office.

If I walk in there, I might end up wearing this thing, I thought, and then suddenly had all these visions of all the wild stuff I'd seen on the internet. Being blindfolded. Being tied up. Being whipped, or spanked or, like, whatever it was that people who were into this stuff did. I couldn't imagine being one of those people. People like me didn't do things like that, so I had *no idea* why Natalie thought that I'd be into this stuff.

Then again... I supposed people like me didn't generally kiss scary union lawyers suddenly, either, did they? I'd somehow managed that. And I'd also agreed to out myself to my entire company to save Henry's reputation and then actually done it, *and* I'd sent Natalie that kind of sexy picture of myself when she'd asked. I'd done a whole lot of things people like me didn't do, and things that I could *never* have imagined myself doing. On top of that, I *had* just basically agreed to have casual sex with her. I supposed it kind of made sense that Natalie thought I might be into this.

I looked down at the blindfold, facing off with it for a few seconds. I didn't know how I felt about the prospect of using it, but I'd come this far. It seemed silly to leave now. I drew a long, deep breath, and took a step into Natalie's office anyway.

Inside, one set of the overhead lights had been turned off; the odd half-light gave the room an after-hours atmosphere, like something out of a horror movie. Because there was no one else in, it was quiet. All I could hear was the whir of her computer fan, the muffled sound of Natalie talking way down the hall, and the hum of the traffic outside. I felt like I was trespassing, so I tip-toed across the carpet into the centre of the room.

I'd been too stressed out about seeing Natalie and the whole Henry affair to really appreciate her office last time I'd been here; it was huge and spacious, there were locked filing cabinets up one side of it, and glass shelves with meticulously chosen knick-knacks on the other. The knick-knacks matched the art prints on the wall, and everything matched the carpet. The only thing that stood out were the red business cards in a little stand on Natalie's desk.

An innocuous photo frame beside them caught my eye. It was facing away from me. Curious, I gingerly walked around the desk to the window side to inspect it.

It was Natalie in jeans and a t-shirt—which she still managed to make look stylish as hell, by the way—with a little girl, maybe five or six, in a pink tutu. The girl had Natalie's dark hair.

What? That made me pick the frame up to have a closer look. They had the same smile too—I thought, anyway? *Wow.* I exhaled. I mean, I didn't know why I was so surprised; if she was 36 and the average Australian woman had her first child at 29, it made perfect logical sense that she'd have a child about this girl's age. ...if she *was* actually Natalie's child, that is. I tried to tilt the picture towards the light so I could see better, but before I could make a decision about her, there was movement at the door.

"Surprised?"

Shit. I jumped and immediately put the picture straight back down on her table, standing to attention with my heart pounding. I could feel my face turning the same colour as Natalie's business cards.

Natalie herself was standing in the doorway looking amazing (of course), leaning a casual shoulder on the doorframe as she watched me. I couldn't read her expression.

She'd caught me spying on her *again*. I gulped. "I'm sorry!"

She didn't acknowledge that. She just regarded me neutrally for a moment and then slowly, confidently, approached me. All the hair on my body stood on end.

She stopped when she was nearly toe-to-toe with me again, eyes on mine for just a little bit too long. Beside us, she lifted the picture frame up and glanced down at it, spent a moment or two appraising it. "I still really like this picture," she decided, and then put the frame back down, looking right back at me. "So what do you think, Gemma, did you pick me for a mother?" She looked smug.

I didn't know how to answer that without saying something *really* wrong. If I said no, that Natalie didn't seem like a mother at all, I'd be the asshole. If I said yes, and then it turned out that girl *wasn't* actually Natalie's daughter, I'd look stupid.

She was waiting for an answer. I was practically sweating. "I don't know..."

She watched me. "Sure you do. You immediately thought, 'there's no way Natalie's her mother', didn't you?"

Now I really *was* sweating. "I really don't know..."

"Gemma." Her tone was deceptively casual. "I'm interested to know what you think." Gosh, her eyes were *hard*. She was steel. Why was she smiling? She shouldn't be smiling. I didn't want to answer or— "*Gemma*. Just say it."

Oh, no. I did—*gosh*, her face was so close, I couldn't—but I had to say *something* or—"No," I managed. "No, I think maybe... I don't know, it doesn't seem right? You never talk about her..."

For a moment, there was silence. I searched Natalie's face for even the smallest sign of anger.

Then, after what felt like eternity, her smile deepened and she chuckled. "Good guess," she told me, and then laughed a couple of times, glancing down at the photo. "Lucia, my niece. You see, middle-aged men in the industry I represent like to bond over talking about their kids, and I can't be bothered justifying my lifestyle to them most of the time."

"Oh." But I thought... "Don't gay people sometimes have kids, too?"

I must have caught her by surprise, because her eyebrows went up and she laughed. "'Lifestyle' meaning 'I'm not interested in having a family'."

My cheeks were *burning*. I felt like the biggest, stupidest wreck in front of this completely calm, highly-accomplished and super-hot woman. "Oh..."

Her eyes dipped to my red cheeks. After what seemed like eternity, she cracked a smile. "So, does that make 'one' for me?"

I didn't know what she meant by 'one', and I didn't want to risk asking in case I said something else stupid.

It must have been obvious I was confused, because she explained, "Henry said your friends keep a highly competitive tally of how often they get a blush out of you."

My eyes widened; *ugh*! Of all the things for Henry to tell her about! Her knowing about that made my blush even worse. "Yeah..."

She observed my reaction. "Two," she said. "He told me he wasn't sure what number they were up to, but that he thought Min was probably winning."

"Sh—*he* definitely is."

Her grin deepened and she nodded once. "For now, anyway," she said casually, and then locked eyes with me. "Because I think after what I'm going to do to you tonight, I'll have beaten him."

O-Oh. My lips parted.

She spent a few seconds enjoying my reaction to that, and then her hands lifted to the buttons on my coat. "Why don't we make you a little more comfortable?"

Oh, no, here we go... I thought, taking a sharp breath.

Very slowly and deliberately—her eyes on mine the whole time—she undid my buttons one by one, in a neat line down my front. After my coat hung open, she slipped her fingers under the shoulders of it, brushing against the bare skin underneath, and pushed it down my arms. It fell in a pile at my feet. I glanced down at it, wondering if I should pick it up.

"Leave it," Natalie told me impassively, her eyes travelling down my body. I could practically feel the weight of them on my skin. "Huh," she observed. "You wore the dress I like." She looked impressed. My stomach fluttered; I felt absurdly delighted that she approved of it.

She took a step back. "Turn around, Gemma. Show me properly how it looks."

Breathless, I followed her instruction. It was such an odd feeling, knowing she was *staring* at me.

When I was facing the window, she said, "Stop." I did, and she was silent.

Outside, the sun had set. Past my own reflection in the window, I could see the building opposite us across the road still had its lights on, with the odd person still at their desk. On one of the floors, a cleaner was vacuuming already. I wondered if they could see us.

I couldn't focus on them, though, because in the window, I could see Natalie's reflection, too. She had a knowing smile. "Do you like the view?"

I could hardly breathe. "Yes."

313

"I do, too." She wasn't looking out the window, though. She was looking down my body. Again, I felt that rush of delight that she found me attractive—delight, and *terror*. I had no idea what she wanted to do to me. It didn't seem like she was going to tell me, either.

She spent a few long moments admiring how I looked from behind in my little red dress, and then took a few steps forward until she was almost right up against me. I could feel her breath on my bare shoulders. She didn't touch me, though. She was just looking down at my skin. I watched her in the reflection.

"You don't do this very often, do you, Gemma?" I shook my head. "How long has it been?"

Oh, goodness... I didn't think Mikey counted because we hadn't actually done anything in the end, and before that, well, what year was it...? I grimaced.

She glanced up to observe my reaction in the reflection. "Three," she said, and then looked back at my body. "A while, then." I nodded, and she really enjoyed that answer.

She lifted one hand and trailed her fingertips very lightly and very theatrically over my bare shoulder. "Tell me, Gemma," she began, as I tried not to visibly shiver at her touch. She was giving me goose bumps. "How far down do these freckles go? Because I can see them here," she touched my shoulders, "and here," her fingers trailed down my arms, "and here," she touched my hands.

I didn't know how to answer that. I definitely had freckles in other places than my arms.

"Are there freckles under that dress of yours, Gemma?"

I was watching her lips in the reflection. "Yes."

That was clearly the right answer, because they smiled. "Show me."

I inhaled sharply. Just like that?!

"I'd like to see them, Gemma."

If we'd been in the privacy of my bedroom, I might have pulled down my dress for her right then. But beyond our reflections, I could see at least a dozen people—maybe more—

314

in the building opposite us and I had no way of knowing if they could see us or not.

"I said I'd like to see them."

I—I couldn't just— "But there are people in that building..."

She looked unfazed. "Do you know them?" I shook my head. "Are you likely to meet them again?" Well, I didn't think so... "So why do you care if they see?"

I looked across at them. I didn't know why, I just did.

Her smile faded and she stepped away from me, her reflection disappearing. I could hear her footsteps leave towards the door and for a second, I panicked. I'd already begun to try and figure out if I *could* actually do it in front of a bunch of strangers when her reflection reappeared behind me.

She looked smug, lifting both her arms towards my head. What was she—?

Before I knew what was happening, she put something over my eyes.

The blindfold.

She tied it around my head; I didn't stop her, even though my heart had started racing. I put a hand out to the window in front of me, bracing myself against the thick glass so I didn't fall over. My mouth was open.

"Don't worry about those people," she told me. "They don't matter." Then, she was silent for a moment. I could hear her breathing. One breath, then another. I don't know what she was waiting for, but when her fingertips touched my shoulder again, I *jumped*, and then felt silly for being so dramatic.

"Four." Her lips were beside my ear, much closer than I thought they'd be. Slowly, very slowly, her fingertips trailed down my arms to my wrists, and then back up again. Then, she lifted her fingers from me; all I could hear was her breathing and my pulse in my ears. When she touched me again it was my waist—I hadn't expected that—*again*, I jumped. "Five," she said, "Gemma. You're making this far too easy for me."

"I can't help it," I murmured.

"I know," she said. There was a smile in her voice. "That's why it's so much fun." Her fingertips trailed up my torso towards my chest, and—

"Six," she said, when my jaw opened. She stopped short of my breasts on purpose. Everything she did was *so* deliberate.

There was another pause for a moment where nothing happened. I was holding my breath; I had no idea where she was going to touch me. It could be anywhere, I knew she wasn't shy. It made my skin sing with anticipation.

When her fingers hooked into the back of my dress, my breath caught. I knew what came next.

She didn't tug the fabric down straight away, though. She paused. "I'm going to pull down your dress," she said in a calm and clear voice. "Is that okay, Gemma?"

I was so spaced out, so aware of my hammering pulse and how close she was, but I somehow managed a breathy, "Yeah..."

I felt the dress move. She was slowly pulling the fabric down over my body; slowly, until she reached my ribcage and I could feel the gentle office aircon on my bare chest.

I was topless in her office.

I was topless and blindfolded in a corporate workplace. I was also standing in front of this massive floor-to-ceiling window and I had no idea if anyone could see, but *she* could. As aware of how this must look to other people, something about having the blindfold made it difficult for me to focus on anything outside of me. I was aware of my whole body—of *her* body behind me. Of my pulse, my breathing, and the goose bumps on my skin.

I could hear her breathing, too—or rather, I could hear her holding her breath. I wondered what she thought of what she was looking at; I didn't have her round breasts or sumptuous curves. As if reading my mind, she made an appreciative noise. "Very nice. Very, very nice."

I released a breath I hadn't been holding; I think I may have smiled slightly.

Now they were out, I expected her to reach straight for my breasts—that had been my experience of previous partners—but she didn't. She didn't do anything at first. I don't know what she was doing—waiting. Watching me.

I *jumped* when she suddenly touched me again. Both sets of fingers started at the base of my neck, trailing outwards; down my arms again, slowly up them. Along my back, and along my torso. Every time her thumbs stroked up my ribcage towards my breasts I inhaled, expecting her to finally *grab* them, but she didn't. She'd get close, *so close*, and then move her hands down again.

And her lips... they were so close to the sensitive part of my neck, hovering of my skin. Hovering, but never *fucking* touching me.

She was standing so close to me and yet not quite close enough; touching me, but not quite enough. And she was *chuckling* deep in her throat. She was really enjoying it, and it was torture. Sweet, glorious torture.

I was lightheaded. I was *panting*. If I hadn't braced myself against the window with that hand, I might have just flopped into a hot mess at her feet.

She pulled away for a moment—I heard the rustle of fabric?—and then when she stepped up against my back I felt lace and hot skin against mine. She'd taken off her blouse.

"I have an event to go to tonight," she murmured into my ear. "I don't want my shirt to get sweaty from what we're about to do."

She pulled me right against her and, one hand on my jaw, she pushed my head to the side, exposing my neck. She exhaled heavily across my skin, her lips hardly touching me. My mouth was open. My head was lolling on a shoulder. I felt like I hadn't taken a lungful of air for eternity when she finally—finally!—pressed her mouth firmly against the skin of my neck. Dragging her lips against it, biting down gently just under my ear and, embarrassingly, I *groaned.*

I could feel her laugh more than I could hear it. She paused to say, "Seven," before diving back in on my neck.

Her hands rose to my breasts, roughly cupping them, searching out my nipples and rolling them between her fingers. I was so aware of her—of her lips, her body against mine, how quickly she was breathing—that I didn't notice I was leaning so heavily against the window until my forearm fell against it, too. To stop myself from just collapsing, I put my other hand to the glass as well.

Her lips still on me, her fingertips crept under the hem of my dress, but it was too tight for her to do much. I wanted her to pull it down properly, I wanted to kick it off so her hands could get at the rest of me, but she made pulling it up to my waist such an agonisingly slow and deliberate process that Christmas was going to come by the time there was any chance of me joining it.

When my dress was finally bunched around my waist, when she'd finally rolled my stockings down to the middle of my thighs and commented, "Nice underwear," softly into my ear, she took her hands off me and stood back a moment. I could hear her walking around me—fingers trailing casually along my arms and shoulders as she went—probably checking me out from all angles. I could almost *feel* the smirk I knew she had.

Here I was, nearly naked in her office while she was almost fully-clothed. That's when it hit me like a tonne of bricks: 'she'. It was a *woman* doing this to me. The person who was stepping up against me from behind again, body-to-body, skin-to-skin, was a woman. I was getting it on with a woman, and there was something *so* naughty about that. It was hot. It was *so* hot. I was so turned on, and every nerve in my body sang with how ready for it I was.

When her fingers drew a line down my torso, trailed down my stomach and *slowly* slipped inside my underwear, I was ready for it. I was ready for the deep chuckle she gave me when she found how wet she'd made me, and I leant heavily on the window, knowing what came next.

There was nothing to look at with this blindfold on. I couldn't see how ridiculous I probably looked, I couldn't worry about all the people who might have been able to see, all I could do was focus on her fingers. Her lips. Her other hand dragging along *my* lips while my head lolled to the side.

The moment she started to give me hand... wow, did she ever know what she was doing. Not that operating me was a fine science, exactly—but, *wow,* she knew. My own hands might as well have been down there for how responsive she was. She knew when it wasn't working, she knew when it *was* working and, boy, did she jump right on that when it was. Every movement, every circle and every line she drew, it was all I could focus on. My world narrowed and all that mattered was her hands, and the sound of me taking each breath, and the hammering pulse in my ears, and—how much my legs wanted to shake and how close I was—and then she'd pull back, chuckle, wait, and start again. And again, and again, and again...

The last time she did it I wasn't sure she was going to finish me, but I was so close, so close I could feel my cheek against the cool glass window as I fogged it with my hot breath, so close that my knees felt like they were going to collapse underneath me, so close I felt like this woman would probably let me *die* before she'd let me actually get there and I found myself mouthing, "Please," half-against the glass. "*Please*...!"

She laughed at that—once, triumphantly—and then her lips were on my neck again and her fingers were inside me and I was being *mashed* against that window, pushed up against it as it all built up inside me and built and built and built and then finally—when I thought it would never happen she finally *brought me there* and my mouth opened and muscles *shook* and all I could think about were those fingers on me and what she was doing to me and that I was doing it with a woman—

such an incredibly hot woman!—and her body was against me and her lips were on me and, *fuck, fuck,* it had taken me so long to get here and it was *amazing...*! It was so *good*, so *natural*, so *everything* I'd always felt was kind of lacking every other time I'd slept with someone. It was *right*. It was so *right*. I pushed every part of me against every part of her, letting her guide me through it all.

She let me down slowly afterwards. Giving my neck slow, leisurely kisses, toying with one of my breasts. I listened to our breathing begin to slow, to my pulse stop drumming in my ears. Our bodies starting to relax against each other.

I'd let my eyes fall shut under the blindfold, just enjoying the feeling of being gently touched and kissed by her when she stopped. "Be back in a moment," she said quietly, planting a kiss on my shoulder and moving away from me. I heard her walk out of the room and down the hall—then there was the squeak of a bathroom door opening and closing. Water began to run.

I didn't want to move.

Everything about me felt still—my mind felt blank, like someone had hit a reset button. I felt like I was somewhere else; somewhere far away and peaceful. I almost could have slept like that, against the window.

It didn't take her long to come back, though. I heard her stop by the door. There was a long, obvious pause. "You can get dressed, you know, Gemma." She sounded amused.

Whoops. I was still bent double against the window. Cringing, I pushed myself to stand upright on my weak legs, and with shaky arms, I lifted the blindfold.

She was walking over to where she'd draped her blouse, looking smug.

I was too distracted by the fact she was about to put on her blouse to fully appreciate the fact she was nearly topless. She was going to put her shirt back on already? But wasn't it her turn? "Don't you want—" Spit it out, Gem. "I mean, don't you want me to...?" I made a very, very vague hand gesture towards her.

It made her laugh, which made me blush. "Eight," she said, and then shook her head. "I'm good, thanks. I have to speak at this event and there will be a couple of ministers there, which means there will probably be cameras. Given that, I don't think it would be very prudent to get up on stage looking like I've just been fucked between meetings by a gorgeous redhead."

I gaped at her.

She clearly found my expression very entertaining as she put her blouse back on. "Thank you, though," she said, walking up to me with her blouse still hanging open. "That was *exactly* what I needed." She cupped my jaw in both hands and kissed me firmly.

That was exactly what I needed, too, I thought, kissing her back and not sure what to do with my free hands.

When she pulled back, she stood in front of me for a moment, making sure I copped an eyeful of her big breasts and how fabulous they looked in her lacy bra. She waited too long, long enough to make it obvious she was waiting for me to react to them. I did.

"Nine," she said triumphantly, and then her eyes dipped to my bare chest for a moment. She made that appreciate noise again. "You are one very attractive woman, Gemma," she told me matter-of-factly, and then walked past me to her desk drawer and took out her handbag. "Anyway, I need to re-do my lipstick and read over my speech, so I'm going to head off." She paused by the door, giving me one indulgent once-over. "Don't hang around; the building alarms switch on at midnight," she said like she was dismissing an employee. With that, she gave me one last wink, and casually walked out.

I stood there in her office for a moment, half-naked, listening to the 'ding' as she called the lift. Then, once it had left, there was only the hum of traffic and the whir of her computer idling on her desk. I was alone again.

I exhaled, looking down my body at my bunched up dress, my rolled-down stockings and the coat in a pile at my feet.

I'd just had sex with a woman.

I let that sink in: me, Gemma Rowe, had just had sex with a woman, and not just 'a' woman, with possibly the hottest woman in Sydney, in her office, and afterwards, she'd thanked me and told me I was gorgeous. I repeated that to myself a couple of times, hardly able to believe it had actually happened.

Light-headed, I collected my coat off the floor and pulled my dress and stockings up, sparing a moment to look apprehensively behind me at the building opposite.

I wasn't sure what I expected to see, people gaping at me, maybe? Nothing had changed over there, though. People *weren't* staring. The cleaner was still vacuuming, and the people working at their desks still had their eyes glued to their screens like I didn't even exist. I felt a bit silly for worrying about them.

I looked back at my reflection for a moment—it was obscured by hand-prints, face-prints and what could accurately be described as 'signs of a struggle'. *Ten*, I thought, ignoring my pink cheeks and hurriedly rubbing the window with my coat to make it less extremely obvious what we'd been doing against it.

The toilets were just down the hall from her office; I walked in and got a proper look at my reflection. 'Disarray' was an understatement. My hair was messy, my dress was twisted, and I had red lipstick *all over* my pale skin. It couldn't have been any more obvious what and who I'd been doing if I'd actually been caught in the act. I kind of liked it, though. It felt like proof I had a sex life.

I knew exactly who would find this version of me super entertaining, too. I took my phone out of my coat pocket and snapped a mirror selfie, sending it to Sarah. *"We just talked, honest"*.

My phone practically went off in my hands before I could put it back again. *"OH MY FUCKING GOD YOU DID NOT. YOU DID NOT. OH MY GOD. GEM. IS THAT IN A RESTAURANT??? DID YOU JUST LITERALLY GET NAILED IN A TOILET???"*

I laughed. *"In her office."*

"!!!!! YOU TOTAL HUSSY OMG!!!!! That's it, I'm coming over after work. I don't care how late I finish, you'd better be awake. I need to know everything, Gem, EVERYTHING. Prepare flow-charts and powerpoints, I need all the intricate details!!!!"

"Lol, okay!" I told her, remembering now that she'd been like this last time I'd slept with someone, too. It had been a boy way back then, but her reaction now was exactly the same as it had been back then. She was just as excited for me, and just as desperate for all the details. The fact it was with a woman this time made absolutely no difference to her. Nothing had changed between Sarah and I at all.

I ordered an Uber before I put my phone away and looked up at the mirror. I had a great big smile on my face, and I was practically glowing.

I felt so fucking good. So good that I felt like I could have thrown my arms out and just flown home on this feeling.

I never thought things could turn out this way. I never thought I'd have Sarah this excited for me after I'd come out to her; I just always thought I'd have to give that up, but I didn't. I didn't have to give anything up. I'd just had amazing sex with a woman, I wanted to tell her all about it, and she wanted to hear it. I just felt *so good.*

Still with a roaring smile, I cleaned up, fixed my dress and washed all the lipstick off me. My undies were a lost cause and I hadn't thought to bring a spare pair, so instead of facing the prospect of being stuck in them for 30+ minutes in a stranger's Uber, I just took them off and left them in the bin. Sarah had said I probably shouldn't wear underwear with this dress anyway, right? Besides, I had dark stockings on.

Outside, it was warmer than I remembered; probably too warm for a coat. I didn't really want to wear no coat at all—because my dress *was* tiny, even for eveningwear—but I let my coat hang open so I could feel the breeze.

No one cared. They didn't even give me a second glance. People were on their way home from work or out with friends and all dressed pretty similarly. I didn't stand out at all.

I was a bit worried about what my Uber driver would think of how I looked, but he turned out to be a tired middle-aged man who was clearly working his second job. As a result, he hardly even noticed me. He was polite but distracted; checking his dash-mounted phone at every intersection and staring blankly forward at traffic. Talkback radio played in the background as we drove back over the bridge to the North Shore and back home. I half-listened, smiling through my reflection at the city beside us.

My flat was quiet when I got home—well, except for Mr Grump who was complaining about being fed late. As I let myself in, feeling like a completely different person, he curled around my feet and I very nearly fell over him in my heels. I took them off and fed him, and then wandered into my living room, feeling fantastic.

My living room didn't look as fantastic as I felt, though. In fact, after being in Natalie's big, open and meticulously clean office, it looked like a truck had backed up to my living room and just tipped out all my belongings out everywhere. The state of it hadn't bothered me before, but after I'd had a shower, I found myself frowning at my crap everywhere. It bothered me now.

Well, I had to stay up late for Sarah, right? I might as well use that time to clean this place up. I put some music on and set to work.

Singing to myself, I picked up all the photos one by one, pulling the Blu-Tac off the back and laying them carefully in an old shoe box. They were everywhere—on my couch, on the floor, on the table—and I brushed the cat hair off them and put them safely away where they wouldn't get ruined. Next, I set about putting my clothes back in my actual wardrobe (I think it had probably been years since they were all in there), and moving all the empty wine bottles in recycling.

I was just hunting around the couch for anything I'd missed before I vacuumed, when I came across something long and black buried in the cushions. I didn't recognise it—was it a belt? I didn't remember buying a belt like that.

I stood up, pulling it out of the couch in one long thread. It was only when I turned it over that I realised what it was.

It was Mikey's tie.

CHAPTER TWENTY-SEVEN

When Sarah burst through my door at midnight with a huge smile on her face, I expected to immediately get the third degree on sex with Natalie. Instead, the words died on her lips. She stopped dead in the middle of my clean living room, gaping like she'd seen a ghost. "Wow," she said, giving me a stunned look. "You actually had carpet underneath all that junk? I can't believe it."

I scoffed. My place had never been *that* bad. "You've seen it clean before!"

Her eyes were still wide. "Yeah, in the winter of 1903. That's the last time I saw your couch not covered in clothes and cat hair." She took a few more steps so she could lean in through my bedroom doorway and peek inside. "Wow, and you didn't just pile all your laundry on your bed, either." She turned back to me. Her eyes were twinkling. "Well, I guess now that *you're* no longer in your closet there's plenty of room for clothes."

I groaned. "*Sarah.*"

She laughed and wandered back into the living room, looking around us. "This place looks so different now! I bet it feels good too, right?"

Well, it probably would have felt a whole lot better if I hadn't found Mikey's tie right at the end of cleaning everything. I was sitting on the couch with it, not feeling as good as I probably should have.

Sarah frowned at me. "Okay, Gem, you've just had sex for the first time in a hundred years and your place looks amazing, why do you look like a kid who's just dropped their ice cream?"

Because I *had* dropped the proverbial ice cream, so to speak. I held up the tie and said with gravity, "I found this in my couch while I was cleaning."

"A tie?" She looked at me blankly. "Is it Min's?"

"It's Mikey's."

Recognition dawned on her face "*Oh*," she said. Then, she laughed. "Oh my god, of course you've found something to beat yourself up over, I forgot who I was dealing with!" She kicked off her heels and flopped down on the couch beside me. "You've just had amazing sex with an ethereal being and instead of swinging from the chandeliers, you're stressing about this one thing that happened that one time."

"It wasn't 'that one time', it was last week," I pointed out, and then sighed and nodded at the phone in my other hand. "It gets worse. I just thought I'd check Facebook to see if Mikey was seeing anyone else already..."

"And from your down-in-the-dumps expression, she clearly is."

I shrugged. "Well, she unfriended me so I can't see her updates, but some of her friends have public profiles, so I just thought I'd check her comments on their posts in the last week. She's acting like nothing happened." I sighed. "Maybe it didn't mean as much to her as it meant to me?"

Sarah gave me a tired look and slung an arm across my shoulder. "Gem," she began, "I love you, but you're overthinking this. Let me tell you how this is going to go: instead of being creepy and stalking Mikey on Facebook, you'll send her another friend request, then you'll kiss and make up and live happily ever after. And *now*," she said ceremoniously, changing the subject, "you need to tell your best friend *everything* about sex with Evil Lawyer Women, because it's past midnight, I'm pregnant and exhausted, and I've been trying to figure out for nearly three hours how on earth she managed to convince you to have sex in an office when the planets basically need to align for you to even agree to have sex in your own flat."

Sarah wasn't going to let up on me until I told her all the dirty details, so I did: right down to how Natalie put the blindfold on me. She stopped me at that. "Oh my god," she said, "you didn't just have *crazy* sex. You had crazy, *kinky* sex in an office where people could see and then came home and cleaned your flat? Who are you and what have you done with my best friend?" Incredulous, she shook her head. "Anyway, don't stop there. Did she get naked before you did the dirty, or what? Is everything on her real?"

I shrugged. "She took her top off so she didn't get it sweaty, but that's it. I didn't really see that much of her."

Sarah looked unimpressed. "Okay, wait, so she's happy with people maybe seeing *you* naked, but not her?" She paused. "*You* were happy with that?"

"I don't know if they actually could? No one seemed to notice, and she's told me before how careful she is about that stuff."

She pressed her lips together. "Hmm," she said, clearly unconvinced. "Oh well. Maybe I've been hanging around with you and Min too much and now I'm stressing over nothing. Honestly, though, I still literally can't believe this happened: *you*, Ms Wallflower of the Year, had kinky sex with some crazy hot lawyer woman *and* you didn't find an excuse to chicken out. You actually went through with it. That's pretty damn cool of you, Gem."

That made me smile. It *was* 'pretty damn cool', wasn't it?

She noticed my smile and shoved me. "That's better! Stop looking so miserable! You should be posting your sex hair all over social media right now so everyone knows you're finally getting some. Maybe I can even get Bree to bake you a 'Congratulations on the Sex' cake or something, too."

Sarah looked like she was totally ready to bake me that cake herself, despite the fact her cooking was infamously bad and she barely knew how to operate her microwave.

We went over the finer details of sex with Natalie *again* so she could make exclamations about how un-Gemma-like it was and how happy she was for me—even if she *was* mildly disappointed that I hadn't beaten Natalie up for her and disguised it as BDSM.

Despite the fact that she was ecstatic, though, she couldn't stay very long because she hadn't been home last night and didn't want to wear the same suit *three* days in a row.

I said goodbye to her and was getting ready for bed when my phone buzzed. I didn't think she'd text me so soon after just leaving, and Natalie had probably already gotten what she wanted from me, so I didn't think it would be her either... so for a second, because I'd been doing recon on Mikey's Facebook all night, my heart kind of fluttered and I stupidly thought, '*Maybe it's her!*'

It wasn't Mikey, of course. It was Sarah. "*Btw, Gem, I don't want to spend the next five years watching you beat yourself up over messing things up with this Mikey person. If you're not going to hook up with her again, at least apologise to her so she can forgive you and you can let the whole thing go.*"

I stared at that message for a moment, both amazed and annoyed that Sarah knew me so well. Then, I exhaled, put my phone away, and got ready for bed. I was too tired and sore from having sex (I loved being able to say that) to face the thought of sorting things out with Mikey right now.

The following morning, I needed to have another shower to get all the residual lipstick off my neck and shoulders, and, just in case I still smelt like kinky office sex, I washed my hair too.

Sarah and I had planned to catch the train together this morning, but when I ran downstairs, late again, Rob's old ute was pulled up in front of the building. Sarah gave me a little wave from the passenger seat.

Sarah and Rob were picking me up; that put a *big* smile on my face. I couldn't climb in fast enough!

I hadn't had much sleep for two nights in a row, so despite the fact it was nice to be driven to work and really nice of them both to think of me, I found myself drifting off against the window to the rattle of Rob's car engine and the hum of traffic. It was only when Sarah said to Rob, "Hey, babe, could you drive through Hyde Park? I just want to check something out," that I woke up. I'd been there last night; Natalie's office was near there.

Rob obliged, and, to my alarm, Sarah directed him *right* past the Heiser & Anderson building. It made me nervous; I didn't know what she was doing. With Sarah, you could never be sure.

While we were stopped at a set of lights beside it, she rolled her window all the way down and craned her neck all the way up at the skyscraper beside us. I didn't understand what she was doing—and I was worried she'd jump out and go and confront Natalie or something—until she exhaled at length, wound up her window, and twisted back to me with a relieved smile.

"One-way windows," she said simply. "You can't see in from outside."

Oh. I *knew* it! I *knew* Natalie wasn't the bad guy Sarah still sort of thought she was, even if the strike was causing Marketing some major dramas.

At work, there were a lot of bleary eyes and jumbo coffee mugs because of the strike; I think everyone who was on Sarah's project hadn't slept much. She disappeared into a meeting with management as soon as we got to work, leaving me to head off to my desk alone and wonder what I was going to—

I stopped in my tracks. There was a huge mixed bouquet lying across my keyboard.

What was *that* doing on my desk? My immediate thought was that it was either a mistake or someone messing with me. The latter seemed unlikely, though, because the bouquet was clearly one of those expensive luxury ones. No one would buy one of those for a prank.

Embarrassed—people were surreptitiously watching me out of the corner of their eyes—I went to investigate.

Because of how expensive the bouquet looked, my first thought was that Natalie had probably bought them for me as some sort of courteous 'Thank You for the Sex'-present. When I turned over the card, though, it *did* say '*Thank you so much, Gemma*', but also, '*and I'm sorry*'.

'Sorry'? There was only one person who'd say both 'thank you' and 'sorry' to me: these could *only* be from Henry. I held up the bouquet and inhaled deeply; they smelt gorgeous. It was a nice gesture, even if I'd told him a million times he didn't need to be sorry.

Unfortunately—or fortunately?—expensive flowers appearing on my desk fed into the brand new rumour I'd very effectively planted by kissing Natalie during that teleconference.

I'd almost forgotten about it until a head appeared over the partition. Mark, I think his name was? "Those are nice flowers," he commented. There was something cheeky in his tone of voice.

Uh, oh. "Um, thanks," I told him, going red and putting the bouquet off to the side of my desk where it was difficult for other people to see. Then, I sat down and tried to pretend to be very busy so he wouldn't say anything else about them.

It didn't work too well, though, because a colleague of Mark's casually found a reason to come over and 'notice' the flowers. "Those are nice, who are they from?" he asked, even though it sounded like he already thought he knew the answer. He and Mark glanced at each other, and I knew *exactly* what he was going to say. "That MEU lawyer, maybe...?" They both tittered like schoolgirls.

My poor cheeks. Still, this gossip was kind of the point, wasn't it? This was what stopped people talking about Henry and me, so I should probably feed it. Oh, gosh. "Well, it, uh, doesn't say who they're from," I answered honestly.

It sounded like a lie, and they clearly thought it was one. They looked at each other, and then one of them got a bit more brazen. "Is it true you and that lawyer were going at it during a teleconference?"

Before I could answer, Mark shoved him. "Mate, you can't talk about crap like that at work, it's sexual harassment." He sounded like he was quoting a policy manual.

"What, so it's *not* harassment for them to actually go at it during a meeting, but it's harassment if I ask about it later?" He looked back at me, unfazed. "So did it happen?"

RIP, my entire face. "Well, I didn't know she was in a meeting..."

Their reaction was *perfect*—or perfect according to Natalie's design. They both looked like they were about to explode, made excuses to leave, and joined their colleagues in other parts of Marketing. For the next few minutes, everyone had their heads together and were trying to pretend they weren't looking at me or my flowers.

The hairs on the back of my neck stood on end; they were *all* talking about me.

I sat there waiting to feel what I'd expected to feel: shame, humiliation. Waiting to feel horrified about what they were saying about me. *Everyone* knew my deepest, darkest secret, and now they were all talking about it with each other. The whole company would be talking about it soon. I waited for it, I waited for that horrible, sick feeling.

But to my surprise, it never came.

I stared forward at my clasped hands on my desk, chewing my lip.

I... actually wasn't ashamed. How could I be, really? I'd done this on purpose, they were talking about me because I wanted them to, spreading rumours because I wanted them to, and that made a world of difference. Instead of feeling humiliated that people knew and humiliated they were all talking about it, I was sort of *proud* that I'd had the guts to out myself to them all.

I did this, I thought, feeling eyes on me, *I did this just like I promised Henry I would.*

I'd done this big thing for Henry by coming out to Sarah before I thought I was ready, this big thing by coming out to everyone at Frost, and then I'd gone out and taken this big risk and slept with someone I was attracted to but super intimidated by. Never in a million years would I have thought

I could ever do any of those things, and especially not in the way I did them. I didn't think I was that sort of person.

However, as evidenced by the people gossiping behind me, apparently I *was* that sort of person, after all. I was the sort of person who could stand up and do what needed to be done.

I sat there at my desk, feeling a smile growing across my face and letting it all sink in: I'd done it. I'd done the right things, the hard things, the things I wanted to do and the things I was afraid of, and I'd done them all *myself*. No one needed to do any of them for me. I looked down at the flowers and the *'Thank you'* and just beamed.

I was still on cloud nine when Sarah came out of her meeting.

From her expression, she definitely didn't feel as good as I did. "Guess what I'm doing this weekend," she said grimly as she walked towards me. "I'm sitting by myself in a stuffy warehouse trying to pack $100,000 worth of print advertising to be shipped by Monday so we don't need to dump it."

By herself? "Won't these guys help?" I asked, nodding at our gossiping co-workers.

She scoffed, not looking very impressed by them. "I doubt it, they mostly think it's outdated anyway and would *love* to see me need to dump it so they can say, 'I told you so'."

That didn't surprise me. "Well, I'll help," I promised her. "And since Min designed it all, she probably will, too. And maybe some of our old friends from uni? They'd definitely help."

Sarah's expression changed; she'd caught sight of something hidden by the partition on my desk. "Maybe," she said vaguely, obviously distracted. She leant over a little further before I remembered there was a big bunch of flowers down there. She made an elated noise when she saw them. "Oh my god, Gem! She's sending you *flowers* now?! Jesus Christ!" She reached out to examine the bouquet.

"Don't get too excited," I whispered to her. "They're not from Natalie, they're from Henry."

She made a silent 'ah' shape with her lips. "Well, I bet everyone else thinks they're from Natalie anyway." She nodded at our co-workers. "Look at them all; whoever says men don't gossip has never worked in an office, I swear to god. It was the first thing they asked me about this morning, too."

I was confused. "About my flowers?"

She shook her head and gave me her best gossipy Marketing clerk voice: "'Is it true that hot MEU lawyer is sleeping with your friend?'"

Oh; I blushed a little at that. "What did you say?"

"Duh, I told them you totally were," she said with a smirk. "They also asked if I knew anything about you and Henry, I just kind of blurted something out about him trying to plug you for information about the MEU because you're with Natalie. I hope that's okay."

I pressed my lips together; it was kind of perfect, actually.

We spent a couple of moments watching our co-workers glancing at us and completely losing their minds over what they were discussing. One guy looked directly at me with this expression of *total* shock—even from across the floor, I could see it was *Nate*. Sarah and I both snickered to each other over it. She couldn't hang around for long, though; she was busy as hell.

Because of the strike, I hardly saw Sarah all day. I ended up catching the train home by myself, too.

It was really jarring arriving home to a clean house; I'd totally forgotten about it so when I walked in and there wasn't crap everywhere, I had this momentary panic I'd been robbed and all they'd left was my grumpy old cat and the generic-brand TV. I really liked how it all looked, though, like this. Neat and clean, swept and vacuumed, like it belonged to a happy, functional adult. It actually made me feel like I could be one.

It was bittersweet, though, because I couldn't shake one last nagging thought from my mind: I wished Mikey had seen *this* version of my house. Clean, and without the shrine to Sarah on my walls. Maybe things would have turned out differently.

There's no 'maybe' about it, I told myself, changing into my pyjamas in preparation for another productive evening correcting logic mistakes on Reddit. *If Mikey had seen this version of my flat, I'd still be with her.*

But... as nice as it was to imagine that I'd brought Mikey back here to a clean house, if I'd done that, none of the other stuff would have happened: the stuff I'd been smiling about all day. I wouldn't have come out to Sarah, I wouldn't have come out to Henry and everyone at Frost, and I wouldn't have had the courage to even *talk* to Natalie, let alone the courage to have casual sex with her.

The more I thought about it, the more part of me was sort of glad things turned out the way they did, even if I really regretted screwing things up with Mikey. Really, that mess-up with her was the only thing left that I regretted about all of this.

I exhaled, and looked across at my wardrobe. Mikey's tie was hanging on its handle.

I wonder if she knows she's left it here? I thought, forgetting I was halfway through buttoning my pyjama top. Half-dressed, I abandoned the buttons and sat on the edge of my bed and grabbed my phone, deciding that I *would* message her on Facebook.

After staring at an empty text field for ten minutes, though, I gave up and flopped back on my mattress. There was no guarantee even if I'd managed to write the perfect message that she'd even read it anyway: it would be hidden away on Facebook in the place where messages from non-friends went, and I'd spend the rest of my life wondering if she'd ever read it.

Besides, I didn't want her to read a message from me and then close it and lock her phone again. I wanted to talk to her properly.

While I was lying on my back, staring at the ceiling, an idea began to crystallise in my mind: I could go to her work and give her tie back to her in person. That really conveyed the 'I want to talk to you'-vibe, didn't it?

In person, though? It was a *huge* risk, and part of me went cold at the thought of it. I'd never even normally *consider* doing anything like that. But 'I've never done anything like that' didn't seem a good enough reason to not do something anymore. I'd fixed a lot of things lately by throwing myself in the deep end. This one thing with Mikey was all that was left.

I took a breath, slowly letting all of that sink in.

Maybe I *should* take Mikey's tie back to her?

I looked at the clock just to check if I had the time; it was 6:30pm, and Mikey got off work at 8pm on weeknights. It gave me half an hour to get ready and a good, safe hour to get back into the city. I could make it, easy. I'd even washed my hair this morning, too, so it would be soft and easy to straighten.

I can wear another dress, I thought, wondering which one I should choose. *Something nice*, I decided, *nice enough that she knows I dressed up for her*. I stood up off the bed and went to my wardrobe, leafing through my dresses for 'nice' until a came to a pretty pale green one I hadn't worn since Sarah's 25th. I took it out; I wasn't even sure it would still fit.

I figured I should just quickly try it on to find out; it was a tiny bit tighter that it used to be, but it was still comfortable. I looked across at myself in my full-length mirror, taking a deep breath.

My stomach fluttered. I was really going to do this, wasn't I?

I already knew my answer: *of course* I was. Sarah was right, I would beat myself up over this forever if I didn't. Even if Mikey wouldn't talk to me, even if she was angry with me, at least then I'd know. At least I could give her tie back to her, look her in the eyes and say, 'I'm sorry' and have her know I meant it.

I still dressed up for her, though, just in case. I still hoped she'd notice my earrings, or how they matched my sparkly shoes. She'd commented last time how nice my bra was; I put the same one on again, just in case. It was stupid, but it made me feel like I was doing the best I possibly could to give myself

335

the best chance with her. I didn't want to walk away from this not having given it my everything.

When I was done, I stood back and admired myself in the mirror. "Here goes nothing," I said to my reflection, snapped a mirror selfie, and then went outside to catch my Uber.

The traffic wasn't too bad and I ended up making really good time back into the city. On the way, I texted Sarah the mirror selfie and, *"Wish me luck: I'm about to take Mikey's tie back to her at the restaurant…"*

"Whoa!!" was the response. *"Will Gemma Rowe finally get nailed in a restaurant toilet after all?? ;) Kidding. Good luck, Gem. I love this new side of you—I'm sure she will, too <3 PS, take flowers."*

I looked up. Flowers? Wasn't that overkill, especially when I didn't even know if she'd talk to me?

In the end, I decided that it was a risk worth taking, so after the Uber dropped me off near Chez Phillipe, I spent the fifteen minutes leading up to 8pm scouring a nearby florist for appropriate flowers.

The clerk insisted on helping me. "If you're apologising to a *partner*," she said, using the gender-neutral word I'd used with suspicious intonation, "then it has to be roses. Long-stemmed roses, all the way."

Roses seemed kind of forward and presumptuous but… well, what the hell, right? I needed to try. I needed to try everything. I bought twelve crisp long-stemmed roses and let the lady wrap them for me, and then walked back to Chez Phillipe with them across my arms.

When I stepped inside the building, however, I caught sight of myself in the polished stainless steel of the lift door. I looked ridiculous, dressed up to the nines and sporting long-stemmed roses like I was about to propose to someone. It was *way* over-the-top.

Oh, shut up, brain, I thought, and pressed the '25' button. My brain wouldn't shut up, though; it kept worrying how Mikey might react to all this. What if this whole dramatic gesture act was creepy rather than genuine? What if she was *angry* with me for being so presumptuous?

Well, it's not long until I find out how she's going to react, I realised, my knees shaking as the lift neared the 25th floor. *I'm about to find out what's going to happen.*

CHAPTER TWENTY-EIGHT

When the lift doors opened and I stepped into the foyer outside Chez Phillipe, my knees were shaking. It was busier than it had been last time I was here, and outside the restaurant there was a queue of people waiting to be seated. As I went to stand at the end of it, people turned around to glance at me, their eyes lingering on my flowers.

It's because you look ridiculous, I caught myself thinking as I went bright red, and then I shoved that thought back where it came from. So what if I *did* look ridiculous! I had to do this, it was important!

Trying as hard as I could to ignore the attention and how much it was making my palms sweat, I squinted through all the tables at each of the waiters, looking for a familiar face. I didn't recognise most of them, and just as I was worrying Mikey wouldn't even be here tonight, I spotted short brown hair ferrying some drinks to a table. I inhaled sharply.

It had only been a week, but all the details looked so familiar: her cheekbones, the way her fringe flopped over one of her eyes, her slender figure with her server's apron double-wrapped around her middle. She was having some sort of light conversation with the table she was waiting on, too, so I was treated to a glimpse of that cute smile of hers as she merrily chatted with them. She was just like I remembered: *gorgeous*.

While she was taking their orders and I was dumbly gazing at her, another server passed by her and whispered something in her ear. She looked up immediately, right towards the line where I was standing.

She couldn't miss me.

We locked eyes, and my heart *leapt* into my throat.

Please be happy to see me, I mentally willed her. *Please be happy to see me*!

I saw her eyebrows rise and her face *lift* like she was about to smile back, and my lungs filled up with air and my breath caught in my throat as I anticipated that gorgeous smile—but it never came. Something passed over her eyes. Apprehension, I think. Maybe hesitation. Whatever it was, she didn't look happy to see me.

A knot formed in my stomach.

She glanced self-consciously at the table she'd been serving just before; all of them were looking between us with considerable interest. She went a bit red, nervously pushing her long fringe behind an ear, and nodded pointedly towards the clock by the cash register. It read 7:45pm, not 8pm when she finished. Then, she took a deep breath, pulled herself together, and got back to taking orders like nothing had happened.

I watched her for a moment, deflating. Even though her cheeks were still pink, she was deliberately not looking towards me, and that made my heart sink. What if I'd made a big mistake by coming here, after all?

It's not a mistake, Gemma, I reassured myself as I went to take a seat on the benches near the lifts to wait for her. *Even if she isn't happy to see you and doesn't want to give things another shot, at least you'll know.*

I lay the roses across my lap and repeated that to myself a few times: *whatever happens tonight, happens.* The important thing was that I didn't just leave things open-ended so I'd always have to wonder what could have been.

It wasn't much comfort, though, because I couldn't get her apprehension out of my mind. I mean, I suppose it made sense—did I really expect her to be happy to see me after she basically discovered a shrine to another girl in my house? I'd probably feel a bit weird if I showed up, as well.

Those fifteen minutes inched past at what felt like a continental pace: I took out my phone and tried to find stuff to keep me busy until 8pm. I couldn't concentrate, though. I kept role-playing imaginary conversations with Mikey in my head; in some of them she was angry, in some of them she was upset, and in some of them she just threw herself into my arms and we kissed right here in front of the restaurant. Most of them were anxious, though. I imagined fighting with her in front of all those people, and I imagined her laying into me about what a hopeless person I was and me just standing there in the middle of the restaurant, crying while all those people stared at me.

At least you'll know, I told myself, closing my eyes and repeating to myself that it would be all over soon.

"Gemma?"

I gulped a breath, snapping my eyes open. Mikey was standing opposite me, arms crossed nervously across her chest. She looked as worried as I felt; there was a big, deep crease in the middle of her forehead. I didn't know how long she'd been standing there.

I went red, jumping up. Automatically, I went to greet her, except just as I opened my mouth, I realised 'Hey!' didn't seem appropriate. I couldn't think what was appropriate instead, though, so we stood there awkwardly for a moment, silent.

She spoke first. "What are you doing here?" she asked eventually.

Well, at least she was listening, I guess. "I-I wanted to talk to you."

She looked around us; the queue for dinner had thinned, and no one was coming out of the lifts. It was private enough. She nervously tucked her fringe behind her ear, and then crossed her arms tightly again. "Okay..."

"Well, um, for starters, I wanted to tell you that you were right."

She looked a bit taken aback. "I was?"

I nodded. "Yeah, about me having a thing for Sarah. I didn't want to admit it to myself, but... yeah."

Her face *fell*. "Oh..." She didn't look very happy about being right.

"But," I took a breath, "I came to tell you that that's all behind me now."

Her frown deepened, and she gave me a pretty cynical look. "So, what, last week you had a thing for her and this week you don't?"

When she put it like that... "Okay, I know how it sounds, but it was never going to go anywhere with me and her, anyway. I always knew that."

Her voice was dry as a bone. "Like that's ever stopped someone from pining after their best friend before..."

Okay, she had a point. "I guess not, but it made it easier to get past my feelings," I told her. "Honestly, Mikey, I've had such a big week this week. I came out to Sarah, to everyone at work, and made all these other changes in my life, too. I'm in a different place now, so..." I looked down my body at the roses and my party dress. "Well, I-I just wanted to come and tell you that. That's why I'm here."

Mikey looked a little sceptical. "Okay," was all she said, though.

That wasn't the reaction I'd hoped for. "Okay?"

She crossed her arms even tighter. "I'm not sure what you want me to do? I mean, I'm happy for you, I guess, but it's pretty clear to me that I was just a rebound."

My eyebrows went up. "You think you were just a *rebound*?"

Her lips were pressed in a tight, thin line. "It's hard to feel like I was anything else."

"I made you feel that way?" I couldn't believe it "Because I thought things were going really well before you came back to my place! Even *after* you did!"

It was only at that point that I noticed her bottom lip was trembling. "Yeah, I really thought that, too," she said. There was a note of melancholy in her voice, it was heartbreaking. "I'd met this *amazing* girl, I'd never clicked with anyone like that and I was totally and completely head over heels for her… and then I see this wall covered in photos of another girl, and I realise she's been texting that girl all night. Even when we were about to sleep together, it turns out she'd rather stand in the living room and text this straight girl who can't love her than come to bed with me." There was a raw note in her voice.

Ouch… I'd never thought of it like that. It was awful. "Oh… I guess that *does* look pretty bad."

"So, yeah," she said quietly "I don't want to feel like that again."

I didn't blame her. That was an awful night, that whole Sarah thing was a mess, and she didn't deserve to get caught up in it.

"I'm sorry," I told her, hoping she could hear how much I meant it. "I'm really sorry I made you feel like I wasn't into you, Mikey."

She wasn't looking at me, but her lips parted a little; I saw her inhale but not exhale. She was listening.

My heart lifted. I took a deep breath: I didn't come this far to hold anything back. "No one's ever made me feel as special as you made me feel," I told her, a bit breathless from the admission. "I was having a really great night too, and I was head over heels for you too, and I totally shouldn't have texted Sarah, I know that," I promised. "It's just that I wasn't out to her last week, and she could tell I was hiding stuff from her and she was upset. I was texting her because I felt guilty about that, not because I wanted to be with anyone but you right at that moment."

She listened as I said all that, digesting it. I could see it ticking over behind those big green eyes of hers. It must have been the right thing to say, because I could see the tension in her arms easing. She wasn't clutching them so tightly across her chest anymore. Something was still bothering her, though. She swallowed, protesting, "But… you have that whole photo wall thing of her…"

341

"Had," I corrected her. "It was about time I took it down."

That surprised her. Her eyebrows went up. "You took it down?"

I nodded. "Right after you left. Being with you made me look at it differently."

"Wow..." she said, considering that. She was silent for a moment as she watched me, but I could see the fog was lifting.

It gave me hope. It gave me hope that I might actually win her over.

My heart fluttering, I tried to think of other things that had changed. "I cleaned my house too," I told her, hoping that would impress her as well. "I even put all the clothes from everywhere back in my wardrobe—" Saying the word 'wardrobe' reminded me of what had been hanging on it this evening. "*Oh!*" Gosh, how could I have forgotten why I was here? "Your tie!"

She blinked at me, looking really confused at the sudden topic change. "My tie?"

"Yeah, you left your tie at my house. You know, the skinny black one? I found it while I was cleaning, that's what gave me the idea of dressing up and bringing it back to you in the first place." Awkwardly, because I had the roses over one of my arms, I unzipped my handbag to retrieve it for her. "Let me just quickly give it to you before I forget."

"Thanks," she said vaguely. I think she was still a bit confused. "I figured Patrick had borrowed it and lost it *again*..."

"Nope, it was buried in the deep recesses of my couch," I told her, feeling around in amongst all my toiletries and makeup for where I'd put it. There was so much junk in here, it was really embarrassing. "...and now it's buried in the deep recesses of my handbag."

She bit her lip as I said that. She could probably see how much crap was in here. "Maybe you should have cleaned your handbag, too."

I paused momentarily to give her a tired look, but I was secretly overjoyed. She was teasing me; that was a good sign, right?

After several seconds of rummaging around and not finding it, though, the joy started to fade and my cheeks started to go red. It was kind of embarrassing how long it was taking me to find it; if I was trying to present a façade of being a new and improved responsible adult, the state of my handbag wasn't helping.

I tried to burrow a bit faster, but in the process of doing that, I forgot to keep the roses balanced on my elbow and they nearly fell out of my arms. Mikey darted forward to right them just in time, but in my alarm at the sudden movement, I jumped and spilt a bunch of crap out of my handbag onto the floor. It scattered around my feet. "Shit!"

I bent down to grab everything, half-stuffing it back into my handbag and half-feeling through my handbag again for *anything* that felt like a tie. "Sorry, it's got to be in here somewhere..."

Except I'd looked through these pockets like three times now and hadn't found it, had I? It was looking increasingly like it wasn't in there, and so I stood back up again, holding my bag to the light and peering into it.... when it dawned on me that I couldn't actually remember putting it in my bag.

...It was still hanging on the handle of my wardrobe, wasn't it?

Shit. Aghast, I looked up at her. "Oh, no, I think I left it at home!"

Her eyebrows were in her hairline. "Wait, so you came here to give me back my tie, but forgot to actually bring it?"

Yup. That *definitely* sounded like me. I blushed a deep, flaming red, and nodded. I must have looked horrified.

She took one look at my expression and my red cheeks, and the ice finally melted and she *laughed.* It was a really pleasant sound; it echoed off the corridor walls and showed me all of her beautiful white teeth.

She was standing closer to me because of catching the roses, so before I could do something else super embarrassing, I stood up and pushed them at her. "Well, at least I can give you these," I told her. "You should probably take them before I leave them somewhere, too."

343

She accepted them. "Thanks," she told me, "they're really beautiful." She was looking right at me as she said 'beautiful'.

Oh...

I couldn't stop a nervous smile from rising to my lips.

We were both silent for a moment; all I could hear was the clink of cutlery and the hum of conversation from the restaurant inside. She was looking at me. It filled my stomach with butterflies.

"Every time I see you, you always look so nice," she said eventually. "I wish I'd dressed up, too. I promise I can look nicer than I do in a waiter's uniform or some old t-shirt."

I didn't know what she was talking about, because I loved how she looked. I didn't doubt that she'd look amazing dressed up too, though. "I bet you look great."

She took a little, hopeful breath. I could feel her eyes on me.

I think I knew what was coming next—at least, I hoped I did. I *hoped* I knew what she was going to say next.

"Would you... like to find out how I look dressed up?" She stole a little shy peek up at me.

My lips parted. I *was* right.

She was going to give me another chance.

We stared at each other for a moment while my heart *pounded* and my spirit *lifted* all the way up into the sky. Did I want to see her dressed up?! It didn't matter! It didn't matter what she wore! She could even wear an ugly canvas sack and I'd want to see her in it, just as long as the 'see her' part was included. I wanted to jump up and down, and shout and shriek and whoop, but all I managed was this tiny little breathy, "Yes."

It was enough to make the smile nearly crack her face, though. I'm sure I looked exactly the same. I could already hardly breathe, but when she glanced around us to make sure we were alone, and then stepped forward, briefly wetting her lips...

I couldn't look at her. I knew what was coming, and I couldn't look at her. I couldn't stop smiling either. Her free hand touched one of my hot cheeks, and I could smell delicious French food on her skin and from her uniform.

When she leant in to touch her lips to mine, we were both smiling so much we had to pause there, laugh nervously at each other, and take another breath before we finally kissed.

It took a moment for me to really register what was happening. She inhaled sharply as I opened my lips to hers, pushing our bodies together. Before I knew it, I was wrapping my arms around her slender waist and crushing the roses between us.

She tasted like chocolate—comfort food, maybe?—and I think I heard the lift ding at some point, but I didn't care. This was *everything* I secretly hoped would happen when I'd decided to come here; this was everything I'd wished for. 'Whatever happens, happens', pfft, this was what I'd *really* wanted!

It felt surreal and impossible that she'd forgiven me—like the universe had given me this big, beautiful gift after everything I'd been through: another chance with someone I was into. With someone who was into *me*. My heart sang and my pulse raced and I just couldn't believe it had turned out like this.

I don't know how long we actually kissed for—probably not that long, really, but we were both breathless when we stopped. We didn't step away from each other, though; we stayed silently together, her cheek brushing mine. Her eye lashes tickling my skin, and her breath warming my neck. Our breasts were together—well, apart from the roses squished between them. I didn't care. I didn't want to lean back to free them. I didn't want to be apart from her at all, not now.

I took a little breath and murmured into her ear. "You could... come back to my house to get your tie?"

She chuckled at that. "Smooth," she said. "If you hadn't looked so shocked before, I might have thought you left it there on purpose."

"Can we pretend I did?" I asked her. "So I don't look as hopeless as I really am?"

"I like how you really are, I don't want to pretend you're different," she told me. "I've never met anyone who's such a fun combination of 'terrified' and 'impulsive' before. You're pretty unique."

That I laughed darkly at. 'Unique' was a kind way to put it. "I think you mean 'statistical anomaly'," I told her dryly. "Everything about me is such an outlier characteristic my whole data set would probably be omitted in any proper study."

She froze for a moment, stunned by what I'd said, and then *laughed*.

I went red; so much for being 'smooth'... "Um, can we just pretend I said 'thanks' instead of all that nerdy stuff?"

I could still feel her smiling against my cheek. "It's fine, I took maths in HSC too," she said, and then paused. "And you can skew my data any time."

I had to laugh out loud at that—she was actually pretty damn good! "Now who's being smooth?"

We both giggled over that for a few moments before she exhaled at length. "I don't know how much you were joking about me coming over before—because I probably would, but I have a personal training session tonight back in Fairfield and I've already paid for it."

"Oh," I said. "Well, when does it finish?"

She chuckled. "Late. And you have work tomorrow."

"Who needs sleep?"

She ignored me, but she was smiling again. "Maybe we could do something on Saturday?"

I'd opened my mouth to say that it would be really nice to see her then—and then I remembered Sarah's predicament with the strikes and *groaned*. "Oh, I would, but work has this big strike on at the moment, and I promised Sare I'd help her pack, like, thousands of brochures into envelopes to be sent out by Monday." Then, because I didn't want her to think it was just me and Sarah, I said, "All of our friends will be there."

"Huh," she said, thinking. I was worried she'd comment on the fact I was ditching her for something to do with Sarah, but she didn't. The opposite. "Well, do you need any extra help?"

Oh—I considered that. Well, actually, Sarah would probably be happy to have another set of hands. "I guess? Sare said we could use all the help she could get for it. But it will probably be really sweaty and gross, because it's in a warehouse."

She shrugged. "I play soccer. I'm used to being sweaty and gross. Where's the warehouse? I might be able to rope a couple of other friends into it, too."

Unfortunately, I had to step away from her to get the address of the warehouse off my phone, and she gave me her number so I could text them to her before she had to head off for her PT session.

"I'm so glad you came here tonight," she told me with gravity as we said goodbye for, like, the fifth time, and then kissed a couple more times while she was waiting for the lift because it took ages to arrive.

Hand-in-hand and on top of the fucking world, we walked a couple of blocks to the station, and she blew me a kiss as she went through the turnstiles to her platform. It made me blush again—so many people saw!—but I could just not get this huge smile off my face. I practically floated all the way home.

When I got there, it was almost a shame to take off my lovely green dress, wash all my makeup off and get into my pyjamas, but I kept having glorious flashbacks from tonight—Mikey's smile. Her laugh. Her hands on my waist. Every time I caught a glimpse of myself in a mirror I was smiling.

It wasn't all just for Mikey, either. I mean, it was amazing I had another shot with her, and I couldn't believe she'd decided to take me back, but that wasn't the only reason I was so happy: I couldn't believe I'd had the guts to go there and speak to her in the first place. I'd dressed up and marched in

347

there, totally prepared to make a fool of myself. I hadn't, but that wasn't what mattered. I'd done it. Just like I'd done it when I came out to Sarah. Just like I'd done it when I'd come out to everyone at work and saved Henry's job.

It had all worked out—all of it. I'd fixed all of it by myself, and there was no feeling in the world that matched how good that felt.

It was a shame to come back down to earth again, but I needed to confirm with Sarah that it was okay for Mikey to bring a couple of friends to help ASAP so she had time to ask them.

As predicted, her response was immediate. *"OH MY GOD TELL ANYONE WHO WANTS TO BRING A FRIEND THAT THEY'RE WELCOME,"* she messaged back. *"I'LL PAY THEM IN PIZZA. PIZZA, AND MY ETERNAL, UNDYING GRATITUDE."* There was a pronounced pause. *"Wait, you said MIKEY offered to help? Does Mikey offering mean you two are back on again????"*

There was my smile again. *"Yeah,"* I told her. *"We are."*

My phone rang in my hands and startled me. Trying not to drop it, I answered. "Hello?"

It was Sarah. *"This is so awesome!"* she hissed into the receiver; I could tell her hand was over her mouth; she as trying to be quiet. "I'm so happy for you! This is so fantastic, oh my god! Tell me *everything*!"

She went and hid out in the women's toilets so I could go over all the details, and when I reached the part where Mikey and I kissed, she practically *cheered* for me. "That's my Gem!" I could hear her voice echoing off the tiles. Then, she reconsidered. "Well, not *my* Gem. But you get what I mean."

I did know what she meant. But it was true anyway: I wasn't hers, not anymore. And realising that—really realising it—put me back on top of the world again.

I was feeling so good that I decided to clean out my handbag. I put all the junk I never used in a drawer I never used, and was just planning on rolling up Mikey's tie and putting it neatly in the nice, clean interior of my newly spotless handbag when I thought twice about it.

If her tie was here at my house, she'd have to come *back* to my house and get it on Saturday night. Grinning ear-to-ear, I left it on my wardrobe and spent the rest of the evening imagining what would happen when she came to retrieve it.

Those thoughts carried me on a cloud through the work day on Friday. On Saturday, after I woke up and rolled over and texted Mikey good morning, I spent a great deal more time than I needed to stressing about which bra and undies to wear (just in case Mikey *did* come back here tonight!) and then headed over to Sarah's so she could drive me and Rob to the warehouse. Mikey said she'd meet us there because she was coming from the other side of the city.

Sarah, Rob and I were still the first people to get there; Min and Bree were coming in a separate car and hadn't arrived yet. I helped Sarah and Rob open the heavy roller door at the side of the building (not that big, burly Rob needed much help with it), and then we wandered into the warehouse while Sarah hunted around for the light switch.

When the lights came on, what was in front of us was a pretty sobering sight.

There were pallets and pallets of print material stretching all the way from the roller door to the back of the warehouse. I couldn't get over how many there were; I don't think I'd really appreciated the scale of Sarah's problem until right at that moment. It was *huge.*

One thing was certain: there was absolutely no way the three of us—or six of us, when the others got here—were going to be able to finish it. Not in two days. Not even though a couple of our other friends from uni were going to help out for a few hours tomorrow. It would take a whole team of admin staff to do this in that time.

Sarah knew it. She exhaled at length, her eyes veiled. "Well, that's what $100,000 worth of print material and my fading job security looks like," she said somewhat bleakly.

She sighed. "Okay, well. Let's at least get as much of it done as we can, yeah? I want to dump as little as possible."

We'd pulled up a work bench, and Sarah was just explaining to us what to do when there was a knock at the side door.

"Hi!" That was Bree's cheerful voice, and a head full of blonde curls poked through the door. "We're here!" Behind her, Min was carrying a very welcome sight: a cardboard tray with big takeaway coffee mugs nestled in it. She placed one neatly in front of each of us as we greeted her, and then straightened, giving the *huge* swathe of pallets a bit of a wide-eyed stare.

"That's a *lot* of advertising material," she commented neutrally. "We've got our work cut out for us."

Bree didn't look quite as bothered as her partner. "Oh, well. I suppose it will be easier with the others helping."

Sarah made a face. "'The others' is only the Matts and one of their partners," she said. "Liz is still up in Newcastle. And they'll only be here for a few hours tomorrow."

Bree looked confused. "But what about the girls outside?"

Sarah gave her a really strange look. "What girls outside?"

"Oh—they're not your uni friends or something? I just kind of assumed they were..." She shrugged, looking a bit disappointed. "Oh, well, I guess they're here for something else, then. That makes sense with what they're wearing. It's a pity, though, because they're all *totally* hot." Behind her, Min grimaced.

While Sarah was giving Bree a deep frown, something occurred to me. "Oh! It might be Mikey?" I realised, reaching into my pocket for my phone and noticing I had several unread messages. "Yeah, it's probably Mikey. She said she was going to bring a couple of friends to help out, they're probably waiting out front."

Bree's eyes were wide. "A couple?"

I jumped up from the work bench. "I'll go grab them," I said, and headed outside. Sarah was hot on my heels—"I've been waiting three whole years for you to finally hook up with someone, I want to meet her."—so we both went out the side door around to the parking lot to see the girls that Bree was on about.

As we got to the back of the building, I noticed a couple of extra cars parked along the fence—and then another two, and another two... and then as we rounded the corner to the car park, there was talking, and laughter, and... a whole crowd of women, all dressed in matching blue tracksuit pants and chatting to each other while they stretched. They all had variations on Mikey's athletic figure, and they all looked *super* fit.

Sarah and I stopped dead in our tracks, staring. There must have been a dozen of them.

Mikey wandered out of the crowd towards me with a *big* smile on her face. "I hope you don't mind," she said, looking maybe a little smug. "But I invited my entire soccer team to help. It's off-season, so we'd only be running laps and doing drills anyway..."

"Yeah, and we don't get free pizza at training!" Someone called out, and someone else piped up with, "And we don't get to meet Mikey's first girlfriend there, either!"

Mikey blushed a little. "*Guys*," she hissed at them, and then turned back to me and Sarah. "I'd like you to meet the Northern Thunderbirds."

I normally left all the talking up to Sarah when we met new people—she was always good at that stuff— but when I looked beside me at her to see why she wasn't, she was frozen in place, staring at them, speechless.

There was at least twelve women in front of us, maybe more, I didn't know how many people there were on a soccer team. But one thing was for certain: these women were going to be the difference between Sarah dumping $100,000 worth of print material and never getting picked as a project lead again, and Sarah *nailing* her project and putting herself in line for further promotions. She was choking up with emotion; I think there were tears in her eyes.

Her project *wasn't* screwed up, after all.

Unexpectedly, she took a few steps forward and threw her arms around Mikey, even though she'd hardly met her. "*Thank you*," she said quietly. I could hear emotion in her voice.

Mikey looked a bit stunned—I don't think she was really a very huggy person, normally—but she didn't push Sarah away. She just blushed a bit more and smiled shyly at me over Sarah's shoulder.

As I watched Mikey stiffly patting Sarah's back, I realised it: that she'd done all of this for Sarah, despite the fact Sarah was the cause of our whole mix up last week. She'd put all that aside and done it anyway.

I didn't know if it was possible to fall in love with someone in just one week—but, right then, right at that moment, I was well on my way.

When Sarah finally let Mikey go, she turned towards me, and pointed directly back at her. "Marry this one," she told me half-teasingly, even though I knew she *really, really* meant it. "You officially have my blessing. She's a keeper."

Mikey was grinning. "Actually, I'm a striker."

"Yeah, I'm the keeper!" A thick-looking brunette called from behind everyone. "You can tell by all my bruises!"

They all laughed, coming forward to meet me one-by-one, all telling me they'd been waiting for the day when Mikey *finally* got her first girlfriend, and then they all piled inside to be given instructions on what they were here for.

Min and Bree pulled up another couple of work benches to make space for everyone and generously sat at the very back (although, secretly, I think they wanted to set themselves up in a place where they had a view of all the cute girls), and then we all set to work, unloading the pallets, bundling up the materials specified on the shipping spreadsheet, and addressing boxes, envelopes and letters to places all over the world.

It was hot, sweaty work—Sarah hadn't been wrong about that. But there were so many people, and everyone's spirits were so high that despite all the papercuts I was giving myself, and despite the fact I wasn't getting any alone time with Mikey, I was having so much fun.

At the end of the day, after all the pizza we'd ordered was gone and we'd arranged a time to meet on Sunday to finish what was left, Min sidled up to me for a moment. "She's really nice," she said quietly, her eyes on Mikey. When she looked at me again, her smile was every bit as warm as one of Henry's. They were so alike. "I'm so happy it turned out this way for you, Gemma."

I returned her smile. I was, too. "Thanks for being there for me before it did."

She nodded and gave me a little salute. "Any time," she said, and then went to help Bree clean away all the empty pizza boxes. I watched her thoughtfully for a little while.

When the clean-up was finished, Mikey ducked out to say goodbye to her teammates while I finished addressing one more envelope.

"You're letting her go home by herself?" Sarah asked me as she stiffly got up from her work bench, one hand on her lower back. She was smirking. "After that workout, she's going to need a nice, long massage..."

I went a bit pink. A massage hadn't exactly been what I was planning. "No, no, she *is* coming home with me," I corrected her. "We'll just get an Uber or something after she's said goodbye to everyone, and I'm just finishing this one envelope."

Sarah looked insulted. "You most certainly will *not* catch an Uber home," she said firmly. "Rob can drive you both! That's the least we can do after she basically saved my career."

Hearing his name, Rob wandered over. "Yeah, it's no problem as long as you two don't mind being squished together in the back of the ute."

Hah. I definitely did *not* mind the idea of being squished together with Mikey, that was for sure. "Okay, I'll ask her when she's done saying goodbye to people."

Sarah nodded, following Rob out of the warehouse. "Good, we'll go wait in the car—I need to sit somewhere other than on these horrible work stools. Can you pull the door shut in here and turn the light off when you're done with that envelope?"

I nodded, and then paused for a moment to watch Rob and Sarah give each other a vague peck on the lips, and then wander back to the car together, arm-in-arm. She was complaining about how sore she was, and Rob was promising her he'd make it better when they got home. I listened to their voices disappear up the side of the building, deep in thought.

Normally, seeing how happy they were together would have made me feel left out. Tonight, I didn't.

I *didn't* wish Rob was up in Broome or away on some other worksite, and I wasn't looking for excuses to stay over at Sarah's place. I didn't even mind that she and Rob were really in love. In fact, I was happy for her—especially after today, it was wonderful that she could sleep peacefully knowing her career was safe. I wasn't jealous at all.

It had been so long since I felt this way and it was so liberating to be free of it, like I'd finally climbed out of Sarah's pocket and I'd taken my first glimpse at the rest of the world. It looked different than I expected.

Of course it did: Sarah was the perfect statistical representation of 'typical' that I'd ever met, and I was a female redheaded maths nerd who worked in the mining industry. I was also gay, which kind of explained why I hadn't married some guy at 28.3 and I wasn't pregnant with my first child already.

There wasn't much research on age landmark norms for Australian lesbians (believe me, I'd checked), but I didn't care. It didn't matter. I already knew my score for the most important index there was.

You see, the average Australian woman may have rated her overall happiness a 7.7, but right then, as I switched off the lights and walked out of the warehouse towards a car with two amazing women in it, my happiness score was easily a *perfect* ten out of ten.

THE END

***

ALSO BY THE AUTHOR

Under My Skin
Flesh & Blood
Solve for i

Want to read more stories by this author? Visit <u>aedooland.com</u> for free content and news about future web series. You can also follow her on <u>Twitter</u>, <u>Facebook</u> or <u>Tumblr</u>.

A FINAL THANKS TO OTHER FINANCIAL BACKERS

Dora 'ikeeptalkingonmyown' & Phine 'Demandypants' Humphrey, and:

Deb WW

Niki Sims

Alex Ayres

Anne Farmer

Jodey Sanders

M. 'Mikey' Cohen

Agnes Price

A. J. Winter

Eden

Lauren Thomson

Steenium

William Hillary

Diana Pinguicha Connors

Heather Ott

Elizabeth KW

C. A. Tomlinson

Kal

Genevieve H.

Alba Arrieta

Ivan 'Noelemahc' Kostin

April Damiani

Tuna Re

Cindy Alex Nguyen

Regina Fletcher

Aleksandra Borowska

Alec Fowler

Zeal

Alex Chevallier

George C.

Mathew Westwood

Tamzin Walker

Thomas Carlsson

Patrizia Bregant

Rachael V. and Jordan H.

Hannah Hunter

Elena S.

Caroline Spence

John Morgenstern

Wilhelmina Richards

E. Catedral

Jess Heyne

Zeal

Chris Bergeron

www.ingramcontent.com/pod-product-compliance
Lightning Source LLC
Chambersburg PA
CBHW071158020726
47502CB00002B/462